OF ICE AND STEEL

By

D. Clayton Meadows

Published by Leatherneck Publishing
A Division of Levin Publishing Group, LLC
http://www.leatherneckpublishing.com

Publisher: Lt Col H. Neil Levin, USMC (ret)

Edition: 10 9 8 7 6 5 4 3 2 1 SAN: 256-8799

Library of Congress Control Number: 2006928551

ISBN-13: 978-0-9771431-2-2
ISBN-10: 0-9771431-2-0

Cover, Background Photo: Steve Neill. www.sneill.com

Cover Composite: Randy Galloway, DreamWorx Graphix
Cave Creek, Arizona

Printed and Bound in Ann Arbor, MI 48106
United States of America.
This Book is printed on Acid Free Paper

Author's Note

This is a work of fiction. The tactics described are in no way representative of the United States, NATO, or Russian tactics, past or present. The descriptions of ships, weapons, weapon systems, and other details have been purposefully modified to protect sensitive information.

Acknowledgements

The idea for this book was born when I was a young sailor. It was May 6, 1986. My submarine, USS RAY SSN-653, along with the USS ARCHERFISH SSN 678, and USS HAWKBILL SSN-666 had just surfaced together at the North Pole. The event was the first ever surfacing of three submarines at the Pole. It has been twenty years since then, and at last, the seed of inspiration planted that day in the Arctic has born fruit.

I would like to thank my father, Reverend Donald C. Meadows for instilling in me a love for writing, and maybe a little genetically transferred talent.

Without the dedication, inspiration, and constant urging of my mother Diane Clark, *Of Ice and Steel* would have never been created.

A special thanks to my Grandfather James Atkins. As a child I spent hours asking question after question about his time in the Navy. It was from this giant of a man I gained a fever for the sea and a love of the Navy.

My Mother-in-law, Esther Ballard, was and *is* an inexhaustible source of encouragement. She pushed me along when I was at the end of my rope.

No task, however small or great, can occur unless you have behind you a family that supports and encourages you. My wife, Susan, has been there through it all. She has played the roles of both Mommy and Daddy during my weeks and months at sea. She believed in me and put up with more than any woman should. Her love and dedication are without match.

For the first years of my children's lives, "Daddy" was a framed picture lovingly placed by their beds. Despite my absence, or maybe because of it, Donnie and Andrew have become two of the finest young men I know. I am so very proud they call me Dad.

A word of dedication and respect also goes to those under any flag, and throughout mankind's history who have sailed, fought, and died under the sea.

Dedication

For Carl Ballard who loves history
and a good story.

To the memory of Hans Goebeler, crew
member of U-505, and my friend.

"Good and noble sailor, your watch is over.
Rest your oars."
A Sailor's Farewell

Unknown

"I have a reactionary Army, a National Socialist Air Force, and a Christian Navy."

- Adolph Hitler

"Isn't there some way we can avoid our first exchange with a Russian submarine — almost anything but that?"

-President John F. Kennedy
October 27, 1962

Eternal Father, strong to save
Whose arm hath bound the restless wave,
Who bid'st the mighty Ocean deep
Its own appointed limits keep:
O hear us when we cry to thee,
For those in peril on the sea.
Lord God, our power ever more
Who arm doth reach the ocean floor,
Dive with our men beneath the sea;
Traverse the depths protectively
O hear us when we pray to thee
For those in peril under the sea.

-The Navy Hymn

Preface
The Submariner

Only a submariner realizes to what great extent an entire ship depends on him as an individual. A land man doesn't understand this and it can be difficult to comprehend, but it is true.

A submarine at sea is a different world and in consideration of the protracted and distant operations of submarines, the Navy must place responsibility and trust in the hands of those who take such ships to sea.

In each submarine, there are men who in an hour of emergency or peril at sea, can turn to each other. These men are ultimately responsible to themselves and to each other for all aspects of operations of their submarine. They are the crew. They are the ship.

This is perhaps the most difficult and demanding assignment in the Navy. There is not an instance during his tour as a submariner that he can escape the grasp of responsibility. His privileges, in view of his obligations, are ludicrously small, but nevertheless, it is the spur, which has given the Navy its greatest mariners.

It is a duty, which most richly deserves the proud and time-honored title of—Submariner.

Chapter One

Fire and Ice

"War is the science of destruction"
-John S.C. Abbot

August 20, 1944

U-761 floated still and silent. Her slender, graceful lines, and shark-like bow, blurred to translucence by billows of freezing mist. Daggers of ice hung like teeth from her rails and guns. The worn gray camouflage on her sides and conning tower, melded into a lifeless slate sky. She lay there, the perfect predator, hidden in a field of jagged, broken ice.

Shivering on the U-boat's bridge Kapitanleutnaunt Manfred Becker peered into an empty frozen ocean. At 34 he was considered to be one of the *old gang* of U-boat commanders. His five foot-nine inch frame was thin, yet his shoulders broad. His face was pure Prussian. A noble nose jutted from proud smooth cheeks. His mouth was thin and turned down to a permanent frown. Stung by the angry mist, his normally pale blue eyes, now red and swollen, strained to spot movement or even a shadow on the bleak, dead ice. An occasional gap in the swirling clouds of mist would open like a shutter, only to slam closed seconds later, as the sky fumed and frothed.

Becker felt the cold wrap around him. Frigid air seeped past his felt lined parka through his woolen sweater until the chill pricked at his skin. His feet had long since gone numb. His legs ached as the cold made its way through his body.

Becker turned his head to check on the lookouts stationed behind him. “Everyone okay?” he asked. His words sounded strangely muffled as if the Arctic air absorbed the sound of his voice.

“Yes, Captain,” they replied through chattering teeth.

Becker stepped to the open bridge hatch. Bending slightly, he peered down into the submarine. Warm air rising from inside the U-boat caused a trickle of melted ice to run from his beard across his throat and onto his jacket.

“Frimunt,” Becker called.

“Yes, Captain,” a voice replied from inside the U-boat.

“How long have they been out?”

A long pause. “One hour, twenty minutes, Captain.”

They should be back by now, Becker thought.

U-761’s engineer officer, Chief Edel stuck his head out of the hatch, “Captain?”

“Yes, Chief?”

“Sir, we need to start the engines. Lube oil is getting cold. The intakes may be freezing.”

“Not yet. Let’s give them a few more minutes.”

“Sir, I think…”

Becker stopped him. “Not yet.”

"Yes sir," replied the engineer. He started to slide down the ladder.

"Wait, Chief," Becker said, bending further down. "What is our guest doing?"

"He's the same, sir. Sitting alone on his bunk, staring at the clock." The engineer stuck his head farther out the hatch. "Seems nervous."

"Me too," whispered Becker. "Okay, Chief."

Edel grinned and disappeared down the hatch.

Becker was about to call for coffee when the port lookout shouted, "Captain. There they are." The lookout's gloved hand waved over the port bow.

Becker saw only shadows cast from tortured mounds of lifeless ice. He wiped at his eyes clearing the mist from his face. Then translucent manlike shapes appeared from the swirling mist. As if being painted on canvas, the shapes formed silently into men. "What the hell?" He felt suddenly flushed, his blood hot. "Why are they running?" *Like drunken phantoms,* he thought.

His men stumbled and picked themselves up, only to fall again. U-761's commander tore the cap off his head, his brown hair in a wild tangle, while he watched his men crawl on the ice.

"Frimunt, the guns," Becker's voice echoed off the ice. "Get up here, now. I need help aft."

Within seconds, the gun crews hammered at the ice covering the twin barreled 3.7cm weapons. Showers of ice shattered from the creaking, groaning weapons as they swung over the tower side.

Becker heard the welcome sound of ammunition covers slam home and feeding thumb-sized bullets into the chambers.

"Ready, sir," the gun captain reported.

"Stand by." Becker swallowed hard at the sight of his men, clawing toward the U-boat and safety.

Only six meters from the boat, all strength gone, the first man collapsed. Another crawled beside the prone man and then fell on the hard ice. Three others staggered a few steps farther and they too went down.

"Frimunt, take over," Becker barked as he slid from the bridge onto the after-casing. The galley hatch clanged open. Nine of her crew clambered up slipping and sliding on the frosted deck.

Becker knew seconds meant U-761's fate. Calculations filled his head. *Can I get the landing party onboard, before whatever they ran from found its way here? It takes thirty seconds for U-761 to submerge. Leave them? Five men dead to save thirty-eight?* "No," he said aloud. "Everyone comes home."

Those shivering on the after-casing called to their shipmates, urged them on and pleaded with them to get up. The U-boatmen looked to Becker. Their bodies coiled like spring steel ready to get their shipmates back.

"Go," Becker commanded.

In unison, all nine leaped from the U-boat. They tumbled on the ice, then on their feet again as if they rehearsed this act a thousand times. Becker looked back to the bridge. "Contacts?"

"No, Captain. Nothing," Frimunt answered.

Becker turned. With groans of effort, they retrieved their nearly frozen shipmates, hauling them aboard. Soon all five lay in gasping heaps on the deck.

"All on board?"

"Yes, sir."

"Where is Volker?"

"Here," answered one of the shivering rescuers.

The Captain stepped over two of the men and knelt by the third. Becker gently placed his hand under the gasping man's head, raising it slightly. "Volker?'

Volker's eyes fluttered half open. "Sir?" he managed in a weak thin rasp.

"What happened?"

"Captain?" his words a struggle. "All dead."

"Who's dead?"

"All," he whispered, forcing his lips to move.

"Volker." Becker wiped the man's face, his lips, blue from frostbite. "Lieutenant Volker."

Again, the eyes fluttered and muscles twitched with an effort to keep the eyes open. "All dead. Shot-burned...."

Becker felt the man sag in his hands. "All hands below. Prepare to dive."

He heard a clamor of thudding felt boots, orders shouted, metal groaned, and the mist continued as the landing party was quickly lowered down the hatch.

The last to leave the casing, Becker shouted, "Frimunt, secure the guns. Dive the boat in five minutes."

Frimunt cupped his hands around his mouth. "Yes, sir."

Inside the U-boat, Becker pulled and tugged until he threw off his blue-gray parka. His steps labored as his legs complained with needling surges of pain. After what seemed a mile, he stood in the control room. "Diving stations."

Edel came forward taking his place behind the

planesmen. "Three hours left on the batteries," he said to the Captain.

Becker turned to Oberbootsmann Brendin Hamlin. "How far to open water?"

"Twenty kilometers, sir."

Becker then looked at the engineer, Edel. Being their fifth patrol at sea together, the two men needed few words between them. He knew his Captain's question.

"Please go slow," Edel urged.

U-761's captain nodded as he opened his mouth for the order to dive, a voice called out, "Halt."

Every face in the control room looked at the forward hatch. SS Major Lambert Von Gerlach stepped into the control room as if walking on air, graceful, silent and menacing.

"Captain, on whose authority are you submerging?" his voice soft, yet as lifeless as his black eyes.

"Major, our mission is over."

"Why, Captain, do you say that?" asked Gerlach, his black eyes narrowed.

Becker disliked few persons, but this arrogant secretive little Nazi with his polished boots, black parka and perfect straw colored hair earned a place among the few. His voice caused anger to form a lump in Becker's throat. "The landing party reported everyone is dead."

Gerlach polished his fingernails against his jacket. "All?"

"Yes, all."

"Unfortunate," responded Gerlach.

The lump of anger grew. “Major, the ship is in danger.”

“Yes. This is a setback.”

The Captain’s anger left as fast as it had come, replaced by a mix of curiosity and fear.

Becker stepped toward Gerlach, pointing to the hatch. The Major ducked his head under the steel circle into the next compartment with Becker close behind. Away from the crew, Becker grabbed Gerlach’s collar, shoved the Major’s small frame into a recess forward of the U-boat’s toilet.

“Major, I command this boat,” Becker hissed.

“First, Captain, take your hands off me.” Gerlach ordered stiffly.

Becker released his grip.

“Your mission,” his voice cool and lifeless like the ice, “ is over when I dismiss you.” He paused as if to let the words sink in. “Your mission is half complete.”

“Major, something up there is killing people and I don’t know what it is,” Becker wondered if this SS Major had the slightest idea of what was going on.

“Captain, the mission is far from over.”

Becker felt anger rise again. “What is our mission, Major?”

“That is not your concern, Captain.” He met Becker’s eyes. “And, yes, you are the Captain of this ship. But until we both fulfill our missions, I am in charge.”

“What happened out there?” Becker pointed to the ice.

“I don’t know.” Gerlach’s mouth cracked into a thin smile. “Trust me. If what your men say is true, this ship is in no danger.”

"What?" asked Becker, trying to make sense of words.

"We remain here till I tell you otherwise." The Major pushed passed him.

The Captain controlled his breathing, rubbed his throbbing head and suddenly felt more tired than mad. He could not remember the last time he'd closed his eyes. At last, his breath slowed. He forced his stiff aching legs to move. Back in the control room, Chief Edel looked at him, puzzled.

Becker slammed his fist on the chart table. "Secure from diving stations."

Becker moved the periscope. "Chief, start the engines. Charge the batteries. And get some heat in this coffin."

"Aye, sir," replied Edel as he headed aft.

"Hamlin," the Captain called.

"Sir."

"You have the bridge watch. And Lieutenant," Becker drew the young officer close, "you see anything¯anything at all, dive the boat."

Hamlin nodded in understanding.

Becker went aft and felt the familiar and welcome rumble of the U-boats twin MANN diesels growling to life. Soon, air, driven by blowers, warmed by the engine's exhaust manifolds flowed through the cramped hull.

The Captain stepped into the tiny wardroom where the landing party, shaken but alive, rested in bunks or sprawled on a thin bench along U-761's curved hull. Stripped of their parkas, shirts, pants, and boots, they shivered under rough gray blankets.

Berdy, the cook, ladled steaming, red soup into cups held by trembling hands. Radio Operator, and U-761's medic, Waldron Roth examined and fussed over all five men. Apart from slight exposure, exhaustion, and dehydration, the men seemed fine.

Kruger, the big torpedo mechanic, pushed by, his large greasy arms laden with bottles of apple juice. He handed a bottle to each of the landing party.

"Wish it was beer, huh?" Kruger grinned. "Well, it *is* cold."

Becker smiled and thought, *such a large serious looking fellow to tend to his shipmates like a coddling nurse.*

"Good, Kruger." He slapped the torpedo man's back.

The Captain caught Roth's eye. "Volker?" he asked.

Roth's head motioned to a top bunk.

Becker gently pulled back the wool blanket. "Volker?"

"Yes, Captain?" A drop of Berdy's soup rested on his chin.

"You look better than last time I saw you," grinned Becker.

"My apologies, Captain," Volker chattered.

"No need for that. How are you feeling?"

"Still a bit weak, but I'll be okay."

"Good. I thought Germany had lost her best tennis player."

"No sir, I always carry my medal." Volker smiled and raised his hand. His 1939 Olympic gold medal wrapped around his still trembling finger.

Becker admired the medal. "Brings you luck?"

"I hope so."

"What happened out there?"

Volker lay back, staring at the maze of pipes and cables above him. "Captain, I have never seen anything like it." Volker shook his head. "We reached the camp and I signaled with the light. I didn't see any reply. I signaled three more times, still nothing. I thought they couldn't see the signal in the fog. I ordered the men forward." Volker coughed violently.

"Kruger, some juice over here."

Becker took the bottle, held it to Volker's lips while he drank down great gulps.

"Thank you, Captain."

Becker handed the half-drained bottle back to Kruger. "Now tell me."

"The entire camp was gone ..." he stammered.

"Gone?"

Volker trembled. "Tents, equipment, metal buildings all blown apart. Bodies everywhere."

"What bodies?"

"Captain," he bit at his lower lip, his eyes darted. "There was a large fence, or enclosure, more like a cage. I counted fifteen dead there."

"What?" Becker's stomach knotted in fear. "Our men?"

"No sir, I think they were Russian."

"You mean POWs?"

"Yes, sir. It looked like some escaped. I found a hole under the ice on the backside of the cage. We went on and saw German and Russian bodies. Our men were beaten, stabbed, or shot. Russians had our weapons. I think there was a fight and someone shot a fuel tank. Outside one of those buildings was a big hole. I could smell burned petrol. I imagine that was the fuel depot."

"You're sure everyone was dead?"

"I don't know. We checked the bodies we could. Others were too burned. I counted seventy." Volker paused. "I thought there could still be Russians hiding in the ice. We were unarmed, so I ordered the men to run."

"You did the right thing. Get some rest." Becker turned to go.

"Captain," Volker moved his arms till he raised up. "I went in one of the metal buildings and saw large canisters. Twelve, I think. Each large enough for a man. They had windows cut into the front and hoses coming out of the top." Volker's brow crinkled. "What happened, sir?"

Becker ran his hands through his hair. "I don't know, but I am going to find out. Now get some sleep."

Becker moved to the hatch. "Roth, check for messages," he whispered. "Find out what the Major is doing and report to me."

"Aye, sir," responded Roth.

Becker walked forward into the torpedo room. The mechanics came to attention as he entered. Becker waved them to carry on. His men moved about in silence tending to the sleek sinister looking *fish.* The sleek shapes of the torpedoes filled most of the space. Their dull bronze bodies and greenish warheads, held captive by straps, secured them to the hull. The upper torpedo stow held the new secret Leche torpedo, a meter smaller than the regular G-7e, with a soft black nose.

Instead of running straight to a target, this weapon listened for its quarry, then turned to attack. If it missed on the first try, a thin wire connected to the U-boat could send a signal and steer the torpedo to its victim. *Takes all the fun out of it*, Becker thought.

Above his head, heavy chains dangled from massive steel beams. Narrow bunks, used after a number of *fish* had been fired, formed of thin steel tubing, were lashed up along the white painted hull. Boxes of tools lay strapped to the diamond patterned deck. To use every millimeter of space, loaves of moldy bread and greasy sausages hung everywhere. Canned foods, stacked and tied in neat bundles, hung in rows lining whatever space remained.

The torpedo tubes stood at the head of this jumble. Becker picked his way carefully till he stood between the tubes. He peered over the maze of pipes and cables to a small space behind the equalizing control manifold. There, wrapped in a dull silver blanket-like material, was the Major's cargo.

Becker ran his hand over the cool, damp silver covering. He pressed down on the tight, thick green webbing, but felt nothing.

The Captain thought of what the landing party saw, the Major, this cargo, the secrecy. Nothing fell into place, nothing made sense. *Why me? Why this boat?* Becker rubbed his head and trudged aft, hoping a message from C-C headquarters would send them home.

Becker knew he needed sleep. *Just a few minutes*, he thought. *Machines get rest, pumps, batteries, the diesels, and now it's my turn.* Ducking through the hatch, Becker turned toward his cabin.

Directly across the narrow passage, Roth sat at his folding chair hunched over the radio receiver. As Becker brushed past, he could see Roth poured over the top secret *Enigma* coding machine, careful to copy each letter correctly.

"Anything for us?" asked Becker.

"No sir. Routine messages." Roth looked at his messages. "Sir, there is one message I don't understand."

"Oh?" yawned Becker.

"Never received a message from the Japanese."

"The Japanese?"

Roth read the message. "*All Vessels Of The Combined Imperial Fleet, Merchant Vessels, and Allied Vessels of Japan Operating In The Northern Pacific.*"

"Let me see that." Becker snatched the message and studied the words. "Get Frimunt," he ordered.

Roth stepped quickly around the corner and ducked through the control room hatch.

Becker read the message again. *Maybe this was some type of code,* he thought.

Frimunt stepped through the hatch with Roth close behind.

Becker handed him the paper. "Read it."

Frimunt cleared his throat, then read aloud, "*An earthquake of great intensity has occurred from the American held Aleutian Islands to the Bering Sea. This earthquake continued along the sea of Okhotsk to the tip of the home islands. All vessels operating in these waters are warned of intense wave action, including waves of Tsunami force. Vessels operating in the service of His Majesty will use all precautions. In the name of the Emperor, Admiral Mineichi Koga, Commander Combined Fleet.* What does it mean?"

"I hoped you would know." Becker took the message back. "Okay, carry on."

Frimunt disappeared into the control room.

Becker limped to his bunk again and let his frame fall onto the thin mattress. "Here," Becker said as he handed Roth the message.

"What do you think, Captain?" he asked.

"That's on the other side of the world," Becker answered. "We have enough trouble on this side."

"Yes sir," Roth nodded. "TS-UN-AM-I," he sounded out the unknown word. "Oh, Captain, the Major decoded a message from Berlin."

Becker bolted upright. "Did you look at it?"

"No, sir. He destroyed it after decoding."

"Anything else?" Becker tried to hide the fear in his voice.

"He tore up his code book. I think he dumped it over the side."

Becker jumped off his bunk. "Where is he now?"

"I don't know."

"Find him." Becker stumbled into the passageway. "Get the Chief, Frimunt and the other officers here now."

Becker heard a faint popping sound, then another, followed by a scream. Then a screech of high-pressure air filled the hull.

He knew the sound of the 9mm rounds. *A Luger.* He thought of the gun Gerlach carried on his belt.

Shouts and curses ran through the hull. Becker pushed through a tangle of sailors to the control room.

The control room mechanic saw the Captain. "Torpedo room," he shouted.

Flying through passages and hatches, Becker entered the Torpedo room. Two men lay bleeding on the deck. Shipmates tore off the shirts to stop the flow of blood. Mechanics searched for the valve to secure the screaming air. Then Becker saw Kruger, the giant Torpedoman.

The deafening scream of escaping air slowly died. Orders rang out. But Kruger stood silent between the tubes, only his back visible. Becker saw the muscles on Kruger's back ripple and flex. Kruger's right arm slowly rose and his plate-sized hand gripped another hand, clad in black and holding a pistol.

"Kruger," Becker shouted as he ran forward.

The Torpedoman made no sound. Becker grabbed the pistol, then saw Kruger had Gerlach's throat in his left hand, his face, now purple, his black eyes wide and white. The fingers squeezed like bands of steel, sinking into the SS man's tender neck. Gerlach's mouth opened and his tongue hung out.

"Stop," Becker grabbed at Kruger's arm and pulled. The arm flexed again and the fingers tightened.

"Kruger. Stop *now*." Without thinking, Becker backed up and with all his strength plowed his fist into Kruger's side.

The big man turned his head.

"Kruger, let go," Becker order. "I have the gun."

The fingers relaxed. The Major crumpled, his tortured lungs gasped for air. Streams of crimson spit dangled from his blue lips. His head hung as limp as the rest of his body.

"What have you done?" Becker bent over the Major.

Gerlach gurgled.

"Get him out of here," shouted Becker.

"What do we do with him?" a voice asked.

"Tie him up in the engine room. And for God's sake, put a watch on him. Where's Roth?"

"Here, sir."

"How many wounded?" Becker's own breath came in gasps.

"Two. None serious."

Another shout. "Captain."

Becker's head turned to the voice. One of the wounded pointed to the torpedo on the upper port rack.

"The warhead. Under the warhead," The wounded man rasped as his arm jabbed at the air.

Obermechaniker Aldo Baldric, the Weapons Warrant Officer, closest to the torpedo, peered under the *fish* and gasped. "A bomb," He backed away almost tripping over his own feet.

Becker's mind swam and everything seemed in slow motion. From the corner of his eye, Becker saw Edel jump over the wounded man to the weapon.

Thrusting his thin hand under the warhead, Edel grunted, strained and pulled at the attached explosive then a sickening sticky sound echoed in the Torpedo room. The Chief withdrew his arm with an explosive in his hand, slightly smaller than a loaf of bread, wrapped tightly in brown wax paper and a steel pencil-shaped fuse. The fuse slipped through his fingers. With one hand holding the explosive, Edel reached into his back pocket for a rag, wrapped the fuse in the rag and pulled, but the fuse stayed. Angry wisps of gray smoke jetted from the fuse.

"Get it off the boat," Becker shouted.

"Out of the way." Baldric shot forward, grabbed the bomb, and in an instant, gone. Becker followed.

Men dove to the side, slamming themselves against steel hull. At the control room ladder, Baldric reached for the rung. Suddenly, the bomb slipped from his greasy, sweaty fingers. With a dull thud, the explosive charge landed on the deck. The fuse hissed louder.

With no emotion, Baldric reached down and snatched the bomb. His boots clanged loudly as he climbed the ladder into the conning tower with Becker close behind. The fuse spurted sparks and blue-white jets of fire as Baldric thrust himself to the bridge.

Becker felt the icy wind rush down the open hatch. The Captain's legs cleared the hatch when he heard the Warrant Officer's booming voice. "Get down."

Pain shot through Becker's back as the lookouts fell on him. Pinned against the hatch and the periscope fairing, Becker struggled to turn his head and saw Baldric launch the bomb to starboard, his arm moving in a graceful arc.

For a few seconds¯silence. *A dud?* thought Becker.

Splitting the air, the explosion expanded into a fireball three meters across. A pressure wave moving three times the speed of sound, slammed into U-761, rocking the submarine as if a toy.

The blast tore the air from Becker's lungs and pressed his eardrums to the point of rupture. His body lifted, then slammed into the deck. The explosion echoed in waves, then carried its report across the broken ice. Then silence.

Slowly the men who pinned Becker rolled to the side.

"Stay down," Baldric shouted. "Cover your heads."

Chunks of black ice rained over the U-boat and pelted those on the bridge. Broken ice the size of footballs, smashed down onto the casing. Upon impact they exploded, sending deadly shards in all directions. Larger pieces of blasted ice, splashed alongside the submarine then finally silence.

Becker craned his neck. "Anyone hurt?" he asked as touched each man.

Slowly they picked themselves up, weak-kneed and dazed.

"Baldric?" Becker asked.

"Sir," he panted, "I need a new job."

"I hear the Army is hiring," Becker answered.

Baldric grinned. "Thank you, sir. I will keep that in mind." He groaned, took hold of the bridge handrail and lifted himself up.

Edel thrust his head from the hatch. "Everyone okay?"

"Yes, Chief," Becker responded. With the help of the lookout, Becker regained his feet.

"My God, look," shouted Hamlin.

The explosion created a crater six meters across and a meter deep in the ice. The ugly black hole marred the clean ice with jagged dark gray fingers shooting in every direction. Chunks of dead black ice littered the once clean icescape.

"How much longer for the batteries?" Becker asked Edel.

"Another half hour."

"Good. Check the boat for damage, then we'll get out of here."

Edel disappeared down the hatch. Becker lowered himself down, every muscle ached. "Coming Baldric?"

"Yes, sir." He smiled down at the Captain. "First time I've been out of the boat in a month."

Back in the control room, the men staggered about, shaking their heads from the concussion of the blast. Charts lay scattered on the control room floor. Electricians replaced fuses and checked wires. Shards of broken cups and bits of blasted bulbs littered the gray steel.

Roth appeared by Becker's side. "Sir, I checked the wounded," reported Roth. "Torpedo mechanic Henning grazed in the upper left arm. Machinist Mallman, a bullet went deep into the buttocks, but I managed to get it out. But sir, it's not them I'm worried about. It's the Major. Kruger almost killed him. His breathing is not very good. I think his trachea is swelling shut."

"Damn." Becker closed his eyes. "What can you do?"

Roth chewed his thumb. "If the swelling gets worse, I will have to open his throat. I make a cut here, then put a tube inside his windpipe to breathe through until the swelling goes down."

"And you've done this before?" asked Becker.

"No, but I have the book, and it may be the only way to keep him alive." Their eyes met. "Sir, if the Major dies... "

"Let's just make sure he makes it. Okay?"

"Aye, Captain." Roth turned and went aft.

Becker sat again on his mattress. He drew the flimsy blue curtain shut. He lay back sank into his mattress as if melting into the best thing on earth.

"Captain?" came a voice outside the curtain.

"Yes?" *I knew it was too good to be true.*

"Sir, it's Berdy," the voice whispered. "I brought you some food."

Becker swung his feet off the bunk and pulled the curtain aside. There stood Berdy, tray in hand and as always, that infectious smile on his round face.

"Here, Captain. Some corned beef with gravy. Freshest bread on board and a bowl of tomato stew. Looks like you need it, if I may, sir."

Becker smiled. "Yes, I do." Becker reached up and unfolded the small table from its recess.

Always the professional, Berdy gently lowered the tray to the table.

"Thank you, Berdy."

The ship's only cook bowed slightly. His small hand drew the curtain as he left.

Becker dug into the steaming plate. The beef was good, a little salty, but warm. He quickly finished the heaping mound of beef. Becker then pushed the hard crusty bread into the gravy. Soon the plate was clean. Now for the stew, Becker thought as he picked up his spoon.

Suddenly the bowl shook and the red liquid vibrated small waves radiated from its center. Becker felt U-761 shudder. The submarine rocked from bow to stern. Becker jumped to his feet. The tray, plate and utensils crashed to the deck. He headed for the control room, dodging men as they fell, unable to balance.

A deep rumble ran through the hull and grew till it drowned out the sound of the diesels. The submarine pitched up and down.

"Captain. Captain to the bridge," the frantic cry, almost a scream.

The U-boat bucked and Becker slipped on the ladder. It took all his strength to hold on and climb the ladder. He pushed his head over the bridge where a gale of hard wind tore at his face. "What is it Hamlin?" he shouted above the growing roar.

Eyes wide and full of terror, the young Lieutenant slowly raised his shaky arm over the bow of the U-boat.

Blood drained from Becker's face and his knees weakened. The ice around the submarine danced, great plates lifted and fell, roared and screamed. Large cracks opened along the ice, then slammed shut. Each convulsion of the ice sounded like a thunderclap.

"My God." His brain tried to process the sight.

Less than a kilometer from U-761, a wave of ice rushed toward them. The wave lifted great house-sized blocks of ice, flipped them like playing cards. As if feeding on the dying ice, the wave grew ten meters high, then fifteen. Thousand-ton slabs of ice rolled and churned in the wave, and the roar grew louder than any thunder. Pressure within the ice exploded, shards and boulders of ice hurled hundreds meters into the gray sky.

"Clear the bridge," Becker bellowed above the roar.

A lookout stood transfixed by the site of the mounting wave so Becker grabbed him by the arm and shoved him toward the hatch. The men tumbled down, landing on one another. "Alarm," he yelled.

The wave towered over the U-boat. Becker looked one last time before slamming the hatch. As if alive, the wave boiled, grinding the ancient ice into powder. Bullets of blue white ice crashed into the U-boat. Automobile sized boulders of ice splashed along side of the submarine, throwing her onto one side, then the other. Each time U-761 fought to right herself, she was rocked by another boulder of ice.

Becker landed in the control room with a heavy thud. He pulled himself upright braced himself with the chart table. "Chief, 200 meters now," he screamed.

"Open the vents," Edel shouted over the roar. "Stand by on the motors."

All eyes watched the depth gauge. It didn't move. A shout rang out from the back of the control rooms.

"Vents will not open."

Edel's eyes widened. "Override the control. Operate them in hand."

The stern of the U-boat sank slightly, the shark-like bow jutted up as if challenging the oncoming wave.

"Forward vents must be clogged." Edel looked at the Captain. Their unspoken words told the terrible truth.

"Hold on," Becker shouted.

Then a slab of three meters thick ice, slightly smaller than a city block slid under the upturned bow. The entire hull left the water. U-761 fell to port. Unable to bear the weight of the submarine, the great slab cracked and U-761 fell two meters and landed in a V of broken ice.

As the wave rushed over, tons of ice pushed U-761's hull, further into her ice cradle, burying her. The bow remained up, but the stern dropped again. The ice broke again. The ice resisted, but the pressure of the wave was too great, and the ice started to spin. It spun faster as the pressure increased. Millions of tons of ice and steel spun like a top.

Inside U-761, men and machines tumbled through space. The lights flickered then went out. Objects hung in the air only to be bashed into dust against the hull. Emergency lights came on, but they too went dark as the submarine turned and rolled. Equipment crashed and sparks from blown fuses lit the air in flashes. Like rag dolls men slammed tossed through air as if gravity was no longer an earthly force.

Becker strained to hold onto the chart table. His arms felt as though they might rip from his shoulders. Over the roar, he heard screams, but couldn't tell which was his.

Chapter Two

Trapped

"All you that would be seaman must bear a valiant heart."
Martin Parker, d 1656

August 21st 1944

It died as quickly as it had come. Shuddering, moaning steel quieted. The roar of the furious wave faded into silence. Becker opened his eyes into complete blackness. His head felt as if solid lead had replaced his brain, his body rigid, every muscle coiled and sore. The Captain strained and grunted as he slowly lifted his chest off the chart table. He craned his neck, but could see nothing in the inky dark. Ghostlike moans and whimpers filled his ears. With great effort, Becker forced himself upright. His rubber boots slipped on the damp deck. He found a hand-hold and moved his foot forward. The boat listed to port.

My God, he thought. *A ballast tank has ruptured.* Becker heard a curse as an arc flashed blue-white from behind the main control room lighting panel. Grudgingly, lights glowed till they peaked to a sickening yellow.

Once his eyes adjusted, Becker glanced around at

charts, logbooks, broken dishes, spare parts, clothing and men lay everywhere. Bundles of red, black and green wire lay in a tangle, along the deck, or dangled from broken panels. Thick black cables hung from the overhead, as if the very guts of the submarine lay strung out. A reeking stench of bilge water, sweaty men and rotting food filled Becker's nose. He shook his head to clear the dizziness in his skull. "Damage reports."

Around him, men stirred and struggled to their feet. Their breath came in pants. Becker carefully pulled himself to the depth gauge. *Where are we? He thought.* His memory came back in a rush. I *ordered us to dive. If the vents opened, we could be falling beyond crush depth.*

Becker scanned the depth gauges again then at the main gauge with its plate-sized white dial. His brow wrinkled. The thin black needle indicated zero.

"Chief." Becker turned, almost losing his boot's grip on the tilted deck. "Where is Edel?"

"Here, sir." Edel wedged himself up using the silver periscope barrel for support.

"I need a full report."

"Yes, sir," Edel mumbled as he limped aft.

Becker noticed his men with their eyes blank, mouth open taking in the foul cold air. Becker recognized that vacant look, the look that always preceded panic.

"Okay, let's get this sty back in order," he bellowed. "Come on men, nap time is over." Becker clapped his hands.

"Frimunt," he called.

"Sir," the reply, weak.

"Frimunt, where are you?" Becker saw boots lying behind the barrel like gyrocompass.

The boots moved. Frimunt rose to his knees. A trembling hand reached for the top of the compass. Frimunt groaned and with effort, he pushed his shaking frame upright. "Sir …" He staggered a step, his legs wobbly.

Jarman, the control room electrician, dropped his tools and stepped up the sloping deck just as Frimunt's legs collapsed. Jarman put his chest into the Lieutenant's, holding him up. Frimunt's head slumped over the smaller man's shoulder.

"Help here," Jarman pleaded.

Two crewmen reached out. The three of them lowered the injured officer to the cold slanting floor. Jarman pulled the oilskin hat from Frimunt's head. Frimunt's usual light auburn hair matted with thick oozing blood, the left side above the ear was caved inward. Dark blood dripped from his left ear. His body shook and his eyes glazed.

Becker looked at Lieutenant's ashen face. "Frimunt," he shouted.

The Oberleutnant's legs slowly, flailed on the deck. The eyes regained some color. He tried to move his head.

"Frimunt, don't move," Becker whispered. "Just look at me."

The Captain saw Frimunt's eyes try to focus. The pupils grew smaller.

"Frimunt?" Becker whispered. "What is our motto?"

Becker wiped blood from Frimunt's forehead and

turned to Jarman. "Get Roth. Now." Back to Frimunt. "Stay with me." Becker took the man's hand, the grip weak and pulsing. *Keep him awake. Make him talk.* "Come on, man, what is our motto?"

Frimunt's lips moved, "Every... "

"Yes that's it. Say it with me."

"Every on ...one. Everyone comes home."

"Yes. Now say it again. Everyone comes home."

Frimunt swallowed. "Every ... one... comes home."

"That's right. You keep saying that. You hear me, Lieutenant?"

"Ye ... yes, sir."

Roth, knelt down to examine Frimunt's head.

"Get some help over here," Roth called. "Jarman. Get a litter."

Machinists Waller and Burhardt dropped their tools and moved up the sloped deck. Gunner's mate, Nefen also crawled toward Roth.

"We need to get him to a bunk," Roth whispered and wiped his lips on his sleeve. "Waller, take his feet. Burhardt, and Nefen take a side. I'll support his neck and head."

Moving carefully, the men positioned themselves. Jarman stood ready with the green canvas litter.

"Put that in front of the hatch." Roth pointed to the open circle of steel then put his hands under Frimunt's head. "Okay. On three, we lift." They looked at each other nervously and nodded. "One, two, three.... Keep him level." Roth urged. "There. Now easy, easy. Set him down."

Becker squeezed Frimunt's hand, then folded it over his chest.

"Okay, let's move," Roth ordered.

Becker's mind flashed back to U-432. He forced the thoughts from his head, but, still his hands shook. He tried to calm his breathing, which came in short shallow inhalations. Becker closed his eyes, fighting the rage. He hoped the crew didn't notice. *God, they're scared enough*, he thought.

Edel came through the hatch, silently slipping next to the Captain. "Sir, I have a damage list. A coolant leak in the starboard diesel, three lighting panels tore off their mounts. One cell in the forward battery cracked. Number two lube oil purifier has a cracked base plate. Our compressor's second stage relief valve is jammed. Fuel oil transfer pump blew a packing. And, our air banks are depleted."

"How long for repairs?"

Edel pulled the cap off his head and scratched the tuft of his remaining hair. "Give me two hours. Three at the most."

"Injuries?" Becker asked.

"It could've been worse." Edel flipped the page in his tired leather notebook. "Other than Frimunt, a few broken bones, some cuts, and bruises, but nothing life threatening."

Becker nodded, "Good."

"The younger you are, the more you bounce," Edel offered.

Becker grinned, then his face turned serious. He pulled Edel close, his voice a whisper, "Are the vents open or shut?"

Edel looked at the indicator above the planesmen seat. "Open," Edel whispered back.

"Are we submerged?"

The Engineer swallowed, and tapped the depth gauge's glass face then moved to the periscopes. Reaching high above his head, his hand found the green handled valve. "Let's see if there is any water in the periscope housing." Slowly he twisted the valve and a hiss of air escaped then silence. Edel moved to the depth gauge valve. His hand reached for the special wrench still in its holder. Behind a maze of pipes, he fit the wrench on the valve and opened the tiny port. A faint wisp of air spurted from the valve, then silence. Edel twisted the wrench to shut the test fitting. He sat back, face puzzled.

"What about the control room strainer?" Becker asked.

"Good idea." Edel stepped around the periscopes, dropped to one knee to the left of the scope. He carefully removed the dull brass cap from the sea strainer, pulled the locking ring retainer and slowly twisted the end. After three turns, the bronze plug came off. He peered into the hole. "Nothing."

Becker took in a deep breath and let it out slowly.

Edel replaced the cap and screwed it down hard. "Captain, we have no water under us." Edel stroked nervously at his wiry brown beard. "The hull must have been forced over the ice."

"The stern is down. It could still be submerged."

"Could be," Edel shrugged.

"Maybe we can use the motors and back out."

Edel moved his hands to his hips. "One way to find out." Edel took the control room microphone. "After Torpedo room."

Static crackled through the speaker, then came a voice. “After Torpedo room.”

“After Torpedo room, open the tube flood valve for tube-five. Then, open the tube inboard vent.”

A few seconds passed. Again static. “Control, the valves are open.”

“Is water flowing into the vent drain?”

A half minute passed. “Control.” This time the voice seemed puzzled. “There is no flow from the vent.”

Edel’s eyes looked up. “Captain, we’re trapped.”

Becker took a full deep breath. Try the periscope. See what’s out there.”

Edel nodded. “Better use the sky scope. The Attack scope is thin.”

“Careful, Captain,” Edel warned. “If we break that scope barrel...” He placed his hand on the frosted steel periscope. “That’s an eighty centimeter hole right to the ocean.”

Becker nodded his understanding. “Up scope.”

Edel pushed the orange handle of the lifting hoist. The lifting cable went tight as the scope slithered up. Edel and Becker then felt the scope shudder, then stop, not quite halfway up.

“Damn.” Becker swore as the scope screeched to a halt. He heard the lifting ram whine, straining to lift the heavy scope.

“Captain, lower it some and try it again. Probably a lot of ice to push through,” explained Edel.

Becker moved the handle down. The scope slid back into its pit. “Here we go again.”

When the periscope lifted, it vibrated and twisted with a crunching noise that caused the conning tower to shake. Becker grit his teeth as the scope moved higher, slowed, then stalled.

"Stuck again." Becker was about to lower the periscope, when, it screeched then the two ton barrel slid to full height with a shudder.

Becker turned his white cap till the brim was at the back of his neck. He stepped forward and lowered the scope handles. He peered into the eyepiece and his shoulders sagged. "My God."

The Chief Engineer remained quite. He wiped his hands over his filthy shirt.

Becker moved the scope as if dancing. He swung it left, then right, only to stop and swing it back.

"Well, what is it?" Edel asked.

Becker rested his arm on the black handle of the periscope, he then let his chin fall onto his arm. "The ice is just under the scope head."

Edel gasped.

Becker motioned for him to see for himself. Edel took the scope and looked into the tiny optic window. After one rotation, he hung his head,

"Maybe we can cut ourselves out," Edel suggested. "Use the cutting torch. Pry open the bridge hatch, over the side and melt the ice under the keel."

"Do we have enough gas for that?"

"I don't know," he shrugged.

Becker lifted the cap from his head. "What about a scuttling charge?" Has to be a way."

"Explosives," Edel mumbled. "That might open the ice enough for us to slip out. Go out the forward tubes. Our bow is up. Use the torch, melt a hole far enough from the hull, set a fuse for ten minutes."

Calculations ran through Becker's mind. *How much explosive?* "Can you think of anything else?" he asked.

Edel took in a long drag of foul air. "No."

"Okay. Let's try the explosives." Removing his cap, he let the palm of his hand run over his dark brown hair.

Edel limped to the forward compartment.

"Captain, I have a report on injuries." Roth's voice was as weary as his face.

Becker turned his head to see Roth. Only nineteen, Roth looked old and tired his eyes sunken and his once freckled skin now gray. "Go on."

Roth cleared his throat. "Arnwolf has a broken collar bone. Lambrecht has broken his left arm, just below the shoulder. Lutz has a bad cut above his right eye. Meinrad broke his nose. Kulbert twisted his ankle." Roth finished. He looked at the Captain waiting for a reply. None came. "Captain?"

"I heard you Roth," his voice soft, eyes, distant.

"Sir, most of the crew has minor cuts and bruises. And I am running low on morphine."

"How is the Major?"

"The swelling is down. He is awake, but weak. He can talk, but not much."

"And Frimunt?"

"He needs a doctor. His skull is fractured."

"Okay, Roth. Thank you." Becker lowered his head. "Roth?"

"Yes, Captain?"

"How many special pills do you have?"

Roth's eyes went wide. "Sir … I …"

"How many?" Becker insisted. "Enough for everyone?"

Roth shook his head.

"Good." Becker managed a smiled. "And Roth, when we get home, I'm putting you in for a Knight's Cross."

The young radio operator blinked in disbelief. "Thank ... thank you, sir." Roth turned and faded into the stale air of the U-boat.

Becker closed his eyes. His still throbbing head hung till his chin touched his chest. Scenes floated through his mind. Suddenly, he was at Frimunt's wedding. *That was what, three months ago?* Becker smiled to himself. *What a good looking couple*, he thought. The scene shifted to his first meeting with Erich Kruger and he smiled again.

After U-761's third war patrol, they floated safely in one of the huge U-boat bunkers in Lorient, France. Kruger, sporting his dress uniform, with three attractive nurses in tow, strode along the quay as if he were Donitz himself. Crewmen on the forward casing stood stunned. The big man leaned down and kissed each in turn. Like a scene from a motion picture, Kruger tipped his cap to the giggling nurses, threw his sea bag over his massive shoulders and strutted onto the deck.

One of the torpedo mechanics stuck his head from the forward hatch. "Captain?"

The sound startled Becker back to the present. "Yes?"

"The Engineer needs you in the Torpedo room."

Becker groaned, then hefted his dead tired body from the seat. "I'm coming."

The Captain moved slowly forward, passed the Senior Enlisted mess. Becker glanced at the clock, mounted to the rich honey colored paneling. *Another day,* he thought. Entering the torpedo room, Becker heard clanging of heavy chains of the controlled chaos of loading and unloading torpedoes.

The upper tube door stood open. The twin counter-rotating propellers of the torpedo looked like curved knives. A two-piece steel bracket clamped over the propellers provided both protection and a means of attaching a block and tackle. Once the block mated to the bracket, a thick rope of the finest manila ran through the block. At the end of the rope, a stainless steel C clip had been carefully spliced. This clip slipped into a neatly cut hole in the tube's locking ring. The remaining line lay stretched along the deck.

"All ready?" Baldric called.

"Ready," the men replied in unison.

Baldric pointed to the tube. "Unlock the weapon."

Another Petty Officer pulled a long curved handle. "Weapon free."

"Heave," Baldric shouted.

The manila went tight, then inch-by-inch, the dull olive colored torpedo slipped from its tube. Covered in thick black grease, the weapon crept silently inside the torpedo room. Once the blunt bronze nose cleared the tube door, the men worked quickly. Heavy canvas slings stretched under the fish. Once wrapped around the torpedo, chains were latched to the slings. Three heavy-duty hoists hung under the lifting beam, then linked the chains to the hoists.

Becker heard the hoisting tackle ratchet, as the

lifting beam took the weight of the three-quarter-ton torpedo.

The torpedo gang were as one. Under Baldric's watchful eye, the weapon came gently to the deck and rested on three evenly spaced cradles. Rubber lined steel straps laid over the weapon then quickly locked to the cradles and tightened with wrenches.

Baldric and Edel peered down the throat of the gaping tube. "Pass a light," Baldric snapped. One of the torpedo gang handed Baldric a battle lantern.

Becker stepped toward the tube, just as Baldric flipped on the light. Becker, Edel and Baldric crowded around the tube.

"No damage to the outer door." Baldric removed his dirty peaked cap.

Edel squinted into the large black hole. "Yes, the gasket seems tight."

"Sir, request permission to remove safety locks and open the outer door."

"Do it." Becker placed his mouth an inch from Edel's ear. "Are you sure about this?"

"No, sir."

Baldric reached in his pocket and removed a set of four steel keys. He flipped the keys till he found the one stamped TUBE #1. "Captain, if we're wrong about this, and there is water out there … "Baldric shook his head. "We're dead."

"Unnecessary crew aft," Becker ordered. "Last man out shut and dog the hatch."

Within a minute, only four men stood on the leaning torpedo room deck. Becker, Edel, Baldric, and little Penn, stood in the cold damp air.

Becker could see the worry in Baldric's face. "Go on."

Baldric moved to the side of the tube. Reaching over his head, he placed the key into the mechanical safety that made it impossible to open the breech and the outer door at the same time. He rotated his wrist, and with a sharp metallic click the safety device rotated downward. "Safety unlocked."

Edel moved his hand to the large red lever to open the torpedo tube outer door. "Ready, sir?"

"Do it."

"Stand clear of the door," cautioned Baldric.

The three men moved to the side of the open tube.

"Opening." Edel rotated the curved rod. With creaks and groans, the outer door folded outward while the protective shutter door swung inward.

Becker looked first. "Not a drop."

"Good. We need to get working." Edel motioned for Penn to come closer.

Becker thought, n*o way Penn was eighteen.* Smaller than his shipmates, this boy could not even grow a beard. Penn sported a full head of jet-black hair, which hung over his eyes and framed his baby face.

Edel moved two green tanks in front of the tube. From his back pocket came a length of thin rough rope. Using the rope, he lashed the tanks to the tube door.

Baldric had the cutting torch and hoses in his hand. "You sure you know how to use this?"

Penn nodded and took the thin bronze torch.

Becker placed the lantern in the rim of the tube. The beam reflected off the smooth white ice, causing it to shimmer on the tube walls.

"Penn," called the engineer, "put this on." Edel threw him a heavy oilskin coat. "It's cold in there."

Penn slipped the coat around him.

"We could put two of you in that coat," Baldric laughed.

Edel handed Penn the cutting torch and the striker. "Penn you know what to do?"

"Yes, sir."

"Good. Get at it," Edel replied.

Little Penn stepped in front of number one torpedo tube.

"Here you go." Baldric and Edel picked him off the deck.

Penn took hold of the breech-locking ring, ducked his head and slipped into the black tube. The engineer fed the supply hoses down the tube, as it snaked out behind Penn.

Becker saw a flash inside the tube as Penn lit the torch. "How much gas do you have?"

Edel stepped back and wiped the frost from the gauge. "I say about an hour's worth, maybe less."

Becker shrugged. "Will it be enough?"

"I hope."

Baldric looked over. "It's a race. What will run out first, the gas or the air?"

Becker suddenly shivered and saw tiny icicles hanging from overhead pipes and wires. The Captain stepped to the hatch. His tired muscles strained against the dogs as he opened the heavy circular door. He stuck his head into the CPO quarters. "Bootsmann Hewett. Get the men into warm clothes. It's getting cold in this tub."

"Yes, sir." Hewett answered. "Captain?"

"What is it?"

"Is it working?"

Becker rubbed his beard. "Don't know yet, but I think it will."

Hewett nodded, "Thank you, skipper."

"Edel," Becker called.

Edel stepped over the torpedo."Sir?"

"How's it going?"

Slowly his left foot traced small circles on the deck. "Slower than I thought. I hoped he would be at 3 meters by now."

Becker's thin dark eyebrows rose. "Damn. How far is he?"

"Meter … meter and half."

"We need at least seven meters." Becker pushed his white cap to the back of his head. "Any less and we could damage the bow planes or put a hole in the ballast tanks."

"Or worse."

Becker looked at the tube. A steaming trickle of water sizzled as it dripped from the tube onto the cold deck. Becker lowered himself till he sat on the rim of the compartment hatch. "How much air do we have left?"

"That torch is eating a lot of the oxygen." Edel scratched his head. "We may have to use escape appliances in forty-five minutes," he tapped the cold skin of the U-boat. "That ice - hard as our hull."

"Okay, Chief." Becker stepped to the tube. The blue white flashes of light blinded him as the flame of the torch reflected off the ice.

"Here, sir," Baldric offered the Captain a pair of tinted goggles.

Becker slipped the goggles over his eyes and peered down the tube. Like something from a fable, the Captain gazed at the smooth glasslike tunnel. Not quite a meter wide, the tunnel snaked to the left and up.

Like a faceted diamond, the ice reflected Penn's image as he worked at the face of the ice tunnel. The Captain was about to turn when the reflection and the light of the torch died.

"Penn," Becker called.

Edel was at his side in a second. "Baldric, get the light."

Baldric handed Edel the lantern.

"Penn," Edel called.

From the dark maw of the torpedo tube, there was only silence.

"Damn it, damn it," Baldric yelled as he looked around him. "Rope. I need some rope."

"What's wrong?" Becker demanded.

Edel leaped over the resting torpedo to the port side and tore down a hammock of crusty bread. Stale brown loaves flew through the rank air, landing in a pile. Stepping onto the bread, Edel reached around the port upper tube.

He groaned as he reached further behind the tube. He struggled a moment, then leaned back as his hands found a neatly coiled length of rough hemp rope. He stepped over the rotting bread and in two more steps, he stood over the torpedo, his hands unwound the rope. By the time he reached Baldric, Edel had fashioned a slipknot in the line.

Baldric saw him coming and raised his arms. With one foot still in the air, Edel slipped the loop of rope over Baldric's arms. As the rope slipped to his chest, Edel pulled the knot tight.

Baldric hefted his foot to the top of number three torpedo tube. Using the locking ring as a step, he slithered into the darkness of the greasy tube.

Edel unwound the rope from his arm as Baldric moved up the tube.

Becker peered in the black hole and heard Baldric struggle, his breath coming in pants.

"Pull," Baldric shouted through coughs and gasps. His voice echoed off the tube walls, making his shout seem more like a moan.

Becker grabbed the rope's free end. Edel dropped the coil and grabbed the rope's middle. "Now, Chief." Both men pulled. The rope went tight but would not move.

Edel strained, "Harder." The engineer braced his right foot on the lower tube door. He pushed with his legs and pulled with his back.

Then the rope moved. Slowly at first, then faster, the line snaked from inside the tube.

Becker wrapped a length of the line around his waist. Leaning back, he applied more force. Baldric wheezed and coughed his lungs desperate for air. He pulled again, as the coughing got louder.

Suddenly, a boot appeared at the tube. Edel dropped the line and went for the boot. He pulled and another boot flopped out of the tube.

Becker dropped his end of the rope and moved like a cat next to Edel.

Baldric's gray-green trousers emerged. "Hurry," he wheezed.

Edel grabbed at Baldric's pant's pocket, the Captain his leg, and pulled till Baldric's head came out of the tube. The three of them reached into the tube and pulled Penn's limp body slipped out of the tube and into Edel's arms. Baldric fell to one knee gasping for air, his face and lips, a sickening blue-purple.

Becker took Penn's legs, as Edel cradled the young man's shoulder and gently laid Penn in the upper starboard bunk.

The Captain leaned over till his face was even with the torpedo room hatch. "Get Roth."

Penn's face had turned blue like Baldric's. Becker pushed on the boy's chest. Penn's eyes and mouth opened. He gasped and sucked in the dank air.

Edel helped Baldric to his feet and to the bunk below Penn's.

Baldric also took in air in great gulps. His color changed from blue to its usual pale cream.

"You okay?" Edel asked.

"Good, sir. Just let me get my breath." Baldric coughed again.

"How is he, Captain?" Edel panted.

Becker did not answer. He kept his eyes on Penn.

Penn's breath came in long, labored drags. Like Baldric, the boy's face slowly returned to normal. "Sorry, sir," he managed between breaths.

Becker smiled down. "Not your fault." *If and when we return to Germany,* he thought, *this entire crew would wear the Knight's Cross.*

Edel moved to the open tube and began pulling the red hose and torch from the tube.

Becker felt that unwelcome rage, slowly spin in his stomach. He worked hard to fight it.

Roth ducked is head through the hatch. “Sir, you called for me?”

Becker did not respond.

“Captain?”

Becker motioned to the two bunks. “Check Penn and the Baldric.”

“What happened?” Roth stepped through the hatch.

“They ran out of air working in the tube,” his voice cold as the air around him.

A sudden metallic clang echoed in the hull. Becker spun on his heels at the noise, his face growing red and his eyes, a burning blue.

“Outer door shut.” Edel announced. He froze as he saw Becker’s face. “Captain?”

Becker did not speak. The rage wrapped around him like a snake. He felt his arms shake. His mind suddenly filled with acid. “Captain?” Edel stepped over the torpedo toward him.

Becker spun on his heels and dashed through the hatch. “Out of my way.”

Edel followed. “Captain?”

“Not now, ” The Captain barked.

Sailors moved from their Commander’s path. The passageway cleared as if by a force of nature.

He stopped at his cabin. Behind the pillow lay Gerlach’s Luger. Becker threw the heavy feather pillow to the floor. For a second he looked at the polished evil-looking weapon. In another second, the gun in his hand, Becker racked the action. A spent casing flew from the chamber landing silently on the bunk. Becker pushed the magazine release. Skillfully, he moved his fingers under the Luger's handle and caught the magazine. He looked at the black rectangle and counted the shinning brass shells. In the same motion, Becker slammed the magazine back into the gun and pulled the action. This time a live shell entered the chamber.

Becker turned. Edel stood, arms outstretched, blocking the way into the passage. "Captain," he said softly.

"Out of my way," Becker shouted.

"Sir, please."

"Get out of my way." Becker's lip curled. "That's an order."

Edel dropped his arms. He moved his hands in front of him, palms up, "Please, Captain."

Becker could not hear. He pushed the Engineer aside. Once in the passageway, Becker looked aft. He no longer felt pain in his legs, or fatigue, only the rage swam in his veins.

His steps thumped on the deck gratings. He passed the hatch to the diesel room, his boots boomed on the hollow floor of engine room. He ducked as he passed into the electric motor room. His head missed the steel rim by millimeters.

On the starboard side, Major Gerlach swayed in a stinking wadded up canvas hammock. His head lay to the side, propped up by a blanket slightly less filthy than the hammock, his hands tightly bound over his head. His eyes watched every move through their bruised and blackened lids.

Becker grabbed Gerlach's black coat below his

battered throat. "Now, Major." he hissed through clenched teeth. "You will talk or your brains will be all over my ship." Becker shook the Major's head. "Why are we here?"

His bloodshot eyes stared at the Captain without emotion, his mouth tightened,

Becker's rage grew as Gerlach turned his head away. "Damn you to hell."

He slammed Gerlach back down, only to grab him up again. "Because of you, my crew is half dead. I want to know why we have to die here?"

Becker shoved the black barrel into Gerlach's mouth. His eyes on fire, Becker moved his thumb and slowly brought the hammer back.

Chapter Three

Water Bears

"I am a man under authority, having soldiers under me: and I say to this man, go,and he goeth: and to another, come, and he cometh."

Matthew, VII, IX

August 21, 1944

Becker felt his hand tremble as his finger slowly pressed the thin curved trigger.

Gerlach gagged and sputtered when the Luger's barrel pressed the back of his throat. The Major's neck twisted in reflex then he choked on the gun's muzzle. Blood mixed with thick spit dripped in long red strings from his lips.

"Bastard," Becker shouted. "Is this how SS men die?"

Gerlach's eyes spun wildly in their sockets as if looking for salvation. He gurgled when his swollen throat took in what air it could.

Suddenly Gerlach's body went limp. He exhaled a long bubbling breath. His eyes shut in acceptance of the end and waited for the bullet.

At the same time, Becker's mind went numb. Images of Frimunt's wedding again appeared, then his own wedding. He could see his new bride that day at Lake Constance. Through the lace of her veil, her dark blonde hair shimmered in the late May sun. He thought of the way she fussed over him when he was home on leave. She always knew what do, what to say, what not to ask. And how she silently cried each time he boarded the train for France ... and the war. *Wonder what she is doing now? What is she now - six or is it seven months pregnant?* He wondered.

Then the rage unwrapped itself. The acid in him seeped out. He looked at the gun in his hand. *If I do this, what would that make Ada?* he reasoned with himself. *What would she think? What about our child? Son or daughter of a murderer?* Becker warmed with the thought. *Our child.*

Images of Ada faded, replaced by images of severed arms and bloated bodies. That day on U-432. He shook his head to clear the images.

The trembling in his hand eased. *Too much blood on my hands already*, he thought. "*Too much blood,*" Becker whispered to himself.

A voice, familiar but strangely distant, came to him, "Captain?"

Becker turned his head to see Edel standing behind him.

"Captain, give me the gun," Edel asked with his hand outstretched.

His entire mind and body felt perfectly drained. The Captain closed his eyes.

"Captain? Sir, please give it to me," Edel pleaded.

Becker opened his eyes. He saw Gerlach - not as he had been - but as he was now. Ready to die.

"Major, open your mouth," Becker whispered.

Major Gerlach's eyes blinked open as if a switch turned him back on. He focused on Becker. His lips slowly parted.

Becker lifted his finger from the trigger and eased out the gun barrel.

"Here, sir, I'll take it," Edel urged.

The Captain turned his head, then put the gun gently in the engineer's palm.

"You okay, Captain?"

"Yes, fine now, Chief." Becker nodded to the gun in Edel's hand. "Put that away for me."

"Aye, Captain," Edel's hand closed around the gun as he limped forward.

"Why?" Gerlach rasped.

"You're not worth the bullet," Becker hissed.

Gerlach's bloodied lips curled into a vile grin. "True, but not the reason."

The Captain rolled his head from side-to-side to stretch out the tension. "You know Major, this is it. We'll die here." Becker looked at the hull above him. "In a day - maybe more - we'll freeze. Not much left in the batteries. No way to get any fresh air." Becker sneered. "I wanted you to enjoy it with the rest of us."

"Not a bad way to go, so I understand." Gerlach cleared his throat, turned and spit. "In Auschwitz, prisoners submerged in ice water stay alive for three hours. No pain, in fact, they felt warm and peaceful, then they slipped away. Peaceful and quiet."

"Major, don't push me."

"Why didn't you kill me?" Gerlach's voice almost a taunt.

Becker stood slowly, and rubbed the back of his neck. "Killing you is easy, to let you live is a challenge. I kill you I become you. I let you live, I win."

"Win?" Gerlach coughed, "Win what?"

Becker's cheek twitched. "My soul."

Gerlach shrugged, "Oh, come now, Captain. A German in the service of the Fuehrer worried about his soul?"

Becker's eyes blazed. "What else do we have? You arrogant little bastard."

"Duty to the cause," rasped Gerlach.

Becker lowered his face inches from Gerlach's swollen face. "You think what you and you're your chicken farmer boss is doing has anything to do with duty?"

Major Gerlach's bruised face reddened further. "You're a traitor."

"Look at my crew. These are the real Germans. My men - or boys, I should say. A thousand miles from home, rotting in this stinking sewer pipe, ready to die. Die for what? So boot lickers like you can reign over the planet." Becker caught his breath. "The worst part of it is, I am just as guilty. Every patrol, I take boys to sea. When I went to sea, I learned how to reef a sail, tie a bowline. But, what do I teach? I teach death. I give lessons on how to kill other young men. Does that make them acceptable Germans?"

"It is their duty to the Fatherland," Gerlach hacked.

"Duty? Becker snarled. "They cheer when our torpedoes sink a tanker or freighter. They paint flags for each ship we send to the bottom. They cannot see what I do in the periscope. I see other young men -

British, American, Russian - arms torn off, legs gone, some on fire. They fall into the ocean choosing to drown rather than fry. No, Major there will be no victory. And us? We'll just be part of a statistic. Major, I do care. The reason we will lose is that people like you, don't."

Gerlach could not speak, the arrogance drained from his face. "Germany will lose this war. You talk of the things you have seen," Gerlach swallowed hard. "That is nothing, compared to what I have witnessed."

The Captain held up his hands. "Please, Major, I don't want to know."

Gerlach turned his face to Becker's. "That's the problem," Gerlach's voice cleared, he tilted his head back. "Soon the whole world will know." Gerlach gagged again, turned, and spit. "When that happens, Germany will be erased from humanity. Just like us," Gerlach whispered. "Germany is doomed. You should be grateful you won't live to see it. "

"Well, I'm not," shouted Becker. "If there were any way to save my ship, I would."

Gerlach stared. "Captain. There will be no Germany, no home, nothing."

"No, Major, I can't believe that. I have something you don't."

Gerlach looked at the Captain, puzzled. "What would that be?"

"Hope."

The Major rolled his eyes. "I wish it were so."

Becker reached down and tore the party emblem from Gerlach's coat. "Not all Germans think like you. Most are good people. You think they hate the British, or Americans? Your ideals feed on hate. You add hate, throw in some lies, sprinkle it with uniforms, stir it with propaganda, bake in a useless war. You keep hoping the cake will taste good. Not so tasty, is it, Major? Besides, half the American soldiers have German names. Although I will never see it, my child will know the real Germany, and hopefully, a better world."

Gerlach remained quiet and rested his head against the woolen blanket. The Captain rose to his feet and turned to go.

Gerlach's eyes shot open, "Captain."

"What?"

"You are right."

Becker laughed.

"No, Captain, you don't understand. There is hope."

"Maybe in the next life. But I won't be seeing you there."

Gerlach coughed. "Maybe, I can get us home."

Becker moved next to Gerlach and sat down. "Okay Major, how?"

"You wanted to know about my mission? I'll tell you," Gerlach coughed. "Germany is going to lose. Everyone knows that - some knew it from the beginning. The war started too early. Some think Hitler is way ahead of his time."

Becker looked puzzled. "We all know that."

"This trip was part of an experiment to preserve Hitler until the nation and the world would be ready for his ideas."

Becker felt the hair on the back of his neck go straight and his guts tighten. "What?"

"Yes, Captain its true."

"How?" Becker hissed.

Gerlach took a deep gurgling breath. "Have you ever heard of an animal called the water bear?"

Becker shook his head.

"A very tiny animal, so small you need a microscope to see it. These animals live in moss, under rocks, in trees, mud - everywhere. Captain, even on this boat there are millions. They may be the oldest living creature on earth."

Becker tried to understand, but this did not make any sense. "So what?"

"What makes these animals important is that they never die," Gerlach said.

"What?" asked Becker.

"If you take a water bear and freeze it, the animal will shut its body down. If you starve its oxygen, same result. We even placed a water bear in boiling water and the little bastard just draws in its legs and goes to sleep. Breathing, heartbeat, all stop. Even frozen, without air or even boiled, the water bear reanimates when conditions returned to normal. Captain, water bears have been revived after one hundred and twenty years."

The pieces neatly fit the puzzle, the camp, the canisters Volker mentioned, the Russian prisoners. Becker felt faint.

Gerlach went on. "A doctor in Munich discovered he could remove the protein that provides the water bear with this talent. Better yet, he discovered how to make the same protein."

"And used those Russians for guinea pigs," Becker mumbled.

The Major looked down. "Yes."

Becker's features turned hard. "So when the ice camp was blown away, you were to destroy all evidence of the experiment?"

"Yes."

"Are you saying that our cargo is that protein?"

"The code name for the operation is *The Forever Project* - not just the protein. It is combined with agents that assist an organism's survival." Gerlach beamed. "Our scientists created a gas that floods the lungs, blood and tissues of the test subject." Gerlach stopped to clear his throat. "A dog was placed in a solid block of ice for six months. No food, water or air. When the ice thawed, the animal seemed no worse. No tissue damage. Organs and blood -everything - operated just as it should."

"So, this was to be the first test on humans?"

"One of the first," Gerlach replied. "We had other items we wanted to look at also."

Becker interrupted, "What if a person were injured and then frozen?"

"If that person were frozen, they would be dead." answered Gerlach.

"But, you said…"

"What I should have said is cold is used to trigger the reaction in the organism. The gas does not freeze the subject. It triggers hibernation - more correctly - we call it suspended animation. Other additives in the gas protect tissues, organs, and such." Gerlach paused. He smiled. "Captain, I understand your question. Your Navigator, Frimunt, would remain just as he is, until qualified doctors could assist him."

Becker thought a moment. "What if all these tests succeeded?"

"If my report came out positive, the leaders of the Third Reich would have been smuggled here."

Becker's jaw dropped. "In the name of God, *why*?"

"Dr. Goebbels convinced the Fuhrer the time is not right for him. Too many Jews and Communists. Too many weak links in the chain. Why should Germany fight the war? So Hitler is to be placed into suspended animation. Once the leadership is hidden away, Himmler will sue for peace."

"Sue for peace? Then, we will have lost."

Major Gerlach sat back. "Only the battle, not the war."

"Major, this is crazy. You don't make sense."

"How long do you think the Americans and the Russians can get along?"

"I have no idea."

"Let's just say that after a peace is in place, there are those whose duty it is to help get World War Three started."

Becker's mouth gaped. "What?"

Gerlach shook his head. "Oh yes, this war is just the beginning. From the ashes, Germany will rise again."

"What if you reported the gas didn't work?" asked Becker.

Gerlach waved his hand. "Then the war would end and Germany would pay a heavy price."

Becker's mind raced. *This could save the crew and Frimunt. Nevertheless, what would the lives of fifty men mean to the world?*

Gerlach pulled himself upright. "Captain, you have to decide."

"If this does work, what will you do?"

"I told you, you were right."

"What does that mean?" Becker asked.

"This boat, these men. This is Germany. We seem to kill more of our own than the enemy."

Becker's head dropped. "Maybe your bomb was the answer."

"No, Captain. The *Forever Project* is a gift."

"A gift?" asked Becker. "But who gets to open it?"

Gerlach again leaned back and shut his eyes. The bruises around his neck darkened. "That depends on you."

Becker felt the weight of the decision slowly press on him. *It's not fair*, he thought. *This is not what I am trained for and this is not what war is about ... is it?*

U-761's Commander looked around. The U-boat's batteries pushed what little energy it had left through the wires and the yellow lights dimmed. The air grew worse, with each breath men poisoned themselves. In dark corners, the film of ice became a sheet. It grew each moment while it crept along the hull. A strange quiet hovered inside the U-boat. Like the silence in a tomb, U-761 was dying.

Chapter Four

The Forever Project

"A man is no sailor if he cannot sleep when he turns in, and turn out when he is called."

R .H. Dana Jr. Two Years Before the Mast, xxxiv, 1840

August 21st 1944

"How do we use the gas?" Becker asked.

Gerlach rolled his head slowly. "Time is against us now, Captain. The men need to make themselves as insulated from the steel as they can. Pile blankets, sheets - whatever they can - and be sure their skin is completely covered. They need to eat as much as they can."

"How do we get the gas in the boat?" Becker asked.

"Put one canister in each compartment and turn the handles."

"That's it?"

Gerlach chuckled, "Sorry, it's not more technical."

"Major?" Becker asked. "What will it be like?"

Gerlach let out a long gurgling breath. "I don't know."

Becker thought, *am I making the right choice. What if it doesn't work? What if it does work?* Becker realized the fastest way to kill a U-boat was to let emotion dictate action. As *a German naval officer with honor and tradition. I can hold the crew together. They trust me. They had seen me at the periscope, seen me smile as the sea around them exploded with depth charges. They believe and trust. They fought with and for me. Not for the Reich, not for Hitler, not even for Donitz, but for me. Such dedication, such bravery, deserved life. These men earned the right to live, or at least have a chance at life.*

Gerlach halted the Captain's thoughts. "Commander, the air is going fast."

Becker looked at the bruised and battered man. "I know. You will help?"

"Yes, sir, I will, but remember our deal."

U-761's Captain wiped his face. "I remember."

"Ulrich," Becker shouted down the narrow passage between the two electric motor controllers.

"Yes, Captain?" came the faint reply.

"Give me your knife."

Ulrich, the electric motor operator, hurried along the deck, his boots muffled by their felt soles. From his pocket, the young sailor brought out his folding knife and handed it to Becker.

"Thank you," Becker said, taking the knife. "Ulrich, have the officers, and Petty Officers meet me in the Torpedo room."

"Yes, s-sir," he stammered, his forehead wrinkled. For long seconds, he stared at the Major.

"Hurry up, man," Becker urged.

"Yes sir. Sorry, sir." Ulrich disappeared into the dark passageway.

and the engine went to full power. At fifty knots, the distance closed to fifty meters. Cavitations from the screw of the *KILO* sent a command to the warhead.

Before the first blast had generated the massive over-pressure, the second torpedo detonated under the *KILO'S* battery compartment. Superheated streams of plasma took only milliseconds to vaporize the high grade steel of the hull. As both explosions developed, her own weapons detonated. The sea flashed into a brilliant white fireball, its energy radiating in all directions.

Sections of the *KILO* not vaporized by the blasts were torn into fist size chunks by the pressure of the ocean. From the center of the boiling angry ocean, bits of the dead submarine rained toward the sea floor.

VEPR turned and headed deeper when the pressure wave hit and lifted the damaged stern plane. The flow of water across the surface caused it to drift back. The remains of the rotted pintle fell apart, as the eleven-ton plane moved upward. With no guide bearing and no support, gravity caused the plane to droop. Hydraulic pressure could no longer move the sagging plane. A signal sent to the control valve required too much pressure to move the control surface. A separate signal went to the plane control station that caused the control panel alarm to flash a warning. When pressure in the systems spiked, another valve opened and emptied the fluid into the emergency reserve system. Automatically the plane control now shifted operating modes.

During the two-second delay the wobbly plane slipped from the yoke assembly and jammed at a fifteen-degree dive angle.

In the Command Center, the planesman yelled his controls no longer responded. The automatic system engaged and again pressure built up. The control surface jammed and twisted the control arm, fractured then splintered like an old log. The emergency system continued to build pressure, while the hydraulic lines swelled, and one after another, the main lines ruptured. Atomized hydraulic fluid filled the engine room. One by one, the control surfaces lost pressure and flapped uselessly in the slipstream of water.

Then the rudder and bow planes failed. With no hydraulics to her control surfaces *VEPR* heeled to the right. *VEPR* pitched on her nose.

"All back emergency," Danyankov screamed..

"Emergency plane's control not working," shouted the watch officer.

Danyankov looked at the depth gauge; 190 meters and falling fast.

The propeller stopped, shuddered and started in reverse.

"Captain," a voice shouted. "The array is out."

The engineer grew pale. "Hydraulic rupture in the engine room," he yelled above all the other noise. "Permission to activate fire suppression?"

"Activate fire suppression," he shouted.

"The array," a voice shouted.

VEPR backed over the array. Like a giant bobbin, the long wire wound its way around the screw as the submarine reversed. "Jettison the cable from the winch."

The sonar officer activated the release mechanism, but the array wrapped tighter around the spinning propeller. As the end whipped, it lodged against the hanging stern plane. It held tight. Again the propeller shuddered and stopped. *VEPR* had no propulsion, no way to steer or control her angle. Pressure on the hull grew and she picked up speed as she dove toward the bottom.

Inside the *Akula,* men held on to what they could. The angle increased to twenty-five degrees. Anything not attached or restrained crashed to the decks. They passed 210 meters.

"Fire emergency ballast system. Blow forward, trim for five seconds, then open the vents by hand," he ordered.

Inside the ballast tanks of the damaged *Akula,* gas generators fired and blasted the water from the tanks. Mechanics stood by to operate the forward vents when the angle of the ship reduced. As the water left the main ballast tanks, the *VEPR* grew lighter. The descent slowed and the angle eased.

"Open forward vents," Danyankov ordered. *VEPR's* bow pitched up. The ballast control panel showed them open with massive bubbles of air leaving the forward vents. Shouts of joy rumbled through the ship. *VEPR* leveled somewhat, her bow gently rose to a ten degree up angle. With the remainder of the ballast tanks dry, *VEPR* lifted toward the surface. The speed of the ascent increased, the numbers on the digital depth gauge appeared as a blur.

"Surface contacts?" Danyankov shouted over the sound house sized bubbles.

"Sonar is blanked out, I can't hear a thing," responded the sonar officer.

Danyankov felt the sweat pour from his face.

Twenty seconds later, *VEPR* broke the surface. Her hull heaved itself clear of the ocean, only to fall back again with a thunderous smack. Carried by her own momentum, she submerged again. This time she sank to twenty-five meters. There she stopped. For thirty seconds she hung in the sea. Slowly, gravity yielded to buoyancy and *VEPR* rose, and her streamlined, whale-like body broached the surface. There in the moonless cold night, she bobbed gently in the slight swell.

Inside the helpless *Akula,* lights turned from white to red. The shaken men went about their work.

Danyankov looked around at the young faces. With a sudden rush, a feeling of pride came over him. Those near the commander's console saw him lift the microphone to his lips, and braced themselves for the tirade.

"Men of *VEPR*," he started. "You have performed with great distinction and bravery. You are all a credit to the Navy and to Russia. And this is something I do not say lightly as you all know. Thank you, men." He gently placed the microphone back in its holder.

Men looked at one another with mouths open and eyes wide. Is *The Prince of Darkness*, human after all.

"Radio to Captain," came a voice over the speaker. "Ready to transmit our action report."

"Good," responded Danyankov. "Come up on clear voice from the satellite. Tell them we need a tow and an escort."

Chapter Seven

World Affairs

*"Which of you, intending to build a tower,
sitteth not down first, and counteth the cost,
whether he have sufficient to finish it?"*
Luke, III,5

October 14th

Satellite News Today (SNT) interrupted the eleven-forty weather report with breaking news. Weather reporter Stephanie Marshall's pleasant face, was suddenly replaced by a black screen. A second later the news desk appeared. A stern faced, anchor sat before the camera with the proper air of seriousness.

"Hello this is Brent Bacus. We have a breaking story just in to SNT. Earlier today in what can only be called a coup, Russian President Kenshanko was removed from office, by military force. We are still trying to get more information on this story. We have some video we can show you."

The screen showed shaky images of Russian T-80 tanks rolling along on an unknown highway on the outskirts of Moscow. The scene then cut to pictures of droning HIND attack choppers nervously darting across the gray sky.

Bacus reappeared. "We have now on the phone our Moscow correspondent Dale Shevley. Dale, what can you tell us?"

"Brent, can you hear me?" a voice asked.

"We can hear you, Dale. What can you tell us?"

"Brent, this is a scene right out of 1917. Russian forces have taken over the Kremlin. Tanks are inside the walls and block the gates. Earlier we heard both small arms and tank fire. The firing is sporadic now. I can see the top of the Kremlin, and yes-yes the red flag with the hammer and sickle now flies at the flagstaff. The flag of the Soviet Union."

"Dale, have you talked with anyone in government?" Bacus asked.

"We have not been able to move very far from the hotel. For the most part the streets are empty of people and traffic. We will try to get more on this when it is safe."

"Thank you, Dale. We now have Pam Brenner, our associate Pam Brenner in London."

Again the screen flashed to the attractive yet business like face of long time reporter Pam Brenner. "Dale, this is indeed a revolution. The governments of Latvia, Georgia, Belarus, and Russia have been overthrown by military force. Fighting was intense earlier, but now there is a strange quiet. I'm getting word that a military spokesman in Latvia is declaring his country and Russia are merging."

"Pam, what does this all mean?" Bacus asked.

"Dale, for years the nations of the former Soviet Union have struggled with capitalism and free market. Crime is rampant, and living is hand to mouth at best.

All the signs point to a rejection of Western ideals. It looks like the Soviet Union has returned."

The image flashed back to Bacus. "Thank you, Pam. It is unclear what this means to the world and to the United States in particular. One thing we can be sure of, this news is not what the administration needed right now. We'll have more as the day goes on. This is Dale Bacus, SNT." The image of a worried looking Bacus faded into a commercial for the latest pill for erectile dysfunction.

Hours after the news broke, protesters took up stations outside the White House. One group demanded the President support the new Russia with economic aid, while on the other side of the street, groups demanded the United State's military restore the Democratic government. Some protesters had no idea of what was going on and latched on to the side that had the loudest speakers.

Iran

In the capital of Tehran, meetings took place. This Russian affair could go two ways. If the United States suddenly found itself distracted by a war with Russia, the way could open for Iran to join its brothers in Iraq. The dream of one holy Islamic nation could come true. Surely the United States would have its hands full and not want two wars at the same time. But on the other hand, Russia would be hungry for oil. Tehran had a good working relationship with Moscow, but this new leader might see the American weakness and take the oil. That scenario would place Iran in the uncomfortable position of asking help from the United States. Still, this was at most a setback for Iran. She had her own plans.

Pyongyang, North Korea

By noon their meetings started in that country. The deterrent of the United States might be weakened by a conflict with Russia. It would be a sworn duty to assist Russia's communist brothers. The Great Leader, pushed his glasses further up his nose as he reviewed his options and strike plans. Generals sat nervously hoping that this mad man would let this crisis pass. Unfortunately the Great Leader went further. North Korea possessed two missiles capable of hitting the West coast of the United States with 25 megatons each and targeted Bremerton, Washington, and San Diego, California would cause a devastating blow to the Pacific military might of the United States. Bremerton with its nuclear missile submarines, and San Diego home to any number of American Naval and air combat units. The Great Leader hypothesized that with most of its Pacific assets turned into radioactive ashes, America would not retaliate. In his mind the American's would want to protect what they had left in case the Russians got out of hand. With America so weakened an invasion of the South would be a simple matter of overwhelming waves of humans. Why stop at South Korea? Maybe now would be the time to extract some revenge on the Japanese. From hidden mountain caves, mobile launchers emerged. The heavy trucks had no lights, and no markings to identify their purpose or cargo. Upon leaving their secure underground facilities, the launcher vehicles split up. They crawled along shabby worn roads, to remote locations. Once on station the crews began fueling long range nuclear tipped missiles .

Beijing, China

It rained when the ruling council of the People's Republic of China met. The talks were heated and frank. Some members welcomed the new Russia and demanded China throw her vast military support behind her. Other more practical thinkers called for no reaction. They reminded the war hawks that China was very much - though regretfully - dependent on American trade. Any move that put that relationship at risk was financial suicide. Finally, the talks calmed and the council agreed China would sit along the sidelines and see how the game played out. One quiet delegate reminded his fellow party members that a new Soviet Union emboldened with victory might as before challenge China's rule of the Pacific. China went on alert.

United Kingdom

The House of Lords filled with shouts that afternoon. The Prime Minister of Britain reported on events and the British reaction. Questions of blame and bad policy argued back and forth. Most knew that, like the U.S., the British markets would be at the mercy of the news from Russia. Little headway was made during all the shouting, although England had already made some moves unknown to the general population.

From Faslane, Scotland, three of England's Trident armed submarines slipped quietly into the Firth of Forth, and as the sun set, they disappeared into the Atlantic. From Portsmouth and Plymouth, sleek warships of Her Majesty's Navy moved into the English Channel. Once cleared of the harbor, the ships divided into Hunter-Killer groups and one group sailed south and the other north.

From air bases around the United Kingdom, maritime patrol aircraft lifted from the runways. Airborne tankers followed, ready to keep as many aircraft aloft as needed.

NATO Headquarters
Brussels

Stung by the lack of fore-warning, NATO held an emergency conference. British Major General Kale Mayborne, was appointed NATO on scene commander. Each member nation placed what assets it could afford under his direct command. Polish tank brigades rolled toward her border. Spain deployed her aircraft carrier, and escorting frigates to guard the approaches to Gibraltar, least a Russian submarine ambush supply or warships entering the narrow chokepoint. The United States redeployed the new aircraft carrier *George H. Bush* to an operating area south of Norway. Four battalions of Italian mountain troops mustered at air bases around Italy awaited orders. The German Navy deployed to protect shipping lanes to and from the Baltic.

The Vatican, Rome

At nine in the evening the Pope offered a message

of hope for peace. From the Vatican, the Holy Father delivered his message and an offer to mediate should the need arise. Leaders around the world knew his predecessor had done his part to bring down the Soviet Union. Some wondered how the Russians would handle this Pope.

Eastern Europe

Villagers from the Balkans to the Carpathians received word of the revolution - not on the news - but by actions. Borders were suddenly sealed. Throughout their history, these tiny remote villages turned their thoughts to family. Many of the older members fought in the Great War. These people knew the horrors, the loss, and the futility of war. The fields they now tended were bathed in blood and tears.

Elders of the villages directed everyone to gather stores of food, fuel and blankets. Some families took to the mountains and others made room in cellars and basements. Others cast worried eyes to the North.

Airports Around the World

Word of fighting between Russian forces caused a panic in the world's airlines. European vacationers wanted to get home. Air traffic adjusted routes and layovers rearranged. Insurance carriers refused to cover some of the air routes. Gridlocks in airports developed. Security tightened, causing further delays. In Rome, a near riot broke out when the World Cup challenger and the long shot favorite Polish soccer team, was delayed on a plane for Athens. They were to play Greece in two days.

The Kremlin
October 16th

Lieutenant General Evgeni Moiseev strode to the great doors of the President. His boots still muddied, thudded with sharp reports on the worn marble tile. Guards at the door, attired in shoddy wrinkled suits, made from cheap wool, stared under black heavy brows, their faces pocked and scared and hands, thick and powerful, hung at their sides, fists clenched.

"Tell your boss I need to see him," the General barked.

The guard to the right appraised the general and reluctantly, he took a small walkie-talkie from his belt. "Moiseev is here."

"Send him in," a voice spoke back.

The man on the left opened the ancient door. "General."

Moiseev entered the office and let the heavy doors clang shut behind him. The stench of Cuban cigars mixed with cheap cologne, filled his nostrils. The heavy smoke made the already dimly lit room even darker.

On the sofa where Stalin once rested, a pudgy balding man slouched. Obviously half-drunk, the little man stared into the smoke as his thick lips puffed on a half-smoked, half-chewed cigar. Around the office, other men lounged in chairs and sofas. Most little better looking than the men at the doors.

At the great desk sat Viktor Paslav, a tall stout

man with deep kind eyes that betrayed a cold ruthless soul.

"General," Paslav smiled warmly. "How goes the war?"

Moiseev did not return the smile. "My units have control over most of the country. There was resistance in an area of Kiev, but nothing too troubling. Still we may have an issue."

"Oh?"

"The North is a concern. The Army for the most part does what its told, same with the Air Force. The Navy is another story. The Pacific fleet is under control, but we have problems in the Kola."

Paslav's eyes narrowed. "What kind of problems?"

"Two attack submarines refuse to return. A Frigate was sunk. Fleet air is divided and the carrier *Kuznetsov* is making for open water. Her intentions are unknown."

"This *Kuznetsov*? Is she a big ship?" asked Paslav.

"It's an aircraft carrier. She sailed with her escort last night. Two cruisers, three *Udoly* destroyers, and her supply ship."

"Umm," Paslav grunted. "Tell me, what does that mean?"

General Moiseev removed his hat. "That we have a hell of a lot of fire power loose."

"What will they do?" Paslav asked.

"I don't know. They could launch strikes at our supplies or our troops. I just don't know."

Paslav looked around the room. "Will they return to port as ordered?"

Moiseev scratched his pale forehead. "You have no idea what you're doing, do you?"

Paslav's eyes narrowed and the smile faded. "General, I'm no politician or a military leader. What I am is a businessman and I surround myself with those who have answers. I thought you would be the man to handle my military affairs. So far, you've done the job. Now, I wonder if you can carry it through." Paslav let his words taper off for effect.

"Don't think you can threaten me," Moiseev hissed. "It was my tanks and troops that got you here. You are the one who had better carry through. Look out your window. Those tanks sitting in the yard have bigger guns than these thugs and I am the one with my finger on the trigger."

"General, come now." Paslav smiled. "We are in this together. When it's all over, we're going to be very wealthy men."

Moiseev leaned over the desk, his arms rested on the antique wood, his face inches from Paslav. "I am not in this for money. I want my country back."

Paslav leaned back in the great chair. "General, I am in this for the money. Your patriotic notions mean little to me. In a few weeks, maybe a month, there will be a free election and I will step down. Of course, the new President will be one who, shall we say, has a tendency to overlook certain activities."

"Do think the world is turning a blind eye to this?"

"What are you talking about?"

"You've set the whole planet on its ears. There are three United State's aircraft carrier battle groups on the way. Oh, and those are also very big ships."

"This is none of their business," Paslav shouted.

"Well Comrade, I suggest you tell them that,"

Moiseev laughed. "I suggest you do something other than have my troops hunt down your enemies."

"You make a good point, General. I am the leader of Russia and I should speak for Russia," Paslav stood and stared at the line of T-80s just below his window.

"What about the people? What do you tell them? All those soldiers and sailors have families. So far, I don't think you have made much of an impression."

Paslav clasped his hands behind his back. "The people needed this. I will eliminate criminals from the streets. I'll give them bread and get them respect."

"Spoken like a true Stalinist," Moiseev mumbled.

"So, General. What would you have me do now?"

"Talk to the world. Tell them you are a man of peace. You had to commit to this to save Mother Russia from corruption and to prevent financial ruin. You're a good liar, you can pull this off. The longer you wait the more nervous people get."

"Nervous? Why? I have done nothing to anyone outside Russia."

Moiseev rubbed his temple. "Are you that ignorant? What you have done is upset the balance. The West had a good relationship with us. Of course, a bit one-sided. Nevertheless, now that is gone and upset the balance."

Paslav looked puzzled. "So, the West is in it for the money also?"

"Money is the cause of most wars," Moiseev shrugged.

Paslav cocked his head. "War? You think this could lead to a war?"

Again Moiseev laughed. "I can just about guarantee it."

"Hmm, I see. I will make an announcement. Give them a smile."

"Why not have the Ambassador hand-carry a message to the Americans?" asked the General.

"That will not be possible," Paslav responded with ice in his voice. "He was a weak link in the plans. He had second thoughts. He might have given us all up."

Moiseev took a deep breath. "So he is dead?"

Paslav raised his chin and loosened his tie. "Yes."

The General shook his head. "You better have a silver tongue, Paslav. If you are linked to killing the Ambassador, you lose all credibility," Moiseev let his words taper off. "Oh, I might also suggest you do more research on your victims."

"Why is that, General?" Paslav sighed.

"The Commander of the *Kuznetsov* battle force. His uncle was the Ambassador."

A sudden look of fear crossed Paslav's face. "My God."

The General placed the cap back on his head, making sure it was square with the line of his thinning gray eyebrows. "I'll be looking forward to your announcement."

Paslav said nothing as Moiseev turned for the door.

Moiseev then stopped. "Oh, I almost forgot. Should anything happen to me, say some unforeseen accident, those tanks on the parade grounds have orders to crush you like an insect."

Paslav remained silent as the door shut behind Moiseev. Even with the doors closed, those in the great office of power heard his boots thudding down the long marble hall.

Paslav returned to the seat. Others in the room stared at him, waiting for direction. The leader of the Revolutionary Soviet State picked up his phone. "Get Troschinsky," he spoke into the mouthpiece.

There was a pause. "Yes, Colonel Troschinsky, listen to me. We seem to have some navy ships out off the Kola who might have to be dealt with. The *Kuznetsov*. Yes, she has other ships with her. I have no idea, but Moiseev thinks they may hit us. Can your Air Force take care of that? Good. Tell me when it's done. Oh and Colonel, I think maybe you are the man for Minister of Defense. No, Moiseev seems to be having second thoughts. I am counting on you," Paslav placed the receiver back on the hook.

The White House
October 16th

The President had been up since before daylight. Around him, advisors and staff waited for his decision. An emergency meeting of the United Nations Security Council was to begin in three hours.

"We can't trust him," the President started. "This whole thing is a sham."

National Security Advisor Brian Metz nodded his head. "I agree, Mr. President, but what are the options?"

Kim Bennet, White House Press Secretary, waved her hand. "Listen, if we don't say anything, the folks over at the UN will have a field day. The offer seems reasonable. Everyone pulls their forces back."

Defense Secretary Samuals spoke next. "Problem is Paslav has no idea of what he's doing. He's a thug, and using this to kill off other thugs. This revolution against crime and poverty make good press. What we have to worry about is *who is really* calling the shots. The army may have been duped, but someone is using Paslav."

The President looked over to Secretary of State James Hollinger. "What does the world think?" asked the President.

"Mixed, sir. Some think it's good. NATO though, has doubts. I have a feeling we may wind up with a new world order," offered Hollinger.

"All it will take is a mistaken border crossing, an accidental bomb release, or some Russian private taking a piss on the wrong side of the fence. Then who knows where this could wind up," said Samuals.

"Okay, we'll officially accept the offer of a pull back of forces. I want open communications with Paslav. CIA and State, get to work on finding out what the hell is really going on," the President said, hands on hips.

"How much of a pull back?" Samuals asked.

The President closed his eyes. "Make it look good."

Chapter Eight

Friends and Foes

"Set ye Uriah in the forefront of the hottest battle."

II Samual, XI,15

Russian Carrier *KUZNETSOV*
220 Miles Northwest of the Kola Peninsula
October 17th
The Present

Her gracefully curved bow lifted and fell in a moderate swell, the Russian aircraft carrier *Kuznetsov* turned into the wind. Heeling slightly to port, the giant ship brought the fifteen knots of wind over her flight deck. As if somehow connected, the escort ships turned with her in perfect unison. Once steady on her new course, the 1,000-foot carrier settled while the shriek of jet engines pierced the evening stillness. One by one, *SU-25 Frog Foot* ground attack jets lifted from the carrier's deck. Once in the air, the attack planes formed tight wedge-shaped formations of four aircraft. Three wedges formed, then slowly orbited the carrier. Stiletto shaped fighters raced from the ski slope bow of

Kuznetsov. Like the *Frog Foots*, the *SU-27 Flankers* formed formations in curved defensive arcs. Twenty-six aircraft, circled the carrier. The fighters rose to their stations at 18,000 feet. Once at altitude, they split into two elements. Their arc formation unfolded into two angled lines of sleek fighter jets. The entire mass of aircraft moved East toward land and their targets.

After launching her planes, *Kuznetsov* again turned toward the open sea. As before, her escorts followed into the dying light.

Northwest of *Kuznetsov*, and over one-hundred miles away, an American four-engine P-3C Orion, code-named ANVIL 23, hung in the sky. The Allison turboprop engines purred in the twilight when the plane banked slowly to the East.

In the cockpit, Lieutenant Commander Sandra Neely eased back on the throttles. Looking at the center console, she checked the fuel status. "Good for another three hours," she nodded to her co-pilot.

"Slow circles to nowhere, commander," replied co-pilot, Lieutenant Mike Devin.

Neely looked out her side window. The sea and sky merged in shades of dark purple as twilight gave way to dusk.

"Two more patrols," she said.

Devin rolled his eyes. "Go on, Boss, rub it in."

"Oh, don't get me wrong," she teased. "I'll be thinking about you guys freezing your asses off in Scotland when I'm strolling on the beach in Pensacola."

"They found someone to replace you?"

Neely snapped her head toward the Lieutenant. "Replace me? Replace the best in the Navy? How can you replace perfection?" she grinned.

"You are so full of it," Devin grinned back.

"I really will miss you bunch of idiots." Her grin evaporated.

Devin looked down and spoke quietly, "You taught us a lot, Boss."

"Yeah, well just remember half of it and you'll do fine."

"Commander?" a voice called through her headset.

"Go ahead."

"Looks like Master One, the carrier, just launched," the young male voice answered.

Out of instinct, Neely again scanned her instruments. "Okay, people, looks like we have some activity," she called into her throat microphone.

Devin looked to the digital compass. "Heading now is 090. Next turn will be in five ... course North."

Neely pressed the microphone button. "What can you tell me back there?"

A female voice came into the earpiece of Neely's helmet. "Count is twenty-six fast movers on course 045, true. Our tape is running."

"Roger that. What about classifying?"

An older male voice answered, "Commander, no radar emissions. These guys are staying quiet."

"Okay, stay on top of it, we don't need any surprises," Neely advised. "Radio, send our data to LINK so TWEETY can see."

"Roger that, Commander. TWEETY is now on line," answered another voice, with a deep southern drawl.

Six hundred miles from the lone P-3, an E-3A AWACS also circled. Code-named TWEETY, the large jet was filled with highly sophisticated radar and communications equipment. Atop the fuselage, a twenty-foot diameter saucer slowly rotated, as it fed radar information to the hundreds of processors and dozens of glowing screens along the plane's interior. TWEETY could monitor air traffic for a thousand square miles. At her present position just north of the Faeroes Islands, TWEETY scanned almost the entire North Sea.

With ANVIL 23 sending a LINK, the AWACS could see even further. What Neely's radars saw was transmitted directly to the operators flying TWEETY.

"ANVIL 23, this is TWEETY," a voice came over the radio.

"Go ahead, TWEETY," Neely called back.

"Roger ANVIL 23. We have good copy of your LINK."

"TWEETY, understand. Break. What is the situation?"

"ANVIL 23, analyzing now."

Neely again pressed the microphone button, "Roger TWEETY, ANVIL 23 out."

Devin turned to his pilot. "Analyzing? Does that translate into *We don't have a clue?"*

"I'm afraid so."

"Man, suddenly I feel really alone up here." Devin, adjusted his helmet.

"What's wrong, Lieutenant? Getting a little spooked?" Neely smiled.

"A little."

"Just remember who's flying this thing."

"It's not that as much as *who* the hell is flying those other things."

Neely faked a yawn to hide her own worry. "Hey, we have anymore coffee?"

"I think so." He reached under his seat for the thermos.

"Hope so. I need a good jolt right about now." She yawned again.

Devin found the dull silver thermos and held it close to his ear. He shook the container hoping to hear the welcome sound of lukewarm coffee splashing around. "Yep, just about a cup left."

"Bring it on," Neely held out her hand.

"Commander," a voice almost screamed into her headset. "Ten boogies at seventeen miles, course 220. Fast flyers headed our way."

"Okay, calm down," Neely urged. "Can you classify?"

"Negative, Commander," answered the *ELINT* operator.

"Are they from the carrier?"

"No, these are new contacts. Larger aircraft. The contacts have increased speed. Wait. Now I have six more from the carrier," the radar operator suddenly sounded nervous. "Uh, Commander, one element has broken away from the carrier's first launch. New course of those aircraft is 310. They will intercept our track in seven minutes."

"Patch me to TWEETY," she ordered.

"Hard to make contact. We're being jammed," the female voice called back.

"Get on COMSAT, they can't jam that." Neely tried not to let her fear be apparent.

"Okay, we're on with TWEETY."

"TWEETY, this is ANVIL 23."

"ANVIL 23, ANVIL 23, this is TWEETY, we see. Maintain course and altitude," came the reply.

Neely bit her lower lip. It would be easy to stomp the rudder pedal, dive to the deck and get the hell out of there, but she had orders. Besides, she told herself, they were in international waters.

"Classified," the male voice with the southern drawl yelled. "New contacts are classified TU-160 bombers. Classification based on DOWN BEAT Radar."

"Shit. They're going after the carrier," Neely shouted.

The male voice reported. "Commander. SLOT BACK radar."

"SLOT BACK?" she asked.

"Carried on SU-27 and MIG-29 fighters," the male voice reminded her. "Commander, they're lighting us up."

Neely pressed her microphone. "TWEETY, this is ANVIL 23. We are being painted by SLOT BACK Radar, please advise," her voice desperate.

"ANVIL 23, this is TWEETY, come to new course South, descend to 2,000," the voice directed her, calm, but forceful.

"Roger, TWEETY." She immediately kicked the left rudder pedal and pushed the control stick forward.

The nimble ORION obeyed at once. It turned in a graceful arc toward the South. Neely pushed the four throttles to the limit and the Allison engines roared.

Descending rapidly toward the ocean, the P-3 was twenty degrees from her new course when Devin screamed.

"Pull up, Pull up," his voice cracked with fear.

Neely yanked the control stick to her chest. "What is it?" she screamed back. Out her window, she saw the sleek razor-like shape of a TU-160 bomber pull along side her. She looked over to her co-pilot. Another giant bomber rode the right wing. Leaning forward, she looked up. She let out a yelp as her eyes focused on the glowing exhaust of a third Russian bomber.

"We're surrounded," Devin yelled.

"Commander, now picking up BEE HIND gun control radar from the bombers."

"I can't maneuver," she announced. "TWEETY, this is ANVIL 23. I am surrounded by bogies, please advise."

"ANVIL 23, wait," came the reply.

"Wait," Neely screamed. "Wait for what?"

"ANVIL 23, ANVIL 23, this is TWEETY, hang on. Norwegian F-16s have been scrambled."

Neely didn't reply.

"Commander. Second group of SLOT BACKS are painting the bombers." the *ELINT* operator announced.

"Oh Jesus, they're using us as cover," Devin shouted.

"What?" Neely asked.

Devin's voice cracked, "The bombers hope no one will to risk hitting us."

A long slow exhalation came over the intercom.

"Commander, now picking up PLATE STEER air search radar from the carrier," the ELINT operator calmly reported. His voice rose in a higher pitch, "Multiple missile control radars just came on. Radars are high pulse mode. Believe these radars to be also from the carrier and at least one *KRESTA* class cruiser."

"How far are we from the carrier?" Neely asked.

"Forty miles," came the reply.

"Okay Lieutenant, these boys wanna fight it out. Fine, but I'm not sticking around. I'm going to slow down and nudge our way out of here," announced the thirty-two year old mother of two.

Devin only nodded.

When her hands reached for the throttles, the missile warning alarm flashed.

Now the *ELINT* operator screamed, "Inbound missiles. Count is eighteen - no wait, six more. Too many to classify, some are from the carrier groups, most are air-to-air."

"TWEETY, this is ANVIL 23, we are under attack."

"ANVIL 23, this is TWEETY. Evade, evade."

"No shit," Neely screamed back.

A blinding flash lit the sky. A missile had found one of the bombers.

Neely, watched as if in slow motion. The sharp nose of the dying bomber lifted, then tore from the fuselage as flames shot from the decapitated body. The right wing crumbled, then erupted in a fireball. As the remainder of the jet tumbled toward the waiting ocean, another huge explosion and, only hand-sized pieces of burning aluminum splashed into the cold Norwegian Sea.

The Orion shook when the pressure wave of the explosion washed over it. Neely fought the controls to keep the P-3 from colliding with the other bombers.

Three great flashes again blinded her. She shut her eyes, hoping her vision would return to normal.

"Bombers have launched missiles," the *ELINT* operator yelled. "AS-7 KERRY anti-ship missiles."

The bomber flying over the left wing banked away from the P-3, when it was hit with another huge explosion. One of the Flanker's scored with an AA-11 ARCHER air-to-air missile.

The blazing jet rolled toward her, and instinct took over. Neely slammed the control column forward. She heard the rush of the burning plane when it passed fifteen feet over her head, the jet tore apart.

Chunks of aluminum slashed into the P-3. Warning lights flashed. Neely felt the right wing dip. She tried to correct the sudden roll, but the ORION would not respond. She pressed the rudder to the left, but the rudder pedal was sluggish. More explosions around the aircraft lit the cockpit. Neely heard a rush of air in the cockpit. Now another flash lit the right wing. Neely saw the entire right side of the cockpit gone, only Devin's lower body remained. The legs twitched and convulsed and finally stilled.

The roll increased and Neely managed to look out the right wing at a mass of fire.

"Mayday, mayday," she screamed.

The roll continued until the P-3 was almost on its back. The flaming wing collapsed then folded back and crashed into the tail, severing the ORION into two pieces. Another flash of light billowed as the fuel cells exploded. Neely and her crew knew nothing more.

Chapter Nine

Vitus

"A man trusts his ears less than his eyes."
Herodotus, 484-424 B.C., Clio,I,8

The Kennedy Space Center, Florida

October 18th

"I don't like this one damn bit," exclaimed Nelson Evers.

Public Relations Manager, Charles Rawlings raised his hand. "I know Nelson, but listen, it's taken us five years to get here. Let's not blow it now."

"Okay, what are the rules?" Evers ran his hands through his bristly gray hair.

Rawlings flipped through his yellow notepad. "All they ask is for a few intelligence people to be around whenever we do the mapping," he said soothingly.

"Okay, but this is my satellite." He pointed to his chest. "I'm flight director, and I'm the boss."

"Of course, Nelson, we all know that."

"VITUS goes where I tell it to."

"Come on Nelson, calm down. You keep this up, and you'll have a stroke."

“This whole damn idea was mine.” His face flushed. “I’m the one who got the grant. Me. What in the name of holy hell does the military want with it?” Ever’s hands waved about while he talked. “Hells bells, they didn’t think it mattered a damn when I asked them to pay for it.”

“Hey, Nelson listen, you are the smartest man I know. Use that brain and listen for a second,” pleaded Rawlings.

Evers crossed his arms and let his chin down till it touched his chest. “What?”

“I don’t know if you read the papers or watch the news, but the world is different now than forty-eight hours ago. Hell, the Russians shot down one of our planes yesterday then blew one of their own carriers to hell.”

Evers looked up, surprised. “Really?”

“Yeah. So you can see where the military would be concerned. Think about it,” Rawlings urged.

“You are about to use an untested system to shoot a 500 megawatt laser from space. And just to make it even more exciting, you’ll aim that laser not far from the Norwegian Sea.”

Evers reached up to rub the back of his neck. “Okay, they can watch, but the first GI Joe that tries to tell me what to do is going to get this size seven shoe up his ass.” Evers broke into a rare smile. “Well as long as he isn’t too tall.”

Rawlings laughed, “Good, so we’re on the same sheet of music?”

“I guess,” he sighed. “God, I need a drink.”

“No, you don’t.”

"Yes, I do."

"Can it wait?"

"Are you my PR man or my mother?"

Rawlings shook his head, "Sometimes I wonder."

Evers looked at his watch. "Is there anything else before I go shoot my rocket?"

The veteran public relations man winced. "Well, there is another little request we need to talk about."

Evers spun on his heels, his face again reddened. "Oh, I damn well knew it. Here it comes. Go on, Chuck. Tell me. No, wait. Let me drop my pants and bend over."

"Please, don't."

"What is it? What the hell do they want? Wait, let me guess. Umm, some General's grandson wants to push the launch button? Get a good picture of Little Johnny Hungfunny pushing the big red button? Bullshit."

"Will you stop?" Rawlings demanded. "No, nothing like that. The military wants copies of the mapping printouts."

"Hell, we put those out on the Internet."

"I know, but they would like to see them first."

The VITUS satellite designer calmed. "Okay, no problem."

Rawling's mouth fell open. "Well, that was easy. Come on. Ten minutes till launch."

Both men walked toward the door to mission control.

"Did you mean what you said? Am I the smartest man you ever met?"

"No."

Ever's eyes narrowed. "I don't like you."
"Yes you do."
"No, I don't."
Rawlings pulled the door open. "You do."
"Maybe a little."
"Good enough for me."
"Up yours."

The Security Council
United Nations, New York
October 18th

"Fellow council members," American Ambassador Gene Tullman announced, "the world has changed over the past few days. The clock has turned back." Tullman let his words trail off so the translators could keep up.

"We face an uncertain future. Freedom for millions and the lives of twice that, are in jeopardy. Already, thousands are dead. I need not remind this council of the past. I do however, remind this council what the result of inaction can be." Tullman paused. "More than a few of you have been victims. How much suffering will this body allow? How many have to die for us to act? I ask you to consider these points when we vote on this resolution." Tullman made eye contact with each member of the council.

"How many times has this organization failed? This resolution serves not only Russia, but sends a message to those who endanger the respite from fear of nuclear holocaust. It sends a message to those who cannot defend themselves. The message says the world will not tolerate tyrants, will not tolerate injustice. Some of you, I know, prepared your statement. Any nation has the right to choose its own form of government. Let the people decide what kind. I'll tell you the United States agrees.

"This must be more than a resolution, but a statement of our unity and our commitment as outlined in the founding charter. I second this resolution, and ask that it be ratified, and imposed at once."

United Nations President Diego Prez leaned over his microphone. "The chair now recognizes Ambassador Sergi Atopov of Russia."

A slight built man with fatigue in his face rose from his chair. He marched sternly to the microphone.

"Mr. President, fellow representatives, this is indeed a time of change," Atopov spoke softly. "My country has for the past two decades been ruled by liars and criminals. To say that my people did not choose this new government is false. They demanded it. Our economy is staled, while the cost of basic needs made it unbearable. In many ways, those in favor of this resolution are to blame for these conditions. Crime rules the streets. Food used as a weapon and a tool. Already many who perpetrated these crimes have accounted for their actions. This is justice. Russia seeks only peace and the ability to survive with the rest of the nations of the world." Atopov eyed the council members.

"There is no need for this resolution. We have agreed to pull our military forces back and only wish to secure what has always been Russian. The past is just that - the past. We look forward to a better future. But let me say this - Russia will defend herself. Russia will not be told what her government will be. That is for Russia to decide." Again, he paused. Now his face grew stern and his eyes narrowed. "We indeed regret loss of life and regret the destruction of the American patrol plane, but please, understand; passage of this resolution will not deter my nation from her goal of safety and security. This resolution will serve only to push back the clock to a time when the world lived under the threat of a nuclear exchange. I reject this proposal as far too dangerous and far too self serving for those who created it."

Silence fell in the council chamber. A tension hung in the air.

The Kennedy Space Center, Florida
October 18th

"Oh crap," Nelson Evers gasped when he saw the waiting reporters.

"Come on, Nelson. You're a success. The rocket went up without a hitch. Give them a word or two," Charles Rawlings urged.

"I'd rather wear my grandmother's underwear as a ski mask."

"Nelson, you have issues, you know that?"

"Okay, a few words? Oh, here you go - eat shit." His face reddened. "Damn leaches. Those asshole reporters were here in case the damn thing blew up."

Rawlings sighed. "I'll talk to them."

Evers nodded his head. "Hurry, I want a systems test within the hour. And I'm hungry."

"Sure, Nelson. Why don't you just find a corner

and wait for me. Catch some flies and pull their wings off or hey, maybe you can find a kitten to kick."

"God, I hate you."

"I know," Rawlings responded. "Wait here. Smile and wave when I point to you, okay?"

"How about when you point, I flip them off?"

Rawlings clenched his eyes shut. "Yeah, that would be great. Remember last time you flipped people off?"

"How the hell was I supposed to know they were Girl Scouts? They were in the wrong area."

"Maybe so but, NASA had to buy six hundred boxes of cookies and you made front page of the paper."

"I'll be good, but hurry," promised Evers. "Oh and by the way, smart ass, I like cats."

Rawlings smirked and stepped toward the waiting reporters.

An attractive young reporter made her way to the front. Her jet-black hair framed a tanned, yet flawless face. Wide, perfectly shaped eyes set off her dark skin and hair. Her lips pouted under a well-formed nose.

"Mr. Rawlings? I'm Brenda Santos, WJSC-TV 9. Can you tell us how the launch went?"

Rawlings smiled. "The booster lifted the VITUS satellite from the launch pad right on time. A great shot."

The pretty, young reporter continued, "Will you tell our viewers what VITUS is about?"

"Of course, VITUS carries with her a new mapping system."

"What does this new system map?" Santos pressed.

"VITUS will show the Arctic in a way never seen

before. We will be able to see in three dimensions, ice formations, movement and thickness."

"Why is that important," Santos asked.

"To help predict weather patterns, to answer questions about global warming and the age of the ice."

"What does the word VITUS mean?"

"VITUS is named after an early explorer of the Arctic…."

Before he could finish, another microphone pushed in front of Rawling's face. "Robert Thorpe, WAKO Progressive News 3," the reporter said.

Brenda Santos's lip curled into a sneer when this new reporter shoved her out of his way.

"Is there any truth to rumors that this satellite is in fact a weapon system capable of disrupting communications over a wide?" Thorpe asked.

Rawlings blinked his eyes in disbelief. "VITUS has been in the public eye for five years." He chose his words carefully. "There have been PBS shows about ice research and the role this satellite will play in exploration of the Arctic. The data collected is for everyone. There is no military use for VITUS."

Thorpe's eyes glowed like a hunter with its prey cornered. "Mr. Rawlings, if that is so, why are members of the Armed Services in mission control?"

"Mr. Thorpe, as I just stated, VITUS is shared by everyone. You are just as welcome as anyone to be in there. When can I set you up an appointment? I believe your station could use the ratings. If there are no other questions, I'm going to lunch. Thank you. Tell your viewers to log on the web site and see VITUS in action."

He passed Thorpe, his right hand brushed the reporter's side.

"Hey, Thorpe," Brenda Santos called.

Thorpe turned to her and she raised her middle finger in his face.

Rawlings returned to the door to Mission Control. Inside, his mouth fell open when he saw Evers talk, not scream, to a tall Navy Commander. "Oh God," he scowled and rushed to his side. "Everything okay, Nelson?"

"Yeah, fine. Hey, me and the admiral here went to the same grade school in Texas."

The Commander smiled and extended his hand. "Commander Greg Dunn, I'm with Naval Intelligence."

Rawlings accepted the hand. "Chuck Rawlings. I'm handling Public Relations for the VITUS mission."

"Nelson here explained how this thing worked."

"So anyway," Evers continued, "what I did was use a software-driven system to control pulse length and spread the laser light in a fan shape. The energy is the same, but the light pattern covers a wider area. When the laser hits the surface, it penetrates and expands. It's a matter of recording the wavelengths of reflected light, and computing those with the pulse length. The colors reflected indicate ice thickness. I can determine which way the ice moves. The information is processed and displayed in three dimensions on our printouts and at the same time overlaid on a chart."

"Most interesting," remarked the Commander.

"Oh, very much so," added Evers. "VITUS will do the first mapping in about ten minutes. The solar panels have extended and the batteries are charged."

"I am looking forward to this," Dunn answered.

Evers smiled back. "Always glad to help our men in uniform."

Charles Rawlings almost choked.

Three-Hundred-Twenty Miles Above the North Pole

VITUS stabilized in a perfect geostationary orbit. Each of the satellite's systems worked to perfection. Black solar panels fed hungry batteries and powered the navigation computer. Inside a maze of circuits and components, the electronic brain sent and received signals to VITUS's master in Florida.

The sun faded from the Florida coast. VITUS started her work.

In Mission Control, Nelson Evers scanned his screen. "Okay, folks, this is it."

Around the room technicians monitored their screens and computers.

Evers took a deep breath. "In five-four-three-two-one, firing." Evers pushed the execute button.

For ten long seconds there was silence. Then the screen flickered and data flowed in. Evers leaped from his seat and went to the three dimensional chart.

"Good God in Heaven. Look, it worked," shouted Evers.

Others then gathered around. The display showed a perfect model of a section of the Arctic ice. They saw the ice as if it had been split down the center and they stood in the middle. Shades of blue, orange and violet marked thickness.

"Look, the blue indicates one meter thickness, all the way to 15 meters here," Evers bubbled then pointed to the image. "Switch to a profile view," he ordered. A few seconds passed before the image changed. "My God, look at this."

The image showed the bottom of the ice to its surface. "This section of ice extends to eighteen meters. Look, you can see where the ice plates slide under other plates."

Chuck Rawlings stepped up. "Nelson, how big an area are we looking at?"

Evers held up a finger. "Wait, let's see." He punched a few buttons. Numbers appeared next to the glowing image of the ice. "We have data on about fifty-eight square miles."

"Wow," exclaimed Rawlings.

"*Wow?* Understatement of the day, there, Chucky boy."

"Don't call me that."

"Sure, how about asshole?"

Rawlings nodded. "Anyway, good job Nelson."

"Calm down, Chuck, just bustin' your stones."

Evers returned to his computer screen. "All right. I am moving the map grid to 12.32-584. Now, we wait so VITUS can focus."

His monitor showed the cursor move toward the new map grid. A green light indicated VITUS lined up and ready. "Here we go again in 5-4-3-2-1 firing," he announced.

New data flowed, and again an image of the ice projected onto the chart. "Hot damn. Even better. Looks like eighty miles."

Commander Dunn stood by quietly. He noticed a small black space in the far right hand corner of the chart. "Nelson," he pointed to the black space, "what's that?"

Evers looked puzzled. "Looks like something blocked the light reflection. Here, let me magnify it." Evers commanded the image to view the area in question.

The computer updated the requested information. A fuzzy image appeared - long and narrow, tapered at the ends.

"Interesting," Evers said calmly. "It appears man-made."

Dunn stepped closer. "Why do you say that?"

Evers pointed to his glowing model. "Only steel or iron could absorb or block light that way. If it were wood, the image would show some light."

"Can you tell how long it is?"

Evers typed a function into the computer and numbers flashed across the bottom of the image. "I'd say anywhere from three to four hundred feet."

Dunn swallowed hard. "What it is?"

Evers looked again. "No idea. Could be an old shipwreck. A lost whaler … who knows?"

"Is there anyway to tell where it is in the ice. I mean, on top or under the ice?"

"Sure, just a second." Seconds later the numbers alongside the image updated again. "Uh, hard to tell, but I'd say it's under the ice."

Dunn walked to Rawlings, busy writing his statement at his small desk. "Chuck? Is there a secure phone I can use?"

"Sure, in the preparations room. Anything wrong?"

Dunn forced a grin. "No, just need to check in."

Rawlings pointed to a heavy gray door at the end of the Control Room. "In there, Commander. Oh, you'll need a password. Type in *drop dead*."

"That must be Nelson's."

"How could you tell?"

Thirty seconds later, Commander Greg Dunn was on the phone with the watch officer of the National Security Agency.

"Captain, this is Dunn. Yes, sir, weather here is great. Sir, I have an image taken from the VITUS satellite. Sir, this bird snapped an image of what I think is a Russian boomer snuggled up under the ice, about 350 miles North of Bear Island.—Yes sir, I can hold," Dunn bit his lower lip. "Yes sir, I'm still here. Are you sure, we have accounted for all Russian SSBNs? Sir, this is a submarine, no doubt about it. I think it may be a DELTA III. I know the Russians agreed to pull back. Captain, I have high confidence in this image. We may be in the cross hairs of a first strike," Dunn kept his voice barely audible.

"No sir, no one here knows what it is. It just all adds up, Captain. The image sits right next to a good-sized polinya. Oh, sorry sir, polinya is a large hole in the ice. Yes, Captain. If this is a Russian boat, all she has to do is move two hundred feet, pop up and launch her missiles. Yes sir, I know we also agreed to pull back, but this is big. Yes sir, I will leave here now. That will put me back there at 22:30."

Dunn replaced the receiver, and took a deep breath. He opened the heavy door to the control room. "Hey Nelson," he called.

"What's up, Commander?"

"Think I could get a printout of that last shot?"

"Sure, but the next series will be even better. I have some ice keels almost a hundred feet," Evers said proudly.

"No, this is the one I like most."

Three hours later, Commander Dunn's plane touched down on a special runway at the West end of Dulles Airport. An hour later, analysts at Fort Meade looked at the image. A half-hour later, phones rang in Washington, D.C., Norfolk, Virginia and Groton, Connecticut.

Chapter Ten
Second Chances

"He that ruleth over men must be just."
II Samual, XXIII

October 19th
Pier 3, Naval Submarine Base
Groton, Connecticut

Rain pattered around them, as they stood silent at the head of the pier. Rear Admiral Burke Tarrent had a long history with this pier, when he reported to his first boat, USS SCAMP, and as Executive Officer of the 637-class attack boat USS POGY. The summer of 1990 found Tarrent at the same spot. On a miserably hot July day, the then Commander Tarrent took command of USS DALLAS. His exploits on Dallas put him on the fast track now as Commanding Officer Submarine Group Six.

The rain steadily continued and mist slid from the surrounding hills into the Thames River. Admiral Tarrent stood silent and stone faced. Soon sailors, line handlers from the surrounding submarines walked onto the concrete pier. Headed by a burly Chief Petty Officer, the men took up stations and waited. A muffled engine noise floated across the silent pier. The Admiral and his party moved a few paces further down the pier. A huge yellow crane parked itself close to the edge as deemed safe.

Splashing along the soaked pier, an officer approached. Captain Cavin T. Farmer stepped up and saluted. "Sir, the families have been briefed."

"Thanks Gav. Any problems?" asked Tarrent.

"No, sir."

The admiral smiled proudly. "Bless them all."

"Sir, we have made arrangements for the body to be taken up the hill for autopsy."

Tarrent looked at the puddles around his shoes. "I want him released to the family as soon as possible."

"Of course, sir."

"Damn it," Tarrent swore. "Of all things."

An ambulance pulled onto the pier.

"Master Chief?" called Tarrent.

"Yes, sir?" Nick Bisetti answered.

"There are going to be lots of questions. Questions which are best answered by someone besides me."

"I know sir. I have it covered."

The mist thickened, although just short of noon, in crept a damp darkness. Mercury vapor lamps clicked on. In the channel, the river seemed to evaporate as fog settled over it.

To the East, the top of the Gold Star Bridge was barely visible. "There she is," Bisetti kept his voice low.

Out of the fog, USS MIAMI SSN 755 emerged. The shroud-like mist failed to hide the nuclear submarine. Two powerful tugboats latched on and gently nudged her through the narrow waterway. With short hoots from their whistles, the tugs expertly handled *Miami's* 360 foot length. Her sail passed the pier when her rudder swung hard right. Another short toot and the tugboat pushed the 6,900 ton submarine toward the line handlers. The second tug, cast off from the starboard side, reversed its engine, and drew astern. Once clear, its diesels rumbled as it moved forward to aid its sister. From the curved deck, heaving lines snaked through the air. Those on the pier caught the lines and attached them to the thick nylon mooring lines. Within minutes, Miami was home.

Both tugs cast off and scooted back down the river. A crane then lowered the dull aluminum brow to the sub's deck.

With lines made fast and the ends neatly coiled, a whistle blew. The ship's Ensign was hoisted when it reached the top, it was slowly lowered to half-mast. The crew moved about the deck, lifelines were mounted, floats, like those used to mark the deep end of pools, lowered into the water until they surrounded the entire waterline of the Miami. The men moved quickly and with purpose. They took the brow canvases, with USS MIAMI SSN 755 emblazoned on each, unfolded and lashed them to the brow. Absent were the usual smiles and jokes when a boat comes in. With their tasks complete, the sailors disappeared back into the submarine. Only one remained. The Topside Watch.

The Captain's representative and the ship's first line of defense, a young man no more than nineteen, stepped off the brow in his dress blue uniform. At his hip, a 9-mm pistol hung in a stark white and black leather holster.

Tarrent approached the young sailor with a thin smile. "Hello Petty Officer Barkley."

"Mornin', sir." Barkley noticed Bisetti and Captain Farmer. "Master Chief, Captain," he said with a nod.

Bisetti stepped forward and clamped the young petty officer on the shoulder. "You okay?"

Petty Officer Barkley looked down at his rain soaked shoes. "I been in the Navy three years and this is the worst day of all them," Barkley said in his deep Kentucky drawl. "He pinned on my dolphins."

"I know. Trust me, I know. He was Engineer on the *Saint Louis*," responded the Master Chief. "I know he taught you to be as he called it, *Fast attack tough.*"

Barkley smiled. "Sure as hell did. Told us we should chew steel and shit bullets."

All four men shared a muffled chuckle.

"Reckon ya'll need to see the XO?" Barkley asked.

"Yes, we do," Tarrent answered.

Barkley picked up the microphone for the general announcing system or 1MC. "Submarine Group Six, arriving," he announced. "Come aboard, Admiral. The officers and Chiefs are in the wardroom."

"Thanks," offered the Admiral.

Bisetti and the Farmer followed Tarrent down the rain slick brow. At the narrow hatch aft of *Miami's* sail, the men lowered themselves into the submarine. After a ten-foot climb, they landed in operations compartment middle level, directly behind the crew's mess. Chief of the Boat, Danny Norse waited for them.

"Hello Admiral," Norse said and motioned for them to precede.

"COB," Tarrent offered his hand, "your guys did a great job bringing her in."

"Thank you, sir."

Tarrent walked forward. Master Chief Bisetti waited till the officers passed then gently tugged at Norse's arm.

"How's the crew, Danny?"

"Pretty shook up, but these guys will get through it."

"What the hell happened?"

Norse moved out of earshot of the crew's mess.

"We surfaced in a state four sea. Pretty damn rough. The bridge was rigged and the mid-watch came on. Radar picked up a merchant at 11,000 yards closing our track. The Officer of the Deck maneuvered to open the range, but the contact maneuvered toward us. We slowed, and damned if the contact didn't turn toward us. The OOD called for the skipper. Captain came out of his stateroom and up the ladder. About three rungs from the top, the boat took a big wave over the sail. I guess he slipped and fell. He was dead by the time Doc got to him."

"Jesus," exclaimed Bisetti.

"Doc did everything he could, but the skipper's head was smashed."

"Okay Danny, let's get this over with and put your people on the beach. God knows they deserve it."

After meeting with the officers and speaking with crew, Tarrent returned to the pier. From the hatches, the crew of Miami came topside. Each Officer, Chief, and Sailor wore their dress blues. They formed two lines from the weapons shipping hatch, along the sail and off the brow, ending at the waiting ambulance.

The flag-draped body of Commander Joshua K.

Upman passed gently hand to hand along the submarine. Each member of the crew worked as a team to bring their skipper ashore for the last time.

As the body left the brow, Petty Officer Barkley sounded the ships bell. Four sharp but solemn rings, echoed off the fog mist and rain. Barkley placed his mouth next to the 1MC, and pushed the button, "*Miami* departing."

The rain fell harder. A stiff breeze swept up the river and caused fog to swirl. It grew darker. Bisetti drove the white Ford sedan. Admiral Tarrent and Captain Farmer sat in the back.

"Miserable day," remarked Farmer.

Tarrent said nothing, just stared out the window.

"Admiral?"

"We have a problem," the Admiral muttered.

"Yes, sir, we do."

"I can't hand this mission to just anyone. Sending another boat won't work either. Too many commitments too few submarines." Tarrent removed his hat.

"We need someone with Arctic experience."

"That's a tall order these days. We all but stopped going under the ice when the Russians cried *Uncle.*"

"The world changed. We were caught up in shallow water operations, Special Forces delivery, and fifty types of *specops*. We forgot about the basics. How were we to know?"

Tarrent remained quiet. The car passed the Navy Exchange, eased around the corner and headed up Hospital Hill road.

"There is one man," Tarrent said.

Farmer turned his head to the Admiral. "You mean McKinnon?"

"He's qualified for command. I think he's still down the hill at Sub School. Teaching navigation last I heard."

"But Sir, I…"

Tarrent cut him off, "God knows he has time under the ice."

Farmer shook his head. "Admiral, this mission … I mean this is dicey."

"I've known Grant McKinnon since he was a Junior Officer on *Pogy.* That's been what - twenty years?"

"But Admiral," Farmer argued.

"But what?"

"Well, isn't McKinnon *damaged goods*?"

"Yes he is," the Admiral glanced at Farmer. "I'm the one who damaged him."

Basic Submarine Officer Training Building
Naval Submarine Base, Groton, Connecticut
October 19th

Grant McKinnon alone at his desk, poured over charts for the next days class. A man of medium height, and narrow build Mckinnon would look at home in any environment, be it a corporate office, a little league ball game, or on the conn of a nuclear submarine. His high forehead and receding gray hair accented green eyes that though kind, held a spark.

Tomorrow his new group of students would plot a safe course through a shallow choke point, determine the best course, best time to make their move and decide if the passage could be made at all.

These new guys get smarter all the time. Or maybe I just get dumber, he thought. McKinnon swiveled in his chair when he heard footsteps outside his office.

The Petty Officer of the Watch stuck his head in the door. "We're about to lock up, sir."

Commander McKinnon looked at his watch. "19:30. Wow. Okay, I'll be finished in a second."

"Thanks, Commander."

McKinnon thought, w*ell, I guess it's gonna be a potpie night.* He folded his charts and listened to the guard lock up. He dreaded going to his huge house, a beautiful yellow ochre Victorian, with wrap-around porches, along the Mystic River. The beauty of the house's exterior couldn't compare to the interior. Antiques filled each room of the one hundred-fifty-year-old house. Handmade canopy beds, early American chests of rich walnut or mahogany made the home at 13 Ocean Avenue look like a postcard from the past. In most rooms, Tiffany lamps bathed the house in a warm inviting glow.

Along the south wall of the great room a mammoth size fireplace, made of river stone had once been the only source of heat. Hundred-year-old Persian rugs bedecked the polished pine board floors. The enormous kitchen had all the modern tools of cooking, the kitchen retained the original wood burning oven. The house had everything, including memories he dreaded.

With his charts secured in a heavy steel safe, Grant McKinnon picked up his hat and keys. Outside his office he checked the door, then turned and went down the steps to the Quarterdeck. The Petty Officer of the Watch sat at his tiny desk, the duty phone to his ear.

McKinnon smiled and waved goodnight to the watch as he opened the door that led to the parking lot.

"Wait, Commander," called the Petty Officer.

McKinnon turned and walked back toward the watch.

"Yes, sir. He's here." The Petty Officer said into the receiver then handed the phone to McKinnon. "For you, sir."

McKinnon put the phone to his ear. "Commander McKinnon."

Office of Admiral Burke Tarrent
Commanding Officer, Submarine Group Six

"Grant, why haven't you ever called me a son-of-a-bitch?" Admiral Tarrent asked.

"Never thought the term fit," McKinnon answered.

Tarrent pressed his hands on his desk. "I sure as hell felt like one."

McKinnon frowned. "Drop it Admiral. We've been down this road."

"Commander, I need answers."

McKinnon felt the hair in his neck stand up. "Sir?"

Tarrent leaned back in his chair causing the springs to groan slightly. "Why did you stay in the Navy?"

"What Admiral?"

"Cut the Admiral shit, it's just you and me."

McKinnon leaned forward. "Burke, what are you doing? There is nothing to forgive."

"Forgive? I'm not looking for forgiveness," Tarrent said softly.

"Then what?" McKinnon said confused.

"Why did you stay in? You knew you would never command."

"This is all I've ever known."

"That it?"

"Okay, listen, I stay here because I wanted you to know they made a mistake. I respect the hell out of you and you made a tough call. But, when you pulled my recommendation for command, it was the wrong call. Hell, Burke, I wanted to you to know that for once in your life you were wrong."

Admiral Tarrent folded his arms across his chest. "Maybe I am looking for forgiveness."

"My wife and son were dead for three months before you told me. For three months you knew that life as I had known it for nine years was over," McKinnon shifted forward.

"What could you do?" he asked. "You remember where we were? Sitting on the bottom of the White Sea, listening and watching the Russians launch the SS-N-20s. Was it worth it? I think so. Our Intel sure gave President Reagan the ammunition he needed. Brought the Russians to the table again, and maybe, at least I hope, made the world just a bit safer."

Tarrent looked across the desk at a man he wished he could be. "I pulled your recommendation because if it had been me, I would have killed someone. I would have never been all right - ever. The Navy shrinks agreed. Trust me, Grant this was not an easy thing to do. I had to think of the crews and the fact you might carry around about a thousand mega-tons of nuclear weapons. And believe it or not, I did it for you."

McKinnon paused, lowered his eyes. "I know that

and I won't lie to you, Burke. It was hell, pure unending hell. The first year, I was a basket case. But I managed. I never blamed you or the Navy."

Tarrent stood and put his coat on. "Now, I'm the admiral again, so listen up. I'm giving you *MIAMI*."

McKinnon felt every nerve in his body shoot impulses to his brain.. "Sir?" he managed to mumble.

"You are the only one I trust with *MIAMI*'s next mission. Maybe it will make my record of good decisions perfect again."

"When?"

"We'll bury Josh Thursday. Monday morning, I want you on that boat. You sail on Tuesday."

"What will Admiral Jennings say?" McKinnon asked.

Tarrent chuckled. "Grant, the President of these United States approved your orders three hours ago."

"How did you know I would accept?"

Tarrent's smile faded. "I don't remember asking you… This won't be easy, Grant." He picked up his phone. "Gav? I need you in here."

Captain Gavin Farmer stepped through the door, his left hand holding a chart, his other held a plain leather briefcase.

"Commander McKinnon," Farmer smiled.

"Captain, good to see you."

Farmer extended his hand. "Congratulations and well done." He reached in his coat pocket. Gavin Farmer handed Admiral Tarrent a small blue box covered in rich blue satin.

"First things first." Tarrent opened the box. "Commander Grant McKinnon, I take great pride in awarding you the *Command Star.* You are now duly authorized by the Chief of Naval Operations to command a warship in the Naval service of the United States of America." Tarrent held up the star. "Grant, this is long overdue." He pinned the gold five sided star on McKinnon's shirt.

"Okay guys, sit down." Tarrent motioned them to the chairs in front of his desk. "Now Gav, let's show the new skipper what he signed on for."

Captain Farmer pulled Dunn's image from the briefcase, unfolded the map and laid it across the Admiral's desk. "Last night the VITUS satellite took this image,"

McKinnon stared at the image. "I read VITUS only mapped ice?"

"That's what it was supposed to do. This was unexpected," responded Farmer.

"Unexpected, but fortunate," Tarrent added.

"That's a submarine." His finger jabbed on the fuzzy image. "I thought the Russians agreed to pull back?"

"We know their track record for keeping promises," the Admiral grunted.

The new commanding officer of the *Miami* leaned closer for a better look. "Too small for a *Typhoon*. Most likely a *Delta*. I don't know … something's not right. It may be the angle, but the shape isn't right for a boomer, not a Russian boomer anyway," McKinnon answered.

Farmer sat back. "If not Russian, then what?"

"Like I said, it might be the angle. Any more shots from VITUS?"

"They all come out about the same. What has us worried is, if you look, she sits right next to a polinya."

"I see it now," nodded McKinnon. "Of course, you've already gotten a count of the world's missile boats?"

"Everybody's accounted for."

"Maybe not," sighed McKinnon.

Captain Farmer slipped the image back into the briefcase. "We've plotted the location of that *unknown.* It's here." He pointed to the chart.

McKinnon stood and moved around the desk to get a better view. "Bad place for a boomer."

"Why is that?" Tarrent asked.

"It's right at the edge of the Hopen Rise," he stated. "The Lofoten basin meets the rise exactly where our bogie sits. Noise transients would echo off the walls of the basin. You'd be able to hear a fart from two-hundred miles."

"You mean that is the last place you would put a missile boat?" asked Farmer.

"Yes sir, too quiet. Not even the sounds of the ice would do you much good. There is a shallow layer there. Not much for sound absorption. Any noise below the ice will head straight down that basin, nothing to stop it. You'll have a huge negative gradient."

"So, this guy is either the dumbest skipper in the Russian Navy or a genius," Tarrent stated.

"How could he be a genius?" McKinnon asked.

The Admiral crossed his arms. "It would be the last place we would look for him."

McKinnon felt a chill run through him. "The very last."

Tarrent sat up. "Commander McKinnon, you will take *MIAMI* and find that sub. Find out what the hell she's doing."

"Admiral, what are my rules of engagement?"

"Grant, we don't know who is pulling this guy's string. Hell, he may be a defector waiting for the heat to wear off. But, we can't take that chance. If that boat makes a false move, you spank her ass."

McKinnon felt a weight slam on his shoulders, his dream now realized.

"There will be a briefing with you, the XO and Navigator tomorrow at 08:00. Squadron Two will handle your store's load," added Farmer. "Master Chief Bisetti is talking to the COB as we speak."

"Okay, enough for tonight," Tarrent stood. "That will be all."

Back on the road, Grant McKinnon steered his steel-blue Lexus up North I-95, and wondered, *Am I the man for this. Am I really the only one who can pull this off or just expendable?*

McKinnon turned right from the Mystic exit. A mile later, he passed Mystic Seaport Museum. The rain let up some and he could make out the tall masts of the Whaler Charles W. Morgan in the fog. He continued into the sleepy little town of Mystic, crossed the old drawbridge, where he took a left. He traveled two blocks and turned into his small driveway. He turned off the lights and the engine and sat in the silence.

The dark old house looked as tired as he felt. He wished Cathy and Danny were here. Cathy would cry with happiness when he told her he had at last gotten his own boat. Danny would jump up and down and then call Grandma. Then his mind flashed to the Russian waiting under the ice. *Maybe,* he thought, *maybe it's better they're not here.*

Chapter Eleven

Our Own

"I am sure you will be on your guard against the capital fault of letting diplomacy get ahead of naval preparedness."
Winston Churchill

Lapadnaya Lista
Russian Submarine Base
Dry Dock 9
October 20th

VEPR lay cradled in the rusty gray dry dock. In the frigid air the stench of rotting fish, mixed with diesel, paint, and welding, surrounded those at work on the hull of the *Akula*.

Huge gantry cranes set scaffolds around the damaged stern plane. Electric generators roared to life along with compressors and welding units.

Inside the stinking dock, Captain First Rank Valerik Danyankov stepped over cables and around equipment and made his way to the stern of his submarine. Jov Krivaya, the dry dock manager, tried to keep up, but his feet were not as nimble.

"Captain, it is not possible to predict when repairs

will be complete," argued the dock manager.

With great effort, Valerik Danyankov controlled the urge to pitch him over the side of the dock. "Why not?"

"You must understand, parts are a problem. Rail service is slow, shipments don't arrive," the manager moaned.

Danyankov's face went cold as the Artic air. "That is not my problem. I want a firm date and hour for completion."

"Sir, what you ask ..."

"I ask nothing," Danyankov exploded. "That is a front line submarine you have in your filthy box. Do you know what is going on in the world?"

Krivaya stepped back. Above the clank of tools and the hiss of steam, a deep forceful voice called out, "Captain Danyankov."

Both men turned to see Admiral Zivon Vitenka, at the edge of the dry dock.

Again, the baritone voice called, "Captain, a word, please."

VEPR's' captain looked down his nose at Krivaya. "You find a way. Get my ship back in the water." He walked to the Admiral and offered a halfhearted salute, which was returned halfheartedly.

"Please captain, leave Jov to his work."

"The man is an imbecile. All excuses," Danyankov countered.

Vitenka chuckled. "Maybe, but he's the best imbecile we have to repair your boat. Come Valerik, walk with me."

The two men walked through a riveted steel door

cut into the fifty-year-old dry dock. Once outside the steel walls, the noise and smell died away.

Admiral Vitenka glanced toward the rounded tops of the low hills. "Winter looks like it might come early."

"We both have better things to do than talk about the weather."

The commander of Submarine Squadron Seven stopped and turned to Danyankov. "True. We have much to do."

The rather short, but firmly built Vitenka stepped off. Danyankov held back a few paces then followed. "Then sir, if I may ask?"

"You may not ask Valerik," His voice soft. "You may however, listen."

Somewhat disarmed *VEPR*'s Commander remained silent.

The Admiral stopped short of a ribbon of narrow rutted pavement. "You remember your history lessons, Valerik?"

"Yes, Admiral. Some," Danyankov answered cautiously.

"Don't be so paranoid. I have no intention of moving you from *VEPR*. We have been through that many times."

"That is good, sir."

"You did well last week."

"Thank you, sir. I stand ready to serve the Motherland."

"Do you?" The Admiral smiled.

"Of course."

A small convoy of trucks approached the intersection. The large vehicles bounced and thudded along the miserable dirt road that intersected the equally bad pavement. The first dull tan truck passed and Danyankov saw officers crammed into the back. They wore no coats, only dirty yellow shirts. Only epaulettes on their shoulders identified them as officers. The next carried a platoon of Naval Marines. They sat stone-faced, their heads bobbed with the motion of the truck, their hands held the dull muzzles of their AK-47 rifles. Civilians, large men, with shovels and spades rode in the last truck.

"What is that about?" asked Danyankov.

Admiral Vitenka looked down. "Those are the surviving officers of the *Kuznetsov*."

As though lightning struck him, Danyankov stared as the trucks struggled up a small hill and disappeared down the other side.. "My God."

"Yes it is sad," the Admiral sighed.

"And the men?"

"They are safe. They followed orders. Most never knew what happened."

"How many survivors?" Danyankov asked.

The Admiral looked to the hill. "Three hundred men and fifteen officers."

Danyankov mind raced. "But Admiral, *Kuznetsov* carried 1,600 men."

"Let's not talk about that anymore." He waved his hand. "You and I have other matters to discuss."

"Such as?"

"Valerik, I am greatly troubled by all that has happened thus far." The Admiral came to a halt. "My loyalties, as I hope yours, have always been with the Motherland."

"You know that as fact, Admiral."

"These new leaders in Moscow - I wonder where their loyalties are?"

"What are you saying?"

"I think my friend, we are in trouble. These *leaders* have no more concern for the Russian people than the Czars. Will this revolution feed our people? I think this path is the way to destruction. Are our loyalties wasted?"

The rattle of AK-47 rifles echoed off the snowcapped hills. Danyankov winced when he realized the need for shovels. His blood surged and pounded in his ears. He thought, *and what of the KILO?*

Admiral Vitenka lowered his head. "We again kill our own," he whispered.

The echo of the gunfire faded, silence surrounded them. Vitenka stepped forward, Danyankov at his side.

"I am afraid, Valerik."

"But I thought…"

"We have been yet again used and lied to," the Admiral interrupted. "This new leader is a murderer, and a criminal. Most politicians are, but this man—this man is serves only himself. He is very dangerous."

"Where does that leave us?"

"Alone."

"What about the Defense Ministry?"

"Gone. Replaced by men who never served a day. No minds of their own. Russia is in danger, my friend, from both the inside and outside. As for the outside, we have an agreement with the West."

"What kind of agreement?"

"During the fight over *Kuznetsov*, an American

P-3 was destroyed. The war could have begun then. Our fighters and Norwegian F-16s almost came to blows. Fortunately, the NATO commander had insight enough not to make a bad situation worse," Vitenka paused. "I just worry such insight is not at work on our side."

Danyankov thought, *truth be told, I don't give a damn about who leads the country*. For the past fifteen years, the Captain wanted only to hunt his prey, instead he went on few and far between patrols while the money needed to run the Navy shriveled. Most of the once proud fleet sat rusted at the pier.

"It is anyone's guess what will happen in the next days, weeks, or even months." Vitenka continued, "I just want you to remember the Russian navy has always served the motherland, not the politicians."

"I will remember, sir."

"Good, then you will understand what I tell you. Should this whole mess suddenly get out of hand, I will hold your boat in reserve."

Danyankov felt his heart drop. "But Admiral I don't understand."

"Amateurs are at the helm of Russia and unless they get an education very quickly, this nation is headed for war.?"

"If it is war, then I should be out there."

Vitenka's short but powerful arms went to his side. "What is in the minds of these men in Moscow? Who is loyal to whom? There has been little communications between branches of the armed services. One false move, one careless action, one overt act, and it will be over."

"You sound like a defeatist," Danyankov snapped.

"No, a realist. The Americans have three battle groups circling in the Atlantic as we speak." He paused. "How many submarines do you think prowl out there now? If I were them I would say screw the agreement. They never trusted us, why should they now?"

"Still if it comes to that, I …"

"Look out there Valerik." the Admiral interrupted and pointed across the base. "See all those, undermanned, rust buckets. That's what I have to fight with, plus poorly trained crews."

"But why hold me in reserve?"

"When the shooting starts, how many boats will we loose? Half? Maybe more. It is then that you will best serve the motherland. You may be all that is left. I surmise many of those boats will sail, fight and die bravely, but there are those who will reason that life is too precious a resource to be thrown away for a government that couldn't care less."

Danyankov found it hard to form the next words. "You mean mutiny?"

"That has crossed my mind. They have nothing to fight for. We kill our own and there is little pay, less food."

"Still, the numbers do not add up, Admiral. There is another reason."

Vitenka's eyes widened. "Yes. The Russian mind does not consider losing. I fear this may lead to a nuclear exchange."

"The Americans would not dare," Danyankov countered.

"It is not the Americans I fear."

Danyankov's throat tightened. "My orders?"

"When I and only I issue you the order," he paused. "You will render our ballistic submarines combat ineffective."

Danyankov stood shocked. "We will be considered traitors."

"No, Valerik. Saviors.

Suddenly the confusion lifted and the numbers fell into place. "You have been like a father to me, Admiral. I stand ready to do my duty."

Admiral Zivon Vitenka looked into Danyankov's eyes. "As do I." Vitenka cocked his head. "There is another issue that has been brought to my attention again and again," he said smiling. "Evelina asks about you."

Danyankov almost choked and thought, *We just talked about the end of the world and now the Admiral meddles in my love life*? "Sir, I really don't think…"

Vitenka cut him off. "I know you don't think. None of us are getting younger and damn it, I want grandchildren. What? Is my daughter not good enough for you?"

"No, I mean yes. She is good enough, but my work, my boat…." Danyankov stammered only to be cut off again.

"She adores you and I don't think you're half bad," Vitenka thundered. "So Captain Danyankov, you will report to my dasha at 1930 tonight for dinner. And do clean up a bit."

* * *

Meanwhile, Jov Krivaya climbed the shaky

scaffold to the edge of the damaged stern plane. He nearly gasped when he saw the extent of the damage. Only the control arm shaft, bent to an almost perfect forty-five degrees, held eight ton stern plane. During her maneuvers to reach the surface, tons of hydrodynamic force caused the plane to smash into the control surface tearing out tons of high grade steel. What remained of the faulty pintle welded itself to the trailing edge of the control surface

"How long to repair?" Krivaya asked hopefully.

The foreman took a long drag from his cigarette then rubbed his temple. "Three weeks."

"Three weeks," shouted Krivaya over the sudden blast of a compressor's relief valve.

"I have material to repair the control surface," the foreman said. "We can bend the plane back with the press, but control shafts are special to this class. I don't have raw stock to make them."

Krivaya looked desperate. "What do you have?"

The foreman leaned on the scaffold, and threw his smoke over dry dock's side. "We can repair hydraulic lines and servos. The screw is chewed up, but I have one more." He lifted his finger. "Bearings are no problem, but that shaft and pintle are a worry."

"Captain Danyankov wants his boat back in three days," Krivaya shouted.

"Okay, okay," he frowned. "I have a shaft from the *Delta* we did last year. Not the same metal though. I could use welding rods to coat the shaft, then turn it down on the lathe," the foreman raised his voice over the loud compressor.

"Can you do that?" Krivaya brightened.

"Sure, but I don't know how long it will last though. The coating will wear off quickly."

"So?"

The foreman rolled his eyes. "Then you'll have the same problem."

"Just do it."

"You're the boss." The foreman slid down the scaffold.

* * *

Danyankov arrived at the dasha exactly on time. Evelina met him at the door "So, it takes my father to get you here?"

VEPR's Commander offered only a shy grin.

"Do come in, Captain." Evelina Vitenka motioned with her delicate hands.

Danyankov stood transfixed by her sparkling blue eyes and blond hair upsweep that exposed her tender neck. He admired the flowered dress that clung to her slender body and hips. When he followed her to the dining room, his eyes lowered to her shapely legs. *She's built better than VEPR,* he thought.

Chapter Twelve

Whales, Women,and Warheads

"...mighty men of valor."
Joshua, 1,9

USS MIAMI SSN 755
Groton Connecticut
October 24th

Well before dawn, the crew started to bring the nuclear submarine to life. Throughout the ship, each department, each division and each man made ready for taking *Miami* to sea. Deep within the hull, the nukes coaxed the power plant into service. Electronic technicians prepared gear for the transit out. The deck gang rigged the bridge with its portable windshield, life ring, and bridge bag. In the torpedo room, twenty-foot ADCAP torpedoes slid silently into their tubes. A short thick A-cable, linked electronically to the Miami's BSY-2 fire control system, ran from the after side of the weapon to the breech door of the torpedo tube.

The sun inched over the hills of Groton Heights when Grant McKinnon walked onto the pier, well aware, every eye would watch his every move. Pride of this ship welled within him. *She looks uncomfortable tied to the pier,* McKinnon thought. *We'll set you loose soon.*

He greeted the topside watch with a sharp salute. "Morning." His smile stretched across his face.

"Morning sir and welcome," the watch responded. "I'm MM3 Cole."

"Petty Officer Cole, it's good to meet you." His eyes swept his ship from bow to stern. "Is she ready?"

"Not yet, sir. Soon as I get off watch, we'll take the vent covers off and remove the sanitation fitting. We'll get outta here on time though. Always have."

"Good," replied McKinnon. "I'd better get below and pack my bunk. God only knows what the officers are doing." He put his hand beside his mouth. "You know you have to watch those officers like a hawk."

Cole burst out laughing. "Oh yes sir, so true."

McKinnon stepped from the brow to the black curved hull. He looked out over the still dark river. *No wind today*, he thought. *This should be an easy one.*

Inside his new command, Grant McKinnon smelled the fresh brewed pots of coffee. In the crews' mess, a jumble of boxes and frozen foods covered the tables. Mess specialists in checkered pants and blue cotton shirts stored each item according to preset menus.

McKinnon stepped in the pantry behind the wardroom.

"Morning, Skipper," the pantry supervisor smiled. "Care for a cup of Joe?"

"Sure would," smiled McKinnon.

"Name's Stephens, sir, Milo H. Stephens. I take care of the pantry and the O-gang."

"Nice to meet you Petty Officer Stephens."

"Oh no sir, it's Seaman Stephens. I got into a little trouble in Gibraltar last year and lost my crow," the young mess specialist admitted. "How do you take your coffee sir?" He poured the steaming black brew.

"Cream and sugar."

"Oh yeah, blonde and sweet. Just like I like the ladies. Here you go, sir and welcome. *Miami* is a fine boat."

"Thanks Seaman Stephens,"

Miami's Captain entered the wardroom and saw his officers seated around the table.

"Good morning gentlemen," McKinnon started. "First things first. This mission won't be easy. You will be called upon to learn or re-learn skills. We will operate under the ice. For how long, no one knows. We have information that a Russian boomer has staked out a place under the ice."

"I thought they agreed to pull back?" asked the weapons officer, Lieutenant Oliver Dennison.

The Captain pull out the VITUS map. "They did agree, but, there she sits, fat, dumb and happy. Our job is to nose around and see what she's about. As you know, tensions run high. That boomer is in a pretty good firing position."

Miami's navigator, Andrew Duguid, spoke, "Sir, the Russians are really paranoid about their missile boats. They always have a *Vic III*, or an *Akula* riding shotgun. Any sniff of an escort?"

"Not that we can detect, which means we have a few possibilities. One, this boat operates without orders. Two, she waits for her the escort. Three, they plan a first strike. Truth is, we don't know."

"Whatever it is, *Miami* can handle it," announced Executive Officer Brad Gellor.

Wow, thought McKinnon, *these guys really could chew steel and shit bullets.* "Now, let's clear the air." He sipped his coffee. "I talked to some of the crew. Morale is still high and from your record of inspections, *Miami* is the top ship in Group Six. I ask your help to maintain that record." McKinnon liked to see the smiles. "I know what a loss you've suffered. I knew Commander Upman since we were both no older than Ensign Kolter there." He pointed to the reactor officer. "I have no intentions of reinventing the wheel. Business as usual. I will have my standing orders to you soon after we dive. Men, this mission may be the most important submarine operation ever. Keep on your toes. That is all." He stood.

The officers followed suit, formed a line to shake hands and welcome the new CO. Unlike a traditional change of command, McKinnon hadn't received a briefing on his officers and crew and didn't have time to review service records. As they passed, McKinnon searched the faces looking for signs ... of what, he wasn't sure.

At 08:15, with the lifelines plus anything that would cause noise stowed, the *Miami,* 6,900 tons of steel, radiation and enough explosives to level an area, ten square miles, lay ready. The line handlers stood by at parade rest, waiting the word to cast off.

With a soft growl of powerful diesels, the twin tugboats splashed up the river, their blunt bows shoved the river aside in a gush of foam and spray. With nimbleness so unlike their gaudy appearance, the tugs swung into the slip and stopped short of *Miami's* hull. Thick dirty nylon lines passed from the tugs to the deck. The lines from the tugs looped around the sturdy T-shaped cleats along *Miami's* rounded spine.

Standing in the tiny, crowded bridge, Grant McKinnon struggled to contain his excitement. Next to him the harbor pilot, talked into his radio.

Lieutenant Royce Tyler consulted the harbor charts. As tradition Tyler, the newest qualified Officer of The Deck, would receive his baptism of fire by taking the *Miami* down the narrow Thames River and into Long Island Sound.

Petty Officer Barkley manned the JA sound powered phone, relayed and received messages, to and from the bridge.

Tyler checked his watch. "Captain," he said firmly, "the ship is ready to get underway. Request permission to remove the brow and cast off."

McKinnon looked at the young officer and remembered the first time he took a sub to sea. "Mr. Tyler, get the ship underway."

"Get the ship underway. Aye sir," Tyler responded. "Phone talker," he called to Barkley. "To the deck. Remove the brow."

The yellow crane grumbled to life. Slowly and carefully, it lifted the bridge between the land and USS *Miami*.

"Single all lines," the new Officer of the Deck called.

On deck the line handlers, led by Chief of the Boat Norse, removed the wraps of mooring line that secured the boat to the pier.

"All lines singled," reported Barkley.

"Very well," Tyler acknowledged, "Cast off all lines."

One by one, the mooring lines slumped and splashed into the water. The harbor pilot spoke into his radio. At once the tugs churned and growled to pull *Miami* into the channel. Barkley blew a whistle when the last line dropped off her hull. When the shrill note sounded, he raised the flag of the United States from the bridge.

"Helm. Left full rudder. Back two-thirds," Tyler called into the ship control circuit 27MC.

Miami backed smartly into the light chop of the Thames. Tyler ordered all stop. As her backward movement eased, the rudder centered.

Tyler took a sweep around the ship and the river. "Ahead one-third. Cast off the tugs," he ordered.

As her hull surged forward, removal of the heavy lines released the submarine from her tugs. The true form of the underwater warship moved effortlessly toward the open sea. When Tyler ordered the speed brought up to two-thirds, *Miami*'s new master noticed she passed well inside the buoys. Then the wives and children caught his eye.

They stood behind the chain link fence that separated the pier from the rest of lower base. In the chill of an early Connecticut fall, the families saw their sailors off. Some waved, others held babies. These ladies and children understood, maybe better than anyone, of the fear and loneliness ahead.

Grant McKinnon scanned the tiny group, wishing two more cried and waved as *Miami* grew smaller.

**Headquarters
International Whaling Commission
North Atlantic Division
Wick Scotland**

"George," beamed Chester Dalton. "I'm bloody glad you're here." He enjoyed his new vocation. As head of the United Kingdom chapter of the International Whaling Commission, he at last could do something about the slaughter of what he considered the finest animal on earth, the whale.

"Your E-mail sounded as if God himself was coming," smiled Commander George Ladd, a Royal Navy reservist and every part the Naval Officer in her Majesties service. He stood fit and tall, chin square, with the proper touch of gray mixed in his dark brown hair.

"I've got a fix on three Right whales moving south," Dalton announced. "George, I've picked up the whales' radio tags when they rounded the Denmark Straight."

"Well, that's fine, Chester," replied Ladd. "Now what can the Navy do to help these beasts?"

"Right. So we have two females and a calf headed south."

Ladd learned in the two months he commanded Navy District Seventeen, conversations with Chester Dalton took patience. Ladd searched the room till he found a coffee pot simmering on an old electric hot plate. "How old is this stuff?" He leaned over and smelled the yellow stained glass pot.

"Just made it this morning, or ah-ah-was it

yesterday morning?" Chester remained transfixed with the computer screen.

"At least it's hot," Ladd poured a cup and brought the cup to his lips. "Bloody hell. This could damn well be used as paint remover."

"Right," Dalton chuckled. "Must have been yesterday."

Ladd threw the still full paper cup into a nearly overflowing trash bin. The commander noticed other equally full cups lining the bottom of the bin. "So are you going to tell me what is so important?"

"Take a look here, George." He moved aside slightly.

The computer screen projected a map of the North Sea, Northwest of the Denmark Straits, three red blips in the shape of fish blinked. Next to each whale icon a code flashed, indicating the whales tracking number. Another set of data remained lit. These figures indicated course and speed of the migrating mammals.

"Appears these ladies stick close to the surface," said Dalton. "Must have found a good stretch of krill."

"Listen old man," the Commander sighed, "I have a rather full schedule. Can you tell me what is so bloody urgent?"

Dalton peered at Ladd over his glasses. "I'm getting to that." He banged away at his keyboard. "Look."

Ladd pulled up a rusted and bent folding chair, pushed a layer of dust from the seat and sat behind Dalton.

Dalton touched another button and on the screen appeared the black outline of a ship. A dotted line showed the ship's course from the past three days. "That's what's so bloody urgent, George." He tapped the screen.

"A whale ship? asked Ladd.

"Only the most murdering whale ship in the Atlantic. It's the *Beastla*," Dalton wailed.

"I read the reports on that ship. Norwegian, right?"

"Yes, and a cold blooded murdering pirate," Dalton hissed.

Ladd squinted. "Looks like she's in international waters."

Dalton raised a finger. "Ah, but look again." He pushed yet another button. Red lines appeared over the computer map that extended to the coast of Great Britain, then North inside the Arctic Circle, around to the coast of Finland and upper Norway. "See."

"What am I looking at?"

Dalton rolled his eyes. "The Red line marks the present moratorium line for whaling."

"Still, that ship is outside the lines."

"Not for long," His fingers tapped the worn keyboard. "Here is her track over the next two weeks. See. That bloody bastard of a ship will be well inside the lines. Now here is the projection for my *ladies* as they come south." The keyboard thumped and the projected course for the whales crossed the projected course of the whale ship south of the marginal ice zone.

"Chester, are these whales the only ladies in your life?"

Dalton's face turned red. "And what do you mean by that?"

"Nothing, just asking."

"You English bastard," exclaimed Dalton in his low Scottish brogue.

Ladd burst into laughter. "Come now, Chester. I'm only having a bit of sport with you."

"Right then," Dalton responded coldly.

"Tell me, what can the Royal Navy do to assist you?" Ladd asked still chuckling.

"I want you to send one of your ships out there."

"What? We have no authority over whaling. Maybe the Fisheries Ministry, but not the Royal Navy."

"You do have authority," declared Dalton and yanked at the tarnished knob on the old warped desk drawer but it stuck. "Damn thing," he cursed.

His teeth clenched, both hands pulled on the non-budging center drawer, arms shaking. The wood let go and sent the drawer and its contents flying. After the small shower of paper, staples, a finger nail file, two bottles of correction fluid, and month-old mints subsided, Dalton held the now empty drawer up in front of his face. "Bloody hell."

Ladd's face grew red while he tried to stop his laughter. "Careful there, old man."

Dalton dove to the floor picking up the strewn papers, cursing all the way. "Ah, there you are," he exclaimed. "Here you go. Here is your authority." He pushed a rather tattered page across the desk. "See," he nodded. "That Commander is a United Nations resolution."

Ladd read aloud, "All nations which are signatory to the charter and are in good standing within the United Nations are duly charged with protection of any marine mammal as described in the Endangered Species Act of 1972.

"A nation whose vessel is upon the high seas shall provide protection of above mentioned mammals to the fullest extend possible.

"This resolution does not authorize the destruction of a vessel operating illegally, in pursuit or capture of above-mentioned marine mammals. A warship discovering illegal pursuit or capture of marine mammals, may cause said vessel to stop, and be boarded.

"The commanding officer of the warship is authorized to detain officers and crew of the vessel operating illegally.

"Such detention is to be duly reported to the United Nations and to the nation of registry of the illegally operating vessel."

Ladd dropped the paper to his side. "Well I'll be damned."

"I told you so," Dalton smiled smugly.

"I will have this confirmed with London."

"Yes, please do," beamed Dalton. "Then send the whole bloody fleet up there."

"That will never happen, Chester. This Russian problem is getting very tense. Everyone has pulled back. I don't think the Prime Minister will authorize the entire fleet."

"Bloody hell. Send something out there. Destroyer, battleship, bloody rowboat with a pellet gun."

"I'll tell you what. HMS SWIFT is coming out for trials next week. She has a new Captain. I might get the Admiralty to agree to a training cruise in that area."

"SWIFT? Sounds like a damned sailboat."

Ladd chuckled. "Not quite a sailboat, but a very well armed Corvette."

"Well," Dalton sighed. "If that is the best you can do."

"It is the best I can do."

"Are you sure you don't have any battleships?"

Ladd laughed again. "I'm sure, Chester."

Auxiliary Naval Base
***Pechenga* Russia**

With their Naval uniforms supplanted by shabby woolen sweaters, thick canvas pants and antique fur lined rubber boots, the two officers met well past midnight under one of the countless neglected wharves. Each nervously puffed on their stale, but powerful cigarettes. As they talked, small dark waves slapped gently at the rotten timbers of the wharf.

"Captain, you know what will happen if we are found out?" asked Junior Lieutenant Sergi Cheslav.

Captain Third Rank Igor Rurik blew a cloud of smoke into the cold Arctic night. "I know very well, Lieutenant."

"Are you sure this has any chance of working?"

"That's up to us," Captain Rurik answered. "Can you deliver the package?"

Cheslav's eyes darted over his shoulder. "Of course I can deliver."

"Then we are half way to becoming very wealthy men," said Rurik.

"What is the plan?"

"We sail under orders to the North. I figure it will

take some time before we are noticed. Then we tell them we have radio problems," Rurik explained.

"Yes and then?" Cheslav puffed faster on his cigarette.

"When we reach the marginal ice zone, we make all speed to international waters."

"They'll sink us."

"I think not," Rurik replied coolly. "When we reach international waters we broadcast our intent to defect. NATO will welcome us with open arms."

"NATO. How can we deliver our cargo if a NATO ship picks us up?" he demanded.

"We will suddenly have a fire onboard. Of course a distress signal will be sent," Captain Rurik grinned.

"This is suicide."

"Wait, Cheslav. Listen, Our savior is even now sailing up the coast of Norway. An Iranian freighter will happen on the scene. It is there we deliver our package then we are taken to France, where we quickly disappear."

Cheslav scratched his head through the itchy rabbit fur hat. "And what about our money?"

"In a Swiss bank. Untraceable, but available."

"It sounds like a simple plan."

"The best plans are the simplest."

"One thing you did not mention."

"What would that be?" asked Rurik.

"The crew, what about the crew?"

Captain Rurik took a long drag on his cigarette, dropped the glowing butt to the ground and smashed it with his boot. "I told you there will be a sudden fire."

Cheslav's eyes went wide. "You mean we'll be the only survivors?"

"Unless you want to share one-hundred-million U.S. dollars with them."

"I understand." Cheslav smiled. "Are you sure they'll pay?"

"Oh yes, I am very sure. For them, it is a bargain. One hundred million dollars for a 200-kiloton nuclear warhead. That works out to 5000 dollars per kiloton."

Chapter Thirteen

Design and Deceit

"...this horrid disturber of the peace of mankind.

-Lord St. Vincent: Letter, 1812

The Kremlin

Moscow, Russia

October 25th

Viktor Ivanovich Paslav smiled like a cat at a mouse. He slicked back his gray hair. "Good morning, General."

General Eugni Moiseev approached the new despot, appraised him coldly, then sat in the chair across from the great desk. "Mr. Chairman, comrade, your royal highness, or whatever you call yourself," the General said with as much sarcasm as politeness would allow.

"Always a ray of sunshine, General."

"You executed the *Kuznetsov* survivors?"

Paslav returned to his seat. "Of course. They were traitors."

"Traitors against *whom?*"

The smile left Paslav's face. "Russia."

"Russia? You have no idea of what you have done." His eyes narrowed.

Paslav slapped his hands on the desk. "What I have done, General, is to send a message."

"That you did. Let me assure you the message eliminated a threat, but created a thousand more. Remember what I told you?"

"What do you mean?" His brow furrowed.

"Rumors have already started." Moiseev pointed his gloved finger at Paslav. "You are going to lose it all if you don't listen."

"Listen to whom? You?" Paslav laughed. "You don't seem to have your heart in this, General."

"My heart is for the Motherland."

"General, this is a most complicated situation." Paslav nodded. "I am not ashamed to say my own interests play a part in this."

"Let someone take over before it's too late."

The new leader of Russia laughed heartily. "Take over? Who? You? General, now what would the people think? Indeed, what would the world think if they saw a uniformed Russian in the Kremlin?"

"Paslav, you are a dangerous, ignorant man," Moiseev said calmly. "I am not sure which is worse, the danger or the ignorance."

"You're right, I have made mistakes. I am but a man. I promise you though, I will correct those mistakes." Paslav relaxed in the huge leather chair. "You will see, General."

"I hope so."

"You need proof? I can understand that. I've learned much from you."

Paslav motioned for one of his men. The man handed Paslav a folder. His fingers ran over the soft brown leather, then laid it on the desk. "Your tank crews have done their duty bravely."

"Of course. They are good men."

"I watch them, you know? I must say I somewhat envy them. Their only duty is to those steel monsters and to you. They are professionals. I see them eat and sleep on those tanks. Morale is high. At night they gather around the warmth of their cookers and they sing, laugh and they never seem to wonder why," Paslav shrugged. "They just salute and do as they are told. Very good men."

Paslav pushed the folder toward the General. "Take a look, General. I have awarded each Officer and enlisted man, *The Order of the New Soviet Republic.* Of course the medals have yet to be made. Will this help to bridge the gap?"

"It will," responded Moiseev.

"Good, will you present these as soon as possible?"

"Why don't you? I have rewarded and awarded these men many times. It is called leadership. If you want loyalty, then at least introduce yourself."

Paslav thought a moment, then nodded. "Okay, General. I will."

"When?" the general asked.

Paslav again paused, "Would now be a good time?"

Moiseev checked at his watch. "Yes, in ten minutes."

"Why in ten minutes?"

"I thought you said you watched my men?"

"I have," stated Paslav.

"Then you would know that my afternoon briefing is ten minutes from now."

"Ah, General, you should have been a politician."

"No Paslav, I know my limits."

"So you do." He motioned for his aid, an unshaven scruffy looking man with a dark pock marked face and wearing a suit not much better. "Make the arrangements."

The man merely nodded his understanding to Paslav. He stepped to the back of the room and whispered to the two guards.

"General," Paslav stood. "I will see you and your men in ten minutes. Like I said, I hope to correct a few of my errors.

USS MIAMI SSN 755

Submerged in her element, *Miami* slipped through the dark cold sea. Making more than twenty knots, the distance between *Miami* and the mystery sub closed rapidly. Each of the three watch sections traded duties every six hours. The smell of freshly baked yeast rolls filled the nostrils of those on watch and those still awake from the last. In addition to her load-out of ADCAP torpedoes, the *Miami* held a battery of twelve vertically launched Tomahawk Cruise missiles. These deadly accurate policy enforcers sat in the bow of the submarine. Such weapons required constant monitoring and care to put steel on target and on time. *Miami*'s weapon's gang conducted these checks, tending to the birds with great dedication.

New to this ship and new to command, Grant

McKinnon was somewhat bewildered at the mound of paperwork on his desk. Even the daily routine of the ships required his authority. When McKinnon finished reviewing the various logs, reports and charts, he stretched his legs. He looked around his stateroom. *Am I really here?* he thought. *Is this all real?*

Then like a dark cloud, the task ahead of him filled his mind. He envisioned the Russian submarine of black steel pressed against the white ice. *Need to focus*, he thought. He stepped into the small passageway outside his stateroom. He sighed slightly. *Quiet and lonely. The true cost of command, total and absolute loneliness.* He turned to the right and made the three steps into the control room.

"Conn-sonar," came a voice over the speaker. "Gained new contact on passive broadband. Designate contact as Sierra-22. Bearing 232. Range by bottom bounce is three-three-thousands yards. Contact on the right, drawing right. Contact classified as merchant doing 1-2-5 RPMs on one four bladed screw."

"Very well, sonar," responded Lieutenant Frank Addison.

"Afternoon, Officer of the Deck," McKinnon smiled.

"Hello Captain," Addison logged the contact. "Been a busy watch, sir."

"Busy is good," McKinnon nodded. "Makes the watch go by faster."

"Sure does, Captain. Care to review our position report as of 16:30 Zulu?"

McKinnon stepped over the slightly raised area of the control room known as the Conn. "Show me."

The navigation department did their work behind the Conn. Two large plot tables took up most of the narrow space. McKinnon leaned over the starboard plot to look at the chart.

"So far we have made less than 400 miles average speed is seventeen knots," Addison explained, pointing to the neatly laid track lines. Addison then placed a set of dividers on the chart. "Closest land is now Desert Rock, Maine. After we make our trip to periscope depth, we'll come East three degrees."

"Very well," McKinnon nodded. "Looks like you did pay attention in class."

"You remember me?" Addison asked, astonished.

"Of course, Lieutenant," McKinnon responded. "You were class leader that year."

Addison smiled. "Yes, sir."

"Whatever happened to those two guys in your class - you know that...?"

Addison nodded his head. "You mean the two drunks that took the golf cart for a one way trip off the pier?"

"Yes, those two."

Addison giggled. "They're both on tenders, one is in *La Madelina*, the other in *Diego Garcia*."

"Well, the stupid shall be punished. I'll be around the ship. Call if you need me," McKinnon said as he walked out the after end of the control room.

The Kremlin
Moscow, Russia

"As always General, I am impressed," Paslav

whispered as he and Moiseev walked to the small reviewing stand.

General Moiseev said nothing. He glanced to his left to where his men and tanks had lined up. The deadly looking T-80s sat like great insects; turrets square, gun tubes elevated, perfectly aligned. The crews stood in front of their tanks. The slender tough men unruffled by the cold October wind.

Paslav approached a hastily set-up microphone. "Good afternoon men, I am here today to right a wrong and take care of unfinished business. Our struggle for freedom has only begun. I want to thank each of you for the part you have played in this epic event in the history of our nation. This new government could not have occurred had it not been your dedication and your loyalty to General Moiseev. It is for that loyalty that I award you the following."

Paslav's bodyguard inched his way behind the General. In a flash. the bodyguard drew his automatic pistol placed it at the base of Moiseev's skull and pulled the trigger. The general's head exploded in a thick red mist and his body crumpled to the ground. The tank crews stood stunned and confused.

From behind the Kremlin walls, masked gunmen opened fire. The men ran to safety of their tanks, others tried to dive behind the tracks while heavy caliber machine gun bullets from office windows cut them to pieces. Hit in the arm, a tank commander made it into his turret. The tanker swung his heavy gun and pressed the trigger when another round tore out his shoulder that sent blood and bone spewing onto the light snow. Still, the heavy gun echoed. His shots went wide and high, the thumb sized bullets tore craters into the ancient brick and stone. Suddenly a round struck the base of his neck. The echo of the guns faded and the wind blew away the cloud of cordite smoke that hung like a pall over the dead and dying.

Paslav stood emotionless, looking at the heaps of dead and huge blotches of red spattered snow. He turned to his bodyguard. “Finish them.”

The guard nodded and motioned for the other man to join him. They trotted to where the tankers lay, kicking each for signs of life. When a few wounded moaned in pain, pistol shots rang in the air. Within minutes, one hundred and twenty-five men lay dead in the parade grounds. Their tanks stood over them with their guns still raised and their battalion flag still flying.

When silence fell, Paslav took a cell phone from his pocket and dialed. “Colonel Trochinsky, congratulations. I have decided to make you the Minister of Defense.”

Russian Patrol Ship *BARSUK*
Pechenga Naval Base, Russia
October 26th

“You’ve heard?” asked Lieutenant Sergi Cheslav.

Captain Third Rank Igor Rurik looked over the harbor from *Barsuk’s* rusting, obsolete wheelhouse. “The whole country has heard,” Rurik whispered. “But it makes no difference.”

“These murders may make our job easier,” observed Cheslav. “I’ve heard the crew, and even some officers, talk. There is fear.”

Rurik shrugged. "Yes, but now security may tighten. If we have to make our move earlier than planned, can you still get the warhead?"

"It may take a bit more influence, but it will not be that difficult."

"Influence?" asked Rurik.

"Yes. It seems Colonel Sevornon has an addiction to certain pain medications."

"And you keep him supplied?"

"Oh yes, supplied and I also let him know about the punishment for a person in his position," Cheslav said coldly. "He'll play along."

"Why do you think that?' Rurik asked.

"I promised him he can go with us when we sail next week."

Rurik spun and shouted, "You what?"

"Don't worry, Captain, he'll never make it to the ship."

The *Barsuk's* commander looked at the young lieutenant with cold eyes. "Seems I've made a monster out of you," Rurik observed.

"No," responded Cheslav, "poverty did that."

Lapadnaya Lista
Russian Submarine Base
Dry Dock 9

"There is no time," shouted Jov Krivaya. "I'm already three days late. Each day Danyankov has a breakfast of eggs, ham, tomato juice and my ass."

"If you don't let me do the X-rays on those welds, Danyankov might have more than that skinny ass of yours," the foreman growled. "Hell Jov, I don't even know if the control shaft will last outside the harbor."

"I understand, really I do. However, I also understand both Danyankov and fleet command are all over me. Now you. The first two I have no control over, but you I do."

"Hey, we've worked together ten years now. I just want you to cover both our asses."

"Fine, but that boat must be in the water tonight."

"Okay Jov, but please remember this conversation. I surely will."

At 21:00, Dry Dock Number 9 filled slowly and with measured care, the *VEPR* eased back into the dark water of the harbor. On the bridge Danyankov looked for signs of trouble. The water rose to the keel. "Reports," Danyankov demanded.

"All compartments report normal, Captain."

Good, Danyankov thought. "Docking Officer," he shouted.

"Sir," came the reply.

"Increase the flow rate," Danyankov commanded. "We'll be here all damn night.

VEPR's commander glanced over the side. A new rush of water spilled into the sinking dock then he looked over the stern of his ship and strained his eyes in the darkness at the building-size conning towers of the six *Typhoon* class submarines.

The water reached the halfway marker, Danyankov felt a slight shudder underfoot and *VEPR* floated off the wooden blocks. He peered aft and saw the towers of the giant *Typhoons* disappear.

Danyankov breathed in the cold damp air. "Where are the damn tugs?" he bellowed.

"Tugs are assisting another unit, sir," replied the docking officer.

"Another unit? Get their asses here."

Water inched over the bow planes. Lines which held *VEPR* centered in the dry dock went tight.

"Captain, the tugs en route," reported the relieved docking officer.

"Damn well time." Danyankov looked at his watch. "This boat had better be safe at her berth in a half hour, or their asses will hang off my periscope."

The docking officer looked queasy. "Yes sir, I am doing my best."

"Your best?" jeered Danyankov. "That's what worries me."

Now the rough clatter of engines broke in the dark water of Lapadnya Lista. Four tugs, all in desperate need of paint, fumed up to the submerged dry dock.

"Captain, the dock is flooded and the tugs are ready," reported the docking officer.

"Good," smiled Danyankov. "Pass the stern lines to the tugs."

"Yes, sir."

"Oh and be sure you understand," Danyankov sneered. "If you so much as scratch the paint on my boat, I'll use your ass as a dry dock for my foot."

"Yes, sir," the officer trembled.

The stern lines were passed to the waiting tugs. When directed, the ancient tugs reversed. On top of the dry dock walls, powerful capstans eased the forward lines holding the submarine centered. As *VEPR* backed out of the dry dock, new lines were sent from the deck to the other tugs. The capstan lines were cast off and allowed to splash into the icy water.

Ten minutes later, *VEPR* was safely moored to her pier. Danyankov turned to the docking officer and extended his hand. "Well done."

The officer's face turned pure white." Sir?" His clammy hand took the bear-like grip.

"You and your men did a fine job," Danyankov smiled. "Now get the hell off my boat."

"Yes sir, I will."

Danyankov looked at his watch. *Still a half hour*, he thought. *Evelina expects me for a late dinner. Strange*, he thought. *I think of her almost as much as I do my boat.*

Chapter Fourteen
OMSK

"Vain are their threats, their armies
are all vain;
They that rule the balanced world,
who rule the Main."
-David Mallet,1705-1765

The Kremlin
Moscow, Russia
October 28th

"Paslav, my friend. Tell me, why do you look so worried?" asked air force Colonel Adrik Trochinsky.

"I may have gone too far this time."

"You were threatened, no?"

"The West does not think and act as we do. I know those people. They will call it murder. It may give them the excuse they need."

Trochinsky shook his head. "America and its allies have their own worries. A war is the last thing they want. Ask yourself what would you do if America suddenly executed a few hundred officers? Would you risk a war for a few men?"

"Of course not. But with Americans, who knows?"

Paslav lit his fourth cigarette of the hour.

"I think the Americans are tied by their own hands." Trochinsky smirked.

"How so?" Paslav blew a thin steam of bitter smoke from his nostrils.

"The presidency in America is a ghost of what it was."

"I am not a learned man, Colonel. Please, be basic."

"The President cannot make any move without being subject to ridicule, investigation, or flagrant disrespect. His motives are questioned at every turn. Whatever party is in opposition will fight him whether he is right or wrong."

"How does he command? He lets critics make his decisions?".

Trochinsky waved his finger. "The President has certain options, but for the most part he has to beg for permission from Congress."

"A paper tiger then?" Paslav asked.

"These days, yes," Trochinsky shrugged. "Though still, a tiger. You must use caution."

"Colonel, I know the American President personally. We have what the Americans call a history. "

"I know better than to ask how," he laughed

"It is well for you that you don't ask."

Trochinsky round face seemed to slide toward his chin. "You must do as the President does."

"What is that?"

The smile left the colonel's face. "Surround yourself with people who will give you good advice and keep you out of trouble."

"That colonel, is why you are here."

"I thought so. Now for your personal safety…"

Paslav's eyes opened wide. "My safety? Colonel, I have the best men in Russia watching over me."

"The Americans are very good at assassination. Special forces or agents would find a way if ordered to do so. But again, that would be an act the American president would have to answer for."

"Colonel, I think you make much more of this than is needed. I am safe."

"Not as safe as you could be."

"What?" Paslav asked.

"Our reconnaissance aircraft located the aircraft carrier *Eisenhower* off our coast." .

Paslav's face grew red. "They can't do that. We have an agreement," he shouted.

"Relax, let them sail around in circles."

"But what if they attack?"

"This is what we must guard against." Trochinsky moved to the edge of his seat.

"You suggest we attack an American ship?"

Trochinsky laughed. "God, no. It is our right to protect ourselves, no?"

"Of course."

"Should the Americans decide to attack, what could we do?"

"Your jets sank the *Kuznetsov.*" Paslav looked puzzled.

The face turned deadly serious. "Yes, they did. However, an American carrier is another case. My planes would be in flames before they reached their launch points."

"If not your jets, then what?"

Colonel Trochinsky leaned back into his chair. "The Navy."

"The Navy?" Paslav laughed. "If you've not heard I'm not really on speaking terms with them right now."

"That is why you must use them," Trochinsky smirked.

"Explain Colonel."

"Of course, of course. The navy has a submarine, the *Anthey* class. NATO calls them *Oscars,* They have but one purpose - carrier killers."

"Again, I ask. You want to attack an American ship?"

"And again I say no."

"I am lost, Colonel," Paslav admitted.

"If we send this submarine to monitor the Americans, we violate no law. In fact we are obligated to do so."

Paslav rested his arms on the worn material. "I don't know if the Americans will feel the same way."

"How will they know?"

Paslav folded his arms across his chest. "If an attack is launched by the carrier, then what?"

"I think you would have been a good chess player."

"Please Colonel, you can kiss my ass later. Now, I need answers," Paslav barked.

The Colonel shrank into the oversized chair. "Yes, sir. What I tell you is this. We place this submarine near the American carrier. If needed, the submarine can take care of the ship with her missiles."

"That could end up in a war, Colonel," roared Paslav.

"No, no," the colonel smiled. "Sinking the carrier would be blamed on the Navy. Do you see? Your threat from the Americans is eliminated through no fault of your own," the Colonel grinned. "Call it a rogue act, or even an insane commander," Trochinsky explained. "You win no matter what happens."

"The Navy would never agree to this."

"Who says they have to know?"

Paslav's brow wrinkled in confusion. "How could the Navy not know one of their submarines playing games with an American ship?"

"Remember," Trochinsky, said raising his hand, "I am now Minister of Defense. I can arrange it. I'll talk directly to the Commander."

"Do you know him?"

"No, but trust me. The more I tell him how secretive and important this mission is, the more apt he'll be to carry it out. The example you made of the *Kuznetzovs* officers, will ensure cooperation." Trochinsky added coldly.

"This is too big a gamble, Colonel."

"I agree. It is a dangerous move." Trochinsky crossed his legs "You ask for options and this is one." Trochinsky let his words register.

Paslav frowned. "I know this President," he murmured. "The big problem is, he knows me."

"It's your skin."

Paslav wiped the moisture on his brow. "Colonel, send the submarine."

USS MIAMI SSN 755
300 Miles South-East of Greenland
October 29th

Miami slowed as she rounded the southern tip of

Greenland. Cruising at four hundred feet, in water black as her, and a nightmare for the sonar operators.

The warm Gulf Stream met the Labrador Current, mixing warm water with a nutrient rich soup. Marine life from plankton to whales thrived. The resulting noise from shrimp, crabs, fish, and whales caused the acoustic equivalent of an underwater shouting match. With such an abundance of sea life, fishermen from a dozen nations plied back and forth to harvest this ocean goldmine.

Layers of differing temperature and salinity, combined with the drum, click, and rasping biologics, the clank of nets, and diesel engines could mask any transient noise of a slow, well-operated submarine.

Grant McKinnon knew these waters, knew the danger, and knew how to work the environment. After a few hours of slow deliberate zigs and zags, *Miami* found the "sweet spot." The improved 688I followed the Northern edge of the noise wall where the two currents slid past one another. McKinnon placed his submarine in a half-mile wide corridor of perfect silence. *Miami's* BSY-2 sonar listened into the cauldron of noise or by use of bottom bounce, so she could safely venture up, dump her trash, copy her messages, and update her position.

Aboard the Russian Submarine
K-186 OMSK
Five Miles Northwest of the Eisenhower Battle Group
October 31st

"Have you ever been this close?" asked the Navigator on the OMSK.

Captain First Rank Ilya Borysko eyes didn't move from the passive sonar display. "No. I have only dreamed of it."

"Has anyone?"

"I don't think so," Borysko replied with a smile.

"Captain, what are we doing out here?"

"I don't know that either. I don't think Fleet even knows we're here."

"What?"

"The sailing orders came by courier. Delivered directly from the Minister of Defense.

"My God, Ilya."

"Be calm. "I'm sure there is a good reason."

"What were the orders?" the navigator asked barely audible.

The *OMSK's* Captain rubbed his chin. "That is also a mystery."

"Surely you have some directive."

"This vessel has been ordered to defend the Motherland," Borysko shook his head. "We are to trail the carrier as close as possible," his words tapered off. If we observe any hostile actions, we are to engage the carrier."

"My God. Do they want a war?"

"Control," came a voice through the command station speaker. "New contact bearing 245 degrees, estimated range 13,000 meters. Contact is closing. Closest point of approach is in nine minutes. Contact classified as American warship - *Arliegh Burke* Class Destroyer."

"They found us," said the Navigator, his eyes wide.

"Maybe, but I don't think so," Borysko said confidently.

"Sonar," he called. "Can you detect any change in the rest of the battle group?"

There was a pause as the bow mounted *Shark-Gill* sonar listened.

"Captain," the voice came again. "The carrier and cruiser have not altered course."

"What about the second cruiser and two destroyers?"

Again a pause. "Captain," the voice once more came. "There is too much noise from the carrier. The other contacts are being masked."

"Range to carrier?" Borysko asked.

"Range to primary target is 22,000 meters and closing at one hundred meters a minute," came the reply.

"No I don't think they've found us," the Captain smiled. "We'll just sit here like a hole in the water till that destroyer passes."

"Will we run parallel with the carrier?"

"No, not yet. I want to close the range."

"But Captain."

"Please relax, or I'll have you relieved," Borysko said softly. "After all, we are not at war. What could happen?"

Aboard the Arliegh Burke,
Class Destroyer
USS BOOKER DDG 74

"See there, Lieutenant. She handles like a stock car," Commander Dennis Youngren said proudly.

"Yes sir, she does." Lieutenant Malroy, son of the Admiral, said beaming.

"She'll get you into and out of more trouble than you can imagine. Let's see how you do on a ASW pattern."

"Yes sir. I studied the OPORD."

"Good, but the book can't compare to actually doing it. Okay then, here you go. Let's say your helo picked up a sniff. The contact is a probable nuke boat trying to sneak up on the carrier. Now this is not a very realistic scenario, we're too close to the *Bird Farm*, but just for training's sake, show me what you would do."

"First, I order sonar to go active. Full power," answered Malroy.

"Why?"

"To let the bad guy know he's been found. It will cause him to maneuver."

The *Booker's* Captain nodded, "Correct. And why do you want him to maneuver?"

"Because If he maneuvers, he's not shooting."

"Excellent. You must get it from your old man," Youngren smiled.

"I sure hope so."

"Okay, you told me. Now, show me," the Captain smiled as he stepped away from the Conn. "Mr. Malroy has the Deck and the Conn," he announced.

"Mr. Malroy has the Deck and the Conn, aye," the helmsman acknowledged.

"Okay Mr. Malroy. CIC just passed that the helo picked up a passive contact bearing 320. Range three miles. Go."

Like his heritage, Malroy took charge. "Helm, left standard rudder. All ahead full. CIC line up and go active, full power on bearing 320. Master at Arms, sound General quarters."

Instantly *USS Booker* sprang to life. A small rooster tail foamed as her screws bit into the ocean. The new Destroyer's sharp raked bow sliced through the water as she came to her new course. The alarm bell rang and the crew ran to their battle stations.

"Excellent," smiled Youngren. "Now see what information sonar has. Gotta hammer that SOB."

Then the sound of the active sonar ping vibrated through the ship.

"All stations report manned and ready," reported the bridge phone talker.

"Very well," replied Malroy. "Ship is ready, Captain."

Youngren looked at his watch. "Two minutes. The guys get better every day."

A frantic voice came over the bridge loud speaker. "Bridge, CIC. We hold an active return, bearing 312. Range two miles."

Youngren clicked the intercom. "CIC, this is the Captain. This was a drill."

No sooner had Youngren released the switch, when the voice came back.

"Bridge, this is no drill. Hold and active return bearing 312."

A puzzled look crossed the Captain's face. "What?" He clicked the intercom, "Captain to CIC, can you classify?"

"CIC to bridge. Classified contact as definite *Oscar* class submarine."

"Shit," Youngren yelled as he stepped back to the

Conn. "This is the Captain; I have the Deck and the Conn. CIC, continue active. Contact the carrier on bridge-to-bridge."

Aboard *OMSK*

OMSK's Commander heard the powerful acoustic energy that had just bounced off his submarine's hull.

"What?" Borysko, yelled as the active sonar ping rebounded along *OMSK*'s hull. "Diving Control, right rudder to course 110."

"They found us. They'll launch on us now," cried the Navigator.

"Shut up," Borysko yelled back.

"What are you going to do?" asked the near panicked Navigator.

"Give them a narrow angle."

Another wave of sound shook the massive submarine.

"Captain. Contacts increased speed," reported Sonar.

"What about bearing shifts? Give me proper reports."

"All targets are turning ... Wait. Second destroyer, coming this way, bearing 178."

"Where is the layer?" Borysko demanded.

"We are in the layer," called the sonar room.

"Captain, turn around. Get us out of here," pleaded the Navigator.

"We'll scare them off." *OMSK's* Captain crossed his arms. "Flood tubes one through six."

The Navigator went white. "You'll get us killed," he screamed.

"Get him out of here. Lock him in his stateroom."

"Sonar-to-Captain," shouted the unseen voice. "I now hold a helicopter bearing 090, approaching fast."

"Maintain course and speed. Bring air defense to readiness condition one."

At the weapon's control console, the *OMSK's* weapons Officer energized a small fifteen-inch-monitor. He linked information received from the passive sonar to the SAM system. The humming reverberation of the helicopters beating blades fed into the *Sterla* air defense system and a computer took over. It calculated the aircraft's approach, vector, and speed. On top of the *Oscar's* huge sail, five watertight tubes, each holding a single SA-N 5/8 missile rotated, then angled themselves to the proper attitude for an intercept. "Air defense on line, Captain," the weapon's officer reported calmly.

"Tube status?"

"Tubes one through six flooded and equalized. Bow caps are shut.,"

"Good," Borysko put his hands on his hips. "We'll see what they do now."

Aboard USS BOOKER

Two hundred yards off the destroyers bow a SH-60B Seahawk helicopter swooped low over the ocean. Launched only minutes before from *USS O'Brien's* stern, the ASW chopper slowed as her rotors whipped the ocean to foam.

From below the airframe, a small pod was lowered into the sea. Within seconds, the Seahawk's AQS-13 dipping sonar sent information by a link to the *Booker.*

"Okay, let's see what the helo gets." Commander Youngren lightly pounded his fist on the bridge rail.

"CIC to Captain," called a voice over the bridge speaker.

"Go ahead, Combat."

"Captain, the helo has acquired the contact. Bearing now is 276. No change in course or speed."

"This guy is not playing by the rules," Youngren shouted.

"Rules?" asked Malroy.

"He's supposed to go deep. At least try to evade, but he's still headed for the carrier. He has to know we have him nailed."

"It's like he's on a Kamikaze mission," Lieutenant Malroy offered.

Youngren looked at the Lieutenant and suddenly his mouth dropped open. "Jesus. A suicide mission. Get Iron Rod on the line," he shouted then grabbed the radio handset.

"Iron Rod, Iron Rod. This is Hotel Nine. Submerged contact does not alter course. Break. Believe this is a suicide mission. Break. Get your asses out of here. Break. Request weapons free."

Long seconds of silence. "Come on. Come on," Youngren urged.

"Hotel Nine, Hotel Nine. This is Iron Rod. Prosecute. I say again - prosecute the contact," came the answer.

OMSK

"Captain," cried out the sonar officer, "Helo sonar has switched to attack frequency."

"Bastards. I'll show them when to flinch. Open

outer doors on tubes two-four-and six. This will teach them a lesson. Watch them now. They'll turn and run, just watch."

USS BOOKER

"Metallic transients. Torpedo tubes opening," screamed the voice from CIC.

"She's taking a shot at either us or the carrier," Youngren yelled. "Tell the helo to engage. Helm ahead flank come to course north."

Lieutenant Marion Landers heard the order and brought his Seahawk to a dead stop.

"Sir, we have weapons free," called Petty Officer Ted Ferris over the choppers intercom.

"Roger that," Landers replied calmly. "On my mark, drop. Now - now - now."

From under the hovering Seahawk, the stubby slender shape of a Mk-50 torpedo dropped into the water.

OMSK

"Splash detected … Torpedo in the water. Torpedo bears 090." the sonar officer screamed.

"What? No," responded Borysko as his face went white.

"Torpedo has gone active. Range 800 yards."

"Shoot the helo. Match bearings on the carrier," Borysko ordered.

"Weapons ready, ship ready," The weapons Officer called.

"Launch."

In the control center of the massive submarine, a small jolt was felt as the three torpedoes left their tubes.

"Weapon running," Sonar reported. "Torpedo closing. Now bears 084. Range 500 yards."

"Shoot off the decoy," Borysko ordered. "Diving control, both ahead flank. Depth 800 meters. I told you to kill that helo."

USS BOOKER

"Hydrophone effects," called a nervous voice from CIC. "Three torpedoes in the water."

"Wake homers," Commander Youngren said quietly. He did the math in his head. *A forty-knot weapon runs for ten minutes. We were doing twenty-eight knots. Range is 2000 yards*. "Can't catch us."

Lieutenant Malroy swallowed hard. "Captain, there is no way a single Mk-50 will sink that *Oscar*. The chopper only has two."

"Captain," the port lookout cried.

Commander Youngren and Malroy looked out the port bridge window.

For a split second, the ocean glowed. Then a small dart-like shape rose, hung in the air for a mere half a second before a bright flash of orange shot from under it.

"CIC, get the chopper clear. Missile launch."

Those on *Booker's* bridge watched as the missile tipped its nose toward the still hovering Seahawk. With a boiling cloud of angry white smoke trailing behind, the missile lanced toward the helicopter. Less than a second later, the missiles warhead detonated against the helicopter's port engine. The explosion echoed across the water.

Christ," screamed Youngren, as the shattered burning wreck of the Seahawk smashed into the sea.

Youngren looked at Malroy. They both knew what had to be done. "Helm left fifteen degrees rudder."

OMSK

"Torpedo now bears 074. Range two-hundred meters."

"Diving control. Rudder left full," Borysko ordered.

"Captain, decoy was not effective," Sonar reported.

"Launch a second decoy now."

"It has us, Captain. Range 50 meters."

"Brace," Borysko shouted.

The torpedo slammed into the port side forty feet forward of the port propeller. Fifty pounds of RDX type explosives detonated, driving a wave of over pressure like a harpoon into the side of the *Oscar*.

Although it was a solid hit, the design of the submarine saved her. The force of the explosion tore a Volkswagen-size hole in the doubled hull of the Russian submarine. With over twelve feet between inner and outer hulls, the explosion lacked the power to punch through the pressure hull.

In the control center, the explosion sounded like a huge hammer pounded against the side.

"Damage reports," Borysko called. "Sonar, what is the enemy doing?"

"Enemy destroyers are moving off. Bearing 140 and 086," came the report. "Our weapons have acquired both."

"Captain, I have a damage report," said the sweating Engineer.

"Well?"

"Sir, port shaft seal is leaking. Cooling intakes from compartment eight are closed off. I rerouted cooling from starboard, auxiliary compressors damaged. Port shaft lube oil cleaner has been tore off its mounts. Rudder shaft bearings broke, as is the thrust bearing oil casing. The hull flange for number four discharge is also leaking."

Borysko smiled. "That's all?"

"Isn't that enough?"

"Bee stings," Borysko roared. "Attention, these are my intentions," he pronounced. "We have chased the destroyers off. The carrier is moving away at top speed. The Americans are in total confusion. We will come shallow and attack with missiles."

USS BOOKER

"CIC, talk to me," Commander Youngren urged.

"Bridge, detonation on the same bearing as the contact," came the report.

"Where are the torpedoes?"

"Bridge CIC. One weapon is astern. 1,000 yards and closing at five-zero yards per minute. Second weapon is tracking Hotel-Seven, trailing at one-five-hundred yards. Third weapon must have malfunctioned. It shut down soon after launch. Wait ... Regain submerged contact on passive. Contact bears 212, range four thousand yards on the left drawing right," he paused. "She's been hit, sir. Hold metallic transients and increased flow noise."

"You were right," Youngren looked to Malroy. "CIC bridge, deploy the Nixie," he ordered. "That son-of-a-bitch will start lobbing missiles real soon."

Youngren ordered Booker into a tight turn. She heeled over twenty degrees, her gas turbine engines roared at full speed.

"Decoy deployed," CIC reported.

"CIC, go active when you get a steady bearing. Execute Attack plan, Charlie."

"Attack plan, Charlie," the officer in CIC responded.

"Steady course 025," reported the helmsman.

Seventy-five feet below the surface and less than eight hundred yards away from the destroyer, one of *OMSK's* torpedoes hummed along at forty knots. In the weapon's blunt nose, sensors received waves of pressure generated by the turbulence from Booker's wake. When the pressure reduced to one side or the other, the torpedoes electronic brain ordered a slight alteration in course. When the sensors were once again happy with the pressure, the twenty-foot weapon resumed its course.

Suddenly the weapon received a new and larger pressure wave. As programmed, the torpedo altered its course, *tasting* the new information. This new wave of pressure was much larger; therefore, it reasoned, this must be a bigger target. The *Booker* turned to face the oncoming torpedo, her decoy did its job to perfection.

"Torpedo has altered course," came the word from CIC.

"Can they steer those damn things?" Malroy asked.

"Don't think so," Youngren replied quietly.

"CIC to Captain, going active—ASROC launcher on line."

"I want three weapons in the water."

"Three weapon salvo, aye."

"Okay people, here is where we earn our pay," Youngren shouted.

"CIC bridge active return."

Youngren didn't wait for the report on the *Oscars* bearing. "Launch—now, now, now."

From the forward deck of the speeding destroyer, three small hatches slid open. A cloud of orange and black smoke shot as high as the radar mast. The first rocket propelled torpedo, left the ship at two-hundred-fifty miles an hour. Soon as the first was away the second erupted from the launch tube, followed by a third.

"Weapons away," cried the officer in CIC.

"Secure active and listen," Youngren ordered as he lifted his binoculars.

Each weapon was boosted by a powerful rocket to a point determined by the ships fire control computers. At that point, the rocket separated from the torpedo. A small parachute deployed as the torpedoes fell.

Ten feet above the surface small explosive squibs fired, jettisoning the parachutes. At ten seconds intervals, the torpedoes slid into the water.

OMSK

Borysko was unalarmed at the sudden reversal of

the destroyer's course. "He's evading our weapon," he said smugly.

"Our weapon now bears 228, right of the target," sonar reported.

"Damned decoy," Borysko snarled.

The sonar officer's eyes widened.

"What is it?" Borysko demanded.

"Missile launch. One … no two … now a third."

"Diving control. Two hundred meters. Rudder right," Borysko ordered.

"Splashes right above us," shouted the sonar operator. "Torpedoes. I count three … They are active. Range 300 meters. Closing."

"Launch a decoy. Reverse the rudder," Borysko thundered.

"Depth is now four hundred meters," reported the planes operators.

Borysko didn't hear.

"Two torpedoes have acquired us. I cannot hear the third."

OMSK turned and climbed at the same time. The rudder caused a large drop in speed. It also created a huge disturbance of water. The American torpedoes locked on to this sound. In each of the torpedoes noses, their small sonar's pinged faster as the range reached zero.

The first struck just aft of the already damaged section of *OMSK*'s outer hull. The blast sheared the two-inch thick bolts holding the outboard intake valve flange. A jet of water two feet across flooded into the port engine room.

The second weapon approached from slightly

under the massive hull, plowed into the curved underside, and detonated under the main reduction gear for the port propeller. The titanium propeller shaft flexed up and down till a crack formed. The reduction gears slipped from their precision-machined housings, and ground themselves in to a useless pile of broken stainless steel.

The torque from the still spinning propeller twisted the already strained shaft till it snapped, and the entire stern of the battered submarine fell. The last MK-50 slammed into the rudder. As it exploded, superheated jets of plasma welded the hinges, locking the rudder in a hard right turn.

In the command center, the detonations were felt as one continuous rumble. Alarms sounded, and warning lights flashed. The huge submarine lurched to port.

"Flooding in the port engine room."

"Number two reactor scrammed. Loss of main hydraulic power."

"Over voltage trip on port generator."

"Rudder jammed to port."

The 14,500 ton submarine rose like a wounded whale.

USS BOOKER

"Helm ahead two-thirds. Right five degrees rudder," Youngren ordered. "We'll slow down to listen."

"Three hits," shouted the voice from CIC.

"What else CIC?" the Captain asked.

"Too much noise from the warheads," came the reply.

Suddenly a tremendous fountain of black dirty water leaped up a thousand yards astern. In the center of the boiling blackness, a plume of white spray shot higher than a seven-story building. The rumble of nearly a ton of explosives echoed across the water.

"What the hell was that?" Lieutenant Malroy yelled.

"Our decoy just died," Youngren smiled. "The Russian torpedo hit it."

"Jesus," Malroy sighed.

"CIC, what is going on down there?" Youngren asked.

"Captain, sonar is a blank due to the reverbs of the explosions. We can hear some clatter … Wait. Regain contact on passive. Sounds like a train wreck down there."

Youngren shook his head. "God, I hope the reactors didn't rupture."

"Bridge. Contact is maneuvering."

"Give me a bearing."

"Contact is one hundred yards and closing. Contact is coming shallow. Bearing 067."

"Helm ahead flank. Left full rudder," Youngren barked.

"Range seventy-five yards," CIC warned.

Booker's gas-turbine engines roared, her stern settled and the bow rose. The Destroyer turned away from the rising submarine.

"Contact, close aboard. Collision imminent," the officer in CIC screeched.

OMSK rose out of the ocean. The two warships met at a combined speed of eighteen knots. Twice the length and three times heavier, *OMSK* smashed into the thin plating of *USS Booker.*

At just over eleven tons, the *Oscar's* port diving plane encountered little resistance and knifed a gash twenty feet long and nine-feet wide into *Booker*'s starboard side. *OMSK's* high tensile steel hull moved along the destroyer, it crushed and tore as it slid past.

Pressure in the thousands of tons per inch, acted to push the vessels apart. *OMSK* still locked in a hard right turn and moved aft as the destroyer bounced and wobbled to the left.

On *Booker*'s bridge, the collision felt like an earthquake during a thunderstorm. Men and material were thrust upward, then slammed hard onto the steel deck.

Lieutenant Malroy, flung against the plot table, the impact snapped four of ribs, one of which punctured his left lung.

Commander Youngren braced himself somewhat on the bridge chair. The force of the collision was too severe to maintain a grip and he landed hard on his left side.

The helmsman fell, his face struck the control console, smashed his jaw and ripped open his cheek.

Youngren staggered to his feet. He managed a step toward the bridge door when his ship listed slow but steady to starboard. He reached the internal communications station and pushed buttons. "Damage Control," he shouted into the microphone.

"Captain, we're taking water in all compartments. Magazines are flooded. No answer from the Engine room," came a near panicked voice.

The ship listed further on her right side. Lieutenant Malroy pushed himself up holding his ribs. He limped next to his Captain. “What do you need, sir?” he asked. Blood trickled from his lips.

“How bad are you?” Youngren asked.

“Not too bad,” Malroy replied weakly.

“We’re in trouble. Can you make it below? I need to know if we can float.”

“Yes sir.” Malroy struggled for breath then staggered along the tilted deck to the bridge door.

Commander Youngren flipped the switch of the communications system. Bridge to CIC … CIC this is the Captain.”

There was no reply.

Chapter Fifteen

Saber Rattles

"Ye shall hear of wars and rumors of wars."
-Matthew, XXIV,6

USS MIAMI SSN 755
November 1st

Unaware of the disaster off Norway, the *Miami* slipped through the inky blackness of the Arctic Ocean. Ten hours ago she passed through the Denmark Straits on a Northerly course. At midnight, Commander McKinnon turned his boat east, leaving the tip of Iceland roughly a hundred miles astern.

A weary group of officers piled into *Miami's* wardroom. A few officers held cups of black coffee, while others yawned and rubbed their tired eyes.

"Good evening gentlemen, or good morning, I should say," McKinnon smiled.

The officers around the wardroom table nodded.

"I'll make this quick so you guys can get some rack time. Tomorrow, I expect to reach the ice pack. Most of you have never operated under the ice. Two words," McKinnon held up two fingers. *"Be careful.* I want the under ice sonar manned continuously after 06:00. Put your best people on it," McKinnon nodded to the Weapon's Officer. "We'll enter the pack here." McKinnon pointed to a spot on the chart. "This time of year the ice moves a lot, makes a hell of a noise. We have no idea whether or not that Boomer has an escort. If he does, we want to slip around nice and quiet. The noise from the ice should be enough to cover us," McKinnon paused. "Any questions so far?"

"What about comms, sir?" asked Ensign Truluck.

"Good question. When we are deeper than four-hundred feet, we'll keep the floating wire out." McKinnon placed his index finger against his temple "Guys, remember the wire is out. Don't come shallow with it dangling out there," McKinnon warned. "Remember, it floats. You come too close to the ice and it will drag across the bottom."

"How well will the wire work under the ice?" the Weapon's Officer asked.

"Not very well, I expect. That brings me to my next topic. Officers of the deck and sonar need to be alert for holes in the ice. Look for places we could surface. We need to know how big the hole is, and where. Even a small hole is important."

"What about our search plan?" asked Engineer Kenneth Webb.

"Depends on conditions. If the ice has settled down, we'll use the towed arrays. If not we'll do it the good ole' fashion way and use the spherical."

Miami's executive officer waved his hand. "Same rules apply for the towed arrays. Don't go bouncing them on the ice and for God's sake—no backing up."

"Thanks XO," McKinnon nodded. "Okay, anyone have anything else?" he paused. "Get some sleep. You're going to need it."

300 Kilometers From Moscow
0245 Local
November 2nd

A Russian *AN-12BP CUB* transport bounced in the turbulent black sky over the desolate steppe. Flying high enough to avoid power lines, the lumbering plane pushed south against a ten knot wind.

In the dark cavern of the *Cubs* cargo hold, Admiral Zivon Vitenka looked at his watch. So far, he was on schedule. Holding a penlight in his teeth, Vitenka spread his map along his lap. His gloved finger traced a line along the aircraft's route. Another hour and the Volga River will come into view. A slight turn to the right turn, then other fifty-kilometers to Moscow. He looked at the air defense areas marked in large red circles. At any moment, Air Defense Command of the Moscow Military District would pick up the squat ugly aircraft on radar.

"Admiral?" a voice called over the rhythmic humming of the *Cub's* engines.

"Yes Major," Vitenka replied.

Major Valery Gounov, Commander of the 35th Guards Spetsnaz stepped forward, and braced himself against the wallowing airplane.

Dressed not in a uniform, but in jeans and a heavy sweater, the Major plopped himself roughly next to Vitenka. He pulled the large dull orange cap from his head. "Sir, I would like to prepare the men. Do a final check."

"Do your men know what we might expect?" Vitenka asked.

"Yes sir, we do."

"Your communication man, does he fully understand?"

"He does," Gounov assured.

"Good. Prepare the men."

Major Gounov rose and moved back into the darkness. His voice at a low tone gave orders, and eighty highly trained commandos readied themselves.

The Pentagon
Washington DC

"How's he doing?" asked the Situation Room Watch Officer.

Chief of Naval Operations William Flisk looked up from a pile of messages. "He went home for a few hours last night, and returned right back here at zero-five-thirty."

"We have a final count yet?"

The CNO ran his hand through his hair. "Yeah," he lowered his head. "Thirty-five dead - seventeen critical, five missing. The rest—well you can imagine."

"My God," whistled the Watch Officer. "And the Russians?"

"We're not sure. The *Oscar* was still afloat last night. Wouldn't bother me if big bastard went down," the CNO said through clenched lips. "You have anything new?"

"Not really. It's been pretty quiet. The President authorized us to move two Keyhole satellites from the mid-east. At least we can see if they deploy any more units."

"About time," Flisk grunted.

"President's going to speak to the nation sometime this morning."

"I know, Admiral Malroy plans to be there with him," answered the CNO.

"He's tough."

"Yes, that he is."

Lapadnaya Lista
Russian Submarine Base

Snow fell as Valerik Danyankov came topside. The crew stood in neat lines according to department. "Men of *VEPR,* it has been what now—three weeks?" he announced. "Three weeks since you had your lazy asses at sea. The rest of this rusting, shit-pile of a fleet can sit here—Oh, but not us. We have work to do. We will sit here next to this pier and we will train." He hoped his forced smile covered the truth. "Some of you may have heard what has happened over the past few days. That is what happens when you have no training. I will drill you until you want to die. Weapons will be loaded and tested. Engineering systems will be brought on line. It will be as if we are at sea. Radio will monitor all frequencies. I know there are no questions, so get to it. You have ten minutes to report readiness. Dismissed."

"Sir?" a voice from behind called.

Danyankov turned to see his weapons officer saluting. "What is it?" he growled.

"Captain, is it your intention to load live weapons in port?"

"It is," responded Danyankov.

"That is forbidden, Captain," the weapons officer said.

Danyankov swelled with pride. *My lessons are paying dividends after all*, he thought, then looked around till most of the crew hurried below. His eyes narrowed. "Are you telling me what to do? I know what is forbidden and what is not."

"Yes sir," the Weapons Officer yet feared he had signed his own death warrant.

"Walk with me," Danyankov ordered as he started toward the end of the pier.

Five minutes later, they returned to the deck of *VEPR*. "I can count on you then?" Danyankov asked softly.

"I serve the Motherland and *VEPR,* Captain," the Weapons Officer answered. "And I serve you."

Danyankov nodded. "Now get your ass below."

Good men, Danyankov thought. *All good men.* He looked at his watch..

The White House
Washington, DC

Breaking News, flashed across the millions of television screens across the United States. Another million or so throughout the world also tuned in.

"We interrupt our regularly scheduled broadcast to bring you this important news," a monotone announcer said. The blue background switched to the oval office.

"My fellow Americans, we have suffered a great loss," the President opened. "Thirty-five young patriots have paid the ultimate price for freedom. My thoughts and prayers go out to the families of those lost on *USS Booker* and those lost in the air. No words of mine can erase the sadness and loss. I do assure you in this time of sorrow, the entire nation, and indeed the free peoples of the world stand with you.

"Events leading up to the loss of such a fine ship were calculated and planned by criminals, disguised as leaders. I say to them and the world - this: The United States will protect its ships, its citizens and its interests where ever they may be.

"I urge the leadership of Russia to take full responsibility for what has happened and to honor the agreements. Acts such as these can and will have the gravest consequences.

"I have authorized the military to use whatever means necessary to eliminate any threat to our forces. Authority is also given to theater commanders to halt and contain any incursion into a nation's sovereign territory. Let me be sure these measures are fully and completely understood. *Any* means will be used to protect this nation and our citizens and our allies.

"Our thoughts are as always with the brave men and women who serve this nation. We as a people are indeed blessed to have people such as these who guard and defend all we hold dear. I and the American people salute you.

"We as Americans will do our utmost to defend freedom and peace; likewise, we will do our utmost to defeat aggression and tyranny. Our resolve is not wavering and our mission is unchanged. Thank you and God bless the United States."

The Kremlin
Moscow, Russia

"My God, what have you done?" Paslav yelled. "Did you hear what he said?"

"What have I done?" balked the new Minister of Defense Adrik Trochinsky. "I did only as you asked."

"An American ship sunk. What a grand plan."

"Paslav," Trochinsky said in a hushed voice. "It worked."

"What? Are you going to tell me this was a success? The President of the United States just threatened me with nuclear weapons," Paslav paced and puffs of smoke followed.

"Where are the American carriers now?" Trochinsky asked.

Paslav stopped. "I don't know."

"I do. They moved out to sea. Their range is too great to launch any strikes against us. As for the threat of nuclear weapons, surely you didn't believe that. No American President will use nuclear weapons in a first strike. As a matter of fact, it is forbidden by their policy."

Paslav sat down heavily in the large leather chair. He took one last long drag of his cigarette, then snuffed it out." What about our losses?"

"Minimal and expected," smiled Trochinsky.

"So now what?" Paslav asked.

"Now we finish getting the military in line. After that we make this nation what is once was."

"Yes... I see now."

"Our troops and tanks gather on the borders.

Within a month, the hammer and sickle will once again fly across the continent." Trochinsky pointed over his head. "I have also been in contact with several *friendly* governments. The three nations in South America are ready to talk. The Iranians are about to piss on themselves."

"What about our Navy? I still have bad feelings about them."

"We'll start taking care of that today. As a matter of fact, Admiral Vitenka is here to see you."

"Who the hell is that?"

"Commander of Northern Fleet submarines."

"What the hell does he want?" Paslav grumbled.

"Oh, I suppose he'll bitch about us using his submarines without his approval," Trochinsky answered mockingly.

"What do I do with him?"

"Unlike the other services, the Navy has a different set of unspoken rules."

Paslav raised his eyebrows. "Can't you just answer a question? What the hell are you talking about?"

"If he never returns, the message will be loud and clear," grinned Trochinsky.

"What about our other problem?" asked Paslav.

"The Americans? They won't do anything we don't want. They're too afraid of what the rest of the world will think."

"I trust you, Trochinsky. We're going to be wealthy men. Now show the Admiral in."

Lapadnaya Lista
Russian Submarine Base
November 2nd

His crew scrambled from one drill to the next and

Danyankov climbed into *VEPR's* bridge. The wind dropped some, but the snow still fell. Danyankov glanced around to see if anyone was watching.

From his heavy coat, he took a small notebook. Looking West, he noted the location of the *Typhoon* piers. To the South, he checked the weapon loading station. *Good,* he thought, *no missile boats there.* He checked his watch and picked up the bridge microphone. "This is the Captain. Communication Officer to the bridge."

Soon he heard the metallic clank of boots on the bridge ladder. "Permission to come up?" a voice asked.

"Come up," Danyankov growled.

"You sent for me, Captain?"

"Yes. Are all frequencies monitored?"

The communications officer looked puzzled. "Of course sir, as you ordered."

Danyankov looked at the shivering officer. "I expect one of two messages."

"Yes sir?"

"As soon as you get one of the messages, I need to know that moment. Do you understand?"

"I do, Captain."

"The messages will contain only one word. The words are Pandora or Dove."

"Pandora or Dove," the communications officer repeated.

"Now get below and wait."

The Kremlin
Moscow, Russia

"Admiral, tell us what can we do for the Navy?" Paslav smiled as phony and cheap as his wrinkled suit.

Vitenka stood emotionless, his eyes fixed on

Paslav, but in the background saw the bodyguard move behind him. "You will now step down as President of Russia," he said quietly.

The ten or so men around the Admiral, laughed.

Once the sound had died off, Vitenka continued, "Minister of Defense Trochinsky, you are under arrest and will face court-martial."

Trochinsky, still seated, his legs crossed, chuckled, "And what are the charges?"

"Treason, murder, crimes against the Russian people."

Again the men laughed. "Who sent you, Admiral?"

"The Russian people," Vitenka answered coldly. "Time is short. I need you to leave now."

"Leave? Why should I leave?"

"I tell you if you want to live, you will walk out the door."

Paslav's smile disappeared. He gave a slight nod to the bodyguard. "You are a fool, Admiral. Why should I be afraid of you? You're one man. I don't think demands about such matters are up to you," Paslav shouted.

Vitenka remained motionless, his expression unchanged. "Then you refuse?"

"Yes Admiral, I refuse."

The bodyguard stood less than two meters behind the Admiral.

"Unfortunate," Vitenka whispered.

"Yes, unfortunate for you, Admiral," Paslav hissed.

The guard snatched his pistol from its hidden holster, brought it up, extended his arm, the muzzle now even with the Admiral's head.

Suddenly, a pop and a tiny hole appeared in the window glass. The bodyguard's gun crashed to the floor, his body sprawled beside it and a stream of red blood spurted from the side of his head.

Vitenka turned away from the window and squatted, just as the three panes of heavy glass shattered in a deafening explosion. Men clad in black descended into the room with automatic weapons spitting bullets at the men surrounding their President.

As bodies cluttered the floor, one of the commandos pointed his weapon directly at Paslav. "Keep your hands on the table."

Out of either pride or stupidity, Paslav reached for his open desk drawer. A single muffled shot rang out and Paslav's term as President of Russia ended.

Lapadnaya Lista
Russian Submarine Base

"Your village must be missing its idiot," Danyankov yelled. "How long do you expose your scope?"

"I... I... ," stammered the young watch officer.

"You what? You want the ship blown to hell because you got fixated on a target?"

"Seven seconds. Seven seconds. That's all you have. Now try it again," *VEPR's* Captain snapped. "Launch control. Set up the scenario …."

The Communications Officer interrupted. "Sir, the message you wanted."

Danyankov grabbed the folded paper, tearing it open. There was only one word. DOVE. Danyankov closed his eyes. He actually felt the weight lift from his shoulders. The air suddenly seemed fresher. "Thank you," he said softly. "Secure from drills. All officers in the wardroom."

The Pentagon
Washington DC
November 3rd

Captain Scott Lowe walked as fast as he could without actually running. He banged the door open and strode past a startled secretary and marched right into Admiral Malroy's huge office. The Chairman of the Joint Chiefs sat writing the tenth of thirty-five letters. Next to him, a wastebasket overflowed with crumpled papers. Rejected words of grief to wives, mothers, fathers, and a four-year old little girl named Candice.

"Admiral. Phone call, line three," the Captain smiled.

Malroy looked up. "I said no calls."

"Pick up the phone, Admiral."

"Malroy put down the pen and slowly picked up the receiver.

"Admiral Malroy," he grunted.

"Dad?" came a weak voice.

"James. James."

"Yes sir, it's me."

The Captain smiled again, then shut the door leaving father and son alone.

"Thank God, son. Where are you?"

"On the *Ike*. How's Mom?

"She's fine, James. She'll be better today I have a feeling. How are you, son?"

"Pretty banged up, but I'll be fine. Commander Youngren's dead. Lot of guys didn't make it."

"I know, son. I know. How are they treating you?"

"Oh, no complaints."

"I am so glad …"

Captain Lowe came back in, followed by an Army General and an Air Force Colonel. "Sir," the Captain said softly.

"Hold just a second, James," Malroy said into the phone. "What is it?"

"You have another call on line two," Captain Lowe answered.

A look of irritation crossed Malroy's face. "I don't care if it's the President."

"It's not the President, sir. It's the Kremlin."

Chapter Sixteen

Search

"Wisdom is better than weapons of war."
-Ecclesiates, IX,18

The Kremlin
Moscow, Russia
November 3rd

"Admiral Malroy, I speak to you as sailor-to-sailor." Vitenka said in clipped but understandable English. "We leave politics out of it for now."

"The attack on our Destroyer. Why did that occur?" Malroy asked.

"There is little time for explanation. Listen to what I have to tell you. Russian forces are no threat.

Malroy cut him off, "How the hell do you expect me to believe that? I have three dozen families who certainly disagree."

"I have called you to ensure no more killing—no more incidents."

"That's a great idea, Admiral, but what about the nut case you have running the show?"

"Nut case? "

"Your boss,—the boss. Who is in command?"

Again, there was a pause. "Admiral Malroy, Paslav is gone."

"What did you just say?"

"There is no Boss. Paslav is dead." Vitenka said slowly. "For now, I am in charge."

"You've taken over the Kremlin?"

"Yes. I need help. I have not told anyone of this. The country would panic," Vitenka explained. "I, like you, am a sailor who does his duty. You must believe—I have no political ambitions. You must give me time to get control over the military."

"Admiral Vitenka, how am I to know what I am hearing is the truth?" Malroy asked.

"You don't. I have no way to prove to you the truth. You can trust me or you may not. If you do not, then we are all in great danger. I have no control as of yet of the Air Force or Strategic Rocket forces. Commanders are operating on their own. If they perceive a threat, I cannot tell what will happen. Again you must give me time."

By now, Admiral Zivon Vitenka's dossier was open on Malroy's desk. He flipped through the pages. "Trust? Okay, let's see about trust. We have indications that a Russian ballistic missile submarine is sitting under the ice pack. What can you tell me about that?" Malroy asked.

"Admiral, I have no knowledge that any of our strategic units are at sea. Surely, your *Keyhole* satellites have accounted for our submarines. But if this is true … destroy it."

"What?"

"If what you say is true, then I too have been lied

to. A submarine under the ice may have its missiles aimed at Russia rather than the United States."

"Well," breathed Malroy. "I guess that makes sense."

"Admiral Malroy, I ask that you brief our United Nation's Ambassador, then fly him here."

"Why?" Malroy asked.

"What reaction would there be if the people saw a man in uniform leading Russia?" Vitenka asked.

"Jesus, I see your point," Malroy agreed. "Okay, I'll take care of that. You understand I will have to brief my President?"

"Of course, but I deal with only you - sailor to sailor until the Ambassador arrives."

"Agreed. What else do you need?"

"Luck."

USS MIAMI SSN 755
Twenty Miles Inside the Ice Pack

"Okay boys, the tails are out," announced the Chief sonar man, Rusty Masters.

"Damn, that ice sounds like somebody's dumping rocks in a fifty-five gallon drum. How are we supposed to hear anything?" asked the newest sonar operator.

"System will filter most of it out," Masters replied. "Just watch for anything that repeats more than twice."

"Fellas, now we hunt. Looking for a type 2/3 Russian boomer. Don't let me catch anyone in this shack nappin'," Chief Masters warned.

In the control room, Commander McKinnon stood on the periscope stand. "XO, let's go to ultra-quiet."

"Aye sir. Chief of the Watch, rig ship for Ultra-quiet," he ordered.

In every compartment, in every space, any item that had even the remotest chance of makings noise was turned off, ventilation fans secured, hot water re-circulation pumps, the oxygen generator, bilge pumps, even the galley oven went cold. Those not standing watch climbed into their racks.

"Ship is rigged for ultra-quiet," whispered the Chief of the Watch.

"Officer of the Deck, make turns for five knots," McKinnon ordered. "Diving Officer, no angles greater than five degrees."

"Aye sir."

"Helm, no more than three degrees on the rudder."

McKinnon poked his head through the sonar room door. Pale blue light bathed the small cramped space. "We're about ten miles from his last datum. You all set in here?"

"Good-to-go, skipper," whispered Masters.

"Chief, this is all sonar now,"

"Roger that, Skipper. We'll bag this guy, no sweat."

McKinnon smiled. *Wish I had as much confidence,* he thought.

Miami crept slowly forward. Three hundred feet above the submarine, the ice creaked, crashed, moaned and hissed. The BSY-2 sonar system filtered out most of the unwanted noise, although still difficult to pick out any one signal. The automatic tracker for broadband adjusted constantly. Even the towed array sent confused and unusable information.

Three hours later, the *Miami* approached the area where *VITUS* showed the submarine.

"Officer of the Deck, hold a large opening in the ice," the BQS-13 operator reported.

"Very well. Navigation, plot that opening," the Officer of the Deck ordered.

McKinnon checked the plot, and pulled out a clear plastic overlay made from the satellites image. The numbers matched.

An hour passed with only the sound of a billion tons of thousand-year-old ice crashing.

More and more, the sonar operators glanced at the clock to check their time for relief.

"Chief Masters," called one of the operators.

"Got something?" Masters asked hopefully.

"No, it's what I don't have."

"Huh?"

"Look here on bearing 094. Sounds like all the ice is screaming. Except this one area," the operator explained. He touched the area of the screen at a steady dimus line.

"Put me on that bearing." Masters put his headset on and listened. "Like a hole in all the noise," Masters nodded. "Might be our boy."

McKinnon was in sonar in less than thirty seconds. "Talk to me, Chief."

"Skipper, there is a lack of background noise at 092. Might be him - might not."

"Anything on narrow-band?"

Masters shook his head slowly. "Nothing. But if this joker runs at reduced power - maybe on one reactor, we'll not pick up any narrow band for another 2,000 yards. Two-K from a Russian boomer is getting mighty close."

"Okay, I'll start a slow turn to 005. Let the array stabilize, then maybe we can get a sniff."

"Sounds like a plan."

McKinnon turned the *Miami* slowly north. He let the arrays take ten minutes to catch up and send any hint of another submarine to the operator's ear.

A half hour passed until *Miami* settled on her new course.

McKinnon wanted desperately to camp out in the sonar room. He knew though that would be seen as an intrusion or outright lack of trust toward his sonar Chief. Instead he walked to the under ice sonar operator. "What's it look like up there?" he asked quietly.

"Very irregular contours."

God, does this kid's mother know he's in the Navy, McKinnon thought as he looked at the operator's baby face.

"Ice is about three to six feet thick, Captain," the operator added.

"Sounds about right for this time of year," McKinnon said as he stepped to the Navigation plot. *When this is all over,* he thought. *I need to review some service records. These guys can't be eighteen.*

Miami's Captain checked the plot. If the latest pictures from the VITUS satellite were accurate, the mystery submarine sat less than five miles from him. *You're out there,* he thought. *I can feel you. I just wonder if you're alone.*

The White House
Washington DC
November 4th

"Admiral," the President said, "I heard you received some good news."

"Yes sir, very good news." A smile forced its way to his lips

"We may have some good news for everyone. Paslav is dead," interjected Secretary of Defense Martin Samuals.

"Dead?" asked the President.

"Killed by this man." From his briefcase, Admiral Malroy pulled Zivon Vitenka's dossier. "Mr. President, please look at this, sir." He handed the folder across the wide oak desk.

The President leafed through the inch thick stack of papers. "Who is he?"

"Until yesterday, Vitenka commanded Russia's Northern Fleet submarines." Malroy inhaled. "Now he's interim President of Russia."

"How do you know that?"

"He called and told us." Malroy shrugged.

"You've confirmed this?"

"As far as we can ... yes, sir."

A worried look came over the President's face. "When this gets out, it'll be pure hell."

"So far, Vitenkas has kept it quiet. On our side, only about ten people know about it." Samuals lowered himself into the chair across from the President's desk.

"Mr. President, Vitenka is legit." Malroy waited for a reaction. "He asks that the Russian Ambassador to the UN be put on a plane to Moscow ASAP. We have to help him."

Martin Samuals nodded. "I concur, Mr. President. I believe this is the real deal. Those folks have command and control issues and this may be an out for everyone."

The President lifted the dossier. "He's a submariner, right?"

Yes sir," answered Malroy.

"Sneaky bastards," the President sighed. "Sorry, no offense, Admiral."

"None taken sir, but you're right."

"What if this leaks before the Ambassador lands? This could really go south."

"It's about as far south now as it can get - well almost," Samuals gestured with his hand.

Leaning forward, the President picked up his phone. "Anita, where is the Secretary of State? Yes, give him a call and tell him to be in this office in half an hour."

USS MIAMI SSN 755
November 5th

It took *Miami* ten hours to complete the first slow circle, and found only a very large opening in the ice, known by the Russian word *polinya*. McKinnon kept the *Miami* three thousand yards out, making a slow arc, yet sonar remained blank.

The watch section changed. *Miami's* engineer, Lieutenant Commander Kenneth Webb, now had the Deck and Conn.

Executive Officer Gellor slipped silently into the control room. "Captain, looks like you could use some down time," he said out of the corner of his mouth to McKinnon.

McKinnon looked up from the nav-plot. "Sure could, but soon as I do ..."

Gellor chuckled. "Yes, sir. Well then, how about some coffee?"

McKinnon stifled a yawn. “I’ll get some from the wardroom. I need to stretch my legs a bit.”

“Yes sir.”

“Eng...” McKinnon said softly. “I’ll be in the wardroom.” he descended the ladder in the Nav-center

“Aye, Captain,” Webb nodded.

The Engineer looked at the XO. “What you think?

“About what?” Gellor asked without looking up from the chart.

“The Old Man,” the Engineer whispered.

“I don’t know. He seems all right - knows the boat,” Gellor shrugged.

“And the crew?”

Gellor chewed the end of his pen. “Jury’s still out. He’s no Josh Upman, but who could be?”

The Engineer leaned over the plot till nose-to-nose with the Executive Officer. “That’s true.”

Kennedy International Airport
New York
November 6th
02:30

“It will be ... all right,” Ambassador Sergi Atopov smiled to his wife of twenty-six years.

“Why are they taking us away?” she asked, her voice full of fear.

“Kira, you ask questions I cannot answer, right now.” Atopov said gently.

“Have you done something?”

“No,” Sergi Atopov assured his wife.

At the end of dim hallway, the small party stopped. Two agents stood in front of a dull green security door. A veteran of fifteen years, the agent-in-charge could tell the tiny woman with jet-black hair and the chin of a boxer was about to panic. “Mrs. Atopov, please understand, your husband is in no danger.”

“Please, can you tell me why this is happening?” she asked.

Ambassador Atopov wrapped his arm tenderly around her neck. “Please, no more questions.”

“Was it all my speeding tickets?”

“Uh, speeding tickets? No ma’am.” The Secret Service agent almost choked and thought, *Hold it in, Bucko, you can’t laugh at the new First Lady of Russia.*

The agent at the door lifted his small two-way radio, nodded to the agent-in-charge.

“Here we go.” He motioned toward the door. “There is going to be a lot of noise. Follow the agents and do as you are told. Keep your heads low,” he cautioned.

The door opened to a hurricane like wind caused by the rotor wash of a Navy Sea-King helicopter. She faltered for a moment until the agent gently, but firmly, placed his hand in the small of her back and pushed. Ducking, they walked toward the waiting helicopter. Other agents lined the way, their faces turned outward.

A blast of the rotors bounced off the tarmac and caught Mrs. Atopov’s beige pleated skirt. The fabric flew up around her shoulders. In her haste to get dressed, she forgot her underwear.

I could have been a doctor, maybe a lawyer,

deck hand on a riverboat, but no, I had to pick this job, the agent thought as he helped her push the skirt where it belonged.

A minute later, they were strapped in. The aircraft lifted off, climbed rapidly, then turned north.

From New York, the Sea King followed the coast. Two hours later, it touched down in Brunswick, Maine. The passengers were again bundled out and walked to a waiting C-9B Skytrain II jet. The six passengers had no more than sat down, when the whining engines pushed the sleek silver and white jet toward the runway.

Flight time to Norway lasted just under four hours. Once landed, a heavily escorted IL-20 Coot-A ferried the new Russian president to Moscow.

USS MIAMI SSN-755

"Opinions ... ideas?" McKinnon asked.

"I don't know, skipper," shrugged Chief Masters. "Maybe they moved the damned thing."

"We've reconstructed the search and didn't see squat," said the Weapons Officer.

The Executive Officer lifted his hands. "Where would they have moved?"

Next, the Navigator spoke "We also have to ask why would they move?"

"Good question," sighed McKinnon. "One thing for sure, they're not here."

"We need to update our Intel. Maybe that bird has a new picture," the Weapons Officer yawned.

"I was thinking the same thing," McKinnon agreed. "We need to put up a mast."

"If you're thinking of using that big hole out there, I would be very careful," Masters warned. "We never got closer than three-thousand yards. That big bastard might be surfaced."

All eyes in the wardroom focused on Chief Masters.

"The ice around that little lake is four or five feet thick. A boomer at reduced power wouldn't make a beep. The ice absorbs even a small tonal," he explained.

McKinnon paused. *Okay,* he thought. *This is what you wanted. This is your only shot at it. Make a decision.*

"We'll scout close to the polinya. Go deep and listen. Then come up on a reciprocal course coming up two-hundred feet at each pass. At one-hundred feet, I'll use the scope, see if I can pick him up visually. If he's not there, we'll put up the BRA-34," McKinnon said.

Inwardly pleased, he watched heads nod in agreement.

"Gutsy move, skipper," smiled Chief Masters. "I like it."

Chapter Seventeen

Discovery

"War is the realm of the unexpected."
-B.H. Liddell Hart: Defense of the West, 1950

Groton, Connecticut
November 6th

Retired Chief Machinist Mate Carl Blevins sat alone at his computer. He clicked on one of his favorite web sites. "Crap, not updated since June?" he mumbled. "Just as well," he said to his panting Labrador. "Come on Ping, wanna go to the shop?" In a flash, Ping wagged his tail at the door, waiting for his master.

"Okay I'm coming." He rubbed the dog's cinnamon head and opened the door to the chilly November air.

Ping darted outside. Blevins walked slowly in the dim light of a November evening to a very attractive little building the size of a small garage, built in the style of a traditional New England barn. Blevins wiped his feet and turned his key. The side door of the shop swung silently open. Ping followed behind sniffing the ground, his tail wagging. Only a few spots of faded blue filtered through the windows. Blevins flipped a knife switch to the breaker box and overhead florescent bulbs flickered to life.

The first half of the shop appeared more like a museum than work area. Neatly built pine shelves held bits of submarine memorabilia and a small jar with a type written label told the reader it contained melted ice from the North Pole. Next to the jar sat a black fur hat. On front of the hat the insignia of the former Soviet Union shone in the florescent glow. Odds and ends that would mean little to the uninitiated, but a goldmine to a submariner and history buff. On the wall opposite the door hung his medals. The accumulation of over twenty-six years of active service in the United States submarine force.

Blevins walked toward the back where another door stood. He twisted the knob, and pushed. Ping sneezed at the smell of raw fiberglass.

"Sorry about that," Blevins smiled.

Ping retreated out the door, found a nice spot on the rug in front of the recliner and lay down. The retired Chief Petty Officer sat at a stool in front of a rather long and sturdy workbench. On the bench sat his pride and joy, a seven-foot model of a German Type-IXC U-boat, perfect in every detail. Carefully he removed the deck and set it aside. Inside the hull a maze of wires, pumps, and electronics, stared back. "Okay, looks dry," he said aloud. "Let's see if that hinge works."

Through a tiny hole in the clear plastic pressure hull, Blevins pushed a small button. Next, he reached for his radio transmitter. He operated the control stick, watching the rudder turn left and right.

"Good. Now the torpedo tubes." His fingers pushed the joystick. The tubes opened and shut at his command. "Yeah. Looking real good." He switched the radio off. "Another week and you'll be in the water."

USS MIAMI SSN 755
November 7th

"This is the Captain. I have the Deck and the Conn," McKinnon announced.

"Helm aye. Quartermaster aye. Sonar aye," came the responses.

"Dive, mark your Depth," the Captain ordered.

"Eight-hundred feet," Chief Ryan Boyce replied. "Ship is rigged for deep submergence."

"Very well, Dive." McKinnon looked at the status board. The torpedoes were warmed. Their computer brains waited for a bearing. If that boomer made the slightest aggressive move, the ADCAPs would give him a quick attitude adjustment. The Captain focused on the engineering report. Full power line up on the starboard turbine generator, the propulsion plant operated smoothly. Sonar fully functional, Nav systems all green. Satisfied with the ship, McKinnon grasped the stainless steel rail lining the periscope stand. "Rig control for black." The control room lights went out, which left only the dim glow from ship control panel. "Helm, left three degrees rudder steady course two-five-eight," he ordered. "Okay, fellas, this is it."

In the cold blackness of the Arctic Ocean, *Miami* swung slowly to her new course.

"Quartermaster - distance to point alpha?" McKinnon did the math in his head, but wanted confirmation.

"One-five hundred yards," the Quartermaster responded.

"Mark every five-hundred yards."

"Every five, aye."

"Conn, sonar. The second you hear or see anything—call it out."

"Sonar Aye," came Chief Master's voice over the 27MC.

McKinnon watched the remote sonar screen. So far nothing. *Damn.* he thought. *Should I be glad or just pissed off? Just do your job.*

"Five hundred yards," announced the quartermaster.

McKinnon's eyes remained fixed on the screen. "Aye."

"Conn, Sonar—contact, bearing zero-two-four. Hold contact on passive broadband tracker three..."

McKinnon felt every nerve in his body twitch. *Calm down.* he thought. *Something is not right about this.* "Sonar-Conn, I don't think this guy would be a broadband contact."

"Conn, sonar—wait," answered Master's, his voice echoed the frustration they all felt. "Conn, sonar, disregard contact report. Heavy biologics down that bearing."

"Conn aye," McKinnon sighed.

"One-thousand yards," the Quartermaster called off.

"Anything sonar?" the Captain asked hopefully.

"Negative Conn, sonar holds no contacts."

"Mr. Dennison," McKinnon called. "Take the Deck and the Conn. Hold this course till I say otherwise."

"Yes sir. This is the Weapons Officer. I have the Deck and the Conn."

In the darkness of *Miami's* control room, McKinnon put his hand on the XO's shoulder. "Come to my stateroom," he whispered.

Gellor followed as McKinnon opened the door. Both men stepped inside the tiny office/bedroom. The Captain lowered himself onto his bunk. Gellor remained standing.

McKinnon leaned back and turned on the small reading light.

"What do you think, Brad?"

Gellor scratched behind his ear. "Don't know Captain. Maybe they moved."

"Why though? Two weeks—they sat here for two weeks. Then we get in the area and they vanish."

"You think the Navy might have a security leak?"

"Wouldn't be the first time."

Gellor nodded his agreement. "There is another possibility."

"What's that?" McKinnon asked.

"Maybe it was never here," Gellor whispered.

"I thought of that." McKinnon's eyes burned from lack of sleep. "You saw those images. What else could it be?"

"Don't know, Captain. All I know he's not here."

"McKinnon opened his eyes. "Brad, let me ask you a question?"

"Sir?"

McKinnon rested his elbows on his knees. "I'm not Josh and don't want to be. What do you think he would do?"

"Exactly what you're doing."

McKinnon grinned. "I hoped you would say that."

"So now what?" Gellor asked.

"We'll go up in an hour. Stick the antenna up—see if there is any new Intel."

Gellor nodded. "Stanley Cup playoffs started last week, maybe they have some scores."

"Maybe," McKinnon chuckled. "Stand down the extra sonar watches. Have the Weps review the near ice operations procedures. Have any of these guys been under the ice?"

"No sir. You and I are the only officers. COB's been once, but that was in the eighties."

McKinnon thought about leaving the ice before they came shallow. *What message would that send to this crew?* he thought. *They might think I don't trust them, or worse I'm afraid?* "They'll do fine. I'd like you to be in the control room with me when we go up."

"I'll be there."

Lapadnaya Lista
Russian Submarine Base
November 7th

Valerik Danyankov grew to enjoy the late night dinners with Evelina. The roast duck in lemon sauce was outstanding, along with moist and delicious chocolate cake.

Evelina cleared the few dishes from the table, refusing Danyankov's offer to help. She returned quickly, her white calf length skirt flowed as she walked. "Valerik, we always sit at the table after dinner. Can we go to the parlor tonight?" she asked softly.

Danyankov's eyes fluttered while the temperature in the small room seemed to rise. "Of course," he managed.

"Good," she cooed, took his hand and pulled him up. She led him to the warm, cozy parlor, furnished with items that might have been new when Breshnev was in power.

"Sit with me," Evelina said and sat on the old sofa.

When Danyankov sat beside her, the ancient springs squealed slightly. "I've been feeding you too much," she giggled.

"Maybe so," he smiled and leaned back.

"I've been very worried these past few days." She looked at her shoes. "My father ... do you think he is in danger?"

How to answer this? Danyankov thought. *Truth is always the best.* "I think your father is a wise man. He will be fine."

"I don't know what I would do if I lost him," she said sadly.

Danyankov, in uncharted waters, decided to stay quiet.

Evelina Vitenka took his hand, lifted his arm, and placed it around her shoulder. "I don't know what I would do if I lost you either." She brought her lips to his.

USS MIAMI SSN 755

Miami rose slowly, making a huge spiral in the black sea. At three-hundred feet, the blackness changed to dark blue. Two-hundred feet from the ice, the sea turned a light blue.

"On ordered depth one-five-zero feet," the Diving Officer announced.

"Very well," answered the Officer of the Deck and he picked up the handset. "Dive, trim the ship," he ordered as he pushed a button marked CO. The Captain answered.

"Sir, ship is at one-five-zero feet," the Officer of the Deck reported.

"Very well—I'm on the way."

Thirty seconds later, McKinnon and Gellor entered the control room. "How we looking Dive?" asked McKinnon.

"Almost there sir," the diving officer responded. "I want a little extra weight in the ass-end."

"Tell me when you're ready."

"Aye sir."

"Quartermaster, how far to the center of point Alpha?"

"Thousand yards, on this bearing."

"Sonar," the Captain called. "What's it looking like up there?"

"Conn—Sonar, the polinya is roughly four thousand yards wide and six long. The floes seem to move all over the damned place. Recommend coming to periscope depth dead center."

"Sonar, Conn, aye." McKinnon glanced at the XO. "Helm all stop."

"Maneuvering answers all stop," the helmsman reported.

"Very well, helm." McKinnon reached for the orange circular ring that controlled the periscope hoist. "Raising number-two periscope." He twisted the ring and the silver pole slid up silently.

Miami hung in the ocean, her 6,900 tons perfectly balanced. Above the hovering submarine, a clear patch of water shimmered in the Arctic afternoon.

When the periscope limit switch clicked, McKinnon pulled the handles down, and peered through the scope. "Looks clear," he announced. "Officer of the Deck, proceed to periscope depth."

"Proceed to periscope depth, aye sir. Dive make your depth five-four feet."

"Five-four feet," the Diving Officer exhaled.

Miami rose and with each foot more light reflected off the hull.

"One-four-zero," the Diving Officer reported.

"Conn, sonar. Ice getting louder. It might blank the spherical passive," warned the voice over the 27MC.

"One-three-zero."

"Very well sonar. Very well Dive," McKinnon responded. "Conn, radio. Is the floating wire housed?"

"Radio-conn, yes," came the reply.

"I want to get all traffic as soon as the mast breaks the surface. Line up on voice for me also," McKinnon, ordered.

"Line up for voice after all traffic is on board, aye sir."

Through the tiny eyepiece, shapes formed. The bottom of the ice came into focus. Rough and jagged edges hung like knives in the sea.

"One-two-zero."

Sea pressure around the round hull eased. *Miami* ascended a bit faster. McKinnon saw ice floes grind and smash into each other when the submarine passed under. "Wind must be strong."

"Nine-zero feet."

"Officer of the Deck, have the main engines stand by in the ahead direction. I might have to get out of here real quick." McKinnon ordered. He twisted the handle of the periscope until he looked almost directly up to see the waves inside the polinya. "Yep, it's bad up there. Radio I'm going to raise the mast. As soon as you get a signal, let me know."

"Radio aye."

"Seven-eight feet."

"Very well, Dive. Keep coming up, Chief."

"Seven-six feet."

"Conn-sonar, passive is blanked out due to ice noise. On bearing 178 it sounds like the entire floe is breaking apart."

"Sonar-conn aye," McKinnon replied softly.

"Six eight feet."

"Scope is breaking," McKinnon called as a curtain of seawater fell away from the periscope's optic window. "All stations conn, ship is at periscope depth." He swung the scope quickly around a full 360 degrees. "No contacts."

"Conn-radio, have acquired the satellite, downloading all traffic," came the report.

"Five-four feet. On ordered depth," the Diving Officer called out.

"Very well," McKinnon swung the scope around. "Terrible out there," McKinnon noted for the log. "Winds for the north-west speed—I'd say thirty, maybe forty knots. Very overcast, heavy fog or mist. I can just make out the edge of the ice."

"Conn-radio. All traffic on board. Buffer is printing."

McKinnon looked away from the scope. "What are the subject lines?"

The radioman scanned the message headings. "We have two marked *For CO's eyes only.* One is an Intel update, rest are routine."

McKinnon looked over at Gellor. "Radio, did we get any scores?"

"Roger that, Captain," chuckled the voice over the speaker. "I'll have those sent to the XO soon as they print out."

"Thanks radio," Gellor called out.

"Radio, bring the intel update message to the conn," McKinnon ordered. "How we doing Dive?"

"Not too bad Captain. Boat wants to rise."

"Just a few more minutes and we'll get back in the basement." McKinnon resumed his scan.

The Radioman of the watch came around the corner, a clipboard in his right hand. "Message traffic, Captain."

McKinnon pulled his eyes away from the scope and spotted Kolter next to fire control. "Ensign Kolter," McKinnon called. "Come take the scope."

"Yes, sir," the young officer answered.

Free of the "one-eyed-lady," McKinnon took the clipboard. First, he read the message marked *For CO's only.* Suddenly a broad smile came to his face. He turned and picked the microphone to the 1MC. "This is the Captain. We have just received word Senior Chief Rusty Masters is officially old. So old that now we have to call him Grandpa Masters. His daughter Marcy delivered a seven pound, three ounce, boy. Mother and baby are doing well."

McKinnon could hear the shouts and hoots from one end of *Miami* all the way to the watertight door. *Good,* he thought. *Let them blow off a little steam.*

He flipped to the next message. Milo Stephens passed the test, and once again a Petty Officer. When from the corner of his eye, he saw Ensign Kolter go rigid. He opened his mouth when the Ensign spun on his heels.

"Contact," he yelled, his voice cracking.

"What?" McKinnon dropped the message board to the deck and grabbed the handles of the periscope. Through the scope, he saw fog and mist swirling then die down. "Where?"

"Bearing 005, right along the edge of the ice." Kolter pointed at the bearing indicator.

McKinnon swiveled the periscope ever so slightly to the blurred object. He clicked the handle to increase magnification. A gray shape jutted from the ice. As the mist continued to clear, the silhouette of a submarine appeared as if an artist dropped paint on a canvas. The shape took form, the details crisp. McKinnon felt his mouth go dry. "Man battle stations," he yelled.

"What is it?" the XO called.

"Surfaced submarine," responded McKinnon. *Or is it?* he thought. He looked again. With the mist almost gone, visibility increased. *It's a submarine, but not a boomer. Too small,* he thought. "My God. It's not even in the water. XO, take a look."

Gellor stepped to the periscope. "What the hell is that?"

"Looks like it might be a *Whiskey* class," McKinnon shrugged.

“Those went out of service in the seventies,” Gellor responded. “Whatever it is it, it’s stuck. Torpedo tubes are out of the water.”

“How did it get here?” McKinnon asked no one in particular. “This far in the ice? It has to be a nuke.”

“Gellor leaned close to McKinnon. “We need to talk.”

McKinnon nodded in agreement. “Officer of the Deck, take the Conn. Don’t move this ship,” he cautioned. “Nav-center,” McKinnon pointed to the after end of the control room.

“Captain, if that boat out there is a nuke, it means the Russians dumped it here. God only knows what went wrong with it,” Gellor said shaking his head.

“What if it’s not a nuke? Same scenario, but add a nuclear weapon. Maybe they had a problem with a weapon and dumped it here,”

“Why? See it makes no sense. Why bring a problem like that up here? Just sink the damn thing.”

“There are two more possibilities,” he sighed. “One, maybe what’s on that boat has to be in the deep freeze, like a biological weapon. A bug that went bad,” McKinnon whispered.

“Jesus, I never thought of that.”

“Two, maybe these guys tried to get away, wandered in the ice, got lost and then they get stuck.”

Gellor rubbed his chin. “Hmm, Captain, I don’t know. Think we should call this one in?”

McKinnon thought. *If we transmitted, we might be discovered, but maybe worth the risk. No, not enough information to make an accurate report.* “XO, we need to figure out just what this is before we call home.”

Gellor took a deep breath. “Risky, Captain.”

“That what this business is all about,” McKinnon smiled.

“Aye, Captain, that it is.”

“Okay, we’ll creep up nice and slow and get a better look.”

“Want me to start a message draft on what we know so far?” Gellor asked.

“Not a bad idea, we might have to call for help in a hurry.”

“What about battle stations?”

“Not till we know more.”

Chapter Eighteen
Small Boats

"The impossible can only be overborne by the unprecedented."
-Sir Ian Hamilton: Gallipoli Diary ,1, 1920

HMS SWIFT
November 7th

"Bloody hell," Lieutenant Kirby exclaimed. "Never knew this part of the ocean to be this damned rough."

"Rare, but it does happen. How is the crew holding up?" Commander Ladd smiled.

Kirby wiped the icy saltwater from his face. "Half look like they're dying."

"The other half?" Ladd asked.

"Looks like they already died."

"They'll get used to it," he chuckled.

"Weather report says we have another two days of this." Kirby steadied himself against the roll of the ship.

"We'll be out of this tonight. We're going to scout around the marginal ice zone."

"Marginal ice zone? I've never been that far north."

"We've been tasked with guarding a group—oh excuse me, a pod of migrating whales."

"Whales?"

"Yes, Lieutenant, whales. Besides, the seas are calm up that way."

"Good. The men will be glad about that," Kirby smiled.

"It will give us a chance for some navigation training." The HMS SWIFT climbed the crest of another twenty-foot wave. "Hold on."

SWIFT hung on the top of the wave for what seemed minutes. Gravity took over and the frigates bow dropped, smashing into the next wave. The ship shuddered and shook.

USS MIAMI SSN 755
November 7th

"Watch the ice, Captain," Senior Chief Master warned. "Lot of breaking up noise on that bearing."

"Sonar, aye," replied McKinnon. "XO, raise number-one scope—keep an eye on those floes."

Miami inched forward. McKinnon locked his eyes on the strange submarine. "Range?"

"One-thousand yards," answered the fire control operator.

"No movement, no nothing, just sitting there,"

"Helm, all stop."

"Anything moving up there, Captain?" the XO asked.

"Not a thing. Damn spooky though."

Gellor laughed. "Never heard a CO use the word—spooky."

"Yeah, well, that's what it is.

"What do you think, Captain?"

"I want to see it. At least do a radiation survey," his voice low.

"You mean go out there?" the XO asked, somewhat shocked.

"If this thing is a hazard, we need to know. That and I'm just damned curious."

Fifteen minutes later *Miami* surfaced into the choppy ice filled water. Gusts of Arctic wind pushed the improved 688 across the polinya. McKinnon ordered the small secondary propulsion motor lowered, which kept M*iami's* 6,000 tons in one spot.

"Listen up," McKinnon briefed those going topside. "Here's how this is going to work. "I'm going to the bridge, with Chief Berry and a radiac. If he gets a good reading, COB you'll take your team topside."

"I want those exposure suits zipped up tight. This is some serious shit," Chief of the Boat Norse warned. "No grab ass'n."

"COB, you'll get the life raft over the side. When I give the word, head for that sub."

"I want a rifleman in the sail," the Captain ordered.

Norse looked at one of the off-watch helmsmen. "Go get Stephens."

"The cook?" asked McKinnon.

"Best shot on the boat," replied the COB.

"Go figure," smiled McKinnon. "Okay, get aboard and look around." McKinnon pointed at the off watch reactor operator. "Petty Officer Jiminez, see if that boat has any radiation coming out of it."

"Yes, sir," Jiminez responded. "Excuse me,

Captain, it's rough out there, you sure a life raft is safe?" asked the reactor operator.

"Good point. We'll turn the boat to the waves—that will make a lee for you."

"Thank you sir."

"Anything happens, get your asses off that thing and back here. Understand?"

"Understand," Norse nodded.

"Okay, we go in five minutes," McKinnon eyed the control room clock.

Stephens came to the control room, his M-16 over his shoulder. His heavy exposure suit barely fit over his six-foot frame.

"You any good with that, Petty Officer Stephens?" McKinnon hoisted his foot on the first ladder rung.

"Oh yes, sir. Gourmet cook, object of women's desires, and rifle expert. I'm the whole package, Captain. Oh, and it's Seaman Stephens, sir."

"Not anymore," McKinnon smiled. "Here." He handed Stephens the message of his promotion. "Congratulations. It's official." McKinnon zipped the hood of his parka.

"Look out ladies. Milo is coming to town," the cook laughed.

"Let's go," McKinnon went up the ladder. "Captain to the bridge."

A sudden gust almost tore the hatch out of McKinnon's hand. He grunted and hefted himself up into the Arctic air. *Sky is almost clear,* he thought. Instinctively he scanned the horizon. "Okay, come up," he called down the hatch.

One by one, the others wiggled their way through the small bridge hatch.

"Whoa. Granny's panties, it's cold," Stephens shouted.

"Okay, Chief Berry." McKinnon pointed at the gray lifeless submarine, there it is. I need those readings," McKinnon urged "

Berry opened the cover of the radiac, withdrew the probe and switched the power on. He let the meter zero itself. "Here we go." He held the probe over his head and kept his eyes on the meter. "Nothing, sir. Just background."

"You sure?"

"Yes sir."

"Good. Get below, Chief. Have the COB lay topside."

"Aye Captain." Berry stole one last look as he stepped down the ladder.

His voice muffled by the towel used for a scarf. "Russians have deck guns?" he asked.

"Guns?" McKinnon raised his tinted goggles.

"There on the sail, inside that railing." Stephens pointed at the lethal looking weapons.

Wait, Russian submarines don't carry guns, McKinnon thought to himself. *Or do they? I've spent years looking at charts, reactor manuals and sonar, and not once did I ever look at a Russian sub.*

By now, the COB assembled his team aft of the sail, and heaved up the inflatable raft up the hatch. Norse leaned over and pulled the cord. With a whoosh of compressed gas, the orange life raft flopped open. Norse heaved the raft over the side

McKinnon looked down from the bridge and saw the COB look up. "Go."

Another gust of frigid wind slashed from the North East. Norse stepped carefully down the ladder and into the bobbing rubber boat. His hand steadied the small boat. Chief Torpedoman Wendell Rance, Nuclear Machinist Mate First Class, Devin Childers, and Second Class Sonar Justin Maurizio, followed.

Once seated and steady the rubber raft pushed off from the side of the surfaced American submarine. The wind died off and only an occasional gust whistled through the *Miami's* bridge. McKinnon watched the raft plod along and the small folding oars chop at the water. The blunt clumsy boat struggled through the ice-choked water. Norse leaned over the front, moving large blocks of ice out of their path. Halfway, the oars stopped and Childers sampled the air for radiation. McKinnon held his breath. Then the arm lowered and the oars once again dug into the water. *So far, so good*, he thought.

Danny Norse's breath came faster when they neared slender gray hull. "Keep your eyes open," he said loud enough to be heard over a gust. Move us closer to the stern. There aft of the sail."

Skidding awkwardly, the inflatable moved along the hull. Norse held out his hand keeping the boat from contacting the strange submarine.

"Okay, that's good." Norse grabbed one of the limber holes, and tied off the forward line. "Chief Rance, tie up your end." The COB nodded to another of the rectangular openings.

"Damn, I feel like a pirate," Maurizio chuckled.

"Shut up. Quiet," Norse snapped. "Childers, you have any readings?"

Childers looked down at the meter. "Nothing, COB."

"Okay, sit tight. I'm calling the Skipper." Norse unzipped his exposure suit and took out his radio.

"Captain?"

"Go ahead, COB," McKinnon replied.

"No radioactivity. No movement, nothing."

"Roger, COB, any damage to the hull?"

"None that I can see," Norse responded.

"Can you get topside?" McKinnon asked.

Norse looked around. "Yes sir. The deck is about three feet over my head."

"Take one man. Have Chief Rance cover you."

"Aye Captain," Norse answered. "Maurizio, you're with me."

"Me?" Maurizio pointed at his chest.

"Childers has to use the radiac, Chief Rance has the gun. That leaves you Maurizio."

"I feel like I'm in a badly written novel," Maurizio mumbled.

"Come on," the COB motioned. "You can bitch about it later."

Norse balanced himself, then slowly raised his body till his eyes could see along the exposed part of the deck. "It's clear. Follow me." He pulled himself onto the deck.

Maurizio followed and they both crouched. "See anything, COB?"

"No," Norse whispered.

"Hey look," Maurizio, pulled up a small splinter of wood. "This deck is wood."

Norse held it up, turning it over between his gloved fingers.

"Well?" Maurizio whispered.

“So what?”

“Don’t you think that’s strange?”

“This whole day is strange, Maurizio. Wouldn’t surprise me if thing was built outa tractor parts.” He tossed the sliver over the side. “Let’s check out the bridge.”

Both men moved slowly till they reached the base of the conning tower. Norse looked up at the twin double-barreled guns.

“Those ain’t for hunting ducks,” Maurizio quipped.

“Quiet,” Norse cautioned. He slid between the railings, and stayed as low as possible. Glancing aft, he saw Chief Rance, his M-16 already at his shoulder. “Let’s go.”

With Maurizio behind him, Norse duck-walked, forward to another railing with a small deck. “How many floors does this thing have?” He peeked over the bottom rail. “There’s the bridge.” Narrower than the last set of rails, Norse squeezed through while younger and thinner, Maurizio came through with ease.

Maurizio reached down and lightly tapped the deck grating. “COB, steel deck.”

Norse turned his head when something caught his eye. He turned to Maurizio and held his index finger to his lips. “There’s a hatch,” he whispered.

Maurizio leaned over for a better view. “Okay, now what?”

“Go up further and look over the bridge. I’ll radio the skipper.”

“What? Me go up there?”

“Maurizio, will you shut up and just go?”

"I better get a medal for this," Maurizio shivered, "and I don't mean posthumously."

Norse grimaced, then jabbed his finger toward the bridge.

"All right, I'm going." Still crouched, he slowly stepped forward.

Suddenly a loud roar sounded, the deck trembled, then shook. Norse fell onto his side. Maurizio hung onto a ventilation shaft housing. Then it stopped.

"What the hell was that?" called Maurizio, his eyes wide with terror.

"The ice shifted... I hope," Norse replied.

"COB, you okay?" Maurizio asked.

"Fine... busted my lip on the rail."

Norse glanced back. Chief Rance looked a little shaken. "Okay, get up there and take a look."

He again pulled out his bridge-to-bridge. "Captain?" he said into the small radio.

"COB. Is everyone okay?"

"Yes sir, we're good here. I think the ice is shifting."

"It is. We saw it from here. Have you found anything?" McKinnon asked.

"Negative sir, we're on the bridge now. Maurizio checked out the forward deck. This thing is dead, Captain."

McKinnon wondered what "dead" meant. He weighed his options. *This could be an intelligence treasure trove. God only knows what papers, codes, or weapons are on that thing. Is it be worth the risk?*

Fighting off the urges of caution and safety. McKinnon lifted his radio and said, "COB, see if there is anyone on board."

Maurizio returned. “Nothing, COB.”

“Okay, Skipper wants to see if anyone’s down there.”

“What?” His eyes shot open wide.

“Quiet,” Norse grabbed Maurizio’s shoulder. “Calm down. Listen, it’ll be fine. I’ll go to the far side of the hatch. Look, see how it opens? I’ll cover you. You knock real loud.”

“Knock? You mean like on a door?”

“Yes, like a door.”

“What the hell happens if someone answers?” Maurizio chagrined. “What do I say? Hi there. We’re new in the neighborhood or can we borrow a cup of sugar?”

Norse laughed. “I thought you Italians were all macho?”

“Not all,” Maurizio replied.

“Go on, I’ve got you covered,” Norse urged.

“I turn twenty-one next Friday,” Maurizio grumbled but he crawled toward the hatch. “Maybe, that is if I live through this, I want a medal and my own rack in the wardroom.”

Norse took off his right glove, let his hand fall to the grip of the 9mm at his side. “Okay, now.”

Maurizio raised his gloved hand and let it fall on the hatch, with only a muffled thud. “Looks like nobody’s home. Can we go now?” he whispered hopefully.

“Get out of the way.” Norse pulled the pistol out and released the clip. He ejected the one round still in the chamber, then turned the weapon around. “Look out,” he warned and he brought the base of the grip down on the steel hatch. The clanging noise echoed. "Watch the hatch and listen."

They both watched for movement. Norse shoved the clip back in the Beretta. "Here, hold this."

Maurizio took the gun. "COB, what are you doing?"

"Like the skipper said, we're going to see if anyone is down there." Norse put both hands on the hand wheel for the hatch. He twisted. "Put the gun down and help me."

Maurizio set the gun down next to his left knee and wrapped his fingers around the wheel. Both men strained, then the wheel moved, until a hiss escaped around the hatch. "COB?"

"Move back," Norse shouted as the hatch flew open. A stream of ugly orange tinted air rushed up like an erupting volcano. The air rose high above the submarine before being carried off by the wind.

"What the hell was that?" Maurizio panted.

"I don't know," Norse answered. "It's gone now. Maybe built up pressure or an air flask let go. Scary stuff, huh?"

"I about crapped my pants," Maurizio grunted.

Norse took out a small flashlight. "Remember, it's not just a job. It's an adventure."

"I've had all the adventure I want for today," Maurizio whined.

"Everything okay over there," asked McKinnon over the radio.

"We're good, Skipper," Norse responded. "I opened the hatch."

"Can you see anything?" McKinnon's voice asked.

"Not yet."

"COB, watch yourselves. I want you back here in fifteen minutes. Sun's going down."

"Roger that," Norse crawled toward the open hatch. "Come on, Maurizio."

"It's getting colder, COB."

"I know. Let's make this fast," Norse aimed his flashlight. "Nothing moving," he whispered. The white light reflected off the buff-colored interior. "There's a ladder. It goes about six feet down, then another hatch."

Maurizio pushed his face over the open hatch. "Smells like a submarine."

Norse looked around at Maurizio. "They all smell the same." Norse smiled. "Okay, I'm going in. You follow." Norse moved around till his body was in line with the hatch. "Seems small," he whispered. Legs first, Norse tested the ladder then lowered himself down the hatch. "This thing is ancient." The beam of light illuminated the interior. At the front end, at the base of a small black seat, the silver tube unmistakably a periscope ran through it. Norse looked to the right and saw instruments through the light coat of frost. One panel, he saw-twelve circles, lined up six on top and six below, the top row had a green shade and the bottom red. "Must be the torpedo tube status board," he said to Maurizio.

The young sonar technician from Oyster Bay, Long Island, stepped down the ladder. "COB, this gives me the creeps," he whispered in the still air of the unknown submarine.

"Me too," Norse replied. He turned and shined the light into the next hatch. "That must be the control room." His light reflected off the dull stainless steel of the floor.

"Where did these guys go?" Maurizio asked.

"I don't know." Norse slipped into the next hatch. Norse stepped carefully, testing each rung until his feet landed on a solid steel deck.

Norse squinted as his light shined around the space. On the aft starboard side were the unmistakable pipes and valves of a ballast control panel, forward of that another periscope. "Two scopes," he said.

"You see anybody?" Maurizio asked nervously.

"No."

His light danced across a wide flat table. "That must be the nav plot."

Maurizio descended the ladder, his own flashlight bobbing nervously. "I don't see any damage."

"We need to hurry this up." Norse shivered. "I'll go forward—you go aft."

"Alone?"

"Look Maurizio, it's about ten below in here. I don't think anyone is going to reach out and grab you. I think these guys tried to walk home."

"You think they made it?" Maurizio asked innocently.

"The only thing you have to be afraid of is me kicking that skinny ass of yours. Now move."

"I'm going," Maurizio, sighed. He shined his light toward the after-end of the control room, when he noticed something. "Hey COB, look at the lettering on that valve."

Norse's eyes followed the beam of light to the valve. "Yeah, so?"

"It says *öffnen*," Maurizio said curiously. "That's not Russian. His eyes went wide. "That's *German.* It means *open.*"

Norse shined his light around the dark control room. More stenciled signs came into view. "It's all in German." A look of understanding crossed Norse's face. He stepped to the plot table. A leather binder sat neatly in the center. Norse looked down at binder's black leather cover. Carefully, he brushed away a thin layer of frost. Its black leather was embossed gold wording *Wir Fahren gegan Engeland.* Norse gently opened the book. The next page was of good quality heavy linen paper. At the top of the page, more words - *Befatzung U 761 am 24.3.1943.* "Jesus."

"What is it, COB?" Maurizio asked.

"It's a U-boat. A damned German U-boat."

"You mean—as in World War Two German U-boat?"

"Looks like it," responded Norse.

"How the hell did it get here?"

"Hell if I know," Norse shrugged. "Come on, let's check it out."

"You sure about that, COB?"

"Move your ass, Maurizio."

The young sonar technician stood in darkness. "Which way?"

"Forward." He stepped toward a larger hatch.

"Right behind you," Maurizio whispered.

Norse shined his light into the next compartment, then stepped through the opening. "Look how well everything is preserved."

"The cold must have done that," offered Maurizio.

"Hey, these wood panels are real." Norse ran his fingers over the rich woodwork.

Maurizio stepped into a small opening. "What's this?" His light illuminated a blue curtain. He reached for the flimsy looking fabric and gently pulled it back. "Hey COB, check this out."

"What is it?" Norse asked.

"Don't know. Looks like this is the CO's stateroom. Look at the bunk with all the blankets."

"That bottle there, what is that?" Norse said aiming his light at the small cylinder.

"Oxygen?"

"I don't think so. These guys didn't carry O2."

"Hey, there's another," Maurizio said as his light fell on an identical container on the other side.

"This fabric is like new." Norse took hold on the corner of one of the blankets.

Maurizio reached over and felt the cloth. "Strange." He pulled a little more.

The cover fell to the side. Maurizio pointed the flashlight at the top of the bunk. "Oh, shit," he screamed. He tripped backwards.

Norse spun around just in time to catch him as he fell. "What the hell is wrong?"

Maurizio trembled. He slowly raised his finger. "Look."

Norse moved the beam of his light up. "Christ." A face looked back at him.

Chapter Nineteen

Quarantine

"What is a ship but a prison?"

-Robert Burton: Anatomy of Melancholy, 1621

Aboard U-761

November 8th

Norse found it harder and harder to lift the radio. "It's cold, Skipper," he mumbled. "Have you heard from shore yet?"

"Not yet COB, but hang on. Is there anything there you can use for heat?"

"Don't know. Lots of blankets down here with a dead guy under each one."

"Huddle together and save you batteries, we'll figure something out," McKinnon said cheerfully as possible.

"Okay Skipper, we'll be fine. Wait. I've got an idea. Shoot a messenger line over. Then we'll pull across some more batteries and food."

"Great idea," McKinnon said over the radio. "Hang tight and be ready to receive the line."

"I'm not going anywhere," Norse responded weakly.

"COB," called a voice from inside the U-boat.

Norse looked down to see Devin Childers, the nuclear machinist staring up out of the dark. "Yeah?"

"Come down, I have an idea," Childers said, waving his gloved hand.

Norse slowly and painfully lowered himself down the hatch. "What you got?"

"I found the manuals on operating this thing," Childers wiped his nose.

"Good, we can burn those for some heat."

"No COB. Listen. Chief Rance was stationed on a diesel out of Charleston. These manuals are mostly pictures."

"I think we can start the engines."

"You think, or you *can*?" Norse said with enthusiasim.

"Shit, I mean, well, hell¯ what else can we do?"

"You're right," Norse nodded. "Get on it."

"On it now." Childers turned and picked his way aft.

"Where's Maurizio?" Norse asked.

"Here, COB," a voice came from the forward end of the control room.

"You okay?"

"I think so," Maurizio mumbled. "COB, something's not right here."

"There's a lot that's not right," Norse chuckled.

"No, look at this." Maurizio motioned with his light.

Norse moved toward the forward hatch, and stuck his head through. "What's wrong?"

Maurizio moved his light to the face lying

peacefully in the bunk. “How cold you think it is?”

“I don’t know—maybe ten, fifteen below?” Norse responded.

“Watch.” Maurizio stepped toward the body.

“Hey, what are you doing?” Norse asked with alarm. “This is probably officially a war grave.

“Hang on.” Maurizio he moved the blanket, picked up the body’s arm, he raised it, then let it fall. “See? These guys should be frozen stiff—but they’re not.”

The Pentagon
Washington, DC
05:45 EST.

“Yeah?” Malroy said into the phone. He glanced at the glowing numbers of his bedside alarm clock. “What?” He sat upright in the bed. “*Oh my God.*” He glanced over to see Margie still asleep. “Get the staff up and in. I want that Captain from Bethesda in my office in an hour. You know—the bio-weapon’s guy—Okay, make the calls and set up the situation room for a phone conference.” He dropped the receiver back into its cradle.

Within the hour, Malroy checked his watch while he thread his way up the ramps to his office. He took his seat when the rest of the group entered.

“Gentlemen, thank you all for coming in so early.” Admiral Malroy looked at the speaker in front of him. “Admiral Tarrent?” he asked.

“Here sir,” came Tarrent’s voice on the speaker.

“CNO?”

“Here, Mr. Chairman.”

"Fort Meade?"

"Here, Admiral."

"Good." Malroy grunted. "I have here my staff and Captain Andrew Ranon, an expert in chemical and biological weapons. Let's start by bringing everyone up to speed. Admiral Tarrent, if you will?"

"Yes, sir," Tarrent replied, "At 16:20 Zulu, *USS Miami,* located an unknown object locked in the ice, forty-three miles inside the ice pack. At 16:50, *Miami* surfaced. The unknown object was found to be a submarine ..." Tarrent was cut off by murmurs of disbelief.

"Quiet," Malroy said. "Men's lives are at stake here. Let Admiral Tarrent finish. Go on, Admiral."

"Commander McKinnon believed the submarine to be a stranded Russian unit. Four of *Miami's* crew - the Chief of the Boat, the chief Torpedoman, a second-class sonar tech and a nuclear-trained machinist went aboard. After opening the hatch, they discovered a German U-boat from the Second World War. Uh, the U-761. Upon further investigation, the boarding party found twelve canisters, contents unknown.

"Given the nature of her location and the unknown canisters, the *Miami's* Corpsman, Chief Vaughn thought the canisters might contain a chemical or biological agent. The four crewmen remain on the U-boat, to avoid contamination or infection of *Miami's* crew."

"How long have they been onboard?" asked Captain Ranon.

"Almost eight hours," replied the Chief of Naval Operations.

"What's the temperature?" Ranon seemed concerned.

"Oh, I say about ten below," Tarrent's voice from the speaker.

"They don't have long," Ranon said softly.

"Captain, what do you think would be in those containers?" asked the Chief of Naval Operations.

"That's almost impossible to answer. I know the Germans experimented with a few chemical agents, but not much in that area. Spent most of the war developing a nuke."

"So those guys are safe?" Malroy asked.

"No, I didn't say that, Sir. The Corpsman did the right thing. This submarine in the ice could mean whatever they had needed to be kept cold. That leads me to think maybe a biological agent. The Germans didn't seem interested in that either. Of course there is one possibility," Ranon raised his finger. The Japanese were into bio-weapons quite extensively. They spread plague in Shanghai, and they still have outbreaks from it."

"A Japanese bio-weapon on a German submarine? I'm afraid you've lost me, Doctor," commented the CNO.

Ranon sighed. "The Germans and the Japanese shared technology. Germany shipped uranium to Japan. They sent over jet fighter parts. The Japanese even bought a Tiger tank. Maybe this submarine was bringing something home. Something that got out."

"So, how long can a plague live?" Malroy asked.

Captain Ranon shook his head. "Indefinite, if the conditions are right. However, I doubt it. Too primitive, too random. Japan had an entire complex setup to find and develop biological agents. They cooked up some very nasty bugs. If that U-boat carried one of those agents, then the only way to know is from samples."

"Have the men on that submarine reported any unusual looking weapons?" he asked.

"Not that I know of," Malroy answered.

"Gentlemen what we may have here is a submarine that was on its way to deliver an agent to the coast of the United States. On the way something happened and the crew—well I don't know," Ranon reasoned.

"Could that submarine have reached the coast?" Malroy asked.

"Oh hell yeah," the CNO exclaimed. "They damn near blasted us out of the war in '42. My dad told me stories of seeing ships torpedoed within sight of the beaches."

"Okay, so we need to know about the weapons and about the boat itself." Malroy turned to his communications officer. "Get McKinnon on the horn. Tell him we need them to take a look at the torpedoes. Now does anyone know an expert on U-boats?"

"What about the Germans?" one of his aides asked.

"Hell no. This can't get out until we know what we're dealing with. Is that clear to everyone? This gets out and the media will eat it up. Don't forget, we're not even supposed to be up there."

"I have a man, Admiral," Tarrent said. "He's a retired A-ganger. He knows everything about the damn things. Builds models of them. Hell, he even knows some of the old U-boat skippers."

"Okay, bring him onboard. Okay, we'll meet again at ten-thirty. Captain Ranon, I'll need you to stick around."

"There goes my golf game," Ranon smiled.

"Doctors," Malroy huffed.

"I'll brief the SECDEF. He's going to love this," Malroy shook his head. "Gentlemen, if there is nothing else, then we're adjourned."

Groton, Connecticut
November 8th
0845 EST.

Captain Farmer drove up the steep winding lane. "How the hell does he get up here in winter?" he mumbled. The trees overhanging the narrow road opened up and Farmer could see the roof of the house, an inviting place, charming in its simplicity, and natural in the surrounding woods. He brought the truck to a halt next to a rather worn Bronco. He stepped out and went to the door. About to knock he noticed a small hand carved sign hanging from the antique door handle. "AT THE LAKE."

Farmer saw a path leading around the house, so he followed it past the workshop and down a small hill. A glimmer of water shimmered through the trees. He stepped carefully over the loose stones and jutting roots that lined the path. "This place is gorgeous," he whispered. He spotted clearing at the water's edge. In his customary blue-flannel shirt and paint- stained denims stood Carl Blevins. "Carl?" he called.

With a radio control transmitter in his hand, Blevins turned his head. "Well, Captain Farmer, how you doing?"

"I'm good and you?" The captain then noticed Blevins

"Playing with my new toy. Look out there—check it out."

Farmer raised his hand over his eyes to block the glare from off the water. Forty feet from shore, the sleek outline of a submarine cut through the water. From where he stood, the model looked like the real deal. "Wow."

"Took me almost a year to build," Blevins said proudly. "Now watch this." He nudged one of the transmitter's controls, and the submarine dipped beneath the cool lake waters. The miniature periscope left a very realistic feather of water behind it.

"I'll be damned," he smiled.

"You ain't seen nothing yet."

The periscope turned and headed across the small lake. Farmer watched as it stopped and slowly sank.

"Take a final bearing and shoot," Blevins said as he pushed one of the joysticks forward.

Farmer saw a wake of white bubbles erupt from the water as a tiny torpedo headed straight for a peacefully sleeping mallard, and struck under the duck's tail feathers. It let out a loud squawk and she and her companion flapped wildly across the lake. Quacking loudly, they continued to complain about their rather rude awakening.

"Great shot," he laughed.

Blevins looked up at the circling ducks. "Teach you not to shit on my truck now, won't it?" He manipulated the transmitter. The victorious U-boat surfaced and set a course for home. "What brings you out this way Captain?"

Ping ran from out of the woods, his tail whipped

in circles. He came up to Farmer, demanding his head be rubbed. “Hey there, Ping. How you doin’, boy?” Farmer said, as he obliged the big Lab. “Carl, I need help.”

“Oh, with what?” His U-boat gently put its nose on the sand of the lakeshore.

“With one of those,” Farmer pointing to the model submarine.

“You want one of these?”

“No, Chief. We’ve found one.”

Blevins turned around. “Found what? A U-boat?”

“That’s right.”

“Divers find it?” Blevins asked. “Seems more and more of them are turning up. Still there are about twenty or so not accounted for. Bet it was in the Gulf of Mexico, right?”

“No Carl,” he paused, scanned the lake, to make sure no one could hear. “*Miami* found it last night.”

“The *Miami*?” Blevins asked, puzzled.

“It’s been stuck in the ice, north of the marginal ice zone. Frozen since ’44. Crew is still aboard.”

Blevin’s mouth fell open. “What? I mean *how*?”

“That’s why we need your help,” Farmer said quietly. “Grab your boat and we’ll talk in the house.”

U-761
November 8th

Thankful to receive their bags of supplies from *Miami*, the four sat in U-761’s control room eating grilled ham and cheese and drinking hot coffee.

“I don’t like coffee, but damn this is some good shit.” Maurizio sipped the steaming brew.

"Wonder how many Americans this thing killed?" Chief Rance queried.

"Never thought of it like that." Norse munched on his third sandwich. "It was a long time ago. We're all friends now, remember?"

"I know, but still, makes you think," said Rance.

"Only thing I'm thinking about is getting off this pig and back to my nice warm rack." The COB drained his coffee.

"Wonder why they were concerned about the torpedoes?" Maurizio asked.

"Explosives become unstable with age," answered Rance. "When I was stationed in Charleston, they found live shells from the Civil War. Damn things would blow up if you looked at them wrong."

"Wonderful," Maurizio rolled his eyes. "I'm on a submarine, stuck in the ice. It's ten below zero. I've been exposed to God knows what type of chemical. I'm stuck with fifty-four dead guys and thirteen-thousand, two-hundred pounds of unstable explosives. My Mother would die."

Petty Officer Childers spit out his sandwich. "Well, I won't tell her," he chuckled.

"Hey how long till you can try the engines?" Norse asked.

"I want to finish checking the injectors and see if the intakes have water flow. Should be about a half hour. I tell you, for being as old as it is, this boat is almost like new," Childers said as he ran his gloved hand along the bare steel hull.

The Pentagon
Washington, DC
10:30 EST.

"What do we know now?" the Chairman of the Joint Chiefs asked.

"I have here Chief Carl Blevins, the expert on U-boats. He did some digging for us," Admiral Tarrent said over the speakerphone.

"Welcome Chief," Malroy said pleasantly. "What have you found out?"

"Admiral, U-761 is a Type 9-C U-boat. Built by Blomm and Voss in 1943. She made six war patrols. Her only commander was Manfred Becker …."

"Becker, Becker," interrupted the CNO. "I know that name."

Blevins continued, "She sank a total of twelve ships during her patrols. The records list her as missing in August of 1944 - cause unknown. I made a call to the U-boat archive in Kiel. My contact pulled the file on U-761. Everything was normal except for a handwritten note."

"I thought those records were destroyed?" the CNO asked.

"Some were." Blevins answered. "Himmler himself took an interest in U-761. He wrote a small note that said, *Approved to proceed with The Forever Project, H.-Himmler.*"

"What about this *Forever Project*?" Malroy asked.

"That is the big unknown," Blevins responded. "But I think I can find out."

"How?"

"The SS cross-referenced their documents. If anything related to this project they mentioned survived, it could be in the archives in Berlin," Blevins stated.

"Can you get into those archives?" the CNO asked.

"Yes, sir."

"Tarrent, arrange a flight for Chief Blevins," Malroy ordered. "Chief, you understand how important this is and how it must remain secret?"

"I do, sir," Blevins answered.

"What about the weapons?" The CNO asked.

"From what Captain Farmer told me, U-761 carries her wartime load-out of G7e torpedoes. That smaller one in the bow sounds like the *Zaunkönig II.* One of the first acoustic homing torpedoes.

"What?" said an amazed Malroy. "The Germans had smart weapons?"

"Yes, sir," Blevins answered.

Malroy then turned to Captain Ranon. "Captain, you have anything new?"

"If the men were exposed to a toxin or bio-agent, they would have been symptomatic by now." Ranon crossed his legs.

"Could the cold prevent the germs from becoming active?" asked Tarrent.

"I recommend you get the men back to the *Miami* and leave the damn thing alone till we can get a team up there to take a look at just what is onboard."

"Maybe we just sink the damn thing," Tarrent growled.

"For God's sake, no," Ranon answered. "That might release an agent to the four winds."

"Damn, I almost wish it had been a Russian boomer," the CNO added dryly.

Chapter Twenty

Warmth

"The wise man in the storm prays God not for safety,
but for deliverance from fear."
-Ralph Waldo Emerson

Russian Patrol Ship *BARSUK*
Pechenga, Russia
November 8th

"Is everything ready, Lieutenant?" Rurik asked. His cigarette glowed in the cold Arctic night.

"It is done," smiled Cheslav. "The warhead has been removed from the missile. For all they know, it is just a training simulator. The paperwork matches the false serial number. Now it is just a matter of moving the false warhead instead of the real thing."

"Your colonel, is he still playing?"

"He made the arrangements as I instructed. Delivery will be in two days," Cheslav said quietly.

"Good. Our customer is very anxious." Rurik flipped the cigarette butt in the slush of the harbor.

"Do you have your orders to sail?" the young Lieutenant asked.

"No, but it doesn't matter. We will sail no matter what."

"Just think," Cheslav looked into the cold black sky, "a month from now, we'll be where it is warm all the time."

"Yes I have thought of that," Rurik grinned.

"I need to return to the base, the colonel needs help tonight."

"I understand," Rurik nodded. "Keep me informed."

"I will," answered Cheslav. He drew his top coat tight around his neck. "One month and I'll never be cold again." He turned and walked off the *Barsuk's* quarterdeck.

"In a month, you'll be dead," Rurik said under his breath.

U-761
November 9th

"Maurizio, when you hear the engine start, you pull those two handles straight down. Understand?" Childers asked. "That's the main air induction. Without that, the engines won't run and we'll freeze."

"I got it." The sonar technician indicated the two green handles.

"Here we go." Norse held the flashlight as Childers pulled the starting handle. The huge diesel sputtered and shook the steel decking under their feet. A puff of air gasped out of the engine. The camshaft rolled over then a pop. The shaft moved a turn more and another pop. Slowly, as if yawning, the great *Mann* diesel chugged to life.

Childers moved along the length of the engine adjusting an intake or an injector nozzle. The roar of the engine smoothed into a steady rhythmic drone.

"Runs a little rough," Rance yelled over the roar.

"She'll settle out," Childers replied. "Check that RPM gauge." He pointed to the panel behind his left shoulder. "If it holds fifteen-hundred, I can get the motor generator on line." Childers removed his glove and let his hand rest on the giant valve cover. The steel warmed under his nearly frozen fingers.

"I'll be damned," Norse smiled when he heard the engine rumble. A breeze of warm air drifted from the after control room hatch. Norse tore the hood from around his head and let the warmth flow around his face. "We might make it though this."

USS MIAMI SSN 755

"Would you look at that?" Gellor smiled as U-761's engine sent a cloud of condensed vapor high over the U-boat.

"Next thing you know, the COB will want to sail the thing back to Groton," McKinnon beamed.

"The man could do it. I wonder how much fuel they have?"

"As long as they have enough to make it through." McKinnon leaned on the edge of the bridge.

"Captain?" a voice called from the dark bridge hatch. "Flash message sir," the sandy headed radioman said as he shivered in the cold.

"Thanks." McKinnon took the message.

"What is it Captain?" the XO asked.

"Low pressure moving in. We're going to get hammered. Winds of fifty knots or more."

"Great. This ice is moving around enough already. A few knots of wind and we'll have a hard choice to make," Gellor sighed.

"I'm going below and talk to the doc," McKinnon climbed down the ladder.

U-761

"Holding steady at fifteen-o-two," Rance shouted into Childer's ear.

Childers looked back at the gauge and gave Rance a thumbs up. He walked forward till he reached the motor generator room. Holding the flashlight in his teeth, he traced the maze of wires and cables snaking along the hull. His fingers led him to a large handle shaped switch. He pulled down and the switch locked down with a clank.

Suddenly the diesel chugged like a large truck going uphill. Over the sound of the huffing engine, Childers heard the whine of a generator spinning up. He spotlighted the electrical distribution panel. "Generator is spinning," he shouted. "Still a bit low." He adjusted output, and ready lights glowed on the panel. When the last one came on, Childers flipped the breaker and the diesel resumed its rough, but steady thumping.

Dim lights spread as if a curtain opened. The lights grew brighter and the interior of U-761 rose from the shadows.

Childers shielded his eyes since he hadn't seen

light in eighteen hours. He walked forward, ducked his head under the control room hatch. “Well, at least we can see,” he smiled at Maurizio and Norse.

Both men removed the tops of the exposure suits, as the room warmed. “Ya done good.” Norse slapped the lanky machinist on the back.

“Thanks, COB. Didn’t realize how cold it was.”

Norse climbed the ladder to the U-boats bridge. “Captain?” he said into the radio.

“COB, this is the XO. Captain went below. Everything okay over there?”

“Yes sir. Childers got the heat and lights on. All we need is cable television and we’re set for life,” Norse responded.

“Roger that, COB.”

“Any idea when we can come home?”

“Not yet, COB,” Gellor said apologetically.

“Wind’s picking up,” Norse drew the hood back over his head.

“We are expecting some bad weather in about two hours,” Gellor answered.

“How bad?”

“You’ll be back on board by then.

“Sure hope so.”

USS MIAMI SSN 755

“Try again,” McKinnon said roughly.

“Yes, sir,” answered the radioman.

“Sorry. Not your fault.”

“We are lined up with the satellite, but everything is coming in garbled. Sometimes it happens this far north,” the radioman explained.

I know that, he thought, *but I've already almost lost it once with this kid.* "Can we transmit?"

"Yes, sir," came the answer.

"Okay," he said. "Get this message uploaded and ready to go." McKinnon hand-wrote a message on the back of the recent weather report.

"Aye sir." the radioman took the message. "Be ready in about three minutes."

"Good. When you have it loaded, transmit."

"Transmit one, properly released, outgoing, aye sir."

McKinnon stepped out of radio and into control. *Miami* rocked gently. "Captain to the bridge." He pulled himself up the ladder. A howl of wind whooshed down, as if to push him back. *Two hours, my ass,* he thought as he struggled to the bridge.

"It just started, sir," the XO shouted over the moaning wind.

"You heard from the COB?" McKinnon shielded his face against stinging bits of ice.

"They have one of the engines running," answered the XO.

"Radio is out," McKinnon shouted.

"Shit," responded Gellor.

"I've released a message on UHF, asking them to not use the satellite."

Another sound came over the dark ice. A crackling noise like broken tree branches, then the noise turned into small explosions.

"Captain," screamed the lookout. "There."

Geysers of white fifty-foot jets of exploding ice shot skyward then snagged by the wind. Like a zipper, the ice was coming apart. McKinnon watched the hills of ice crumble and fall into a churning sea.

"Jesus," shouted the XO. "We have a problem," he said, pointing to the ice that held U-761.

The pack split at the U-boat's lodged bow. Now broken, the wind pushed on what remained of the three-acre floe and it moved. Unable to bear the millions of tons of pressure, the entire ice floe broke away. Now three acres of six-foot thick ice and one German U-boat drifted toward the *Miami.*

"XO, get them back onboard," McKinnon shouted.

"Sir?"

McKinnon grabbed Gellor's sleeve. "Do it," he shouted.

"COB, get off now," Gellor shouted into the radio.

McKinnon looked at the drifting mountain of ice, then behind his ship. The space seemed suddenly very small. "Clear the bridge."

U-761

"What the hell is that?" Maurizio shouted as the tearing ice shook the hull. Sheets of frost fell from the overhead, smashing like glass onto the deck. The four men held on as the U-boat lurched and bucked.

"Hang on," Norse shouted. "The ice is breaking up."

His radio crackled, and he realized he couldn't pick up the signal from inside the U-boat. The shaking eased and Norse raced up the ladder. He saw the U-boat drifting toward *Miami.*

"COB, get off," he heard through the crashing ice and screaming wind. Norse stuck his head down the hatch. "We're leaving."

The remaining three quickly pulled on their exposure suits. U-761 swayed and rocked as they climbed the narrow ladder.

"Where's the boat?" Rance called over the rushing wind.

"It'd better be there." Norse stepped onto the gun platform. "Stay close, and hold on. Keep moving." He crawled through the conning tower railing, placed his foot on the ice-covered deck, when U-761 lurched to starboard. Norse's feet flew out from under him and he landed hard on the ancient frozen wood.

"COB." Rance called as he stepped onto the after casing, he reached Norse just as the deck lifted.

Norse reached up and Rance's hand clasped around his. "I got you," and pulled the larger man behind him.

Norse pushed his legs to regain his footing. Childers and Maurizio grabbed Norse under the shoulders. "Get me the hell out of here."

Maurizio reached the lifeline supports and held on as the deck continued to tilt under their feet.

"We gotta speed it up," Norse shouted.

Childers reached the inflatable raft. He looked over the side and turned to the others. "Still here." He sat on the sloping deck and dangled his legs over the side of the shuddering U-boat.

The ice shook with the force of an earthquake. The old steel of the German submarine groaned as the force of the insane ice twisted her plates. Explosions of million-year-old ice floes erupted in a thunderous roar.

"Go," Norse screamed.

Childers pushed off the side. He landed roughly, his knees collapsed, when his boots hit the tough rubber of the boat's bottom.

"Here." Maurizio tossed the M-16. Childers caught the weapon just in time.

"COB, you're next," Rance shouted .

The U-boat listed further and for once, Norse didn't argue, sat down and pushed off, and caught the side of the raft. Childers grabbed him before the raft bounced him into the slush and ice.

"We're almost outta time," Rance shouted into Maurizio's ear.

"I know and I don't want your big ass landing on me. Get in the boat."

"You be right behind me," Rance yelled as he too went over the side.

U- 761 fell nearly on her side. Maurizio's feet slid down the deck, as he fell, face first onto the hard after-casing. His fingers managed to grab the sides. He hung with his legs kicking for support or traction.

"She's going over," Rance screamed from the boat.

Out of instinct, he let go of the line holding the small rubber boat to U-761's side. Waves of ice and slush washed around and pushed the boat away from the tipping U-boat.

Norse looked back to see *Miami* growing larger as the giant ice floe moved closer.

Maurizio's left toe found a bit of traction and he pulled himself up to the edge of the deck. The blowing ice stung his eyes and face. He gauged the gap between him and the wallowing raft. The Sonarman from Hoboken shouted his rosary out loud, pushed with his legs and launched his body into the air. He landed in front of the raft. An arm came out of the water and Norse grabbed it, then Rance caught the other arm. Both pulled hard. Maurizio's limp body slid out of the icy water, his face a mask of terror. They dropped the Sonarman in the bottom of the boat. Norse snatched the small oar. "Let's go."

USS MIAMI SSN 755

"Here they come," Gellor shouted above the clamor.

"Chief of the Watch, open the vents," McKinnon commanded.

"You sure about this?" Gellor asked.

"No."

Great plumes of air shot from the *Miami's* ballast tank vents. Almost at once, the submarine settled. McKinnon looked at the oncoming ice. "Going to be close. Come on COB."

The ice holding the long trapped U-boat finally surrendered. Once again, the ice exploded under millions of tons of pressure. She fell off to the side, sliding along the tipping ice as though she were once again being launched as she had so many years ago. As the U-boat slid, her weight caused the edge of the floe to upend. The jagged edge of the floe opened like a mouth filled with deadly white teeth.

"Look," the XO yelled.

McKinnon turned as the huge mouth opened wider. "XO, get below."

The ice towered over the bridge. "Hurry guys," Gellor started down the ladder.

The water rose faster along the deck, with the bow already under.

Twenty feet from the side of the submerging *Miami,* and near exhaustion, Rance grabbed the line tied to the bow of the raft, balled it and with the last bit of energy threw the line toward the men on the deck. The line arced through the air caught by the wind, it hung like a kite tail for what seemed like days, and finally landed in front of the hatch. They felt a tug, as the raft moved on its own. A cliff of wicked-looking ice stood over Norse. Then the raft bumped roughly into the rounded hull of the American submarine.

"Get them on board," a voice shouted.

The rising water lapped at the fairing for the towed array. The crew helped Maurizio to his feet, and down the hatch Billy Handler stood in the hatch and took his young technician by the collar. Gently, but firmly, he lowered the young man down to the waiting arms of other crewman. Norse insisted on getting the job done himself, and tripped the last few feet of the ladder, but the crew caught him. Rance and Childers made it on their own. They fell into the seats of the crew's mess, their breaths coming in heavy gasps of the warm air.

"Hatch shut," a voice called into control.

Gellor checked the hatch leading to the bridge. "All onboard."

The bridge hatch clanged shut. McKinnon appeared out of nowhere. "Depth?"

"Four-eight feet," replied the wide-eyed diving officer of the watch.

"Flood depth control," McKinnon ordered.

At once, the Chief of the Watch slammed the small control stick forward allowing water to rapidly fill *Miami's* trim tanks. The submarine descended faster.

"Five-zero feet," called the diving officer. "Downward depth rate increasing. Shut the vents."

"At sixty feet, start pumping as fast as you can. We'll sink like a rock real soon."

A banging grinding noise raked along the hull.

"We're catching some of it. Pushing the sail," McKinnon said calmly.

"Five-four feet, five-six, five-eight," the diving officer called as *Miami* ducked under.

The sail slid free of the ice. She righted herself, shaking a bit as though staggered by the ice.

"Status of the engines?" McKinnon asked.

"Ready to answer all bells, Captain," the Officer of the Deck reported.

"Good, we're going to need them," McKinnon replied dryly.

"Pumping to sea," the Chief of the Watch reported.

U-761

The U-boat slid back into the water, the sleek hull smashed through the thin ice. The shattered ice exploded under her weight. She rolled in the furious mix of ice and salt water like stretching herself after a long sleep. Once again, her shark-like bow lifted and fell in the swells. U-761 drifted in the newly created polinya, bumping against the smooth side of the overturned ice.

The engine still growled as she bobbed in her new home, its warm exhaust sent radiant heat throughout the compartments. One hour later, the temperature inside reached thirty-four degrees. Drops of melted ice flowed down the rounded interior of the pressure hull.

Chapter Twenty-One

Awakening

"Prepare war, wake up the mighty men."

-Joel, III, 9

Berlin, Germany

November 10th

Soon after 10:00 local time, his flight touched down on the rain-soaked runway of Brandenburg International. He collected his small bag and followed other weary passengers off the plane.

"Now what?" he muttered to no one. "I'll get a cab, or bus, hell anything with wheels, find a hotel," he mumbled.

Blevins followed the signs to Baggage Claim, rounded the corner and noticed a man holding a handwritten sign, "MR. BLEVINS" was marked in heavy lines on a sheet of yellow notepad.

"I'm Blevins," he said quietly.

"Carl Blevins?" the stranger asked cheerfully.

"Yes."

"Sir, I'm Michael Warren." The man held out his hand and shook Carl's.

"Good to be on the ground." Carl commented.

"Yes, sir, it is a long flight."

"Let's get you to the hotel." He led the way down a small flight of stairs.

"Wait here, sir," Warren smiled and waved. A white van pulled to the curb. Warren slid the door open, helped Carl inside then climbed in next to the driver. "Well, Mr. Blevins, welcome to Germany," he said as the van splashed away from the curb.

"Thanks, but just who are you?" Blevins asked.

"I'm Lieutenant Warren, SEAL Team Six. The driver here is Petty Officer First Class, Joseph Moody, also a member of Team Six."

"SEALS?" Blevins asked cautiously.

"We're here to show you around and ensure you get what you need," Warren explained. "Don't worry about a thing. Joe and me, we'll take good care of you. Starting with a little dinner."

U-761
November 10th

The air warmed slowly, but steadily. Along the interior, sheets of inch thick ice dripped away in trickles of water. Bulkheads and stringers creaked and groaned as the steel expanded in the warmth. A fuse for the after-electric motor room blew out in a shower of sparks. The compartment once again fell into darkness. A thin wisp of steam hissed when droplets hit the top of the hammering diesel engine.

Her bow rose and dipped in the slush. The wind lifted great slabs of ice from her deck and conning tower, carrying them away to smash and vaporize on the pack ice.

She drifted with the wind. The U-boat's slender hull nudged the edge of the ice in her tiny harbor. Around her a shroud of fog from her condensing exhaust hung thick even in the near gale of arctic wind.

Hotel *Das Aldalwine*
Berlin, Germany
November 11th

The phone clanged four times. On the fifth annoying ding Blevin's hand reached from under the covers and grabbed the receiver.

"Yeah?" Blevin asked his voice full of sleep.

"Herr Blevins, *Guten Morgen.* It is six-thirty, sir," the heavily accented voice informed him. "Two gentlemen are waiting for you, Herr Blevins."

"I'll shower and be right down."

"Sehr gut, Herr Blevins," responded the voice.

He groaned, pushed himself from the warm soft bed, showered quickly and went in the lobby.

"Sleep well?" Warren asked.

"Yes, just not enough of it," Blevins yawned again.

"Thought we might catch breakfast," Joseph whispered as he motioned for Blevins to follow.

They stepped into the cool air. Along the rather narrow streets, modern buildings shrouded in the dim morning. Glowing fluorescent streetlight glowed in the heavy gray sky, illuminating the stone and brick sidewalks.

"After chow, where do you need to go?" Warren asked.

"National archives," Blevins said as he ducked is head into the same white van.

"Big place," Warren remarked.

They entered a nearby coffee shop. The men spoke little. Blevins ate every morsel of his hearty breakfast while Warren and Joe sipped coffee and smoked a cigarette.

They had little early morning traffic on a short drive to the National Archives. A few bicycles wheeled silently through the streets. Joe parked the van along the street next to a rather young elm tree. Warren remained seated, scanning their route.

"You sure these guys are open yet?" Blevins asked. His foot crunched on the street.

"No problem," Warren assured.

They walked toward the huge stone stairs. "God, I am out of shape," Blevins huffed up the last of the steps.

Inside the door, an older man wearing an aged but well maintained suit of dark gray, watched them. He lifted his hand and unlocked the top catch to the steel and glass door.

"*Guten Morgen,*" the man said warmly. "Please, come in."

Warren bowed slightly "*Danke, Herr Zelik. Wie geht es Ihnen?*

The old man smiled. "See Michael, I told you, with a bit of practice you could speak like a real German. Oh, and I am fine, thank you. Come now out of the cold."

The three followed Zelik inside to seemingly endless rows of books and cases. The great hall smelled of old paper - a musty smell but perfume to an old researcher.

"Herr Zelik, this is Herr Blevins. The man we called about." Warren patted the Chief's shoulder.

"Good to meet you, Mr. Blevins," the balding man said with a genuine smile. "A U-boat … Uh, how do you say, enthusiast?"

"Yes sir. I have done as much reading in my country as I can."

"These two college boys brought you to the right place," Zelik lifted his finger.

"Yes, we met Carl here in Munich," Warren interrupted. "He told us of his research into missing German submarines, so I contacted you."

"Come now. It will take you all day to view the material on our *Ubootwaffe,"* he stated proudly.

The three followed. Joe hung back and glanced back over his shoulder ever so often behind the small party.

Zelik led them down a set of spiral stairs to the main hall with several brightly polished doors, each side-staggered and identified by numbers.

"Here we are," he stopped in front of the door marked 218. "I'll leave the key with you," Zelik handed the key to Warren. "No one will disturb you. Curious, but which U-boat are you interested in?"

Blevins studied the small German. "Ah - U-166," he lied.

"Umm, I remember that one. Lost in the Gulf of Mexico, I think."

Blevin's eyebrows rose, as did Warren's. "Yes, that is the one. You seem to know a bit about the subject," Blevins commented.

"Nein," Zelik smiled. "I watch too much television."

"Oh, ah, I will be sure to share with you what I find."

"That would be most kind," Zelik said with a slight bow. "I will now leave you to your work. If there is any way that I may be of assistance, please call on me."

U-761

Behind heavy eyelids, Manfred Becker saw the fog rush past him. Black billows changed to shades of gray, then white. His body liked the warmth.

The fog then took shape as orbs of light bounced lazily in front of his eyes. He wanted his eyes to open, but they refused. He concentrated on the various parts of his body. The fingers moved. *Good,* he thought. *Now the toes.* Those responded. *What was that noise? A steady drumming sound. Not an unpleasant sound, just strange*. Another sound entered his brain. *Oh, that faucet,* he thought. *Ada left the water to drip again. I meant to fix that. It will have to wait.*

Becker's processed the little information it received and linked it to memories. His brain demanded more oxygen. His lungs responded and drew in more air. The muscles complained as his ribs expanded and contracted. The brain silenced the complaints as more cells fired.

Becker's eyes fluttered half open, and the dim light sent searing pain through his head. Nonetheless they remained open to grasp more information.

Blurry at first, but the retinas quickly compensated and remembered how to focus. Becker saw the maze of pipes and wires above him. While his brain searched its memory for an association with information sent by the eyes. Several memory attempts, but so far, none matched. *This was not home, yet seemed so. There was no family here, or was there? Was it night or day?* The eyes really didn't understand. *Was there danger? Danger. This place knew danger.* The mind could use that. It dug a bit deeper, and pried into instinct. *Okay, some information here. Water... water is dangerous. Underwater—underwater is very dangerous.* "*Why would I be underwater?*" the brain asked. Then the links connected.

Becker's eyes came into perfect focus. His breathing slowed when places, names and faces flashed in his mind and the pieces fell into place. Satisfied with *who* and *where,* the brain sent signals that flowed to long dormant nerves. Muscles tested themselves by a twitch and shudder. The brain reviewed the signals and the rate of information flow increased. Muscle mass degreased some and the signals grew weak at the far end.

Again, the brain checked itself. Energy. All systems needed more energy. A signal flowed to the stomach and it felt suddenly hungry. He moved his legs and his feet and they responded as ordered. Still, the larger muscle structures felt unsure of themselves.

Reluctantly, the deeper functions of Becker's brain gave up control. Memory flooded the section of brain that dealt with reason. An automatic override of instinct quickly replaced fear. Flashes of warnings settled when the higher functions and curiosity returned.

Becker understood he needed to move. He relaxed and took in great breaths of cool clean air. Under his command once again, the brain did as asked and sent commands to the limbs and torso muscles. The muscles obeyed as best they could and the legs moved slowly to the side of the bunk. With little gracefulness, his legs flopped over the side of the bunk.

He rested a moment, let the legs complain until his brain told them to shut up. As though bolted to the thin mattress, he struggled to pull his body upright. He let his eyes move around the U-boat's interior. So familiar, yet not.

He heard other sounds now ... groans and whispers. He felt dizzy and had to concentrate "Can anyone hear me?" he rasped.

"Captain?" a weak voice answered.

"Roth?"

"Captain, are you okay?" Roth asked.

"Ja," U-761's commander responded. "How are you?"

"Can't move," the voice whispered.

"Keep trying," Becker urged as he looked at the deck just a centimeter below his boots.

"How long?" Roth's weak voice increased in volume.

"I don't know?" Becker reached up to stroke his beard. "Funny, though, could not have been too long. My beard has not grown much."

"One of the engines is running, sir," Roth noted.

Becker's head swung till his eyes could see down the passageway. "Yes." *How?* he thought. *I wonder if I can stand, walk*. He took another deep gulp of air and slid his body off the bunk. His legs felt like twigs when they took his weight. He wobbled a bit then slowly steadied. Again, the hunger hit him, this time violently. His mouth watered, his eyes went to the hanging foodstuffs gently swinging in the passageway.

The heaviness of his body faded. Becker leaned against the bulkhead and commanded his foot to move. To his surprise, the foot moved, then the other followed. He let go of the bulkhead. *This is what it will be like to be old one day*, he thought and took another small step.

USS MIAMI SSN 755

"That ice is really making a racket," Rusty Masters reported over the 27MC. "We're almost deaf. I can pick up broadband some off the array, but other than that, nothing."

McKinnon did not like being blind and deaf. "Okay, Senior Chief, keep sharp. I can't go much deeper."

"Roger that," Masters replied.

McKinnon went to the plot to see the chart. "We've got about ten miles to open water."

"Aye, sir," the Navigator agreed. "At this speed, it'll take us about two more hours."

"We have nowhere else to be," the Captain of *Miami* smiled.

The navigator leaned close. "What did you think about that U-boat?"

"Strange things in the ocean—and I thought I had seen them all. To answer your question though, incredible. Just imagine a piece of history like that right in front of our eyes. When I was a kid, my folks took me to Chicago. I saw that U-boat, the U-505," A fond expression crossed his face. "Funny, on that day I knew I wanted to be a submariner."

The navigator's brow wrinkled. "Looks like history has come full circle."

"I guess you could say that," McKinnon nodded.

"What do you think they'll do with her?"

"I don't know. That is going to be a touchy issue. I don't think they'll go public."

"Sad, I sure hope that if I was in that situation, I would be able to come home."

"Same thing I was thinking,"

McKinnon let his pencil fall onto the chart. "I'm sure we'll hear more." He walked forward to his stateroom.

HMS SWIFT
November 12th

"Sir," the Radio Officer said as he came to attention.

"What is it, Mr. Tanner?" the deck officer asked while he scanned the mist and fog.

"We are picking up some garbled transmissions in the two-point-eight megahertz range," Tanner reported.

"Fishing boat?"

Tanner remained rigid when the SWIFT rolled under his feet. "Could be sir, except for the location. Twenty-kilometers northeast."

"What?" the deck officer stepped to the chart. He placed his dividers on SWIFT*'s* position and opened the dividers to the twenty-kilometer range. He traced a light arc. “That puts the transmission inside the ice pack.”

“Yes sir, it does,” Tanner agreed. “If it is a fishing boat, it’s in a very bad situation.”

“Very strange,” the deck officer noted. “Could you make out anything?”

“No sir,” Tanner answered.

“Keep listening, I’ll inform the Captain.”

“Very good, sir,” Tanner turned and left the bridge.

Picking up the bridge phone, the Deck Officer pushed the buttons for the Captain’s stateroom. In his ear, he heard the buzzer sounding. He let it buzz three times.

“Captain must be doing his workout.” He replaced the phone in its cradle. “Quartermaster, enter the radio contact in the log.” He then looked at the radar picture. The ice showed as a blue ragged line not two kilometers to the North. “Bloody bad place to be tonight.”

Chapter Twenty-Two
The New World

"He that shall endure unto the end, the same shall be saved."
-Matthew XXIV, 13

Berlin, Germany
November 13th

"No sir," Carl Blevins answered into the secure phone. "Not much more information than I could have gotten on the web.... Yes sir, I have an idea..... I'll let you know as soon as I find something." He put the phone down.

"Not a man of many words, is he?" Warren smiled.

Blevins scratched the back of his head. "No, matter of fact, he hung up on me," he answered.

"Welcome to the club. Don't take it personally." The SEAL Team leader clamped his hand on Blevin's shoulder. "You said you had another idea?"

"Yes, but we'll have to make a road trip."

"Fine by me," Warren answered.

USS MIAMI SSN 755

With the pack ice eight miles behind her, *Miami* slid toward the surface of a wind-whipped sea. The sleek hull crept upward with her sonar like hands feeling the way in the dark of the ocean. At fifty-eight feet, the round hull rocked with the waves. Her communications mast slid up and pierced the angry sea.

"Conn, radio. Taking hits on the broadcast," the radio operator reported.

McKinnon thought about bringing *Miami* nearer the surface. *No,* he thought. *If we broach, somebody might just be out there looking*. "Radio, this is the Captain. We can't get up any further. Would a course change help?" He steadied himself on the still housed attack scope.

"We can try, Captain," the radioman responded. "Hell, I'll even try some chicken bones."

"Okay, we'll come around to the East. I'll put the seas on the beam. Just be quick. Got some sailors looking a little green up here."

"Will do, Captain."

The *Miami's* rudder swung ten degrees to starboard. Her blunt nose turned, bucking and twisting as the ocean slapped at her.

"You doing okay, Diving Officer?" McKinnon watched the gyro slowly turn to the East.

"I have a ten pucker factor right now sir. Watch the angle," he blurted at the planesmen.

The rolling doubled when her bow lined up with the waves. "Steady on course two-two-zero," the helm reported.

"Okay radio, we're steady," said McKinnon.

"We have acquired the satellite," the radio operator reported. "In receipt of flash traffic. Buffer is printing."

"Subject line?" McKinnon asked.

"Operational orders," came the response.

Chief Engineer Edel trudged along the steel deck, his footsteps heavy and unsure. "Captain," he said softly.

Becker turned his head slowly. "Everything operating?"

"Yes sir, but how?"

"I don't know. Who started the diesels?"

Edel shrugged his shoulders. "Any luck with the radio?"

"None," Becker answered. "Gerlach?"

"He's awake, but very weak."

Becker rubbed his chin. "What now?" he asked mostly to himself.

Edel rubbed the thick stubble of his own chin. "Home?"

"When can we dive?" Becker asked.

"An hour more on the batteries," Edel responded.

Roth stepped through the control room hatch. "Captain, Major Gerlach asked for you."

Becker looked at Edel. Again, their bond needed no words.

"Tell him I'm coming."

"Yes sir." Roth ducked under the after control room hatch.

"I wonder how long we slept," Edel commented.

"I don't know." Their eyes met. "I do know we are alive."

The Captain went to check on the SS officer. kneeled on the deck next to him.

"So Major, it seems your experiment worked."

"I feel very weak," Gerlach said thinly, his face, eyes sunk deep in his skull. "I don't know if it was all we had hoped for."

"Well, we are alive," Becker smiled.

"How long?" Gerlach asked.

"I don't know. The ice has changed. It seems everything has changed." Becker rubbed his head.

"What now?"

Becker stood. "Home, Major. We go home."

"If there is a home to go to," his voice even weaker.

"There is always home, Major, always. Get some rest." Becker stopped and chuckled. "I don't think we need anymore rest, but still …"

Gerlach's lips arced in a slight smile. "No, we don't."

Becker's legs gained strength. Berdy managed a quick meal of canned potato soup and sardines. The effects of the food made his strength return and his mind sharp as ever.

Becker entered the *Zentrale,* where Edel watched the helmsman test the rudder control. "Chief, are we ready?"

Edel turned. "Yes sir," he said quietly.

Roth ducked his head through the Zentrale hatch. "Captain, the wounded are ready, sir. Frimunt is awake and alert. I think it requires a direct order from you for him to stay in his bunk," Roth smiled. "The other two can perform their duties."

Edel gave a slight nod.

"Diving stations," Becker ordered.

Inside the small hull, he listened to the thud of feet. Valves spun open or closed and ventilation systems aligned for underwater operations. The plane's operators took their places, sitting on the bicycle-like seats, their hands rested lightly on the control actuators.

"Volker, how sure are you of our course?" Becker asked.

The young tennis champion nodded his head. "Course is set, Captain. I estimate thirty-kilometers to open water."

"Up scope," Becker ordered.

With a hiss, the silver tube lifted itself from the hull. The optics came up, stopping just below Becker's eyes. He snapped the handles down and peered out. "No contacts. Down scope." Becker slapped the handle of the periscope against the optics. The silver dripping tube receded smoothly into the U-boat's hull.

"Let's go home," Becker smiled. "Chief, dive the boat."

Edel nodded. "Flood the tanks."

At the ballast controls, the Kingston valves opened with a rush of escaping air. Water surged into the ballast tanks. The steel groaned as it became heavier from the weight . Through the thin plates, a gurgling sound was heard as once again, U-761 dipped her nose into the cold sea.

"Five meters," Edel called. "Boat is very heavy. Pump six thousand liters to sea, quick."

"Both motors ahead standard," Becker ordered.

Edel looked at the engine order telegraph, then back to the depth gauge. "Hurry." Edel placed one hand on each plane's man's shoulders. "Fifteen meters and falling."

The dull bronze propellers bit into the ocean and

U-761 shuddered. Her nose dropped ten degrees.

"Stern up ten," the Chief ordered.

"Rudder answers," the helmsman called. "Speed two knots."

"Bow up five," Edel said softly. "Twenty-five meters."

Water slowly flowed over the control surfaces. She responded as if drunk, her hull rolled gently and the bow staggered to level. She lightened herself as water streamed from her trim tanks.

"Boat is stable, trim is good." Edel exhaled.

"Good work to you all. Let's go home." Becker smiled

U-761 pushed her knife-like bow through the cold dark waters. Becker brought her to a southwesterly course, and thought, *the ice formed a large arc in that area. I could cut my time submerged. The batteries need recharging and a saved minute here or there could make all the difference.*

HMS SWIFT

The seas calmed some, but the wind whistled through the gray sky. She sailed west, skirted the edge of the ice, her radar probed for signs of the rouge whale ship.

Her crew recovered for the most part from the lashing the small frigate took during the storm. The old sailors found new ammunition with which to tease and torment younger members of the mess. Tonight the "Blue Nose" ceremony would take place to initiate those who have never crossed the Arctic Circle, afterwards, the planned movie marathon.

After eight bells Arctic fog rolled in a thick heavy mist, laden with ice, and surrounded SWIFT. The order went out to station extra lookouts and man the auxiliary radar. She slowed to eight knots and turned eight degrees south and opened the distance with the ice by three miles, which lessened the chance for an encounter with a stray house-size berg. Ice formed on her upper-works. Armed with brooms and shovels, the off watch cleared the rapidly developing frost so it wouldn't jam the radar or stop the rotation of the automatic turrets. A few less lucky ratings climbed the swaying mast and knocked loose the heavy ice accumulated on the thin wire of the radio aerials.

Rumors spread throughout the ship that tonight would be last night hunting the phantom whale ship. Tomorrow, the HMS SWIFT would turn her fantail to the desolate ice and start the trek to somewhat warmer Scotland and home.

The Autobahn
***Goslar,* Germany**
November 13th

"Warren signaled and pushed the silver BMW into the passing lane. A flat-nosed semi-truck flashed by in a blur. "What do you know about this man?"

"Nothing really." Blevins sighed. "I thought you would have all that information."

Sliding easily back into the travel lane Warren only smiled.

"How long till we arrive?" Blevins yawned.

"An hour at this speed. But I can speed up if you like."

"Hell no. An hour is just fine." Blevins shrank in the seat when Warren again passed a long line of slow moving tanker trucks.

"That sign said *Goslar* is eighty-kilometers," Blevins said as he craned his neck.

"Like I said, little less than an hour." Warren nodded.

Forty-five minutes later, Warren pulled in front of the hotel. "Let's get checked in," he urged and popped open the trunk. "Remember, we're here doing research for a book on ancient Germanic symbols." Warren took out a rather beat-up suitcase.

"I know. Is our contact here?" Blevins put his backpack under his arm.

"No, not till the morning. This meeting has to be hush-hush. This guy is, well shall we say, a person of interest to one of our allies."

"You mean Israel?" Blevins asked in a barely audible whisper.

"Chief, I don't really know your task, but to make it happen, we had to do things you don't need or even want to know about."

"What a beautiful old house," Blevins commented to change the subject.

They walked up a narrow stone path to the rustic looking inn. Warm light glowed from the windows. The entrance like out of a fairy tale had a huge oak door with heavy iron hinges and arched at the top. Warren tapped lightly on the inch thick wood.

Creaking on the ancient hinges, the door swung open and a stunning woman with a bright smile greeted the two Americans, though neither of them really noticed the smile. Her short blonde hair framed a perfect face, her blue eyes wide and lips rich and full.

"Welcome," she said in a mild Bavarian accent. "Please come in. You are the two Americans?

"Yes, ma'am," Warren gulped.

"Please leave your bags by the door. They will be taken to your rooms." She led them to the large dinning room. "Dinner is about to be served." She showed them to two empty chairs at the large table. "I am Frau Shönberg. Please be seated."

Warren and Blevins moved to their assigned chairs at the table. They both exchanged smiles with the other guests. Warren mentally noted each face and expression.

"Lovely place you have," Blevins commented.

"Danke," her voice soft and warm. "Let me introduce you to the guests. Ladies and gentlemen. May I introduce Herr Blevins und Herr Warren?"

Those at the table nodded politely in the typical European way. Frau Shönberg made her exit with her heels tapping on the floor.

U-761
November 13th

Becker opened the war log, he studied the pages and let his fingers rub the paper. *Strange*, he thought, *the paper is brittle.* To complete an entry, he pressed the pen lightly to the paper, but it made no mark. He shook the pen to get the ink to the nib. Again, he tried and again the same result. Becker twisted the top of the pen off and turned the pen upside down. He placed a small scrap of paper down to catch the ink, but it didn't spill out. Becker tapped the pen lightly with his hand. A black powder rained over the small bit of paper. *Strange, I've never seen ink dry out*, he thought.

Roth stepped through the hatch. "Captain?" the Radioman asked. "How have you felt since …?"

His eyes raised to Roth. "Sore, I guess you might say. Why do you ask?"

"Most of the crew have the same, soreness and fatigue," Roth stated with signs of worry on his face. "I don't know sir, maybe it's nothing, but our bodies are not the same."

"What about Frimunt?"

"About the same, I think. He'll make it if we get to a doctor. The Major is healing well, but that is another case I can't understand."

Becker thought, *the crew doesn't need to know everything*. "What do you mean?"

"His throat is healing, but he gets weaker." Roth rubbed the back of his neck.

"And you, Roth, how are you?"

"My bones hurt."

"Could be from the cold," Becker offered.

"I don't think so, sir."

"Keep watching, report only to me."

Edel ducked his head around the corner and interrupted. "Captain, we need you in Control," the Chief said nervously.

Becker walked as fast as his aching legs would allow and tried not to limp.

"The sound room," Edel pointed.

"What is it - a contact?" the Captain asked.

"No, Captain, I don't know what it is,"

Unterwasserhorcher Veldmon answered, "Listen," He handed the earphones to Becker.

Becker held it to his ear then dropped the headset.

"All stop," he shouted. He rushed for the search scope. "Up scope," he ordered. "Chief, go deeper. Eighty-meters—now."

"Both planes down fifteen," Edel barked.

By now, the scope rose enough for Becker to grab the handles. He lowered his body and peered into the sea while the scope finished its upward movement.

Becker spun the scope and tried to focus in the eerie, dark blue. U-761 nosed over when Becker saw a shape loom in front of him.

"Shit," he cursed.

A massive wall of ice hung in the sea like a jagged upside down mountain. What light penetrated the ice above shimmered off the berg, and glowed a sickly blue green.

Becker swung the scope from port to starboard. "Chief, increase the angle. Both engines ahead full." The solid wall of rock hard ice closed in and he estimated his time at less than thirty seconds. "Report speed," he shouted.

"Six knots," the helm responded.

The U-boat dove deeper. The water grew darker and the image of the ice faded into blackness.

"Deeper, Chief, deeper."

"Depth, seventy meters," Edel wiped the wet condensation from his nose. "Flood negative tanks."

The crew braced themselves when the U-boat's nose dipped at a twenty degree angle. Along the entire submarine items fell to the deck. The crew held on not daring to attempt a passage along the still wet and slippery deck. Her hull creaked when the sea pressed on her old steel.

Becker wrapped his arms around the scope to keep himself from sliding forward. The wall of ice moved faster in the optics and grew closer. *Going to be close,* he thought. Suddenly the wall of white evaporated. "Clear water," Becker shouted. "Level off."

"Both planes to zero," The Engineer barked. "Depth one-hundred-twenty meters."

"Lower the scope—be quick," ordered Becker.

The sound of the tormented and surging mountain of ice came through the hull. A grinding terrible noise grew when U-761 passed under.

"Battery?" Becker asked.

Edel looked at the meter mounted above the helm station. "Thirty percent," he said softly.

"We're not out yet. Both motors slow ahead," Becker ordered. The crackle and grind of ice grew louder.

"Estimate three kilometers to open water," Volker shouted over the noise.

Suddenly U-761 rocked from a blow worse than any depth charge. She fell over to port, but quickly, righted herself.

"Taking water from the torpedo loading hatch," a voice screamed over the snap and popping ice.

"We must have been hit by a chunk," Edel yelled. "Getting heavy in the bow."

A shower of sparks flew across the Zentrale and the lights went out. Time dragged till the red emergency lights flickered to life.

"Salt water shorted the circuit," a voice called.

"Bow planes up ten," Edel ordered. The nervous operators tried to focus on their gauges.

"What is happening up there," demanded Becker.

"Thirty percent left on the battery," warned Edel. "We need to pump out the torpedo room."

Becker went to the intercom. "I need answers," he yelled. U-761 dipped again. "Volker, how far to open water?"

"Maybe a kilometer."

"Chief, get our nose up," Becker said calmly.

A voice crackled over the intercom. "Water is stopped. Leak secured. Request to pump torpedo room bilges?"

"Pump bilges," Becker ordered. "Both motors ahead standard."

"Battery is at twenty-percent," Edel said.

Becker looked around at the faces, no longer boys, but veterans. "Prepare to surface."

Chapter Twenty-Three

Contact

"He smote them hip and thigh."

-Judges, XV,8

HMS SWIFT

November 13th

"Radar contact bearing one-nine-five," the young operator reported. "Designate this contact as Romero-one."

The Combat Center Watch Officer stepped to the console. "What do you have, Hopkins?"

"A contact just appeared out of nowhere. Just on the other side of that berg." The operator pointed to his screen. "There it is again."

"Right, switch to high PRF," the officer ordered.

The radar pulse increased, allowing a better picture to develop.

"Bridge combat," the officer said into his headset microphone. "Romeo contact, bearing one-nine five; range two thousand meters. Contact course is one-zero-two."

Commander George Ladd tapped at the keyboard of his laptop computer. He completed the five-page evaluation of the crew and their new Captain when his stateroom phone buzzed. "Yes?" He listened intently, a smile crossed his lips. "Good. Sound action stations."

The veteran Royal Naval Commander opened the stateroom door when the alarm sounded. Its shrill ringing vibrated the entire hull of the small warship.

Ladd emerged from his own tiny stateroom. "Lieutenant Kirby, let's see what your sailors are made of."

"True British tars - every man-jack of them, Commander." Kirby followed the taller man up the small ladder to the bridge. "This bloody fog."

"Situation?" Kirby asked.

"Surface radar contact, sir. No visual yet. Contact bears two-two-zero: speed, four knots. Range to target—one-eight-hundred meters. Angle on the bow is starboard zero-eight-zero. Ship is at action stations, Captain," Sub-Lieutenant Elders reported.

"Very good, Elders," Kirby nodded. "Send a signal in the clear for any ship in sight to turn on lights and hove to," Kirby ordered.

Within seconds, the transmission began. "Unidentified ship, unidentified ship. This is Royal Naval Warship Swift. We hold you on radar. Turn on required navigational lights and stop your engines. Prepare to be boarded."

"Signals report no response, Captain," the Deck Officer informed Kirby.

"Bloody obstinate." Kirby glanced at Ladd for direction.

"Your ship, Captain," Ladd nodded.

"Right. Helm come to new course zero-seven-two."

"Hold visual contact," the port bridge wing lookout shouted then pointed "Came out of the fog," Able Seaman Myers reported. "Gone again."

"What was it?" Kirby asked.

"Not sure, Sir," Myers raised his binoculars to his eyes. "It was long and low to the water. I did see the bow wave though."

Kirby went to the Weapons Officer. "I intend to put a shot across her bow," he announced. "Quartermaster, run up the Ensign. Gun Director, place a shot fifty meters ahead of the contact's last radar bearing."

In less than five seconds the unmanned turret swung the 76mm *Melara* cannon over the patrol ship's side. The battle flag of the Royal Navy slid quickly up the yardarm. The gusty wind caused the flag to whip and snap while it climbed to the peak of the mast.

"Ready to fire," the Gunnery Officer reported.

"Commence firing," Kirby ordered.

"Gun Director, open fire," the Deck Officer shouted.

The compact, but powerful gun erupted and SWIFT shook slightly. The muzzle flash lit the surrounding gloom with a momentary burst of bright orange, ringed in a dull yellow, then fell out of sight.

U-761

The bridge not yet fully manned, Becker wiped drops of freezing water from his face and scanned the surrounding area. The diesels chugged to life, their shafts turning the generator, which fed the power starved batteries.

"Helm, rudder left three degrees. New course zero-eight-nine," Becker ordered softly.

Out of the gloom the rough texture of another large iceberg appeared. Almost invisible in the heavy fog, the berg sat like a hill in the ocean. U-761 answered her rudder and her nose swung away from the jagged ice.

"This will be good cover till the batteries are full," Becker said barely audible. The lookouts took their positions.

"Destroyer," the starboard lookout screamed. A loud boom echoed across the water and the sky lit up in a bright flash, then the round impacted the ice shelf thirty meters in front of U-761's bow. The shell's warhead detonated in the hard ice that sent blasted chunks to rain over the submarine.

"Alarm," Becker cried.

The lookouts scrambled down the hatch. U-761's nose dipped under the frozen ocean while Becker dropped down the ladder and spun the hatch wheel shut. "Down twenty meters," he snapped. "Be quick."

"Herr Kaleu, the batteries are almost empty." His eyes wild. "We can't stay down."

"I know, Chief." Becker's mind raced. *I have only two options. Attack or die.* "Helm right hard rudder. Action stations. Flood tubes one through four."

"Propeller noises," Veldmon called. "Bearing zero-three-zero—closing."

Becker looked up. "He's coming after us."

"Tubes one-through-four flooded, Herr Kaleu," Hamlin reported.

"We'll get one shot,' Becker noted loudly. "Be ready. Helm, steer new course, two-six-eight. Chief, take her to one-hundred meters."

"Contact is slowing," Veldmon said in almost a whisper.

"He'll slow down. He can't risk slamming his nose into that ice." Becker climbed the ladder to the attack center. "Raise the attack scope."

HMS SWIFT

"Contact is gone, sir," the puzzled radar operator reported.

"What?

"Lost it, sir."

"Bloody hell."

On the *SWIFT's* bridge, Kirby and Ladd watched the ice-free channel narrow. On either side of the small warship, the free-floating bergs rose up seemingly surrounding her.

"Combat reports loss of contact, Captain," the bridge phone talker reported.

"Lost?" Kirby asked. "My God, you think we hit it?"

"We would have seen a hit on thermal imaging," the Weapon's Officer responded. "Radar track and the gunnery track don't match either, sir. The round went fifty meters ahead of target."

"Dead slow ahead," Kirby ordered. "Signals, send a contact report to Fleet."

"Kirby, when was the last Intel update?" Commander Ladd asked.

The young commander of *SWIFT* spun on his heels. “I don’t think we received any.”

“Signals, dispatch an urgent request for Intel on submarine activity in this operations area,” Ladd shouted.

“A bloody submarine?” Kirby asked.

“I don’t know,” Ladd said calmly.

“Steady as she goes, helm,” Kirby ordered. “I want to peek around that berg.”

U-761

U-761 slipped through the inky sea, her propellers turning slowly and her motors ate the remaining power.

“We have to come up now,” Edel warned.

“Switch all lighting to lanterns,” Becker ordered from his perch in the conning tower.

“Unterwasserhorcher, what is the contact doing?”

“Slowing sir, propellers sound muffled.”

“Keep listening,” Becker whispered. “Helm, come to course one-eight-zero.”

“Herr Kaleu, that takes us under the berg,” Volker said astonished.

“I know, Lieutenant.”

U-761 slipped under the floating berg. The tip of the periscope coming only meters from the bottom.

Becker felt his blood run hot and hated himself for it. With one eye tight against the periscope, U-761’s Commander peered into the gloom of the Arctic Ocean. Becker suddenly noticed the darkness grow a bit lighter. “We’re clear. Periscope depth now, Chief.”

The propellers stopped. “Battery is gone.”

"Use air, but get me up," Becker shouted.

"Switching torpedo control to manual," *Oberbootsmann* Hamlin said calmly.

"*Unterwasserhorche,* what is he doing?" The gloom grew lighter.

"Very faint, almost stopped." Veldmon cupped his hand around his ear phones.

"Careful Chief, we're coming up fast," Becker warned.

The U-boat barely moved when the scope popped over the surface. Becker moved the cross hairs a few meters and a gray shape filled his view. "There she is. Range eight-hundred meters. Angle on the bow—port zero-eight zero. Bearing zero-two zero."

He felt the swell lift his U-boat and knew he couldn't keep her down without power very long.

"Match," Hamlin shouted. The manual computer indicated the correct interception course.

"Tubes one and three, three degree spread," Becker ordered.

"Set," Hamlin called. "Ready."

"Tube one—*los*," Becker called out.

The U-boat shuddered slightly and the torpedo left the tube. Veldmon heard the weapons motor start. "Torpedo running."

Becker paid no attention. "Tube three—los."

Again the submarine trembled as the twenty-three foot torpedo sped away.

Becker waited a few seconds. He thought, *the next two minutes means life or death but to whom?* "Surface the boat."

HMS SWIFT

"Contact," the radar operator shouted. A blue blip appeared on his screen. "Regain of Romeo-one."

The information digitally linked to the fire-control computer on the bridge. "She bears two-six-zero? How the devil did she do that?" Kirby asked aloud.

On the SWIFT's stern, Midshipman Royce Hill stood at his station and shivered in the angry stinging mist and thought. *This God-awful cold, I spent my first three days throwing up, now this. That sudden cannon blast scared the daylights out of me.*

Reservist Able Seaman Sean Littles stood near the young officer, checking the boats. Hill's eyes followed the small swells that rolled gently off the side of the iceberg and into the blue-gray ocean. He glanced over the side to find the horizon when a shape rose from the sea. "Hey Littles, what do you make of that?"

The older man stopped, squinted, then his mouth fell open. "It's a bloody damned submarine." He moved carefully but quickly to the Boat Deck phone. "Submarine off the Starboard side," he shouted.

U-761

The U-boat heaved herself up from the ocean and water poured from her tower and deck. Becker had the hatch open before the hull cleared the icy water. He thought of having the guns manned, but thought better of it.

"Keep the watch below," he shouted down the voice pipe. He didn't want his crew exposed to the gunfire that was sure to come if the torpedoes missed. His eyes focused on the gray silhouette. Unable to estimate range in the fog, he guessed less than a thousand yards. His mind went to the torpedoes, envisioned their two counter-rotating propellers, the contact detonators fully armed, and waiting to feel the kiss of the small ship's side.

HMS SWIFT

Even with his binoculars, Commander Ladd could not locate the contact. He glanced at the radar repeater screen and confirmed something sat in the ocean.

"Submarine off the Starboard side," a voice crackled over the bridge intercom. All eyes on the SWIFT's bridge scanned for a shape.

At the stern, Midshipman Royce Hill focused on the two blurry objects. An adrenaline rush surged through him when his eyes caught sight of the small mounds of foam, churning toward him like someone drew lines along the ocean's surface. A whiny gurgling sound came from the two lines of frothing water that closed the distance on his ship. "Littles, look at that."

The older sailor's eyes went wide and his free hand clamped on the extra cloth of the Midshipman's coat. "Run," he screamed, his finger pushed the bridge intercom button. "Torpedoes."

"Ahead flank," Kirby screamed.

The helmsman shoved the throttle forward, fuel poured into the cylinders and the twin *Crossley* diesels roared. Her three-bladed screws sawed at the water and sent a plume of icy water rearing up behind her.

U-761's first torpedo struck one meter below the water line, just forward the funnel. The detonator pistol felt the collision and satisfied the force sufficient and released a firing pin, which struck the primer, surrounded by two-hundred and eighty kilograms of high explosives. The warhead shattered and expanded gases drove through the thin hull of SWIFT.

The shock wave pushed the thin plates of the hull inward, till they could stretch no more, at which point they tore. The full force of the warhead entered the ship. The wave of air and water moved at just over the speed of sound. Its sheer velocity caused the surrounding air to ignite.

Inside the ship, the pressure built and the interior of the small ship attempted to hold together. Not yet weakened, the pressure again stressed the already rending metal until it, like the impact point, stretched and tore loose. Two seconds later, the second torpedo found its mark just under the bridge window.

Royce Hill ran and stumbled after the first torpedo struck. His world went into slow motion. He saw the plume of water rise five times higher than the mainmast, and the angry blast of red and orange shoot from the side. The deck jumped from under him and he landed hard on his knees. His mind cleared quickly. The stern disappeared all the way to rear of the funnel. *Where's Littles?* he wondered. Still dazed, he looked over the side. Another track swam toward him, like a snake weaving its way toward him. He tried to stand, but waves of pain from his damaged knees glued him to the deck. He reached out. The ship seemed to fall on her side, then a sudden silence. He felt light as if floating in air, the pain gone. He looked down on his ship and saw it explode into a fireball. *Strange,* he thought. *How did I get up here?* Then his eyes caught sight of a headless body in the air next to him with its arms and left leg missing *That's my coat,* he thought. He knew nothing more.

Chapter Twenty-Four

The Gamble

"If you want to avoid collision, you had better abandon the ocean."
Henry Clay: To the House of Representatives, 22 January 1812

Pechenga, Russia
November 14th

The rutted, neglected road tested the strength of the tired wheels. The five-ton truck, whose best days had been some twenty years ago, lumbered up the small foothill. Sheets of ugly brown and black ice covered the pitiful excuse for a road. The driver, a young conscript from Murmansk, fought the steering wheel. The truck slid over a hill and skidded around a corner. The freezing air found its way into the shabby truck cab through a score or rusted out holes. It blew in and surrounded the driver and his passenger.

Though cold and miserable in the cab, those in the rear of the truck felt even worse. Five of them bundled and braced themselves on the hard wooden bench in total darkness.

"I'm glad there was no breakfast," a voice said. The truck lurched to the side.

"Da," an older deeper voice answered. "But hot tea would be good now."

"Where are we going?" another voice asked.

"To get some package Lieutenant Cheslav needs for our next operation."

"Five men for one package? Must be big," another voice yawned.

"I just do as ordered."

The ancient diesel engine whined and then slowed down. Those in the back saw a glow around them.

"We must have arrived," the older voice announced somewhat hopefully.

The brakes screamed when the truck halted. A slight breeze lifted the canvas flap that covered the rear of the truck. The five men peered out. "Just the same hills and shit," another voice said with little emotion.

In the cab, Lieutenant Cheslav handed a shivering guard his papers.

The guard looked at the young officer and his driver carefully. "Good morning, sir." He held the papers up to the glow of the floodlights.

"Good morning, Sergeant," Cheslav responded with the perfect amount of contempt.

"How many in the back?" the guard asked.

"Five."

"Wait here, sir." He walked to the rear of the truck, lifted the flap and peered into the dark cargo area.

"Hey Sergeant, where the hell are we?" one of the voices asked.

"The ass-hole of Russia," the guard answered.

"Anything to eat here?" another voice asked.

"If you like rocks and ice, there's a banquet." He

lowered the flap and stepped carefully over the icy mud to the cab.

"Smartass," the older voice said in a undertone.

"Sailors," the guard said hiding his own contempt.. He put his foot on the loose running board of the driver's side. "Continue, sir." He gave a halfhearted salute, stepped off the truck and waved the driver forward.

The gears of the truck ground and clanked and the wheels struggled to find traction. The guard unclipped a radio from his belt. "Naval supply truck entering the compound," he said.

The truck neared a high chain link fence and the driver again slowed. A gate slid slowly open and creaked from the strain on its rusted parts. When the gate opened far enough, the driver pushed the transmission into gear. They pulled onto a somewhat less rough concrete pad.

"To the left," Cheslav ordered. The truck rounded a small curve and the road dropped off at a sharp angle that led to a pit of rough gravel. "There." The truck lurched forward till four meters from the side of the hill. "Stop here."

A burst of light from high power floodlights concentrated on the shabby truck and its occupants. From the glare of the light, two forms appeared, then walked toward the truck. Cheslav opened the door and met the two figures.

"Lieutenant," one of the officers said warmly.

"Colonel, it is good to see you again," Cheslav smiled, his hand extended.

The other officer remained silent, his eyes taking measure of the man.

"Ah yes, Lieutenant Cheslav, this is my security officer, Major Tosya," the Colonel smiled.

The major extended his hand without a word.

"Come now, Lieutenant, let's get you loaded. Have your driver pull up and enter the complex."

Cheslav motioned the driver to move forward. The side of the hill slid open. Dim lights came from inside and the young Lieutenant turned with the Major directly behind him.

"So tell me, Lieutenant, what is a patrol vessel going to do with this training shape?" the Major asked.

"Major, this makes little sense to me. I hoped maybe you or the Colonel could fill me in." Cheslav answered.

The Major's face betrayed his puzzlement. "I don't know."

"Sure you don't," smiled Cheslav.

Cheslav and the Major stepped to the side to allow the truck to rumble past and entered the hill.

"Come," the Colonel barked. "I can't keep this damn thing open all day."

Goslar, Germany

Carl Blevins awoke to the soft but persistent rap at his door. "Yes?" he mumbled through dry lips.

"Hey Carl. It's me," Warren called through the heavy oak door.

"Oh yeah, come on in." Blevins let his head fall back into the soft feather filled pillow.

The door swung open barely creaking on its finely handcrafted iron hinges. Warren strolled over the wooden pine planks of the floor, his soft sole shoes silent.

"Hey Chief, it's almost time. Get out of the rack," the SEAL Leader urged.

Blevins opened one eye. "My head fills like it weighs a ton," he murmured.

"Yeah, you tore up that bottle of Schnapps last night. Need you up now, we're going to meet your contact within the hour."

"Okay, I'm getting up." He struggled to pull himself to a sitting position and rubbed at his eyes. "Never again," he said shaking his head.

"Yeah, I've said the same thing myself."

USS MIAMI SSN 755

"Yes, Skipper, I'm sure, nothing makes a noise like that," Senior Chief Masters explained. "The only contact we had was that Brit warship two days ago. Hell, I used it for training my narrowband operators."

"Think we need to sneak back up and take a look?" Gellor asked.

"Not till we know more." McKinnon rubbed his stiff neck. "You have the whole event on tape, Senior Chief?"

"Sure, I always keep the original."

"Good, make a copy."

"Yes sir." Masters stood and walked out of the CO stateroom.

"What do you think, XO?" McKinnon asked.

"Right now, all I have are the facts. One, we passed a small British warship a day or so ago. Two, the sonar gang used the ship for training and followed it. Three, last night we heard it blow up. That's all I know." Gellor slapped his thigh.

"You think we missed a Russian boat?"

"Big ocean out there, Captain."

"Let's get to PD and see what's going on."

"Yes sir. Next scheduled PD trip is in about two hours."

Strategic Missile Assembly and Storage Area Number 3 Pechenga, Russia

The five sailors stood about in the dim cave blankly staring at the walls and roof. Dripping water echoed along the domed tunnels of rough-hewn limestone.

"I thought this place was only a rumor," the older sailor told his comrades.

"I never heard anything about it," a younger crewmen countered.

They silenced when the whine of an electric forklift came through the rock passages. A dull yellow headlight glowed from the oldest of the passageways. The glowing intensified and the sound grew. A rather large lift topped the passage and steered for the truck next to the men. Lieutenant Cheslav rode alongside the driver. Another man, heavier and older, sat opposite the young Lieutenant. On the scarred, dented forks, a large, beat up box bounced slightly as the forklift approached. Its lettering peeled off in some sections and dented areas showed the container had its share of tumbles and spills.

It stopped at the rear of the ancient five-ton truck. Cheslav jumped down while the older man stepped from the lift's tires to the crumbling concrete and approached the younger officer.

"So then, everything arranged?" He tilted his head toward Cheslav.

"Just a few loose ends," Cheslav signaled for the men to come. "Boys, this is our package. Get it in and tie it down—it needs a soft ride, so be careful," he warned.

"Is it dangerous? I mean, look around. Look where we are," the older sailor waved to the walls.

The Colonel heard this and walked over, his gate uneasy. "Just where are you?" he asked coldly.

The senior sailor knew his curiosity overstepped its bounds. He cleared his throat. "Nowhere, sir," he answered nervously.

"Correct," the Colonel rumbled. "Now, get this loaded and you can be on your way." He gently slapped the sailor on his shoulder. "You'll be back to your ship in time for breakfast. Lucky bastards. You Navy men always get the good food and the prettiest wives."

Sighing with relief, the old Seaman turned to the younger members of the work party. "Okay men, you heard the Lieutenant. Get that box in and tied down. Move."

The forklift inched forward and the four guided it inside then secured the load to eyebolts welded to the truck's rusty bed. Cheslav supplied thirty meters of new white nylon rope to tie the box down.

"That green tarp, if you please?" Cheslav asked and pointed to the green foul smelling canvas on the floor of the truck bed. "I have to sign for this thing and get our base passes. Driver, start the engine and wait here for me. Men, get in, we're leaving," he ordered and turned to the waiting Colonel.

"Yes sir," the driver replied and opened the creaky cab door.

The five sailors hopped into the back.

"Looks damn heavy," one noted.

Still timid from his encounter with the colonel, the older sailor pulled the flap down. "Shut up and mind your own business."

Cheslav leaned toward the Colonel. "We can take care of that paperwork now."

"This way, Lieutenant," the Colonel headed toward one of the better-lit passageways. "My office is down this tunnel."

"That Major?" Cheslav asked in a whisper. "What does he know?"

"Nothing. You think me stupid?"

"He worries me."

"He is of no concern. Besides, he will do as told."

"How do you know this?"

"Well, we all have our vices and little secrets, don't we?" the Colonel smiled. "He is under control."

They walked but a short way into the cave-like tunnel when they stopped at a steel door set firmly into the surrounding stone. The Colonel entered his password into the keypad and heard the locking mechanism withdraw the stainless steel bolt. The door swung open a centimeter or so. "In here, Lieutenant." The colonel stepped over the hatch-like threshold.

Cheslav looked around before he followed.

U-761
November 14th

Becker cruised among the litter of HMS SWIFT. Bits of material floated and bobbed here or there. Parts of bodies drifted in the currents. A headless torso bumped about in the chunks of ice and slush. Several large rafts came to the surface and expanded. A large Royal Navy ensign, its edge charred, floated lazily in the gray-green water. Hamlin wanted to retrieve the waterlogged flag, but Becker denied permission, and let the flag drift over the grave of the sailors it recently led into battle.

Although the fog and mist made searching for survivors almost impossible, it offered the U-boat a measure of security from air attack.

After three hours, Becker gave up and retreated to the shelter offered by the large berg. U-761 lay motionless and her Mann diesels connected directly to the generators. Fresh and much needed power filled the starved battery cells.

Becker noticed a chill enter his legs and the familiar ache crawled along his nervous system till the pain found its old home at the base of his skull. He decided to take a break from the bridge and let his legs rest. He descended the ladder slowly. The pain increased. He stopped in Zentrale and held onto the sky periscope for support. The pain eased and he walked forward. He had difficulty getting through the hatch, but managed it without falling. The U-761's commander stuck his head into the tiny radio room.

Roth slowly adjusted the radio frequency dial and

his ears cocked to the side, to pick even the smallest whisper of the world outside of U-761.

"Anything?" Becker sat down on the small folding stool next to Roth.

"Just static, Herr Kaleu. It's like the whole world just turned off." Roth removed the headset and rested his elbows on the tiny table. "Even in Mid-Atlantic we could get some information, some news, anything."

As he picked up the headset, the static broke. A voice sounded. Roth slammed the headset to his ear.

"This is the BBC World News Update," the faint female voice announced in English.

Becker and Roth looked at each other.

"Today's top story is the ongoing war on terror. Protests across the country and continent continue for the third day. An anti-war rally in Berlin turned violent, as police with dogs and water cannons broke up a demonstration in the civic center."

"What?" asked Roth.

"Quiet," Becker barked.

The rather pleasant voice continued, "Protests began last week when the Prime Minister announced six-thousand more troops would be sent to the fighting. Germany announced it will add two-thousand additional troops wherever needed.

"Another suicide bomber claimed the lives of seventy-five Israeli troops at a check point in the disputed Gaza strip.

"Stay tuned here for the latest in weather and sports," the voice urged just as static once again overwhelmed the signal.

"The war is still going on," Roth shouted.

Becker tried to decipher the news. He understood English but the words didn't make sense. "I need to talk to the Major."

Chapter Twenty-Five

The Wage of Sin (I)

"Power is not reveled by striking hard or often but by striking true."
-Balzac, 1799-1850

Goslar, Germany
November 14th

"This whole thing is really starting to freak me out." Blevins walked to the edge of a wooded ravine.

"Yeah, I don't like it much either, but this is where the man wants us to meet him," Warren's trained eyes scanned the area for even the smallest hint of danger.

Tires crunched along on the gravel road.

"That him?" Blevins asked nervously.

"Don't know," the SEAL Team leader responded. "Get back in the trees. We'll check it out before we expose ourselves."

Obediently, the one time submariner moved behind a thin row of bushes covered by straight tall pines. Out of instinct, he squatted to fade among the autumn foliage.

A black armored sedan rolled slowly up the small hill. The car came to halt just short of the two Americans. It remained motionless for a half minute.

The rear window lowered only to expose a black hole of unlit interior then it went back up.

The driver's door opened. A small man, well dressed in a black tweed suit and tie, stood. He looked around and buttoned his jacket. Satisfied with the surroundings, the man stepped to the rear door and gave the window two gentle raps with his knuckles.

The rear door popped open and a shoe found its way to the pavement. The second man, maybe sixty-five, his eyes steel blue, nose chiseled thin and like the driver, his suit hand tailored with a perfect fit for his muscular frame. The older man straightened his jacket, while the driver scanned the area.

"Herr Warren?" the driver called.

The SEAL leader stood up from the brush. "*Hallo*," he said in his best German.

In a flash, the driver's hand flashed a dull silver automatic pistol.

"Easy," Warren shouted.

"Walk toward me, Herr Warren," the driver ordered in a monotone voice. "The other man?"

"He's here," Warren said cautiously.

The driver motioned with the pistol. "Have him show himself."

"No deal." Warren approached the driver. "Put the gun away and we'll talk."

The older man placed his hand on the driver's forearm, pushed the automatic's muzzle toward the dirt and stone. They exchanged a glance and the driver placed the weapon into a holster under his jacket.

"Okay, Chief," Warren called over his shoulder.

Blevins stood and cautiously walked toward the men.

The older man extended his hand and smiled warmly. "Forgive me for the measures I must take," he said bowing slightly.

Blevins took the old man's hand. "Yeah, no problem," Blevins replied.

"One more thing I must ask of you gentlemen," He crooked a finger. "Please, remove your jackets and roll up your shirt sleeves."

"Why?" Warren asked irritably.

"Members of Mosad have tattoos, you see," the old man answered. "The 'All Seeing Eye of Justice' they call it."

"You think we work for the Israelis?"

"I must be cautious at all times."

Warren peeled the windbreaker from his body, unbuttoned the sleeves and rolled the material past his elbows.

"Slowly turn your arms over, if you please." the old man scanned Warren's arms.

"Thank you and now for you."

Carl Blevins did as told and exposed his arms to the old man. "Thank you, gentlemen."

Blevins and Warren retrieved their jackets and put them on.

"Just who are you?" Blevins asked.

"You are Carl Blevins?" the old man asked.

"Yes."

"Then it is you who needs information. Please let us walk."

Blevins looked at Warren.

Warren nodded, "It's okay."

Side by side, the two men ambled down the path with the bodyguards not far behind.

"Because I know any information I give you will be subject to authentication, I will tell you something of myself," the old man said. "But that is all you will know of me and please ask no more. I have a few years left and want to enjoy them in peace."

"Of course," Blevins agreed.

"During the war, I was a young, but highly placed member of the SS. I was what you call in the United States call a 'paper pusher.' I was charged with filing and storing documentation for most of the activities of the research branch of the SS. I also had a few other duties, which I will not discuss with you. When the war ended, I found myself in a situation that many men never have to face. In May of 1945, I was ordered to destroy all the files and documents relating to our special projects. But I thought maybe I could use this information as, shall we say, a life insurance plan."

"So you hid everything?" Blevins asked.

"Yes and so far the insurance plan has paid great dividends."

"I bet," Blevins said coldly.

"I know the information you seek. That file was not even supposed to have been created. However, somehow it did."

"How could you know what I'm after?"

The old man laughed. "Our networks are vast."

"You know what I need then?"

"Yes, and it is a file I myself have not looked at."

Blevins stopped walking. "Why not?" he asked.

"Herr Blevins, if I see a book of matches, I don't have to open them or light them to know they can be used to burn down my house."

"Then how do you know this file is so important?"

"If you must know, and since it seems you have the time, I will tell you. The SS system of records was divided into areas of importance. Routine items were handled in one way, the next sensitive items given code names, the third most secret events and plans. A file had a cover sheet to identify the category for the information. Then files no one could open like those signed for by Himmler himself.

"So why keep them?"

"So many questions, Herr Blevins," the old man smiled. "But our business is done here." The old man reached in his coat and pulled out a CD. "Take this. What you look for is on here."

Blevins took the CD in his hand. "I would love to ask you more questions."

"I'm sure you would," the old man smiled. "I wonder if you would be ready for the answers? Oh and please, Mr. Blevins, forget we ever met. It could be as dangerous for you as for me."

"How do you mean?"

"Ah, I almost forgot." He once again reached in his pocket. "Here you are, this is also for you." He held out a small brown paper wrapper.

"What is this?"

"A treat for your dog, Ping." The old man smiled wide.

"How the hell do you know about my dog?"

"Like I told you, Herr Blevins, our network is vast."

U-761

Snow came down in sheets of blinding white with vicious gusts of Arctic wind. In the lee of the giant berg, U-761 bobbed gently in the small swells around the berg. A beard of ice formed at the blunt top of her bow and the crew chipped it away.

Becker decided to replace the two used torpedoes while he charged his batteries and repaired the damage to the forward hatch. The U-761 nestled between the ice pack and the two towering bergs. Arduous work in good weather, but now backbreaking, the small railroad-like trolley had been assembled and placed on rails running the length of the U-boat. Another set of tackles drew the torpedo from its container. With the trolley in place, they lowered the weapon then wheeled forward to the loading hatch where a set of pulleys took over and gently eased the torpedo into the torpedo room.

Becker sat at the tiny wardroom table with Major Gerlach across from him.

"Are you sure that is what you heard?" the Major rasped.

"Yes," Becker confirmed. "My English is not great, but I did understand."

The Major stared at the pipes and wires hanging over him. "Sounds like the war continues." His lips curled upward.

"What about the statement about Israeli troops?"

"Yes, that is most interesting. The Jews have long wanted Palestine. Perhaps Hitler made a deal."

"There is the possibility Germany has lost."

Gerlach rolled his head slowly toward Becker. "No, I don't think so. The report stated Germany would sent troops whereever needed. How can a defeated nation send troops?"

The Pentagon
Washington DC

"Good morning, gentlemen," Malroy said. "We need to get the facts here."

Royal Naval Captain James Brewster offered, "What we know as of now is the HMS SWIFT was last reported here. Her last communiqué was a request for information of submarine activity in her operating area 15:45 Zulu. At 16:10, a signal picked up from one of the emergency life rafts faded at 16:16. We have been unable to raise her on the radio. It is Her Majesties Government's assumption the ship was torpedoed."

"We share in the grief at the loss of SWIFT and her crew," Admiral Malroy said. "However, we cannot assume anything. We must have facts. What facts do you have?"

"At present, Admiral, we have only the request for activity in her operating area, but we also have a recording taken from our Homeland Defense Acoustic Warning System. I have the recording and will now play it for you."

The Captain punched the buttons on his rather large state-of-the art laptop. They heard the faint hum of a ship's propulsion. Brewster narrated, "This is SWIFT, operating normally, then slows. If you listen, you can hear another set of propellers. Our lads in Faslane determined these noises to be two three-bladed screws."

The Chief of Naval Operations spoke, "I don't know of many countries whose boats still have three bladed screws."

"Neither do we, Admiral," Captain Brewster explained. "Listen further." A faint, but distinct crack similar to mousetrap heard in another room. "That's the ship's main gun. Now, as you will note, the two three-bladed screw disappears."

"Disappears?" asked the Chief of Naval Operations.

"There is a brief pause, where you can hear nothing other than SWIFT. At one point, her screws almost stop."

"If your ship tangled with a submarine, why in the name of God would she slow down?" Malroy asked.

"We don't know, sir," Brewster admitted. "She was in some rather heavy ice. Perhaps that played a part."

"Excuse me, Captain," Malroy raised his hand, "you and I go way back. So please understand what I am about to say."

"Go on, Admiral," the distinguished officer said.

"It sounds like you fired the first shot. Trust me, submarines do not react well to that."

"Bill, I know, and as you know, no warship under the flag of England would engage a vessel without the highest authority or unless she herself were attacked."

"Captain," the CNO said, "if you can, please tell us what operation did the SWIFT conduct?"

Brewster walked around the large table to find the right words. "SWIFT operated under UN charter to protect whales," the Captain said bluntly.

"Whales?" Malroy asked, puzzled.

Brewster tugged at his chin. "Yes, it seems a Norwegian whaling threatened a pod of endangered whales. Her mission was to intercept the whaler and safeguard their passage south."

"So maybe this submarine business is bullshit," the CNO blurted.

Brewster's eyes narrowed. "No, Admiral, we did a bit of checking and found the whale ship in question still tied to her pier in Tromso. A check of her registry also indicated she has housed screws or four blades—not three."

"Could your ship have run into a berg and exploded?" Malroy asked.

"No and of that I have another recording. If I may?" Brewster asked.

"Please, go ahead," Malroy waved politely.

Brewster again keyed his computer. "This is about five minutes after the *two threes* faded.

They listened to the whirring sound of precision balanced screws of the British warship. Then a mechanical clank.

"I'll be damned," Malroy exclaimed. "Tube doors opening."

"Yes," Brewster said. "But there is more."

Again, the room went silent as SWIFT'S last moments in the Royal Navies line of battle played for them. A distant whooshing noise followed by the rapid grinding noise of high-speed propellers.

"Launch transient," the CNO admitted.

"Followed twenty-six seconds later by another," Brewster added.

"Who the hell would cruise in a submarine taking pot shots at ships?" The CNO asked. "Especially warships?"

"Maybe someone with nothing to lose," Malroy offered.

Captain Brewster cleared his throat. "Admiral Malroy, as you said, you and I have a long history. I consider you to be one of the finest officers I know, as well as my dear friend. What I must ask is not easy for me, but it is my duty. Does the United States have any submarines operating in the area?"

"You think we did this?" the CNO blurted, and slapped his palm down hard on the table.

"Easy, Admiral," Malroy cautioned the Chief of Naval Operations. "Captain Brewster, I understand your concern in wanting to get the facts on this matter. Although we are the best of allies, you know I cannot discuss operations that are not being conducted in cooperation with the Royal Navy," Malroy said in his best official tone.

"Please advise your President, Her Majesties government will not stand aside for this unprovoked attack. The Defense Minister is even now discussing with the Prime Minister our options to safeguard the sea lanes," Brewster replied.

"Captain, I'm from Texas, so let me be sure of what you are saying here." Malroy sat upright in his oversize chair.

Captain Brewster beat Malroy to the punch. "What I am saying is that the agreed pull-back of forces seems to have been violated. That puts Russia in default …"

"Wait a minute Captain," Malroy interrupted. "Are you saying you'll pick a fight with Russia? I understand the loss of a ship. Hell, look at our own losses of late. Including nearly having my son killed. Any action taken by your Government in retaliation will have to be without the consent of the United States."

"I will also remind you of the NATO charter."

"Captain, an action, I understand, but one that can

lead to nothing other than total war. I am willing to put whatever assets of the United States into place to find the truth. But I must insist that Great Britain respect the agreement as it stands until all the facts are known."

United States Flagged
Container Ship SS *MINGO*
66,000 Tons

"Anything else on that rescue beacon?" Mingo's Master asked.

The first officer looked at the radio log sheet. "Nothing more sir, it just faded."

"We're near the area of the transmission. We'll slow and take a look." The Master leaned over the greenish-blue radar screen. "Post extra lookouts in the bow."

"Sir," the Navigator interrupted. "Slowing will put us behind schedule."

"It's the law, you know that. We have to investigate any emergency beacon. Besides, if it were me sitting there, freezing my ass off on some damned iceberg, I'd sure as hell hope someone would come looking for me."

"Yes sir," the Navigator agreed. "Still, I am required to inform you."

"Duly noted," the Master nodded. "Ring up dead slow."

U-761

The reloading of the two spent torpedoes went

well. The short day ebbed, the unseen sun slid over the ice and gray and white swirls of fog and mist turned a dark purple.

U-761 moved from her place next to the large berg, to hug the edge of the ice pack until Becker found a safe place to make a break for the open ocean. The diesels purred while the U-boat's sleek bow sliced into the sea. On her bridge, the watch shivered in the freezing air and scanned the nearby ocean.

In his tiny cabin, Becker thought of Ada. He felt somewhat guilty for not missing her more, for not worrying more. *Less than two months have passed since I last held her. What about the baby?*

The clock ticked quietly in the corner. He had Roth work on it for him a few days back. The tiny gears and screws rusted enough to stop the movement. His eyes focused on the clock's face and he thought, *how many times have the hands gone around the dial while we slept?* He suddenly felt frustrated. *It's always about time. Time to do this and time to do that. Be at this grid at this time. Launch a weapon at a certain time. The baby will come at this time. Return to port at this time. All about time, everything and anything—time.*

Berdy came through, his pot and lid clanked. He steadied himself against the gentle roll of the surfaced U-boat. "Herr Kaleu," the cook smiled, "I have made sweet rolls. Would you care for some?"

Becker sat up. The aroma of the steaming rolls filled his nostrils and brain. "You always take such good care of us." The Captain took one of the sticky warm rolls. "Thank you, Berdy."

About to ask how the stores of food held up when

something caught his eye, Becker asked "Berdy, how old are you?".

The cook looked surprised. "Herr Kaleu, I'm twenty-six. You don't remember? We had a cake three days after we left port."

Becker tried to hide his forgetfulness. "Of course … it's just that - your eyes - there are wrinkles."

The cook reached up and felt the corners.. "Just a little tired." His face once again broke into his ever-present smile. "Keeping this crew fed and happy is a hard job."

"Have you been feeling well?" Becker asked.

"Oh Captain, you don't need to worry about me. It is you, I'm worried about."

"Me?" Becker asked.

"Oh yes, Captain. Have you looked? Your beard has sprinkles of gray and so does your hair."

Becker's hand tugged at his beard. "You think feeding these guys is a job? You should be in my shoes," Becker grinned, hoping to end the conversation.

"No Captain, I'll stick to my pots and pans," he laughed. "If you will excuse me, sir, I want to get these to the bridge before they get cold."

"Thank you again, Berdy," Becker bit into the warm roll.

Container Ship SS MINGO

"Radar contact, bearing zero-one zero. Range two-thousand meters and closing," the radar operator reported. "Small contact on the right drawing left."

"Lifeboat?" the first officer asked.

"Can't tell," the operator responded. The radar's invisible beam swept the area again. "Contact fades in and out. It must be low to the water or else this damn mist is causing ghosts."

"Slow to three knots."

The foaming wave at Mingo's bow dropped off. Now only a small ripple marked the Container ship's passage.

"Firming up that bearing now," the radar operator reported. "Bearing now is two-seven-seven."

U-761

"Contact off the starboard bow." the lookout cried.

Hamlin had the watch on the bridge. He raised his binoculars. "What is it?"

"Large gray shape. Looks like a warship, cruiser size."

The outline of a large ship emerged from the gray. *Damn. Heading for us.* "Clear the bridge," he ordered. The bulk of the ship loomed closer. He could see no upper works, no weapons. Only one type of ship fit that description. "Alarm," he called down the hatch.

The lookouts went down the hatch in seconds. Hamlin looked again and the giant ship pointed its huge curving bow directly for them. He cast a last look and dropped down the hatch, landing roughly on the steel deck on the conning tower. He could hear the water race over the deck. He reached the thick rope to the hatch and pulled hard. The hatch clanged shut and he spun the dogging wheel and the ocean closed over the conning tower.

By the time he climbed down the ladder, Edel already at his station, guided the planes men. Becker came through the hatch, his tired eyes wide but confident.

"What is it," he demanded.

"Close," Hamlin panted.

Becker dashed up the ladder to the conning tower. "Chief, hold us at periscope depth."

Hamlin regained some strength and followed Becker up into the conning tower. "Sir, very large ship, believed to be a carrier."

"Carrier?" His eyes went ever wider.

"Yes sir," Hamlin confirmed.

"Up scope," Becker sat on the tiny bicycle-like seat of the attack scope.

The steel tube hissed and clicked as it slid from the top of the U-boat. Becker grabbed the handles and shoved his eye to the monocular sight of the scope. Green water splashed in front of his eyes and the scope continued upward. Three seconds later, the water fell away and Becker stared into a horizon of ice. He pushed a small button with his left thumb. With a soft hum the periscope spun slowly around. He took his eye from the scope long enough to look at the course gyro repeater. The scope turned again and the optics filled with the steel sides of a ship. Becker gasped at the size of the beast looming over him.

His sailor instinct took over. "Right hard rudder," he shouted. The seemingly endless wall of curved steel drew closer.

Volker stuck his head through the hatch. "That is toward the ice, Captain."

"I know," Becker responded.

Volker looked back into the control room and nodded. "Hydrophone reports the contact is slowing."

"Damn," Becker cursed.

"Captain, they're trying to drive us under the ice. Drive us under and drown us."

Becker looked away from the scope. His mind raced. *Why hadn't I thought of that? That's it a Hunter-Killer group found us. That explains the Destroyer we sunk yesterday. Now we've stumbled on the carrier. I could dive under the ice till the ships give up - if that's possible. No doubt, they were less than happy at having one of their escorts sunk. This carrier though - her planes could reach out hundreds of miles in all directions.* The ship in his periscope remained a safe distance *Attack the carrier? Where are the escorts? They must surely be in the area. Maybe even damaging the huge ship would allow us to sneak out from under the Destroyers.*

"Two kilometers to the ice, Herr Kaleu," Volker warned quietly.

Facts and figures raced through Becker's mind. "Action stations," he ordered.

His hunter instinct took over and his actions almost mechanical. "Range, eight-hundred. Bow angle thirty starboard."

Hamlin stood behind him and fed information into the torpedo data computer. "Gyro angle is one-four-three," Hamlin announced.

"Helm left ten degrees on the rudder. Ease me over. Hydrophone?" the Captain asked.

"Screw still turning slow," came the report up the hatch.

"Good," Becker grinned. "Looks like we might have caught this ole lady with her panties down."

"Gyro angle now zero-eight-seven," Hamlin called out in a low tone.

"Keep coming around," Becker said softly. "Open bow caps on tubes one through four. Set up tubes one, two, and three."

"Tubes one, two, and three are set. Gyro angle now zero seven zero."

"Set a three degree spread," Becker ordered. "Torpedo speed thirty. Set running depth at two meters. That should tear her guts out."

"Spread set, depth set. Gyro angle now zero four-eight."

Becker looked again at the U-boat's gyro repeater. "Helm rudder amid ships."

Becker peered into the tiny window of the periscope. His target grew larger. He brought her in line with his waiting torpedoes. He waited until the angle decreased so the weapons would not have to turn, increasing the chance of them running true.

"Rudder zero," the helm announced.

"Match bearings," Becker announced with little emotion. *Something seems wrong with the attack,* he thought. *Something is out of place. The British let this valuable ship fall right in my lap? Is this a trap?*

"Bearings matched," Hamlin announced.

Becker hesitated. *Something just doesn't fit.*

"Captain," Hamlin called softly, "bearings are matched. We are at the firing point."

Second thoughts kill, Becker remembered from his training. A U-boat Commander must decide on his actions and act on his decisions. He placed his eye back to the scope. The light faded and seconds ticked off. "Stand by, tube one."

"Tube one ready."

Becker bit into his lower lip. "Tube one—*los*."

The U-boat's bow rose slightly when the torpedo left the tube. Becker panned down and saw the wake of the torpedo. It sped toward the towering sides of the target. Five seconds went by.

"Tube two—*los*."

The next torpedo ejected into the icy sea. Becker peered at the surface of the ocean. Suddenly his mouth dropped open. The second torpedo malfunctioned and skipped along the top of the water like a stone thrown by a child.

"Shit," he called. He launched the third weapon. "Tube three—*los.*"

"Weapons away." Hamlin shut off power to the Torpedo Data Computer.

Becker saw the wake of the third weapon, running true. He moved the scope around looking for the second when his eyes caught a glimmer on the sea. He froze. The second weapon glanced off a floating chunk of ice and the errant torpedo headed directly for his periscope.

"Chief, get us down fast. Both motors ahead full." Becker shouted.

After what seemed like an hour, Becker felt the nose of his U-boat dip. The entire boat vibrated while the screws chopped at the water. The whining of the torpedo's motor grew louder. "Faster, Chief."

The bow dropped further. Becker took a last look and the waves closed over the scope. The gray air turned to bluish green, Becker caught a glimpse of the torpedo closing in on the U-boat. "Hang on," he screamed. "Get the scope down. The torpedo is coming back."

The U-boat moved deeper. The damaged and ignorant weapon closed, its gyro ordered the tiny rudders to turn. The gimbals that held the spinning gyro in place cracked, which threw the rotation off balance and another signal told the rudders to hold the torpedo on a straight course, unknowingly and uncaringly aimed for its Mother Ship. The gimbals frame, stressed by centrifugal force, broke in half. The rudders locked. The weapon reached its thirty knot speed.

The scope slow retracted into the diving U-boat. Becker, as well as the life of his ship and crew, waited. The steel vibrated while the torpedo motor whirred louder.

Becker closed his eyes. The noise seemed inside the U-boat with them. He thought of Ada and the baby again. *I'll never even see my child,* he thought. *So unfair. Maybe this is the way it should end? Maybe death would indeed bring relief. How many years had death walked behind me? How many times have I felt the cold breath of life's end breathing down my neck, smiling behind him? Looks like you have me this time, and by my own hand.*

Becker held his breath. The whirring of the torpedoes engines faded. He open his eyes and a rush of air came out in relief.

"*Unterwasserhorche*?" he asked quietly,

"Torpedo is fading astern," Veldmon sighed a long labored breath.

"Get us back up." Becker leaned over the conning tower hatch.

"Veldmon, can you hear the other torpedoes?" he asked as again the periscope slid up.

"Five seconds," Volker shouted up the hatch, not waiting for the hydrophone operator.

Becker grabbed the handles and flung them open as soon as the scope lifted from its well. He looked in the optic window, just as the water washed over the periscope window.

"Now," Volker shouted.

Becker saw a plume of white boiling water shoot up from mid-ship. An angry puff of black emerged from the sea at the base of the still growing plume of water. "Hit," the Captain shouted.

"Four seconds on number three," Volker shouted. The rumble of the torpedo detonation filled the dripping interior of U-761.

The plume of water fell. The ship staggered under the hit. A jagged hole of rent steel showed itself. The ship seemed to turn, ever so slightly, away from the incoming torpedo. The last of the explosion fell back into the sea. The second weapon reached the steel hull.

Becker could not tear his eyes away. The huge spray of white water rose along with immense tower of smoke. The rumble of the expended explosives entered the U-boat. Becker looked for additional damage. A bright white flash of light then darkened sky while a cloud of thick boiling smoke blackened the air. The black smoke exploded into a new shade of yellow orange and grew larger, expanding outward and upward. A wave of overpressure pushed at the cold dense air. The rushing wave of air tore the white tops off the small waves.

In slow motion the wave of supersonic air rushed past the U-boat's periscope and Becker saw the large ship's bow dip into the water. The area of the ship where the explosion occurred lifted clear of the water.

"She broke her back," Becker yelled and jammed his eye back to the scope. He peered into the fading light and into the dying ship.

"She's breaking up. I can hear the bulkheads giving way," Veldmon yelled.

Becker suddenly remembered he hadn't scanned the area behind his submariner. *A carrier cannot go un-escorted*, he thought. He swung the scope around. Waves slapped at the small periscope window as the tube spun slowly around. Still, as far as he could see in the darkening gloom, the sea was clear.

"Going down," Veldmon said in a soft, almost sad voice.

Becker swung the scope back to his victim just as the sea closed over the flag flying at her stern flagstaff. His mouth again fell open. Torn and mangled by the explosion, the flag waved proudly until the sea closed over it. Becker felt a huge lump grow in his throat. Becker squinted at the bars of red and white. In the corner, a field of blue covered with stars. "American." he said no one.

Hamlin turned his head. "What?"

"She was American," he said softly. "Chief, surface the boat."

"Surface the boat, aye, Herr Kaleu," Edel responded.

Chapter Twenty-Six

The Wages of Sin (II)

...this war of grouping and drowning, of ambuscade and stratagem, of science and seamanship...
-Winston S. Churchill

Russian Patrol Ship *BARSUK*
Pechenga, Russia
November 14th

"*Barsuk—Barsuk*, this is harbor control. Do you read?" the static filled voice asked.

"Harbor control, this is *Barsuk*—go ahead." Captain Rurik answered calmly.

"*Barsuk,* you are ordered to return to port," the monotone voice stated with no more inflection than a Kiev taxi driver." You have no orders from fleet command and no piloting plan filed."

Rurik put the radio's microphone to his mouth. "Harbor control, this is *Barsuk.* Connect us on this frequency to Strategic Defense Command. Give them your name and rank so they will know who delayed a mission vital to the defense of the Motherland."

Cheslav laughed aloud in the tiny wheelhouse of the aged Russian patrol ship.

"Now, a little something extra, just for good measure," Rurik said. "Harbor control, this is *Barsuk*. Have you made the connection yet? I have the Commanding Officer of Strategic Rocket Command onboard waiting."

A blast of static came from the small radio speaker sloppily welded to the plotting table. "*Barsuk*, this is harbor control. A technical error on our part …uh... continue your mission."

"Thank you, Harbor Control. *Barsuk* out."

"Well done, Captain," Lieutenant Cheslav laughed. "That should buy some time."

"Yes," Captain Third Rank Rurik nodded his head. "Speaking of time, Lieutenant, don't you have something to take care of."

Cheslav looked into the cold eyes of the *Barsuk's* Captain. "Now?"

Rurik shrugged. "This is as good as a time as any. Does the crew know he is on board?"

"No, not yet," Cheslav answered.

"Then it should be taken care of before too many people notice him."

Cheslav looked out the pilothouse window. "It is getting dark. Captain, with your permission, I would like to show our guest around the ship."

"By all means," Rurik answered coldly.

Goslar, Germany

"Man, was that the definition of weird," Carl Blevins sighed.

"I don't want or need to know anything, Chief."

Warren closed the door on the silver BMW.

"Aren't you the least bit curious?" Blevins asked.

The young SEAL Team leader cranked the high performance engine and backed up. "No."

Blevins scratched his neck. "Okay, fine. Tell me something?"

"Sure," Warren floored the gas pedal.

"First, are you trying to give me a heart attack?" Blevins grabbed the dash for support. "Second, is there an interpreter we can trust?"

"I don't know. Truth is, I have no idea of anything you're doing. If you need one, I can see what the boss says."

U-761
November 15th

Sleep came hard for Becker. Although near exhaustion, his eyes refused to close. On the edge of sleep, an image of Ada floated before him. For the first time, a feeling of guilt overwhelmed him. *Why would a man leave his family to go around in a sewer pipe killing other men? A man should be with his family.* It suddenly dawned on him following the latest sinking. Such a great victory would surely mean medals and extra leave for them all yet there had been no celebration from the crew. The entire crew seemed gripped by a type of fatigue. *Is it fatigue, or a sickness brought on by the gas, or do they just want to go home?*

Anton Kruger walked silently past. "Kruger," Becker called from his bunk.

The large torpedo mechanic stopped and ducked his head just short of the hatch. "Herr Kaleu?"

"Your boys did a great job yesterday," Becker smiled.

"Thank you, sir," Kruger grinned.

"How is the torpedo gang?"

Kruger lifted his plate-sized hand to his scraggly beard. "We are well, sir."

"Have you noticed anything strange on this boat?"

"Strange?" Kruger asked.

"The crew? The crew seems depressed."

"Oh no, sir," Kruger said, shaking his head. "I know what you mean though. The men talk more of home than usual, but depressed, no."

"And you, Kruger?" Becker asked.

"I never really had a home. I just seem tired all the time," the giant torpedo man confessed.

"I envy you," Becker smiled. "You are a truly free man. No one to answer to, no worries about family."

"Don't envy me, Captain," Anton Kruger said in a low voice. "I want a family and someone to worry about. It's all about dying."

"What?" Becker asked, sitting up.

"It is strange, I know, but if I die out here, so what? Who will remember me? Who will care?" His usually intense blue eyes softened. "No one," Kruger shrugged his bulging shoulders. "So, did I really ever exist?"

"You're a deep thinker, Kruger. You will not die out here."

"You are the finest officer I have ever sailed with Captain, but you know you have no way of keeping that promise. I just want it all to mean something."

"You're right, but don't let the others know I can't perform miracles," Becker chuckled. "Keep close watch on your boys, we still have a long way to go."

Iranian Cargo Ship
Kangan
200 Nautical Miles North West of Norway

Captain Nasim shivered in the cold air of the North Atlantic while his 300 foot converted water tanker plowed through the swells. He scanned the dark waters ahead and felt uncomfortable with the cold and total darkness. He paced between the wings of the bridge and the out-of-date radar system. He jumped when the rusted door to the bridge wrenched open with a squeal.

A large, dark figure loomed inside from the pale blue light of the *Kangan's* bridge.

"Excuse me," a voice said in perfect Farsi. "That door needs grease."

"Good morning, General Shatrevor." Nasim looked up from the glowing radar screen.

Shatrevor, the third most wanted terrorist in the world, moved closer, his soft-soled shoes making not the slightest sound. He seemed to glide over the steel deck. "The night is dark in this part of the world."

"Yes, General, and cold," Nasim added. *He isn't Iranian, probably Syrian*, he thought.

His dark Arab eyes glowed in the pale light, his face thin and dark skin smooth. His narrow eyes gave his entire face a serious and frightening look. A man that Nasim both feared and respected. The Captain of *Kangan* worried about having a man such as this on his usually friendly ship.

"Are we on schedule for our rendezvous?"

"Yes, General. The sea is building some, but we will reach the designated point in time," Nasim assured.

"Is the welcome ready?" asked Shatrevor.

"We are prepared as you directed," the *Kangan's* Captain said proudly. "All we have left is to get the blessings of Allah."

"That, my dear Captain, we already have."

USS MIAMI SSN 755
280 Nautical Miles Northwest of Spitzbergen, Norway

At four hundred feet, the *Miami* turned invisible like part of the sea. She followed a box-shaped course, slowly cruising the cold deep water. At her stern, the pencil thick wires of her towed array sampled the ocean for any noise or frequency. In her bow, the powerful passive sonar sniffed the water for a hint of anything manmade.

Inside the hull, the warship's crew went about their routines. In the torpedo room, the weapons were withdrawn one at a time from the four tubes, each checked and its tube, then silently slid back in.

In the engine room, the nukes busily calibrated the various systems needed to monitor the reactor. The cold water helped the reactor operate better than in warmer climates. The evaporator and still churned out plenty of fresh water.

In the tiny galley, the cooks readied tonight's dinner. They worked quickly since the lobster tails went fast and not having enough to go around meant disaster. The cooks already suffered one major casualty. The ice cream machine broke down twice. Thankfully, the supply department came to the rescue with a replacement auger and bearing seal. In the Chief's quarters, a movie played on the large television.

All was quiet in the silently prowling American submarine, except for the conversation going on in the wardroom.

"You're sure?" Gellor asked.

"Yes sir, here, look again." Masters flipped back through the sheets of sonar screen printouts. "Here we pick up this merchant." His finger on the first page. "Big son of a bitch, by the sound she made. Two five-bladed screws, turning at thirty-five RPM. That would make her speed about six knots."

"Okay, I see that," Gellor nodded.

"Now once again, here is the overlay from the sounds we heard the other day." Masters flipped through the papers again. "This tiny trace, right here." He stabbed the faint yellow line. "That is something with two three-bladed screws."

"I agree." the XO moved his chair closer.

"Then the rest of the story you know. Suddenly these two screws start giving off a harmonic. Now the only way for that to happen would be for it to be submerged. Look now, at this line. This is a classic diesel engine line. The screws stay, but the line for the engines goes away and we get the harmonic from the same screws."

"But there is nothing in class."

Masters leaned back in his chair and rubbed his tired red eyes. "No sir, but this is a submarine. If it walks like a duck ... "

"Once again, what about yesterday?" the XO asked.

"Here again, the big merchant plods up along this point. What do we have? Those diesel lines again. The big guy slows and the diesel line goes away."

"Nothing wrong with our system?" Gellor asked.

"Negative, no way. I will grant you, this is all based on bottom bounce, but still this is gospel." Masters argued, "Now here you go with two high bearing rate traces that lead right up the big merchant's ass and then BLAMO."

Gellor sighed, "We have to find a hole in this thing. Who would be up to sinking ships and why?"

"Don't know who or why, but what I do care about is the fact that we're sitting on our hands, while some jackass tries to start World War Three," Masters added emphasis by slamming his hand on the table.

"Nothing on class? I don't understand that."

"I don't know either, but sure as hell, there is a diesel submarine somewhere up there."

"Okay Chief, you have at least one believer," Gellor said as he looked again at the traces leading to the dead container ship. "I'll wake the skipper and show him what you have."

Masters nodded. "That's all I ask."

The Pentagon
Office of the Chairman of the
Joint Chiefs of Staff

Malroy had already taken Ibuprofen gel-caps for his throbbing head. After a long day the British calmed down because of the direct call from the President to the Prime Minister. Problems from every branch, lay in the box on his desk. The Air Force needed an additional three tankers sent to the gulf. The Army dealt him a public relations nightmare. A junior Captain got drunk and decided to appear in a video in which she exposed her breasts, while partially still in uniform. *"Oh God, I'll have to make about five hundred television interviews for that one."*

On to the Marines. "At last some good news," he said out loud while reading a report of five new Marines who saved a family of five from their overturned RV. He picked up a sheet of his official stationary and wrote, *"Make the most of this one."* He scribbled his signature on the stationary and shoved the paper along with the message of the rescue into the public affairs officer's box. He was just about to pick up the folder labeled NAVY, when his door opened.

Commander Enright came into the office with a red folder held between the fingers of his right hand.

Malroy looked up. "What's up, Tim? Elvis been sighted¯ The Arabs decide giving us free oil would be the right thing to do?"

"Sir, we have another incident." Enright handed the folder to his boss.

"What now?" Malroy took the folder.

"Looks like we might have another ship down in the area where SWIFT was lost."

"What?"

The Commander cleared his throat. "Coast Guard satellite picked up a distress signal from a raft. The MINGO, a container ship out of New Orleans."

"Shit. We have any conformation on this?" Malroy rubbed his eyes.

"Nothing concrete yet, but she can't be raised on radio."

"What was her cargo?" Malroy opened the folder.

"One hundred and sixty container boxes with everything from Corvettes to furniture, oh and twenty-three-thousand gallons of a new type of jet fuel."

"New jet fuel?"

"Yes sir, I don't know much about it. Supposedly more environmentally friendly, whatever that means."

"How old is this data?"

"Three hours," Commander Enright responded.

"Okay, let's get a chopper over the area. I'll call the Russians." Malroy closed the folder.

"Who do we have in the area?"

"Just *Miami,*" Enright shrugged.

"Damn. That won't work. *Miami* is my trump card if things go to hell up there. I can't play that card yet." Malroy crossed his arms. "Call the Norwegians, have them get a chopper over there."

"Should we wait on a clearance from the Russians?" Enright asked.

"Hell with the Russians. That lifeboat can't keep those guys alive long. I'll bully them some - It'll be fine - Just get that chopper up."

Russian Patrol Ship *BARSUK*
84-Miles Northwest of the Kola Inlet

"Damn pig," Cheslav cursed. He tore off his hat and jacket, went to his tiny washbasin and filled it with cold water. He saw his face splattered with thick dots of blood in the mirror. In the warm air of the stateroom, the blood ran down his cheek and over his nose. He heard the flimsy door open behind him. “Who is it?” he called.

“Just me,” Rurik answered. “Did you give our guest, the Colonel, a good send-off?”

Cheslav turned back to the basin and dipped his hands in the water. “That fat ass bled all over me.” Cheslav threw the water on his face. “I must have shot him too close.”

“He is gone though?” Rurik asked in the dim light.

“Fell right over the side,” Cheslav answered as he scooped another handful of the red water up to his face.

“How close were you?”

“I had the gun right at the base of his fat head.” Cheslav rubbed at the blood on his face.

“Yes, that was too close,” Rurik agreed. “A meter is best.”

Cheslav smiled into the mirror. “How would you know?”

“Oh I don’t, but I will see.”

“What?” Cheslav reached for his towel.

Rurik brought a pistol from behind his back, centered the front sight on the young Lieutenant’s nose and gave the trigger a slight squeeze. A small hole appeared dead center. His head jerked back as a gush of blood and brain spattered the mirror behind him. His legs crumpled and his body dropped to the steel deck like a doll. He twitched and squirmed, but finally, stilled.

Captain Third Rank Rurik stepped closer careful to avoid the quickly expanding pool of blood that flowed and sloshed with the movement of the ship.

"Yes," Rurik said coldly and kicked Cheslav's feet inside the tiny washroom. "A meter is just about right."

Goslar, Germany

Carl Blevins wished lunch could have lasted longer due to the attention he received from Frau Shönberg. His distraction by her caused of SEAL Team Leader Lieutenant Michael Warren's great amusement.

She swished away after serving thin slices of hearty German bread. Her pastel green skirt fell just below her knees. When she walked, the skirt flowed around her perfect shape accenting all the parts men admired most.

The retired Chief, so struck by the vision, he poured an entire carafe of water in his lap. Red-faced, Blevins excused himself and went to his room.

Quickly changing into dry pants, Blevins set up his laptop computer. He slipped the CD into the drive and sat back.

On his screen, a series of files opened. The scanned images were perfect in every detail.

He focused on a word or phrase, but couldn't understand them. Blevins tapped the mouse button until another program opened inside the files. "Okay," he sighed. "Hope this translation program is worth the money I spent." One by one, he highlighted the files and moved them into the electronic brain of the translator program.

The converted files came out with clarity. Blevins's mouth fell open when he reached page ten.

**Norwegian Air Force
MK-43 Sea King
Search and Rescue Helicopter**

Captain Arna Odell scanned what little of the horizon the gray curtain of mist allowed. She guided the bouncing Sea King further north, the visibility closed in as if the air itself shrunk. Two hours into the mission, the crew chief spotted the edge of the ice pack.

The twenty-four year old Odell turned the fluttering machine on a Westerly course to follow the edge of the ice. She watched not only the ice, but also the current and thought, *a boat in that current could drift ten kilometers in a matter of hours.*

"Be alert," she said into the chopper's intercom. "We're almost in area." She slowed the chopper till it moved forward at a walking pace. Chunks of ice rolled in the growing swells. She leaned over, tapping her co-pilot and radar operator on the shoulder. "Anything?" she asked over the scream of the helicopter's engines.

"Nothing yet," the co-pilot shook his head.

Twenty minutes later, a bit of the dead ship passed under the stubby aircraft.

"Okay, we have some debris," she announced calmly. "Check everything you see," she ordered.

She guided the Sea King over the objects, then turned toward the ice. She planned to fly the field from each point of the compass.

"Contact," the co-pilot shouted. "Bearing ten degrees. Range is two-kilometers."

The wind strengthened so the young Captain swung the helicopter around. She pushed the throttle forward and pulled the collective up slightly.

Like a trained animal, the large chopper rose, dipped its nose and moved off. Odell slowed to a walking pace. The tops of bergs suddenly rose up in the front of the Sea King.

"There," the crew chief called. "Two-degrees left."

"What is it?" Odell asked over the intercom.

"Life boat. Can't see anyone on it. It's a fully contained unit."

"Okay, I'm coming around. Guide me in." Odell brought the helicopter to a hover before kicking the rudder. The Sea King spun around.

"Sixty meters. Come left another two-degrees. Forty meters to target. Descend to five meters."

With the Chief's guidance, the lumbering Sea King placed itself directly over the raft. The chief slid the door open and looked down.

The covered orange raft bobbed in the swells and the rainproof top folded and bucked from the helicopter's rotor-wash.

"I can't see any movement," the chief shouted into the intercom.

"Get the swimmer down in the basket." Odell fought to maintain the hover. A new wind came off the ice. The mist and wind caused several whiteouts, but Odell skillfully anticipated the wind and kept the chopper level. "Make it quick, we're running short of fuel."

U-761

November 15th

"I hear it," Becker whispered. He looked above

him to the gray lifeless sky. "I've never heard that noise before. Aircraft?"

"Can't tell," Hamlin whispered back.

"All stop," Becker ordered. His order was relayed in a hush to the Zentrale. Becker cocked his ear and listened. "Watch Officer," he called. "Man the Flak guns."

Within seconds, the gun crews came streaming up. Loaders released the handles on the water-tight ammunition containers. The guns removed locking pins and opened the receivers. Thirty seconds after his order, the guns were ready.

"No one fire until I give the order," Becker reminded them.

The gunners heard a strange beating sound that seemed to hit the frozen ocean and bounce back in the air. They looked nervously around, their gloved hands running over the triggers of their weapons.

"Hamlin, we don't want a fight with aircraft." Becker leaned his arms on the edge of the bridge.

"We should dive, Herr Kaleu."

"Not yet. I want to see just what this is," Becker whispered back.

"What about using our radar?" the third watch officer asked. "At least we should be able to tell where it is."

Becker thought a moment. "Risky."

"What isn't in this line of work, Herr Kaleu?" Hamlin asked cynically.

"Point taken," Becker smiled. "Raise the radar."

Hamlin leaned over to the voice tube and gave the order. With a quiet hum, the FuMO-30 antenna slid up the port side of the bridge.

"Damn thing looks like a mattress spring," Hamlin noted as he looked at the ugly antenna.

"It doesn't have to be pretty, it just has to work. Energize," Becker ordered.

Norwegian Air Force
MK-43 Sea King
Search and Rescue Helicopter

The basket came up slowly. The pencil thin wire wound steadily around the drum and the winch whined under the strain. The crew chief looked down at the rising basket. The swimmer hung on the outside of the mesh and tube steel basket. Inside, a shirtless man clung feebly to the frame. "We have a survivor," he called over the intercom. "Looks burned. Burns are pretty bad."

"Location of the basket?" Odell asked.

"Five meters," the chief responded.

The wind suddenly lifted the Sea King. Odell compensated by rotating the aircraft till it faced the rushing wind.

Odell tried to find the visual horizon. The ice moved closer. Then a slender dark shape appeared. She nudged the co-pilot and pointed at the object. "What's that?"

The co-pilot leaned forward toward the windscreen. His threat-warning receiver went off. "We're being illuminated."

Odell saw the flashing light and fought the instinct to swing the Sea King out of the way. "Chief, where's that basket?"

"At the door."

"We have a bogey out here," she called back. "Let me know when they're in."

Another warning light flashed above the control panel. "Shit, starboard drop tank at zero. Switching tanks." She reached up and toggled the switching valve. "Where are we, Chief?"

"All on board," he yelled over the rotor noise and shriek of the wind.

"Dropping starboard tank. We might need to maneuver fast." Her fingers flipped a series of switches.

The empty ten-foot oblong tank fell away. The wind caught the two stabilizing fins and forced the tank to nose over and head for the ocean.

"Door shut," the Chief panted over the intercom.

"Hang on back there." Odell lifted the collective slightly and the Sea King rose.

U-761

"We've been spotted," Hamlin yelled. "What the hell is that thing?"

"Steady," Becker shouted.

The insect-looking craft moved toward them. Becker more curious than alarmed, saw something fall away from the bottom of the craft. Its nose reared, then dipped. His eyes caught the tail. "Depth charge," Becker screamed. "Open fire."

Norwegian Air Force
MK-43 Sea King
Search and Rescue Helicopter

The shape cleared. At first, Odell thought this might be a fishing vessel. Then the mist opened and she sat back in her seat. "It's a submarine." Suddenly its conning tower seemed to blaze with puffs of orange and red.

Instinct took over and she yanked at the collective. The Sea King jerked as it rose. The first three rounds tore into the underside of the thin-skinned Sea King. One lodged in the wheel well, the next passed through the floor upward, impacting against the basket winch. The third severed the secondary hydraulic line before smashing the lighting control box. The next five 3.7 millimeter shells ricocheted off the helicopter's tough steel frame and spun upward into the cockpit. Two passed into the control panel, sending sparks and fragments around the flight deck. One shell ripped the collective control and the pilot's hand off. The final round entered Odell's thigh above the knee. The shell flattened as it met bone. The resulting hydraulic force exploded her entire leg in a sudden spray of red mist.

Other bullets arched toward the staggering Sea King, and found their marks at the base of the rotor. With the guide arm shot away, the spinning rotor lost balance. Another, deflected by the stainless steel rotor hub, careened back down, punching a fist size hole in the engine. The moving parts of the engine seized, a blast of friction-generated heat caused the yet unburned fuel in the engine to explode. A fireball engulfed the helicopter as it fell into the sea.

Chapter Twenty-Seven
Confusion

'The well-spring of war is the human heart."
-Stephen B. Luce, 1827-1917

Strategic Missile Assembly and Storage Area Number 3
Pechenga, Russia
November 15th

"Captain of the guard," Major Tosya bellowed. Impatiently, he kicked at the door and loosened the hinges from the wooden frame. On the second kick, the screw on the hinges split the wood, and the heavy door crashed to the concrete floor. Tosya slapped at the light switch in the colonel's dark quarters. The light flickered on, filling the room with a cold pale light.

A Lieutenant came around the door opening, his eyes wide. "Major."

Tosya looked up, his eyes filled with both rage and fear. "Lock the facility down."

"Major?"

"You ass. A warhead is missing."

"Where is the Colonel?" his young voice cracked.

Tosya spun on his heels. "He's the one who stole the damned thing."

"My God."

"Now get this place secured. I want a company at each entrance."

"Yes sir." The Lieutenant turned and ran out the door. An alarm screamed along the halls of the cave. Gates slammed down.

Major Tosya knew his next duty would more than likely cost him his life, but duty was duty. He walked to the communications center.

Inside the radio room, the major removed his cap. "Transmit emergency message November-Alpha-One."

Both of the on duty operators stared at the Major.

"Transmit the message," he screamed.

Goslar, Germany

Retired Chief Machinist Mate Carl Blevins checked again. The translation was the same each time. What appeared like formulas made no sense to him and some of the medical terms a bit fuzzy, but if these documents told the truth, even a half-truth, Carl Blevins looked into the window of eternal life.

Taking as many deep breaths as he could without passing out, Blevins forced himself to relax. His finger went numb while he tried to save the translated files. The computer seemed to take forever, but finally the blue bar completed its trek across the screen. Blevins ejected the CD and carefully placed in its case. He stood and walked quickly to the door and out into the narrow hall.

"Mike," Blevins tapped on the door. "Mike, come on man."

"Okay ... okay," came a voice through the door.

Blevins heard the lock turn and pushed the door open, nearly knocking Warren off his feet.

"Mike, we need to get back to Berlin now."

Warren stumbled back a few steps before finding his footing. "Slow down man. What's wrong?"

"Wrong? Nothing's wrong," Blevins huffed.. He moved closer to Warren, and pulled the CD from his pocket. "Mike, this is the biggest thing since ... since ... well, I don't know, but we gotta get this to Malroy."

"What is it?"

"You really want to know?"

Warren shook his head. "Yes, but I can't."

"Well it sure sucks to be you," Blevins smiled. "Get you ass in gear, Lieutenant."

"Okay, I'll be down in five," Warren threw on the shirt.

Blevins grabbed the keys to the silver BMW. "I'll drive." Blevins rushed out the door, shutting it roughly behind him.

"Hey Carl?" Warren called as the door clanked shut. "Carl? Oh Jesus." Warren shoved on his other shoe and followed Blevins out the door.

Russian Patrol Ship *BARSUK*
130-Miles Northwest of the Kola Inlet

"Sir." the steward said quietly. "Dinner is being served in the wardroom."

Captain Third Rank Rurik kept his eyes on the horizon. The patrol vessel rose and fell in the slight swell of the Arctic Ocean. "I'll be down in a moment. Tell the other officers they may begin."

"Yes sir," the steward answered. "Sir, I can't find Lieutenant Cheslav. He does not answer at his stateroom."

"He retired for the evening. Save him a plate if you will."

"Very good sir," the Steward said with a slight bow.

Rurik turned back, as the bow rose and fell.

The Kremlin
Moscow, Russia

The message from Strategic Missile Assembly and Storage Area Number 3 flashed by a secure satellite and went directly to the newly appointed Director of Strategic Forces. In the style of the old Soviet Union, the message was reviewed and its validity weighed. Plans for this had been rehearsed in the old republic and no one thought to update the plan. For three minutes, confusion reared its ugly head. The watch officer, a young Captain from Tbilisi had never been briefed on the plan. Had he acted as the plan directed, he would issue an immediate alert, Russian forces would have been instantly placed on alert condition, and fighters scrambled and submarines leave port with no further orders. NATO would have reacted in kind, and once again, the world would be teetering on the edge.

Like a game of hot potato, the message made its way up the chain. No one wanted the blame for keeping it any longer than their duties dictated.

Ten minutes after its receipt, Vitenka had the

message in his hands, and called the heads of the respective services to his office.

He removed his glasses, folded them carefully and laid them on top of the message.

"What else do we know?" Vitenka asked calmly.

Admiral Ryshenko, Director of Fleet Operations spoke first, "We believe the missing warhead to be on the patrol ship *Barsuk.*"

Vitenka nodded. "Where would they take the warhead?"

Silence … Vitenka paced. "That is a question we must answer. Is there a foreign influence? Is this an act of theft —an act of terrorism —or is this revenge?"

Ryshenko lifted his head. "Sir, I take full responsibility for this."

"That is admirable," Vitenka said. "However, it does not help in the least. We are not here to assign blame. We need to prevent a worldwide disaster and possibly a nuclear exchange. The stakes are far above one man's career or life. We are all to blame for this. We need to solve the problem or at least contain it."

"We need to destroy the ship," Air Force General Norslav hissed. "It is always the Navy causing problems."

Ryshenko's eyes narrowed and his fists clenched.

Vitenka could see the storm coming and like the hand of God, halted it. "This is not the time," he shouted. His sudden anger startled those around his desk. "I need answers, not bickering."

Norslav seemed stunned. "Yes, sir," he answered meekly. "I can have a strike force over the ship in under thirty minutes."

"What of our agreement with the Americans?" asked Commander of the Army, Major General Trofimoff.

"Ah." Vitenka raised his finger in the air. "Another item we must throw into the equation."

"We must tell them," Ryshenko said.

"No," countered Norslav. "That would cause a panic. NATO would over-react."

"We must then be covert," Trofinoff said quietly.

Vitenka's brows rose. "You have an idea, General?"

"We allowed NATO to conduct a search and rescue operation today. How can they refuse us the same courtesy?"

Norslav shook his head. "That was a single aircraft. The chance of a single aircraft destroying the ship is slim. A single aircraft might not even find *Barsuk.*"

"Can we destroy the ship?" Trofinoff asked.

Norslav thick brows rose. "Why not?"

"What about the warhead?" the Army commander asked.

"The warhead is from one of our SS-N-20 missiles. An explosion should not cause a nuclear yield. It would probably sink to the bottom," Ryshenko explained.

"Probably?" Norslav huffed.

"What about another ship or submarine?" Trofinoff shrugged.

"The story of a search and rescue mission would not hold up if we send a submarine," Vitenka pointed out. "But a warship could work."

"It would have to be a fast ship—well armed," Trofinoff said in his quiet, yet forceful voice.

"The Captain must also have a good head on his shoulders," Air Force General Norslav said, waving his finger in the air.

"The Destroyer *Strogiy* can put to sea in two hours," Ryshenko declared.

All eyes looked at the Admiral. "*Strogiy?* asked Norslav.

"Yes, a *Kashin* class guided missile Destroyer. She is both fast and well armed and guard ship of the Northern Fleet this week. Her crew is ready."

"And the Captain?" Trofinoff asked.

"He is my son," Ryshenko said proudly.

Vitenka opted. "What if we fail?"

A hush surrounded the men in the office.

Vitenka broke the silence, "We cannot win this situation, gentlemen. We have to plan for the best way to lose. Either way, men will die."

"We have to act now," Norslav declared. "That ship must be stopped or put on the bottom."

Major General Trofinoff spoke next. "It would be criminal to not inform the Americans if we do not catch or kill this pirate.

"They will forgive us for many things, but not something like this. We can fool ourselves and each other, but we all know where a nuclear warhead will be used and by whom."

Vitenka nodded his agreement. "Then it is settled. Admiral Ryshenko, get the *Strogiy* to sea as soon as possible. Talk to your son personally. This may the most vital mission a Russian warship has undertaken in all her history."

U-761

A cloud of acrid cordite seemed glued to air around the U-boat's bridge. Some in the watch coughed. Finally, the wind carried the cloud of burnt gunpowder aft away from the exposed conning tower. The U-boat altered course south to avoid the last of the flaming Sea King's wreckage. With an angry hiss, the flames drowned and the waves from U-761's wake washed over them.

The gun crews quickly reloaded their weapons. Fresh magazines passed up the hatch replaced the used ammunition, spent shell casing kicked over the side.

"What the hell was it?" Hamlin asked.

Becker could only shake his head. "I don't know, but I think they were alone." he muttered. "Hamlin, take the watch."

Hamlin nodded and stepped to the side. Becker clambered into the Zentrale.

Edel met him at the ladder. "Captain, we need to talk. Quietly."

Becker pulled his brown jacket off his shoulders, and lifted his chin toward an empty area near the ballast control valves. "Over there."

In the somewhat secluded space Edel turned. "There is a problem."

"Oh good, another we can add to the list," Becker sighed.

"Our food," Edel took his greasy cap from his head.

"What?"

"I just talked with Berdy. The smoked meats are decaying by the hour."

"Decaying?" Becker asked as he pushed his cap back on his head.

"Not so much decaying, but crumbling." Edel lifted the cap from his matted thin hair. "That's not all. The canned and jarred foods are turning to powder."

Inwardly Becker searched for answers. "How much food do we have left?"

Edel drew in a deep breath of the stale submarine air. "Another week at the most."

"Talk to Berdy, have him stretch what we have."

Edel nodded and moved off aft toward the small galley.

Becker made his way forward to the wardroom. Volker sat at the small table across from Major Gerlach. Volker had the master sight for the bridge taken apart. He cleaned the precision ground optics. "Volker, can you excuse us," Becker sat at the head of the small table.

"Of course, Captain," Volker gathered the delicate parts in his hands.

"What is it, Captain?" Gerlach asked curiously.

Becker waited till Volker moved out of earshot. He leaned forward till his face inches from Gerlach's. "How long?"

"I don't know," the Major rasped.

"I think you do," the Captain hissed. "I think you're still running your experiment."

"No, Captain." Gerlach sat back. "I already have all the information I need."

"Tell me what you know."

"I know what you know."

"Tell me what you know. Tell me what is going on."

Gerlach smiled slightly. "I know that we are alive. The *Forever Project* was a success. But I wonder how successful."

"Go on," Becker urged, his voice just short of threatening.

"I think we slept for a number of years."

"How many?"

"I estimate twenty—maybe thirty, maybe more. Time seems to be catching up though."

"What will happen?" Becker asked.

"I don't know. Maybe it will stabilize. Of course, it could continue at a faster rate, each man ages faster each day. I just don't know. It could depend on the man, his health ... I just don't know."

"What about our food?"

Gerlach raised his tired yellowing eyes. "I wondered about that myself. Anything organic or natural might age at an accelerated rate, but again I don't know."

"What about you?"

Gerlach smiled. "I'm giving myself morphine injections twice a day. It takes the edge off." Gerlach lifted his hand. "You see, Captain, my disease was also asleep, but now it too is alive and well."

Becker looked at the hand, the color of old parchment. The veins formed small lumps of pale blue, and the fingernails a sickly yellow. "Major."

Gerlach lowered his hand. "There is good news though. Frimunt is doing well. The accelerated aging has also accelerated his healing."

Becker didn't care for Gerlach as a man, but as a person, he did not like to see him suffer. Though he had seen death many times, he forced himself to ask the next question. "How long do you think you have?"

"Another question I cannot answer. A few weeks—less, who knows?"

"What can I do for you?" Becker asked kindly.

Gerlach chuckled. "Nothing, Captain. I hope I see this to the end. This is like a novel you just can't stop reading. You have to know how it ends." Gerlach shivered, then pulled the dirty gray blanket up to his chest. "Tell me Captain, what are your plans?"

"We'll hug to the ice going east. Hopefully, they will have lost us by then. We'll turn south just above Norway, and maybe less activity there. I think the West is blocked. The Denmark Straits are too much of a choke point."

"Then what?" Gerlach asked.

Becker stood slowly. "One miracle at a time."

Headquarters of the Russian
Northern Fleet
***Polyarnyy*, Russia**
November 16th

The order to sortie was flashed via satellite. According to procedure, the order went to Northern Fleet Deputy of Communications and the message and its intent understood as a fleet action. Accordingly, the order went out.

Even with the Soviet Union a mere memory, the doctrines and procedures remained. The Soviets knew if hostilities broke out, their bases came up on the A list of NATO targets. All combat ships were put to sea.

The rotting piers vibrated when the long still warships moved to a pre-determined hold point and awaited orders. Even the massive and beautiful battle cruiser *Peter the Great*, cast off her moorings and slid into the channel.

Within thirty minutes of the order, thirteen Russian men-o-war set a course north-northwest. Sixteen more got underway within the next two hours. Luckily, the order addressed the surface fleet. Sailors on the submarine's berth nearby, watched in amazement.

Office of Admiral Ryshenko
The Kremlin
Moscow, Russia

In his office, Admiral Ryshenko punched at the buttons on his phone for the eighth time. The female recording told him the lines were busy and try again later. He looked at his watch, then to a picture of his son and himself. Taken when the boy was five, it showed a much younger Ryshenko holding the boy in his arms. In the background stood his first ship, the gun cruiser *Admiral Ushakov*. Gently, he picked up the picture, ran his fingers over the boy's face. Sighing deeply, he put the picture back down and again picked up the phone.

The Autobahn, Germany

Mike Warren saw combat in Iraq and Afghanistan. He led and as part of a number of classified operations, but today was the day he thought he would die.

The BMW flew down the pavement as if the laws of nature were but suggestions. Warren cowered in the passenger's seat, his fists clenched on the seatbelt. "Carl, for God's sake, ease off."

"Come on Lieutenant, I can do this with one hand, see," Blevins held one hand up.

Warren went white. "Damn it, Carl."

"Relax, Mike. I got this under control. I'm in a foreign country. I've never driven—let's see—one-hundred and thirty miles an hour before. It's dark and I'm half-drunk. What could go wrong?"

Warren reached for the glove compartment. In the dark of the car, he felt around. Carl looked over to see this tough SEAL clutching a rosary.

"Mom told me these would come in handy." His fingers ran over the beads.

"Can you call ahead and get me a secure line to Malroy set up?" Blevins asked.

"Sure thing. I'll also have a pair of clean boxers waiting on me." Warren whined.

Carl glanced at his passenger. "Wimp."

Chapter Twenty-Eight
Duty

"Blessed be the Lord my strength, which teacheth my hands to war and my finger to fight."
-Psalm CXXXXIV

The Pentagon
Washington, DC.
November 16th

At just before sunup, streams of information fed into the various offices of the United States Military. The bits of information fit together like a puzzle. Computers handled some of the data, the remainder added by humans. The picture that emerged sent a shock through the halls. Secure phones around the nation rang. Pagers found those not close to a phone, and notified leaders along the chains of command. The Russian fleet was on the move.

Chairman of the Joint Chiefs of Staff was again in his office scarcely forty-five minutes after the orbiting surveillance bird code named *Key Hole* snapped images of Russian warships headed for open water.

Admiral Malroy's mood matched the November morning - dark and threatening.

"Where the hell are the others?" he demanded.

"Enroute," the on duty watch officer answered nervously.

"The Secretary?" Malroy grumbled.

"ETA is about ten minutes."

"Damned politicians," Malroy gulped at his first cup of coffee. "Get me a line right to Vitenka's office."

"Yes, sir, already taken care of," the watch officer announced.

"The President?"

The Watch Officer, a newly promoted Navy Captain, shrugged his shoulders. "I don't know, sir. I believe he is Air Force One."

"Shit. That figures," Malroy sighed. "We have comms?"

"God, I hope so," the Captain sighed.

Malroy laughed. "Don't worry, Captain, I'm not usually this big an asshole."

Russian Patrol Ship *BARSUK*
60 Miles From the Edge of the Ice Pack

"Captain, may I ask what are our orders?" the Navigator asked.

Rurik remained on the bridge through the night. "You may not."

"Sir, we are due for communication with Fleet."

"We will maintain radio silence," Rurik hissed.

"Captain, this is highly unusual," the Navigator swallowed hard.

"What is unusual is your attitude,' Rurik barked. "Never question me."

"Yes, sir," he said and returned to the navigation charts.

"Maintain this course and speed for another hour then slow to five knots," Rurik ordered.

Iranian Cargo Ship *Kangan*
25 Miles from *Barsuk*

"It is a great morning," Shatrevor entered the shabby rusted pilothouse.

"Yes it is, General." Captain Nasim smiled.

The terrorist stepped forward, putting his rough olive hand on the Captain's shoulder. "Today we become heroes. Today is a final step to ending the blight on our people."

"Everything is ready, General."

"Good. You have done well, Captain."

"Allah has smiled on us, General."

Shatrevor nodded. "That he has. I am going to look below decks."

"The rendezvous will be in about two hours," Nasim added.

Shatrevor nodded again and stepped down the ladder. On the main deck, the terrorist checked his watch. He then looked into the gray skies and hoped the fog and mist would lift.

Indeed glad the sea calmed, he remembered the first three days on this miserable hunk of steel. His stomach and head finally got used to the constant roll and pitch of the ship.

From the main deck, General Shatrevor strolled to a hatchway. The heavy steel along with years of corrosion, made him strain some, but the hatch creaked open. He pushed till a latch caught and held the hatch open. Shatrevor braced himself against the slight roll of the converted water tanker, then climbed carefully down the next set of steps.

The lower deck a dark cave-like place, reeked of bilge water, diesel and human sweat. The only light came from a string of tired looking bulbs. Shatrevor moved carefully aft. He heard muffled voices and the whir of machinery as he neared the main cargo area.

The light grew brighter and the voices became more distinct. He came to the main cargo deck. Chained to eyebolts along the deck, sat nine T-72 main battle tanks. The squat menacing looking tanks had been painted to match the dull green of the *Kangan's* side.

Around the tanks, the Army detachment checked the gun tubes, tested turret operations and did the last of the main gun ammunition load.

As Shatrevor emerged from the dim light, the tank crews came to attention. A Sergeant rushed forward and gave a stiff salute. "General, we are ready for action."

Shatrevor returned the salute. "I am proud of you all. Today you become instruments of Allah. Your aim will be true and your hearts will show no mercy."

The Sergeant dropped the salute. "We have rehearsed many times. My men are ready to do their duty."

"Show me," Shatrevor stated quietly.

"Certainly, General." The Sergeant trotted to his tank. "Again men," he called with his hands cupped around his mouth.

Men ran to their assigned tanks. Turrets hummed while they traversed to their assigned sectors.

Shatrevor walked over to the Sergeant's tank. "All angles are covered?"

"Yes sir. The ship's crew will be there," the Sergeant pointed to the five sailors standing along the bare steel. "When you give the command, they will use sledge hammers to knock out the pins you see holding the false bulkhead. The bulkheads will fall and my tanks will open fire."

Shatrevor shook his head. "Impressive."

The Sergeant continued, "Each tank has an assigned target. Tanks one and three will target the weapon system. Tanks four and five will take out the bridge and radio. Tanks two and six will use sabot rounds to punch through the hull."

The general looked puzzled. "What of the other tanks?"

The sergeant smiled. "Those gun tubes are loaded with canister shot."

"Canister?"

"Yes sir. Like a huge shot gun. Each round contains five-hundred steel pellets. These tanks will sweep the decks."

Shatrevor gasped, "My God, we are a battleship."

U-761
15 Miles from *Barsuk*

Becker stood over his shoulder while Hamlin plotted the course south. "No contacts in the past eleven hours, sir," the Oberbootsmann reported. "I think we're safe for the time being."

Becker sighed, "We'll see."

"Do we use the radar?" Hamlin asked.

"No, I don't want any transmissions leaving the boat."

"I agree, Captain."

"Well, here we go. Helm, come to course one-seven-seven."

"Where are we going, sir?" Hamlin asked.

"Home, I hope."

The Pentagon
Washington, DC.

"Who can give me a guess as to what the hell is going on?" Malroy asked in none too nice a manner.

CIA liaison Brad Dilmer spoke first, "All we have are pictures. Nothing even hinted at this."

"Okay, since we don't know anything, let's see what we do know," Malroy sighed.

"We know the bulk of the Russian surface fleet sailed last night," the Chief of Naval Operations answered.

"Where are they going?" Malroy asked.

"We did get a request for the Russians to conduct a search and rescue mission," answered Deputy Under Secretary for Readiness, Matthew LaFabin.

"Rescue?" Malroy sat up in his chair.

"Yes, sir. The Russians claim one of their fisheries ships caught fire and about to sink off Murmansk."

"The story checks out?" Malroy asked.

"We didn't check, sir."

"Makes not one bit of sense," Malroy grumbled.

The door to the situation room opened. An Air Force Major entered, a red folder tucked under his arm. "Excuse me, sir," his voice accented with a hint of New Jersey home.

"Yes, Major?" Malroy asked.

The major opened the folder and read. "At 18:20 Zulu, the Norwegians report their search and rescue helicopter - a Sea King is now missing."

"The bastards shot it down," roared Army General Underwood.

"What bastards would that be, General?" Chief of the Air Force Liliton asked.

"The Russians. Who else?" Underwood shot back.

"We don't know that." Malroy slapped the table with his palm. "It is dangerous to assume anything right now," Malroy warned.

"I hate to throw a wrench in an already broken machine," the Chief of Naval Operations interrupted.

"Christ, what now?" Malroy asked.

"We tracked an Iranian tanker for the last week. As of last night, she was positioned seventy-five miles from the ice pack."

"Holly hell. What is it doing that far north?" Underwood asked.

"It's not uncommon for Iranians to move up and down the coast. They do a lot of trading with the Russians, the French and even the Germans," CIA liaison Dilmer explained. "I'll grant you, a tanker that far out of the shipping lanes though, that's interesting."

"Come on people. Let's get this puzzle worked out," Malroy boomed.

"Whatever is going on, we can't sit on our hands,"

Marine Corps General Thomas Skinner observed. "They moved and we need to. At least a *stop gap* force."

Malroy sat back in his chair. "I agree," he said quietly. "CNO, put the fleet in motion. I'll brief the Secretary and the President."

The intercom buzzed. "Shit," Malroy swore. He sat back up and pushed the button. "What?" he snapped.

"Sir," came a business like female voice. "There is a call over the secure line."

"Unless it's the President of the United States or Russia, I'm busy," Malroy shouted at the phone.

"Sir," the voice responded calmly. "It's a Chief Blevins, calling from Berlin. He says it is most urgent."

"I am busy now. I'll get back to him." Malroy pushed the button severing the intercom. "Okay, get the fleet to sea. Slow and steady - nothing that will be alarming. The rest of you, I want a quiet deployment of forces."

"What about the British?" Underwood asked. "They're already pissed."

"I'll talk to them," the Chairman shrugged. "General Liliton, get on the horn with NATO, give them the facts as we know. We are adjourned."

Russian Battle Cruiser
Peter the Great
25 miles off Lista Lanka Island

The ships of the Northern Fleet bobbed around in the heavy swells, and one by one, they headed back to their berths.

On the deck of *Peter the Great*, Captain First Rank

Zinin enjoyed the feel of the icy breeze. "The air is always fresher at sea," he called to the shivering miserable bridge watch. He chuckled at the sight of the helmsman and lookouts. "First time at sea?" he asked.

The seasick watches could only nod.

"Well, you'll get your sea legs. How long have you been aboard?" he asked one of the lookouts.

"Two years," the young sailor answered.

"Two years?" Zinin's eyes went wide with amazement. "You've never been to sea?"

"No, sir," the lookout managed before his breakfast rushed back up his throat.

"Has it been that long since we've put to sea," Zinin wondered aloud.

Those on the bridge were not the only miserable souls wallowing about in the ship. In the machinery spaces, the engineers were both seasick and leaderless. Several of the key Officers had not made it to the ship in time for the emergency sailing. The young ratings did their best, but a lack of training and maintenance showed.

The main lube oil pump for the port shaft lost pressure. As less and less oil was being delivered to the shaft bearing, heat began to build. An alarm sounded indicating the problem, but twice it shut off. The Engineering Officer hadn't sent, instructions down from what the sailors called the ivory tower. Soon the lube pump failed, the packing and seals broke down and blocked oil flow. Each of the ship's two propeller shafts, rated at 75,000 horsepower. Within three minutes the shaft bearings to turn red hot. An alarm sounded, but quickly silenced. Steam and smoke filled the shaft space as the spinning shaft generated friction and the surrounding steel burned. At two thousand degrees, the steel of the shaft softened. Centrifugal force caused the shaft to bow and wobble developed. The wobble transmitted its force through the hull and the entire 24,000-ton ship shook. At three-thousand degrees, the shaft melted in a flash of super heated plasma. The air ignited in a thunderous blast.

On the bridge, Captain Zinin felt the rumble am instant before a blast erupted from the stern of his ship. A plume of water shot high above the tripod-like superstructure. The ship lurched to port.

"My god, we've been torpedoed," he shouted when the wall of water rained down on the wheelhouse and bridge. "Signal Fleet," he screamed over the roar of escaping steam. Smoke billowed from the stern. "Shut the flood control doors," he ordered.

Peter the Great listed further. Reports of damage and casualties came in. Then there was silence as the power failed. Both reactors had scrammed. In such situations, the diesels started automatic operation of auxiliary generators. The ship sailed with three of the four generators out of order. The fourth came to life, but shut down when the generator overloaded.

Most of the ships heard her broken communications about a torpedo. Two *Udaloy* Destroyers turned and pounded the water with *Horse Jaw* sonar. They passed the floundering battle cruiser at flank speed. The first Destroyer *Simferopol* suddenly slowed. In a flash of light and smoke, she fired her anti-submarine rockets.

The rockets arched mere pinpoints then they nosed over and fell. Unlike depth charges, the RBU warhead would only detonate if it struck the hull of a submarine.

In a well-defined chevron pattern, the warheads fell. They impacted the water and sank. Three struck underwater rocks at fifty-meters and exploded. Geysers of furious water bubbled to the surface. The other warheads sank harmlessly into the mud.

The Kremlin
Moscow, Russia

Admiral Vitenka took the reports and tried to make some sense of it all. "Who ordered the fleet to sail?" he demanded.

"The signal was misunderstood," Deputy Minister of Communications Averin shouted above the other equally loud voices.

"It is not important why the fleet sailed," Ryshenko fumed. "We have been attacked."

"If that is so, then by whom?" Vitenka asked.

"Admiral, are you already such a politician that you do not see the obvious?" Ryshenko blurted. "The damned Americans."

"What proof do you have, Admiral?" Vitenka hissed.

"I have a sinking cruiser and five-hundred dead Russian sailors."

"Why would the Americans suddenly attack our ships?" Army General Trofinoff asked.

"Why is not important," Air Force General Norslav shouted. "We have done everything the Americans wanted. We always have and each time, we end up taking it in the ass."

Vitenka shouted back. "Would you have us take a path of no return only to find out later it was all a mistake or accident? As a Russian you can think with your heart, but as a General, you must think with your head."

"We still must be on guard," Trofinoff observed.

"I will grant you that," Vitenka nodded. "We will maintain our fleet at their present location. Order the alert levels raised to level three."

"What of our missile submarines?" Ryshenko asked.

Vitenka thought a moment. "No, those we keep in port. The Americans will surely see them as they pass to their dive points. That could lead to a further escalation."

"What does this new President plan to do?" Norslav asked.

"Hopefully, exactly what I tell him to."

Aboard the Russian *Kashin* Class Destroyer *Strogiy*

Her raked bow sliced through the growing sea, sending up clouds of spray. The ship rocked and shuddered as she smashed into the oncoming waves.

"Captain, we received orders on the fleet emergency frequency," the communications officer announced as he stumbled onto the bridge.

"Well, read it," the Captain urged.

“Missile cruiser, *Peter the Great*, has been torpedoed by an unknown submarine. Alert level is therefore raised to three. All units are to defend themselves as deemed necessary.”

“Is that all?” the Captain asked.

“Yes, sir.” The officer wiped his face on his sleeve.

“Very well. I ...”

“We have gained a new contact.” a report from the radar compartment. “Contact bears zero-two-zero. Course is three-five-eight. Range to contact is five thousand meters.”

The Captain slowly walked to the plotting table. “Quartermaster, bring the ship to action stations.”

Chapter Twenty-Nine

The Day of Dying

A Pale horse: and him that sat on him was Death.
-Revelation, IV,8

U-761

November 16th

Becker emerged out of the bridge hatch, his nerves tensed.

"The sky is clearing, Herr Kaleu," Volker said.

"Yes, it seems so. Get the flak guns manned."

"Aye sir," Volker stepped to the voice pipe at the front of the bridge.

U-761's Commander then walked aft to the flak deck. He looked astern. Squinting in the haze, Becker could still see the ribbon-like line of ice. A half hour later, the clouds of fog and mist evaporated.

Edel came topside. "Captain, the batteries will no longer hold a full charge. The plates corrode faster than I've ever seen. We need to change the electrolytes."

"How long will it take?"

"Four hours minimum, but that's not what worries me."

"I know. The batteries will take most of our fresh water."

"Yes sir," Edel shivered.

"I want you to find Baldric. Have the torpedo gang load our acoustic torpedo."

"Can I ask why?"

Becker pulled Edel close. "I don't think it is 1944. I don't know what year it is. For all we know, it may be 1965. We'll have to use every trick we can to get home. Damn it. I don't even know if we have a home."

"I've noticed things," Edel noted. "The air seems different and the sea has changed. Nothing makes sense."

"How's the crew?" Becker asked.

"They've changed somehow. Matured? I ... I don't know, but they still do their duties."

"I know they do, Chief. I just hope it's all worth it."

Russian Patrol Ship *BARSUK*

"Radar holds a new contact, Captain. Bearing is three-four-eight," the Combat Systems Officer reported.

"Three-four-eight?" Rurik asked. "Are you sure?"

"Yes Captain, target bears three-four-eight."

"That is the wrong direction," Rurik mumbled to himself.

"Is this part of an exercise we're conducting?" the Navigator asked.

"When I tell you, you'll know," Rurik snapped. "Helm, come left."

"We have another radar contact. This contact bears one-seven-eight. Moving slow and closing our position."

"There you are," Rurik smiled. "Helm, zero the rudder. Engine room, make turns for three knots."

The Communications Officer appeared on the bridge. "Captain, we received some strange messages from Fleet and from the Destroyer *Strogiy*."

"Of course you are," Rurik yelled. "We're playing the role of the terrorist ship."

"So, this is all an exercise?" the Communicator asked suspiciously.

"Why else would Fleet use this bucket of rust?" Rurik lied.

"What role does the *Peter the Great* play?"

Rurik looked puzzled. "What do you mean?"

"The missile cruiser *Peter the Great* has been torpedoed and is in sinking condition."

"The Destroyer *Strogiy* has ordered us to stop and surrender or they will open fire."

"Visual contact," the bridge lookout yelled. "Large freighter off the port quarter."

"Officer of the deck, close on that ship," Rurik ordered.

"Is this also part of the exercise?" the Communicator asked.

Before Rurik could answer, another report came in. "Bridge, this is electronic surveillance, we are being painted by targeting radar."

"Seems the good guys have caught us," Rurik smiled.

All stop," he ordered. "What about the contact to the North?"

There was a pause. "Captain, contact has faded."

"Faded?" Rurik asked.

"Aye sir, faded."

"What was the last range?" Rurik asked, somewhat alarmed.

"Range at time of loss was two-five hundred meters," came the answer.

"A contact cannot just fade unless ..." Reality hit Rurik as if he had been punched. "Distance to the freighter?"

"Two-thousand meters."

"We've been found by a submarine," he shouted. "Man, action stations."

"But sir, the exercise?" the communications officer asked.

"A submarine is not part of the drill. Now get to your station."

Iranian Cargo Ship *Kangan*

"There she is, Captain," General Shatrevor smiled. "Bring us alongside."

"Certainly, General. And with your permission, I will have the deck crew make ready to receive our package."

Shatrevor nodded his approval.

U-761

"It appeared out of nowhere, Captain," Volker said between deep breaths.

"What was it?" Becker asked.

"Small warship - maybe a frigate. I've never seen a ship like it."

"Boat is steady at three-zero meters, Captain," Edel reported.

Becker stepped behind Edel. "The batteries?"

Edel looked over his shoulder at Becker. "Forty-percent and dropping fast. We can't be down long."

"Herr Kaleu, I have picked up another ship," the hydrophone operator reported. "Sounds like a freighter. Two four-bladed screws. Closing."

Becker's mind worked on instinct. *I can't stay down long and can't maneuver. That leaves only one thing,* he thought.

"Man, battle stations. Chief, bring us up to periscope depth."

"Periscope depth, aye," Edel answered. "Five degrees rise on both planes."

Russian *Kashin* Class Destroyer
Strogiy

"Target is stopped sir," came the report. "The merchant continues to close."

"Status of the missile battery?" the Captain asked.

"Missiles are still being fueled."

"What the hell is taking so long?"

"Captain, we sailed before the weapons technicians came aboard," the Weapons Officer reported.

"Get people on the fueling detail now," the Captain bellowed. "Take the sonar operators."

Russian Patrol Ship *BARSUK*

"Action stations are manned sir," the Watch Officer on the bridge reported.

Rurik did not reply. "Distance to the freighter?" he asked.

"Five hundred meters," the Navigator replied. "Sir, shouldn't we maneuver?"

"New visual contact. It's the *Strogiy,*" the look out announced.

Now Rurik paid attention. "Damn."

"Periscope off the starboard bow," another lookout yelled wildly.

"Get me a firing solution now," Rurik yelled. He looked aft. The Iranian ship was painfully slow. "Rig the hoist over the hold."

"What?" the Watch officer yelled.

"You heard me. Get it done."

"Captain, this is not an exercise is it?" the Navigator snarled. "What the hell are you up to?" he demanded.

"Solution set," a voice came over the intercom.

The navigator moved toward Rurik. In a flash, Rurik's pistol came up and fired.

The navigator let out his last breath as the bullet dug into his chest. He fell slowly to his knees, then forward, his face slammed into the steel deck.

"Captain," the Helm screamed.

Rurik spun to face him and squeezed the trigger. The helmsman's neck spurted a thick red stream of blood. The dying man crumpled.

Another bullet found its mark just above the sternum of the Weapons Officer. It passed through his body losing little force until it smashed into his spinal cord.

The Quartermaster stepped toward the bridge door,

and the pistol cracked again. The back of his head came apart under the impact.

The freighter moved closer, and Rurik could see men on the deck ready with lines. He saw one of the davits move over the side, a heavy canvas sling dangling from a hook.

Iranian Cargo Ship *Kangan*

"Another warship on the starboard beam," Nasim cried out.

The smile left Shatrevor's face. "What?"

"She is making speed this way," a voice called out.

Shatrevor picked up his two-way radio. "Sergeant, are you ready?"

"We are ready," a voice crackled back.

"We now have two warships to deal with, can you handle it?"

"Allah will guide us, General."

U-761

"Another warship - high speed, closing," Veldmon whispered.

Becker swung the periscope to the left. "I need a bearing."

"Bearing is two-seven-eight moving left."

Becker moved the scope to the bearing as the Russian destroyer topped the horizon.

"Captain, I estimate new contact making thirty-knots," Volker reported.

The scope filled the cross hairs with the *Barsuk.* "She must be re-supplying from that freighter," he said calmly. "Volker, set up a solution for the first and second ships with tubes one-two and three. Set up tubes four-five-six for the new warship. We'll launch the forward tubes, turn and shoot from the stern." Becker took his eye off the scope and wiped the sweat from his brow. "Set the stern torpedoes for magnetic detonation."

Russian Patrol Ship *BARSUK*

Rurik, with his pistol still in his hand, leaped from the bridge wing to the main deck. The sides of the Iranian ship loomed closer. He trotted aft to the main loading hatch. Three sailors cranked the winch that opened the steel door. "Move your asses," he screamed.

The sight of the pistol encouraged the sailors to double their efforts. They looked up just as the freighter ground against their ship.

With the sling over the hatch, Rurik motioned for the davit operator to lower the cable and sling into the hold.

"Secure the box in that sling," Rurik shouted.

"Captain, what is happening?" one of the sailors shouted over the sound of the grinding steel.

His answer came in the form of a bullet in the center of his chest. He collapsed on the deck as blood flowed around his body.

Rurik looked at the other sailor. "Do you have any questions?"

The sailor jumped into the hold, wrapped the heavy sling around the box, fastened the clips and secured the box, he then stepped back under the cover of the deck.

Rurik waved his arms and the box lifted slowly from the hold. Again, he turned and looked at the bridge, and saw a dark bearded man. He smiled and waved. The man returned his smile. Rurik cupped his hands around his mouth. "I am ready to come aboard," he shouted.

The bearded man laughed and shrugged his shoulders, while the freighter's blunt bow opened the distance from the bobbing patrol ship.

"Bastards," he screamed. He lifted the pistol and emptied the remainder of the magazine at the freighter.

Rage overtook him and he dashed for the bridge, he entered the wheelhouse and went to the weapons control station, and almost fell when he slipped on the blood slick deck. He flipped the switch that powered the remote operated 76mm cannon.

U-761

"Weapons set, ship is ready," Volker announced.

"Commence firing," Becker ordered.

At Volker's direction, the torpedoes launched. Volker held the chronometer in front of his face, watching the seconds tick till it came time for the next launch. Eighteen seconds later, tube four sent its torpedo into the sea. "Tube four away," he shouted.

"Helm left hard rudder. Both motors ahead flank," Becker barked as he swung the scope toward the onrushing warship. "Come on, turn," he urged. The compass slowly swung to the new heading.

"Bearings for tubes five and six matched," Volker announced.

"Tube five - *los,*" Becker ordered. He felt the familiar shudder when compressed air drove the weapon out of the tube.

"Weapon away," Volker said not taking his eyes off the chronometer. "Three seconds."

Becker counted the time in his head, "Tube six—*los*."

Again, the U-boat shuddered. Becker snapped the periscope handle up. "Fifty meters fast."

Iranian Cargo Ship *Kangan*

"This is better than I could have planned," Shatrevor shouted. "The problem is out of our hands. Let the Russians now deal with their traitor. Who cannot say that Allah is not at work here?"

Captain Nasim did not seem to share the General's joy. "Do you think they know?"

"What does it matter? We are a poor merchant ship sailing the ocean. They would not board us. We are more or less allied with Big Brother Russia. Is that not true?"

"Yes General, but if they know we have the weapon, I imagine they will attempt to get it back," Nasim said quietly.

"Captain, don't lose your nerve. Allah provided for every circumstance. Remember, you have a belly full of tanks just waiting my word. This will be a great day, my dear Captain."

The smiling stopped when the first of *Strogiy's*

rounds landed fifty meters ahead of *Kangan's* bow.

"They mean to stop us, General," Nasim said nervously.

The smile on the General's face was replaced with evil. His eyes narrowed and his lip curled, exposing his yellow teeth. "Then we will stop," he hissed. He picked up his radio. "Sergeant, the time is now. Aim true."

The entire ship vibrated when the false steel sides fell with a splash into the sea. Instantly the tank turrets traversed to their assigned positions.

Tank two's gunner thumbed his range finding laser and in half of a second, his gun tube belched out its first high explosive round.

Russian Patrol Ship *BARSUK*

Frantic, Rurik jabbed at the switches and buttons for *Barsuk's* gun control. Nothing worked. The aiming system dead.

He screamed in anger and rage when the first of U-761's torpedoes impacted.

The explosion vaporized the center of the ship. The light steel plating crumpled and tore as if made of paper. An immediate secondary explosion followed from *Barsuk's* fuel bunkers. On the bridge, Rurik felt his body being pulled apart, before he also added fuel to the blast.

Russian *Kashin* Class Destroyer *Strogiy*

The tanker aimed true. The 120mm high explosive shell bored into the *Strogiy's* bridge before detonating.

The blast lifted the thin plating of the deck, and peeled it back. Fragments of the shell and pieces of the deck smashed into every living soul on the bridge. Torn bodies spewed blood and gore. They collapsed where they stood.

The second tank round, this time an armor-piercing sabot, punched into the forward 76mm turret. The impact lifted the turret from its mount. The pressure of suddenly superheated air destroyed everything and everyone inside. The forward end of the ship erupted in a geyser of fire. The ship ripped apart when her own ammunition added to the destruction.

Iranian Cargo Ship *Kangan*

"Still worried, Captain," Shatrevor yelled.

Nasim didn't hear him. Flaming wreckage from *Barsuk* rained on his ship. A dozen small fires erupted while his crew tried desperately to put them out..

Nasim picked up the microphone for the engine room when he looked out the bridge window. "General," he said quietly. "Allah has abandoned us." Nasim pointed to the two thin trails of frothing water heading for the ship. "Torpedoes," he announced as if he ordered a glass of water.

"Do something," Shatrevor screamed.

"I will." He fell on the deck and prayed.

The first warhead smashed into the aged tanker's rounded underside. A nine-meter hole opened, allowing the waters of the Arctic Ocean free access to the interior. Almost instantly, the ship fell on her side.

Seconds later, the next weapon bore in. Striking

five meters forward of the bridge and more water surged in. The list increased and the tanks slid on the deck. Their weight plus the sudden in rush of water caused the old tanker to roll till her torn bottom saw the sky. As quickly, her bow dipped under, the stern lifted. For a few seconds she bobbed in the water, her screws still turning lazily. Then as if the sea were tired of toying with her, she went down.

Russian *Kashin* Class Destroyer *Strogiy*

The destroyer moved forward while she burned.. A firefighting team from the repair party tried in vain to fight the magazine fire that raged on the three decks below the flaming turret.

The emergency steering compartment controlled the ship, but no one gave orders. Those fighting the flames topside had seen the flashes of light and heard the rolling explosions, while their intended targets evaporated.

A shout rang out over the screaming alarms. A slender wake swam toward their ship. In panic hoses dropped. Shipmates trampled shipmates in a struggle to get away from the impending explosion.

Ten seconds later the torpedo swam under the hull. In its nose, a magnetic field was generated by a set of batteries. It passed under the hull of the destroyer, the field was suddenly altered. A trip lever moved up and the primer detonated. The shock of this small explosion set off the main warhead.

The sea around the *Strogiy* turned a brilliant white,

and a bubble of super heated gas and steam blew the water from under the ship. The same bubble shot upward tearing into the thin underside. The center of the ship lifted and the sea rushed in at the speed of sound to fill the void left by the explosion. It bent the ship up and down, till her steel screamed, and the ship broke cleanly into two pieces. The two pieces floated apart for some fifty meters before they sank in a surging whirlpool.

The wind picked up and carried the smoke off. The sea quieted once again.

Chapter Thirty

The Brink

"The circumstances of war are sensed rather than explained."
-Maurice de Saxe: 1696—1750, Letters and Memoirs, IV

U-761

November 16th

"Less than twenty minutes left on the battery, Captain," Edel warned.

Becker looked to the hydrophone operator. "Anything?"

Veldmon slowly rotated the hydrophone wheel, his head cocked while he listened. "Clear, Herr Kaleu."

"Helm, come to course north. Surface the boat," Becker ordered.

"We sank them all," Volker announced.

Becker thought,. *we all should be overjoyed, We've destroyed four enemy warships, a tanker, and an aircraft. Why don't we care*"A word, Lieutenant Volker." Becker touched the young officer's shoulder.

Volker removed the chronometer from around his neck and hung it on the peg above the plot table. "Of course, sir."

Becker led the way to his tiny cabin. “Do you notice anything strange with the enemy?”

“How do you mean?” Volker asked puzzled.

“We’ve made how many patrols together?” Becker removed the dingy cap from his head.

“This is six,” Volker replied.

“We’ve seen it all. So tell me, what is different?”

“The enemy seems ... well, sloppy,” Volker shrugged.

Becker nodded his agreement. “Have you ever known the English or the Americans to be sloppy?”

“Perhaps we have been lucky,” Volker offered.

Becker sighed. “Luck maybe, but it’s like they had no idea we were even here. Does that sound insane?”

“They misjudged us before, Captain. Maybe the ice interfered with their radar or ASDIC.”

“You said you have never seen a warship like that before,” Becker probed. “What did you mean?”

“The masts, the guns, all strange. And that aircraft. What was it?”

Becker slowly shook his head. “I don’t know.”

Interstate I-95
Washington, DC.
22:30, November 16th

“You married Petty Officer Jordan?” Admiral Malroy asked his driver.

“Yes, sir, three years. First baby due next month,” Jordan replied proudly.

“Congratulations, son. I was a JO on the *Polk* when we had our first, and I ...” Malroy’s cell phone went off. "Damn, I hate this thing." He flipped the cover up and put the small phone to his ear. "Go ahead," he grumbled.

Lights of cars passing in the next lane cast some light into the interior of the black government-owned four-door. Jordan, out of instinct, looked in the rearview mirror. A truck passed, its lights beamed bright on Admiral Malroy's face. What Jordan saw in that face caused a chill down his spine.

"My God," Malroy gasped. "We have confirmation?"

Jordan tried not to eavesdrop, but with the Chairman of The Joint Chiefs of Staff, not two feet away, made it difficult. A bus passed on the left, when Malroy's voice came in loud and clear.

"All right, I'm headed back now. Hell, that'll take me forty minutes. Get me an escort—now." I'm heading to the White House."

Jordan tensed in his seat.

"Turn this thing around and get me to the White House." Malroy put his hand on Jordan's shoulder. "Son, drive like your ass is on fire." Malroy dialed another number on his cell phone. "Turn around in the median. Floor this thing."

Jordan was from Darlington, South Carolina, where the only way to drive was fast. "Not a problem, sir," he said calmly. "Hang on back there,"

He signaled and whipped the wheel to the left. The car left the pavement, dropping roughly into the median. The sedan bounced, spun and dipped into the low center line. Jordan tromped on the gas, and swung into an open space of oncoming traffic. The sedan's tires screamed when they found traction on the pavement and the Admiral's car fishtailed. A semi-truck hauling two small bulldozers swerved and let go a long blast of his air horn when he rounded the car.

"Hey, that asshole just flipped me off," Jordan complained and straightened the wheel.

Malroy looked up from his phone. "I'll take care of that."

The sedan gained speed and soon alongside the upset trucker. The Chairman of the Joint Chiefs of Staff of the United States Armed Forces lowered his window.

The trucker peered down and recognition crossed his face. His expression change would have made a Pulitzer-Prize winning photo when Admiral Malroy extended his right arm, while raising his own middle finger.

The truck slowed down remarkably fast and the sedan pulled away. Flashing lights came up from behind. "Keep going, Jordan. That's our escort."

Two Maryland State Troopers passed the sedan, then pulled in front. A Metro DC patrol car took up the rear position behind Malroy's car.

"Follow these guys. We're going to the White House."

"Aye, aye Admiral," Jordan smiled. "It's not just a job, it's an adventure."

"Where the hell you learn to drive like that?" Malroy chuckled.

"Back home, sir," Jordan replied.

"Let's just not do it again." Malroy sat back in his seat.

Jordan smiled in the mirror. "Roger that,"

United States Embassy
Berlin, Germany
November 17th

"Carl, I don't think you'll get through," Warren sighed. I just came down from communications. Man, there is a shit storm hitting the fan."

"What do you mean?" Blevins asked.

Warren shook his head. "Intel has it that three Russian ships were sunk by a submarine. A few days ago, a Brit Destroyer got deep six'd, and a day after that, a cargo ship blew up."

"Where?"

"Up north around the ice pack." Warren drained the last of his coffee.

"Do they know what's going on?" His voice cracked some.

"Carl, you okay?"

"Do they know who's doing the shooting?" Blevins drew in gulps of air and staggered forward.

"Hey, come on sit down," Warren reached for the Blevins.

"Do they know?"

"No, no one knows anything." The SEAL said gently. "Carl, what's wrong?"

"They don't know," Blevins reached into his jacket and pulled out the CD. "But I do."

The Kremlin
Moscow, Russia

"This is either an overt act of war or they have a madman in one of their boats," Admiral Ryshenko yelled. Tears streamed down his face.

Defense Minister Vitenka stood and walked around his desk and stopped in front of Ryshenko. He placed his hand on the weeping Admiral's shoulder. "Arman," he said softly, "we will find the truth. I promise you and I promise your son that. But I hope you understand what I must do?"

Ryshenko looked up. "What?"

"I cannot let the situation get worse till we know answers. I must relieve you of your command."

"No," Ryshenko screamed. "I will avenge my son. I will kill them all."

"Please, my friend, do not make this any harder than it already is," Vitenka said soothingly. "We must show restraint. Now go. Your Deputy will assume your post."

"You cannot," Ryshenko blubbered.

Vitenka nodded toward the door. Two uniformed Army officers entered. "Take him to his quarters," he said softly. "Have his wife brought to him. You will use every courtesy."

"Yes sir," the senior of the two responded.

Vitenka returned to his desk and Ryshenko was led by the arm out of the office. The Minister of Defense sat again at his desk, then turned his eyes on the officers around him. "Now, what the hell happened?"

Ryshenko's Deputy, Captain, First Rank Pupynin opened a folder. "Sir, we have lost two ships - both sunk. Missile Cruiser *Peter the Great* is severely damaged. Fleet salvage and tugs are enroute to her now. It is not known if she will remain afloat."

"Casualties?" Vitenka asked.

Pupynin flipped the page. "Count is now at seven-hundred dead. The number of wounded is not yet reported."

"What of survivors?" Vitenka asked sadly.

"There are only a dozen from the Destroyer *Strogiy;* no officers are among them," Pupynin read. "Patrol ship *Barsuk* exploded and sank after being ordered to stop by the *Strogiy.* No survivors. In addition, an Iranian tanker suffered an explosion after which she capsized and sank. Also, no survivors found."

"And our response?" Vitenka crossed his arms over his chest.

Pupynin flipped to the next page. "The anti-submarine Destroyer *Simferopol* engaged a submerged contact near the area where *Peter the Great* was attacked. Her commander reports three hits with RBU weapons."

Vitenka listened emotionless. "Who would do this?"

"It was a deliberate act of war," Air Force General Norslav shouted. "Can you not see that? Two attacks—hundreds of miles apart. Not the actions of one man."

"But why?" Vitenka asked, his voice cool and quiet.

"The West sees a weakness. We are poor in almost everything except the one thing the West needs."

"Oil. Oil is the reason," Norslav yelled.

The Officer's door opened. An older man, dressed in a well fitting suit, strode in and whispered in Vitenka's ear.

Vitenka's eyes flared. "Who ordered our rocket forces to full alert?"

"I did," Norslav hissed. "I have also put up fighters around our bases and Moscow."

"On whose authority," Vitenka screamed.

"On my authority," Norslav shouted back. "I will not sit here and contemplate the reason. My duty is to defend the Motherland. You seem to have forgotten that."

"General, you are a fool. What do you think the Americans will do now?"

"Let them come."

"You have brought us to the edge. Did you know that the Americans and the British lost ships last week?"

"A cover up," Norslav shrugged. "All part of their plan."

"I should have you arrested," Vitenka hissed.

"You are most welcome to try, but I warn you, my feelings in this matter are not mine alone," Norslav said defiantly.

Vitenka's eyes narrowed. "What are you saying?"

"You and your puppet President are inviting attacks. You sit hear and do nothing while Russians die."

"You will kill all of Russia," Vitenka shot back.

"Better to die fighting than conquered. You forget your history, Vitenka."

"What about you?" the Defense Minister asked.

"Sir, I must side with Norslav. Our country is under attack. We must defend ourselves. To back down now would be a further sign of weakness."

"I do agree. We cannot back down now, but not for the reason you give. If we back down, the West will wonder who is in control. Right now that is also a question I would like answered." Vitenka shut his eyes.

Again the door opened and the same well-dressed man came to Vitenka's side.

"The seeds you planted are taking root," Vitenka said with an icy stare. "Three American Battle Groups have left station and are transiting the North Sea. You can be assured their strategic missile submarines are deployed."

"It is not war I want," Norslav said quietly. "We have for too long been against the wall, we must stand up. It is the Russian way."

"What has the Russian way gotten us for the past hundred years? It is time we did things the human way," Vitenka clipped.

"We don't have time to play word games. We are all reasonable men, men of honor. I'll give you this - forty-eight hours - two days - to tell us who is behind these attacks."

"If I do not?"

"Then you will be removed. The stakes here are too high. Force must be met with force."

Vitenka glared. "You'll destroy us all, General."

The White House
Washington DC.

"Sir, I don't think the British would go this alone," Malroy sighed.

"If not the British, who?" the President asked.

Secretary of Defense Martin Samuals shook his head. "We don't know."

"Just for the sake of argument, let's say the *Brits* are not behind these attacks. Could it be the Russian?"

"We can account for all Russian submarines except for one," Malroy announced.

"Only one?" the President tapped his finger on the desk.

"A *Kilo* class, Mr. President," Samuals explained.

"Gentlemen, I was Air Force - what the hell is a *Kilo*?" the President asked.

"It's a small diesel-electric submarine, very quiet," answered Malroy.

"Could that be the submarine causing this damned mess?"

"Best guess—yes," Malroy answered.

"Are the Russians in control or do we have some AWOL sub-skipper out there?" Martin Samuals rubbed the back of his neck.

"Mr. President, I can't answer that," the Chairman of the Joint Chiefs sighed.

Samuals moved to the chair in front of the President's desk. "Whoever's doing this, threatens shipping around the world. What if this jackass decides to hit a few oil tankers?"

"We have bigger problems," Malroy interrupted.

"Like what?" asked the President.

"Your predecessor cut a lot of funding for security. Charleston, Savannah, New York, Boston - hell, any port is wide open. You start sinking ships here and the panic will be unimaginable."

"My God, that'll kill the economy," the President observed.

"That's the good news. A *Kilo* is capable of launching cruise missiles."

"Christ in Heaven. What are we going to do about this?" The President leaned forward. "Martin, put us on DEFCON TWO. I can't take a chance, not until we know what we're dealing with."

"Mr. President, what about the obvious?" the Secretary of Defense asked.

The President's brows arched. "The obvious?"

"Yes sir. What if this is a deliberate attack by the Russians?"

"Why, why would they do that? It makes no sense," the President waved his right hand in the air.

"None of this makes sense, Mr. President," Malroy muttered.

"Should we bring this to the UN?"

"No," Samuals answered. "If we do that, sides will form. We could push the Russians into a corner."

"I thought we trusted Atopov and that Admiral friend of yours?"

"No sir, I don't really trust any Russian. We acted on a request before the whole world went to hell in a handbag."

"Martin, I need answers. How the hell are we going to get ourselves out of this one?"

"Going to the DEFCON-2 might cause their heads to pop out their asses," Samuals shrugged.

Malroy shook his head. "Or it might provoke them into doing something stupid."

"Whatever happens, I want to be ready," the President waved his hand. "Go to DEFCON-2."

Malroy placed his hands on the President's desk. "Let me talk to Vitenka."

"You can do as you wish, but I'm not playing games."

Malroy stood. "I understand sir."

U-761
Edge of the Ice Pack

"I hope this works." Edel stepped along a thin plank. Thankfully, the sea calmed and the U-boat rose and fell gently in the light chop. Once across the plank, he tested his footing on the iceberg. Satisfied, he stepped further onto the floating mountain of ice.

"Send me the torch," he called.

On the deck, the seaman tossed a line. Edel caught the line in his gloved hands and pulled. The hose and cutting head for the torch inched over. He took hold of the cutting head, tucked it under his arm as he untied the line. "Now, the hose and pan," he called and tossed the line back to the U-boat.

"Okay Chief," Hamlin called. "Haul away."

One of Berdy's large pans had a hole cut in the bottom, with a spare valve welded in the hole and a thumb thick hose attached with a threaded coupling. Edel set the pan and hose to the side and took a small hand pick from his waist belt. He hammered at the ice until he dug a meter wide hole out of the berg. He scooped up the chunks of ice and placed them into the pan and continued till it could hold no more. Huffing from his effort, U-761's Engineer dropped the pick and lit the torch. Edel adjusted the flame till it burned a dull yellow. "Ready in cell three?" he called across the ice.

"Ready Chief," a voice called back.

Edel nodded and placed the flame next to the pan. Steam rose, the ice cracked and hissed. Within minutes, fresh water flowed from the hose and into the starved batteries. "It's working," Edel called to the U-boat's bridge.

Becker stood on the bridge, his white hat

unmistakable even in the dimness of the Arctic twilight.

"How long?" he called.

"Two hours."

Chapter Thirty-One

Hard Truths

"If ye go to war ... ye shall blow an alarm with the trumpet."

-Numbers, X, 9

The Situation Room
The Pentagon
Washington, DC.
November 18th

"I want you all to keep your mouths shut," Malroy warned. "I'll do the talking. One wrong word and this could be the last day for a lot of people."

Those around the table nodded. Some nervously fidgeted with standard government pens, others stared off.

"Okay then." Malroy punched the button to activate the intercom.

"Central Communications," a pleasant voice announced.

"This is Admiral Malroy, Chairman of the Joint Chiefs of Staff. Do you have the connection with the Office of the Minister of Defense?"

"Yes sir, Defense Minister Vitenka is standing by," the voice answered.

"Very well, put me on the line," Malroy ordered.

"Connection is complete, sir," the voice said as the intercom switched off.

Malroy pressed the red flashing button on the communications panel. "Minister Vitenka, this is Admiral Malroy. Can you hear me sir?"

A slight pause… "Admiral, I can hear you," answered Vitenka. His thick accent muffled by the connection.

"Mr. Defense Minister, I need not tell you of the recent events in the area of the Arctic Ocean," Malroy said.

"On the contrary, Admiral, you do need to tell me about these events."

"Is it your country's position the United States is to blame for the loss of your naval units?" Malroy asked.

"There are those who believe this is the case," Vitenka answered.

"Mr. Minister, the Royal Navy has lost a warship, as has the United States. Can you give any reasons for these attacks?"

Pause… "Admiral Malroy, I can assure you that no Russian ship or submarine fired on any vessels. I ask if you can answer the same question?"

"You know the United States would never commit an overt action at sea."

"And how would I know that?" Vitenka asked.

"We're not stupid, Mr. Minister. When in our history have we been the aggressors?"

Vitenka chuckled. "We are not getting to the point, Admiral."

"You're right, Mr. Minister. Why did your country deploy its fleet? We had an agreement."

"Admiral, what I tell you now is truth. The signal was a mistake."

Malroy cleared his throat. "Am I to believe that an entire combat arm of the Russian military was deployed due to a mistake? If that is so, is it possible one of your commanders made mistakes?"

"I pose the same question to you Admiral."

"Mr. Minister, this is not getting us anywhere. We know that one of your submarines, a Project 877 class is missing."

A long pause… "Admiral, that ship was destroyed during the coup."

"I see. And you have confirmed that?"

"Unfortunately, yes," Vitenka said sadly. "Admiral, listen to me please. One ship was ordered to conduct a special operation. I can assure you the operation had nothing to do with the security of the United States or NATO."

"If that is so, Mr. Minister, why has your country increased its readiness?"

"Perhaps you already have that answer."

"I can assure you the United States has not attacked any Russian force. We have abided by the agreement you and I made."

"Perhaps you have a rogue?"

"No Mr. Minister, we have control of our forces."

"So, we both are either ignorant or both liars," Vitenka sighed. "Admiral, like you, I need answers quickly before events get - how do you say - out of hand."

"Is that a threat of military actions?" Malroy snapped.

"No," Vitenka retorted. "A statement of fact. Some events are beyond my control at this time."

"Mr. Minister, I have been ordered to bring the armed forces of my country to full alert."

"I have issued the same order," Vitenka answered.

"Okay, let's cut the polite horse shit. If you think we sunk Russian ships, you're wrong. Now I ask you to back down before this thing does get out of hand."

"I cannot do that, Admiral. My country has been attacked by someone. What would you have me do? What would you do?"

"I'll give you that, Mr. Minister, but you must pull back."

Silence. Then Vitenka's voice come through the speaker again, "That is not an option right now. Your forces are closing on our waters as we speak. Will you pull back?"

"Stalemate."

"Yes, it appears so," Vitenka said cooly.

"Let's agree to keep this line open as sailor-to-sailor."

Another long pause... "I agree to that, but I must impress on you the factor of time is not with me. Do you understand?"

"I understand."

"Good, Admiral, I will be waiting to hear from you," Vitenka said. The line went dead.

The Chairman of the Joint Chiefs of Staff blew out a low whistle, and placed his hands behind his head. "He's in trouble."

"You mean he doesn't have control?" asked the Chief of Naval Operations.

"I think he's been threatened. Vitenka is a tough old bird, a cool player. He tried to tell me something. He kept mentioning time."

The telephone in front of the Chief of Naval Operations buzzed. "Yes?—All right, get me more information." He replaced the receiver.

"Something new, Admiral?" Malroy asked quietly.

"Yes sir, our *Key Hole* satellite detected hot spots on the hulls of docked Russian missile boats."

"They're getting the boomers to sea."

"CNO, get some assets to sit on those missile boats. Pass the word personally. No one is to cause an incident. This whole mess can turn into a shit-storm damned quick. I want those boats trailed, but in a nice way. Do I make myself clear?"

"Yes sir."

"What else?" Malroy asked.

Before anyone could answer, the buzzer in front of Malroy sounded. He punched the button on the intercom. "Go ahead."

"Sir, a Carl Blevins is calling on the secure line from the embassy in Berlin."

"Damn it," Malroy shouted. "I'm busy. Tell Chief Blevins his assignment is over and get his ass on the next flight back to Groton."

"Uh ... sir," the voice said nervously.

"What is it?" Malroy bellowed.

"Chief Blevins said, well he said ..."

"What the hell did he say?" Malroy yelled at the unseen voice.

The voice cleared its throat. "Chief Blevins said, '*If that fat son-of-bitch doesn't talk to me now, he's going to fly over here and chicken-choke you till your eyes roll out your ass.*' "

The room went silent. Malroy stared at the communications panel. "Must be important," he said quietly. "Okay, put him through." Malroy punched the button.

"Chief Blevins, I'm a little busy for a report about that damned U-boat. I guess you might have heard we're about a gnat's ass away from the third world war?"

"I know Admiral, and if you'll shut up and listen, I have the answer. I found out what the U-761 was doing in the ice. You'd better sit down for this one."

U-761

"Two cells are beyond repair," Edel panted and climbed from the battery space under the E-motor room. "The plates are eaten away. Nothing I can do."

"How much power will we have?" Becker handed the Chief a filthy rag.

"Good news is the other cells are about eighty-percent functional." Edel took the rag and wiped the grime from his face and arms. "We'll have about seventy-five percent total capacity."

"Only seventy-five?" Becker asked.

"Be grateful for that, Herr Kaleu." He gently lowered the hatch over the battery compartment.

"I am grateful," Becker smiled. "When will the cells be refilled?"

"About twelve hours. Then three hours to recharge."

"You look like hell. Get some rest." Becker said quietly.

Edel looked up. "We need to secure the damage in the torpedo room. I have just enough welding gas left to put a brace over the upper beam. I'll cut an angle out of the compass housing support."

"How long?"

"Give me another hour."

The White House
Washington DC.

"Admiral, if I didn't know you personally, I'd say you've lost your mind," the President said quietly.

"Sir, please, I agree this is the strangest thing I've ever heard, but it makes some sense," Malroy answered.

"Okay, just to re-cap. I'm supposed to believe a Nazi World War II U-boat is alive and well and blowing the hell out of everything in the Atlantic?"

Secretary of Defense Martin Samuals sat silently, his eyes wide and his hands busy buttoning and unbuttoning his blazer. "If this is true, why didn't they just give up when they came out of the ice?" he asked weakly.

"Hell, I don't know," Malroy answered. "How would they know the war was over? Remember when those Japanese troops came out of the jungle a few years back. They didn't know the war was over."

"Okay, let's say this is real," the President said, raising his hands. "What's this guy doing?"

"He has to be low on fuel or food. God only knows what mental or physical shape they're in," Malroy offered.

"That's not an answer," the President shot back.

"If it were me, I'd try to get home."

"What do we know about the skipper?"

"Manfred Becker. I've got some folks checking him out. What I know so far is that he was one of their best," Malroy answered.

"Seems like it," the President responded. "I just can't believe this."

"Sure would make a great movie," Samuals said.

"Shit, who would believe it?" Malroy shrugged.

"Okay, how do we sink the son-of-a-bitch?" the President asked.

"Why sink it?" Malroy blurted out. "Two big reasons I think that would be a bad idea. The first is that this is a German submarine. We're not at war with Germany."

"Not good enough," the President countered.

"Well then, the second reason, this guy wants to get home. Wouldn't you?" Malroy clasped his hands in front of him. "Mr. President, it would be murder. And don't forget one important thing. So far, he's bagged a modern British frigate and possibly three front line Russian warships. If he gets lucky and we lose a ship or two, you'll answer a lot of very hard questions."

"Why don't we tell the Germans?" Martin Samuals asked. "It's their damned submarine."

"God no," the President shot back. "Our relations with Chancellor Niestle are bad enough. They stay out of the picture till we absolutely have to tell them."

"I agree sir," Malroy nodded.

"What about the Russians?" Samuals asked. "They're itching to kill something."

"Oh sure," the President mocked. "I'll just call ole Atopov and tell him, 'Hey listen, we managed to resurrect a Nazi submarine that is sinking your ships. You mind going out and killing that for us?' "

Samuals bowed his head. "You have any better ideas, Mr. President?"

"No, but I … "

Malroy cut him off, "Just a minute - wait one damned minute."

"Yes, Admiral?" the President asked.

"What if we worked together?"

"Who?" Secretary Samuals asked.

"Us and the Russians," Malroy thought out loud.

"I think you need to take some leave, sailor," the President sighed. "I don't believe this bullshit, why would they?"

"It doesn't matter if you or me, or even if the Russians believe it. It is a way we can both agree to a pull back. It will buy time," Malroy explained. "We send a submarine and they send a submarine and everything else goes back to the barn."

"A bit risky, Admiral," Samuals pointed out.

"A lot less risky than where we are as of right now."

"What makes you think the Russians will play fair?" the President asked.

"Well, unless they've all lost their minds over there, I think they need an excuse to back down."

"I don't like it," Samuals grumbled. "But I like a nuclear war even less."

"What happens if you find the U-boat?" the President asked. "How do you communicate with it?"

Malroy looked perplexed for a moment. "We'll try the WQC-2 underwater telephone. If they have a hydrophone, they should be able to pick it up."

"Okay then, what will you say? Do they speak English?" Samuals asked.

"Mr. President, give me the go ahead. I'll get the details worked out. We don't have a lot of time."

"If this goes south, we'll all be looking for jobs," he said quietly.

"If this goes south, there might not be any jobs," Malroy sighed.

Office of Naval Intelligence

"All the shit going on in the world and I get stuck with this," Lieutenant Cliver swore and drained the fourth cup of coffee in as many hours.

"They didn't tell you at the Academy about all the fun we have here, huh?" smiled Commander Austin. "You'll get used to it. Half the stuff we research is bullshit anyway. Then again, who knows?"

"Yeah, well, I think this comes under the total bullshit category." He typed information into the database.

"What are you digging up?" Austin yawned.

"Some dead German,"

"What the hell?"

"Yeah, I know. Some U-boat commander missing since 1944." His screen filled with useless information.

"Find anything?"

"Got his name and date of birth. Schooling and date he joined the German Navy. Wow, quite a war record. Wife's name, one child ..." Cliver stopped, puzzled and stared at his computer screen. "Oh man. Hey, Commander, take a look at this."

"What you got?" Austin walked to the small cubicle.

"Look here." Cliver pointed to the screen.

"I'll be damned. Who asked for this information?"

"Joint Chiefs."

"You'd better send that right along. Better yet, send it over to me. I'll have the CO endorse it. I wonder if he even knows?"

The Situation Room
The Pentagon
Washington, DC.
November 19th

"Admiral, how did you get this number?" a surprised Vitenka asked.

"Now is not the time to talk about that," Malroy said into his cell phone. "Are you alone now?"

"Yes, at least for now," Vitenka replied.

"You will hear a faint buzz as we talk. It's a device that prevents interception of our call."

"Listen to me carefully," Malroy said slowly. "I lied to you earlier."

"I am listening," Vitenka replied.

"We had information that one of your missile boats was hiding under the ice and ..."

Vitenka cut him off, "Where did you get such information?"

"I don't think that's important now, I ..."

"I think it is very important, Admiral," the Russian interrupted

"Okay, listen, I guess we need to trust each other. We have a satellite that found a shape under the ice. We thought it was a Russian missile boat. So we sent an attack boat to check it out."

"So you violated our agreement," Vitenka replied… A long pause... "I would have done the same. But your submarine did not find a Russian, did it?"

"No."

"Then why do you tell me these things?" Vitenka asked.

"Because our submarine found a German U-boat."

"Why would the Germans go into the ice? Their submarines are coastal boats."

"Mr. Minister, you don't understand. It was not a modern U-boat."

"You mean a Nazi U-boat?"

Malroy flipped through his note pad. "Yes, a Type IXC."

"You must forgive me, Admiral," Vitenka chuckled. "I am not understanding what this has to do with our situation. It will be great historical artifact, but I …"

"Wait just…"

Ten minutes later, Malroy finished the whole story.

"I don't think anyone could concoct such a tale." Vitenka observed.

"I have worked out …"

Vitenka cut in, "However, you and I have a trust. I believe this story. Unfortunately, those around me will not believe this."

Malroy yelled into the phone. “You have to make them believe.”

“That I cannot do. There is a great supply of confusion and fear. Why would they trust me? They need proof.”

“Is it that bad?” Malroy asked.

“Yes it is. I have little time to produce answers.”

Malroy sighed. “I don’t know how …” Malroy stopped in mid-sentence. “Will you and the other Ministers be open to an expert in this field?” Malroy asked hopefully.

“I don’t know about the others, but I am,” Vitenka responded. “I will get him here and let him make his case. But I must tell you, time is against us.”

Chapter Thirty-Two

Rivals

"Our swords shall play the orators for us."
Christopher Marlowe: Tamburlaine ,I, 1587

United States Embassy
Berlin, Germany
November 20th

"I'm going where?" Carl Blevins asked astonished.

"Yep, we're going to Moscow, my friend," Lieutenant Warren said as he lifted his small knapsack to his shoulders.

"Wait … It's damn cold there and all I have is this," Blevins protested., holding the bottom of his blue windbreaker.

"Oh, that does suck," Warren shrugged. "You ready?"

"I'll freeze my ass off."

"Oh, you got plenty of ass."

"Very funny, smart guy. Why are we going to Moscow?" He picked up his own worn bag.

"I don't know and don't want to know," Warren smiled. "Oh, but here, this is for you." The SEAL Team leader reached inside his shirt and pulled out a large envelope from his waistband. "Don't open it till we're in the air."

U-761

"What's happening to him?" Becker asked.

Roth shook his head. "He's dying. His condition deteriorates by the minute. He can't eat. There's nothing I can do for him here."

"Can he speak?"

"He's in and out, but you can try."

Gerlach's face turned a sickly yellow. His piercing black eyes lost their intensity, and changed to a dull gray. Gerlach's breath labored.

"Major?" Becker gently urged.

Gerlach's eyes slowly fluttered. With great effort, the SS Major turned his head slightly toward Becker.

"Can you hear me?" Becker asked.

"Yes," Gerlach's voice a hushed whisper.

"Are you in pain?"

Gerlach forced his lips to move. "Doesn't matter."

"Major, is there anything I can do for you?" Becker asked.

"Your promise."

"Major, I can't, I'm sorry."

"I know. Destroy," the Major rasped.

"Destroy?"

"The gas, the canisters - all has to be destroyed."

Becker felt the familiar fear creep down his back. "Why?"

"It worked." His shrunken eyes glazed, his mouth

parted, and his breath rattled from his lungs.

"Is that bad?" Fear took root. No response. "Major?" Becker asked loudly. "Major, what is it? What haven't you told me?"

Roth bent down and looked into the Major's eyes. He felt his pulse. "Captain, it's over, sir. He's gone … Herr Kaleu?" Roth asked quietly.

Becker didn't hear and looked at the wasted body. *Is this how we will all die?*

"Sir," Roth repeated, "what are your orders?"

"He saved us, you know," Becker said.

Roth pulled the wool blanket over Gerlach's head. "Yes, sir," he said softly.

Over Southern Russia
November 20th

"You think this thing will make it?" Blevins asked nervously.

Warren pulled a thin blanket tighter around his shoulders. "Well, I sure hope so. Sit back and enjoy the flight."

"Yeah, right," Blevins huffed. "I wonder if we have a stewardess?"

"Sure we do," Warren answered. "His name is Ivan and he's also the co-pilot. Look up there," Warren said, pointing to the dark area of the flight deck. "That's him pissing in that tin can. Go ask him for some nuts." Warren roared laughing.

"Sometimes you are such an asshole," Blevins fumed.

"Come on there, Chief, lighten up. You'd think you had the weight of the world on your shoulders."

"If you only knew," Blevins muttered under his breath.

United States Ballistic Missile Submarine
USS WEST VIRGINIA SSBN 735
Classified Location

"This makes not one bit of sense." The Captain stared at the message. "Cancel alert status? And this location? We're not allowed in there, are we?"

The Executive Officer shrugged. "I don't know, Skipper, but they are authentic orders."

The Captain folded the message and tucked it in his breast pocket. "Well, I guess someone knows what they're doing," the Captain sighed. "All right then, XO secure alert status." He reached under his left leg and lifted the phone. He pushed the button for the conn.

"Conn, Officer of the Deck," a voice answered.

"Officer of the Deck, this is the Captain. Proceed to four-hundred feet. Make turns for ten knots. Come to new course zero-five-zero. Also, have the Navigator come to my stateroom."

The Kremlin
Moscow, Russia

Their footsteps echoed through the ancient halls of marble and once finely painted wood. Here and there, a bullet hole allowed the cold November chill inside through panes of broken glass. The cold air whistled inside as if it somehow belonged.

Blevins and Warren walked between two not

exactly friendly guards. “Wow, do I feel out of place,” Blevins whispered and struggled to keep pace with the men at his side. “This place is bleak. Looks like it took a beating.”

“Quiet, Carl,” Warren whispered back.

“This sure ain’t the White House.”

“Carl, please.”

“You think these guys are Spetsnaz? “

“I don’t know Carl, but I bet they speak perfect English.”

“We do,” one of the escorts answered.

“Oh sorry,” Blevins replied.

“No problem,” the other responded.

“Anything else you’d like to ask, Mr. Jackass,” Warren chuckled.

The four ascended a set of wide winding stairs. At the top, a guard motioned for them to turn left. The hallway narrowed and the plaster from gunfire lay smudged and trampled. Part of the ceiling had been shot away, allowing the wind inside.

At the end of the hall, a large set of oak doors blocked the way. Another set of guards, armed with AK-47s, stood stone-faced.

The two escorts stopped. “This is as far as you go.”

Warren nodded.

“The Ministers are waiting for you, Mr. Blevins,” the other said emotionlessly.

“Carl, get in there and get your stuff done.”

“But …”

“Get your ass in there, Chief.”

U-761
November 20th

While Roth sewed the body in the blanket, Edel placed a scrap angle iron at the feet to ensure the body sank.

As gently as the confined space within the U-boat allowed, Major Gerlach was carried topside and laid along the deck's edge. Becker thought of saying something, but decided against it. Words for this man seemed out of place. *Still,* Becker thought, *he did save my crew.* "Put him over," Becker said softly.

Two of the diesel mechanics lifted the body. They stepped close to the edge of the deck and let it slide out of their hands.

"Hamlin, the canisters. Throw them over." Becker ordered

The Kremlin
Moscow, Russia

"Mr. Blevins," Air Force General Norslav smiled, "that was very compelling and it does explain much. However, I must ask you one question."

"Yes sir?" Blevins responded.

"Do you believe it?"

Blevins cleared his throat. "General, this world is full of crazy sh… I mean unusual things. I am like you. I have to see to believe."

"A good answer, but not for the question I asked," Norslav snapped.

"First off, General, it's Chief Blevins, and yes, I

believe it and we have the chance to prove it. I also have the feeling that you would rather blow up the world than give us the chance to find this U-boat."

Army General Trofinoff interjected, "Chief Blevins, what are your—how do you say—credentials?"

Blevins scratched his head and sighed, "Well, I'm a retired Chief Petty Officer."

"Retired?" Norslav sat back and folded his hands in his lap.

"Yes, General, I retired last year."

"You were assigned to submarines?" Vitenka asked.

"Yes sir," Blevins said proudly.

"Do you hold degrees from universities in America?" Trofinoff asked.

"No," Blevins replied.

"Then what makes you an expert in this area?" Norslav asked sarcastically.

Blevins cleared his throat, "I build models."

"You build models?" Vitenka sat up in his chair.

"Yes, Admiral, model submarines." Blevin's face reddened.

"You mean to tell me we are supposed to trust the fate of Russia on an American who plays with toy boats?" Norslav laughed. "My time is wasted here." the General stood to walk out.

Carl Blevins, dressed in old jeans and a sweater, and still wearing the thin blue windbreaker, stepped to the right, blocking the General's path. "Sit down, General," Blevins yelled.

Norslav's eyes widened and chubby cheeks quivered in total surprise.

"You heard me. Park your ass and let me talk."

Norslav's head swung to Vitenka, his eyes flashed with rage.

"Sit, General," Vitenka said softly.

Rash-like redness spread across Norslav's face. "My men would never talk to me this way," he hissed, but returned to his chair.

"Thank God I'm not one of your men," Blevins quipped.

"Please go on, Chief Blevins," Vitenka urged.

Blevins watched the General sit down hard in the seat. "Okay, look, I'm no diplomat and God knows I'm no officer. I'm a guy who has done a lot of research. Hell, I don't think I would swallow it myself. It's up to you. Don't forget one important thing. If it is true and we find the U-761, the gas they used is like—like, well hell, it means we might live forever. Or you can listen to the General over there and blow the whole world to hell." Beads of sweat dripped down his forehead even in the chilly chamber.

Vitenka glanced at the other members of his military. Trofinoff nodded, as did the Director of Strategic Missile Defense, indicating their agreement. Captain First Rank Pupynin also nodded. Then Vitenka turned his head to the Air Force General. "General?"

Norslav turned his head and gave a slow nod.

"It is settled then," Vitenka said. "Chief Blevins we will work with the American Navy and find this German submarine, if it exists. Let me say this for the record. Should this prove to be some sort of trick or an attempt to gain advantage, I will have no recourse but to take military actions to protect the Russian people."

"Sounds fair to me," Blevins nodded.

"So, Chief Blevins are you ready to go?" Vitenka asked.

"Go?"

"Yes. You are the expert on this matter and I have none. You will accompany our submarine in the search."

"Wait one minute," Blevins protested. "You mean me on a Russian submarine?"

"Yes, that is what I mean," Vitenka answered.

The two escorts reappeared and each took a place next to the retired Chief. Vitenka spoke Russian to the two men. Both nodded and turned. The taller of the two motioned for Blevins to precede him. The huge doors swung open and Carl found himself again in the hall.

Warren rose from a rickety chair and came to Blevin's side. "How did it go?"

"Oh just fine, and by the way, I just joined the Russian Navy."

Warren's mouth fell open, "You what?"

USS MIAMI SSN-755

With only her number two scope and number one BRA-34 receiving antenna raised, the American submarine remained hidden in a vast empty ocean. She ducked twice since coming to periscope depth. Two fishing trawlers had come too close for comfort. The 6,900 ton nuclear fast-attack rolled gently while the Arctic swells eased at her beam.

In his stateroom, Commander Grant McKinnon sat at his small but efficient desk. The Executive Officer and Navigator stood next to him. “Looks like they’ve agreed.” McKinnon handed the message to Gellor.

“We’re about to re-write Naval history,” the Navigator observed.

“Or end world history,” Gellor whispered.

McKinnon touched the neatly folded chart on his desk. “I’ll need Senior Chief Masters to get a search plan together.”

“Aye, sir,” Gellor responded. “I never thought I would see the day when we would work with the Russians.”

McKinnon looked up. “I bet they didn’t either.”

“What do we do when we find the U-boat?” the Navigator asked.

“We’re supposed to get her to surface and give up.”

“How the hell are we supposed to do that?”

“Good question. We’re getting some pre-recorded sound bites in German. When we get close or think we’re close, we play the tapes over the WQC.”

“Well, at least they can’t shoot at us.”

“Remember the funny looking torpedo our guys found? Well, that is the Great Grandfather of our own ADCAP.”

“You mean to tell me there is a pissed off Nazi running around with a homing torpedo and we’re going to play tapes for him?” The Navigator rubbed his left ear.

McKinnon smiled, “Yeah, strange world, huh?”

“What about the Russians?” Gellor asked.

“You can guess their feelings on the whole matter. Plus they’re pretty trigger-happy anyway.”

"Why couldn't we get something easy like navigate through a nice mine field?" the Navigator sighed. "What boat are they going to send?"

"If it were me, you know who I would send." McKinnon answered.

"This day just keeps getting better," Gellor quipped.

"You think it'll be *VEPR*?" the Navigator asked quietly.

"Like I said, that's what I'd do," McKinnon answered.

"The pissed off Nazi doesn't seem so bad."

"Rules of engagement?" Gellor asked.

"Against the Russians, we can protect ourselves. You know as well as I that getting a shot at *VEPR* will be a ten on the next-to-impossible list. As for the German, we cannot engage."

The Navigator stopped rubbing his ear, "Why the hell not?"

"Here's another part of the puzzle," McKinnon handed Gellor a message marked *For CO eyes only.*

Gellor took the message and read it silently. "Holy shit. Talk about a small world. You think he knows?"

"I don't know, but we might need his help." McKinnon then lifted his right finger. "You know who I wished we had onboard?"

"Who?" the XO asked.

"That Chief who retired last year ... You remember, he builds those models?"

"Oh yeah," the Navigator smiled. "I think his name was Blevins. He would love this stuff."

Chapter Thirty-Three

To Sea

"...Over the wine dark sea."
Homer: The Iliad, c. 1000 B.C.

Lapadnaya Lista
Russian Submarine Base
November 20th

The small room was warm, the lights dim. A cold November wind blowing from the mountains whined as it flowed past the windows and doors. Snow tingled as it struck the old glass. The sun made its brief appearance and night came early.

With the last of the dinner, dishes dried and placed in the cabinet, Evelina Vitenka walked back to the small living room. She seemed to glide over the floor, her feet silent. She sat gently and gracefully next to Danyankov.

Her usual smile seemed muted and her mood somber. She slipped closer to Danyankov, turning her eyes to his. "This frightens me."

Danyankov wrapped his arm around her slender shoulders, drawing her head to his chest. "This is nothing new. You have seen worse with your father," Danyankov said softly.

"No Valerik, this is different."

The commander of the most feared Russian submarine on the sea looked puzzled. "How is it different?"

"Because it's you." Her voice just above a whisper.

Valerik Danyankov, in uncharted waters, his mind searched for the right words or for any words. "Don't worry," he blurted.

"But I do." Evelina let a tear roll down her smooth face. "I don't think I could stand losing you."

"You won't lose me."

"I don't understand and this mission. I've heard the fleet is forbidden to sail. So why must you go, can you tell me?" Her chest heaved.

"You know I can't."

She pulled back. "Father told me not to fall in love with a sailor," she said with a slight grin. "Now look at me."

"I am and you're beautiful." *Not bad,* Danyankov thought. *Maybe I can get good at knowing what to say.* For a split second he thought, *I wish she was one of his officers. I could order her to be happy.* He almost laughed out loud.

"Why do you have to go?" she asked as other tears joined in the flow.

"It is my duty and you know that."

"I know, but still nothing says I have to like it. I'm so afraid."

Danyankov took his arm from around her shoulders. "I am willing to prove to you that I will indeed come back." He fumbled through his pocket till he fished out a small box. nervously opened it.

Evelina Vitenka gasped.

"This is how." He removed the small diamond ring from its red felt-covered box.

"Valerik," she shouted. "Are you asking me ...?"

Danyankov's large hands trembled and placed the ring on her slender delicate finger. "I am ... if you will have me."

She admired the ring. Her body trembled. "Of course I will." She threw her arms around his neck. "You will come back?"

"I have to now, that ring cost me two month's pay," he smiled.

"Stop it," she laughed.

They returned to the worn but comfortable sofa. Her smile brightened the room. He nudged her close, held her tight, and enjoyed a feeling in his heart he had never known. For the first time in his life, he couldn't help but smile.

"My father - has he talked to you? He has not called in days." She nuzzled his neck. "I want to tell him of our engagement," she cooed.

"He is a busy man."

"You men are always too busy."

"Maybe he will call tomorrow."

"I don't want to think about tomorrow," she complained. "All this is new to me."

"To me also," Danyankov whispered.

"Is everything going to be all right?" she asked.

"I hope so."

USS MIAMI SSN 755

With a small swish, the periscope vanished from

the ocean's surface. *Miami* descended into the darkness and turned slightly east.

The evening meal ended and Milo Stephens cleared the last of the dishes, while McKinnon stared at nothing. "You doin' okay, Captain?" asked Stephens.

"Doing good," McKinnon smiled back. "Good meal tonight."

"Glad you liked it," Stephens smirked. "Personally, I hate corned beef."

"You do?"

"Oh yes sir, looks like a Baboon's ass, if you ask me." Stephens stepped into the galley.

McKinnon shook his head and drained the last bit of coffee from his cup. Setting the cup on the wardroom table, he glanced at the Weapon's Officer. "The search plans ready?"

"We have the plan for the *Akula,* she's no problem. The U-boat though …"

"Shit. I forgot we don't have anything on her, do we?"

"No sir, no idea of what she would sound like. I figured on her two-three blades she would sound like the thousand or so other trawlers up that way."

McKinnon rubbed his chin. "What about submerged? If she's submerged, it might sound like a distant trawler. We'd be on top of her before we knew it."

"We'll have to stay deep." McKinnon tapped the table with his index finger

"I agree," said the Weapon's Officer. "Question is, how deep?"

Lapadnaya Lista
Russian Submarine Base
November 21st

The sun achieved a dull cold ribbon of orange. Snow spit out of the dead sky, adding to the dirty brown slush that covered everything. Carl Blevins was up and dressed well before the pitiful sun. He hadn't slept except for a few moments in the old run down room. Here and there bits of plaster exposed the lattice of the wall's interior and allowed in a steady stream of Arctic air. He sat on the edge of the bed, listening to the wind. Unlike most busy ports, Blevins heard nothing. With a sigh and a shiver, Blevins repacked his small backpack and waited. A heavy rap at the flimsy door startled him. "Da?" he answered in his best Russian.

"Mr. Blevins?" a voice in perfect English asked from the other side. "Sir, it is time to go."

Blevins picked up his backpack, went to door and twisted the handle, but the door refused to budge. "Frame is warped," he called.

"You have to use your shoulder," the voice responded.

"Oh, okay. Look out."

With a bit of effort, the door screeched open. Blevins found himself in front of a young neatly uniformed Russian Naval officer.

"Good morning, Mr. Blevins, I'm Lieutenant Shurgatov."

Blevins shivered in the cold air that surrounded him. He extended his hand to the Russian. "Nice to meet you."

"Mr. Blevins, you …"

Blevins held up his hand. "Please call me Carl."

The smiling Shurgatov nodded. "Carl then. The ship will sail within the hour."

"Great." Blevins had goose bumps upon goose bumps covering his body.

"I must apologize for your quarters, but they are the best we have."

"I understand," Blevins lied.

"If I may say, you don't seem dressed for the occasion."

"I know," Blevins replied.

"Not to worry. My quarters are on the way. We'll stop and get you some proper clothes."

"Thanks." He thrust his hands into his pockets.

"Come, we must be fast. Captain Danyankov gets very upset if he has to wait."

Blevins stepped into the thick snow covered slush. "Danyankov?" he asked.

"Yes. You've heard of the Captain?"

Blevins shivered again, but not from the cold.

USS MIAMI SSN 755

"We're about ten hours away," the Navigator said quietly.

McKinnon looked at the chart, his mind drank in the bottom contours and features. "The ice will raise hell this time of year," he mumbled.

"Yes, sir, if we come shallow, we'll have to watch it. Last satellite image we received showed some major bergs in our op area."

"You have them plotted?"

"Yes, sir, but the current is a good five knots, so the damn things are miles from the last known location."

"*Nav*, I want to enter the rendezvous area from the Southeast. Remember, we have to look like we just arrived."

"Sir, what about depth separation between us and the *Akula*?"

"We're the deep boat." McKinnon studied the chart.

"We'll have to watch our asses. Sea mounts rise up here, here and here," the Navigator fingered the underwater mountains.

"Be sure you remind me of that."

Chief of the Boat, Danny Norse entered the Wardroom. "You needed me, Captain?"

"Hey COB, come on in," McKinnon said with a half grin. "What do the troops think of all this?"

"Half thinks it's bullshit, the rest are pretty excited."

"Here's the game plan. Have the tracking party manned in six hours. Battle stations an hour after that. I want a meal served early. Have the cooks get on it. Have the Attack Center and the torpedo room do a check of all the weapons. Everyone else I want in the bunks. God knows when they'll get another chance for some rack time."

"Will do, sir."

"COB," McKinnon stopped him, "what do you think?"

Danny Norse turned back toward McKinnon. He looked down at the white tiled deck of the wardroom floor. "What I saw on that boat ... I can't even put into words. It makes sense. Those guys sure didn't look dead," Norse observed. "They had pictures of their families and girls on the bulkheads. It's strange how submariners are all the same."

"Is there anything at all you can think of that might convince this guy to give up without a fight?"

"Would you give up?" Norse asked bluntly.

Grant McKinnon felt the chill of reality slip like a snake down his spine. "No COB, I wouldn't."

Russian *AKULA* Class, K-157 (*VEPR*)
Lapadnaya Lista
Russian Submarine Base

"Please, we must hurry," Shurgatov urged.

They trudged through a mix of new snow and thick frozen mud. The cold air hung heavy with the smell of rotted wood, and fumes pouring from the antique coal-burning power plant. The two men rushed along a row of squat gray buildings whose once white paint had long since peeled away. At the end of the buildings, an archway of crumbling brick connected yet another stretch of dilapidated structures. With Blevins a few paces behind, Shurgatov entered the archway. Blevins caught up by the time they reached the narrow waterfront.

A small brick guardhouse stood at the head of the second pier, occupied by a lone guard who looked half-asleep. Shurgatov gave the guard a wave and rushed past. The guard yawned and raised his arm in a half-hearted salute. A narrow path clear of ice and snow snaked awkwardly down the center of the rusted, rotting pier. Lieutenant Shurgatov took the lead and they trotted toward the waiting submarine. Blevins gasped when he caught site of the *Akula.*

"My God," the retired American submariner exclaimed. He pulled the oversized fur hat from his head and his mouth dropped open.

A beautiful vessel, her blended sail and hull seemed the work of an artist. The large rudder with its pod gave the whole submarine a look of power and purpose.

Men scampered about the deck, careful of their footing on the icy rounded steel, Mooring lines stowed, the capstan retracted and locked. Cleats and bollards vanished, as did the flag. Blevins looked to the bridge where others raised the plexi-glass windscreen.

Blevins felt a tug on his sleeve. "Please, come now. No time to sightsee," Shurgatov pleaded.

"Yeah, sorry," Blevins responded. Clumsily, he slapped the fur hat back on his head and trotted toward the gangway.

Shurgatov strode up the inclined wooden planks of the gangway, ignoring the stares of the amused sailors. Standing on the deck, he stopped and turned to Blevins. "We made it," the young Russian smiled.

Just then, those on deck went rigid. Blevins stumbled when his foot hit the deck, not noticing everyone else at attention. The hat fell over his eyes, then a hand pushed it back, further up his forehead. With the hat back where it belonged, Carl Blevins found himself staring into the most unfriendly face he had ever seen. The piercing eyes shot through him, the lips turned down at the corners as if made of clay. Even the air around the face seemed menacing.

Shurgatov stepped up, gave a snappy textbook salute. He spoke in Russian to the statue-like man. Shurgatov finished and turned to Blevins. "Chief Carl Blevins, this is Captain First Rank Valerik Danyankov."

Blevins's left eye twitched, his mouth opened, but no words came out. He blinked and cleared his throat. "Captain, it is good to meet you," he stammered and extended his hand.

Danyankov looked at the hand and then back to Blevins's face. Without turning, he spoke again in Russian to the stone-faced Shurgatov.

"He says your uniform is a poor fit," the Lieutenant translated.

Blevins decided to match stares with this legend of the Russian and indeed, NATO navies. He narrowed his eyes and contorted his features into his best war face. It might have worked had the fur hat not again fallen over his face. *So much for that idea,* he thought. He pushed the hat up and looked at Shurgatov. The Lieutenant pursed his lips to keep the laughter down. A droplet leaked from his eye despite his effort.

Danyankov spun on his heels and placed his face right into Shurgatov's. Then the blast of Russian coming from the Captain's mouth echoed off the submarine's hull and compete with steady blowing wind.

Danyankov ranted for what seemed minutes, then stomped off and lowered himself down the forward hatch.

When he had gone, the men moved like stunned survivors of an earthquake or hurricane. Shurgatov took a deep breath. "That is our Captain."

"Wow, I thought I had some bad ones," Blevins breathed. "What was he so pissed about?"

"Oh, he's not pissed. He's in a very good mood today."

Blevin's mouth fell open, "You have to be shittin' me?"

"It is his way," Shurgatov shrugged.

"So what did he say?" Blevins asked.

"He wanted me to welcome you aboard and tell you what an honor it is to be working with a member of the United States Navy."

"Bullshit. Now what did that dick with ears really say?"

Shurgatov sighed, "He said that you are to be with me at all times and that no questions about his ship will be answered. He is not happy with having you on his boat. You will eat after the crew and that I am personally responsible for you. I am to keep you on a leash."

"Is that all?"

"Not exactly."

"Well, what else?" Blevins asked.

"If you get in his way or cause any problem, he will unscrew my head and poop down my neck."

Blevins burst into laughter. "I'm glad he's in a good mood."

Shurgatov chuckled, "Let's get you below."

U-761

Near exhaustion, Edel had the batteries more or less ready for action, although three cells were beyond repair. The torpedo room brace went in with little trouble. The compressor leaked from a tiny fitting located at the bottom of the third stage. His hand wiped at the grime on his face and he thought, w*hen I fix one thing, two other bits of machinery go bad.*

"How bad is it?" Manfred Becker asked.

Edel rubbed at his bloodshot eyes. "We'll need that air. The banks have drained some. I think the check valves may also be leaking."

"What do you need?" Becker asked.

"Time."

Becker sighed, "Again? How long?"

"Give me eight hours."

Russian *AKULA* Class, K-157 (*VEPR*)

The nearly frozen water of the harbor parted grudgingly as *VEPR* slid down the channel. A flight of gulls flew escort for a short distance, their white wings standing in sharp contrast to the dark sky.

Forty minutes past since the streamlined hull pushed away from the pier, the water cast a dark burgundy color. The sun started it's final dip over the distant horizon. *VEPR* rounded the towering rock formations that marked the passage into the open sea, her engines surged. Water flowed over the rounded bow, and splashed against the bottom of the sail. The ship pounded her way forward into the growing darkness and the unknown.

Valerik Danyankov enjoyed the cold wind from the sea blowing on his face. The vibration of the sea and sound of surging water almost made him smile. Still part of him wished he could turn around. That troubled him some.

Chapter Thirty-Four

Rendezvous

"In confidence and quietness shall be your strength."

-Isaiah, XXX, 15

U-761

November 22nd

Becker awoke slowly. A wonderful aroma wafted under his nose. He sat up testing the air. His mouth watered. Looking toward the radio room, Becker saw Roth smiling back at him.

"What is that?" Becker asked.

"The off watch did some fishing. Berdy is frying the catch now."

"I never realized how hungry I am."

"I know, Herr Kaleu. It seems like years since we had a real meal." Roth laughed.

"What are your plans, Captain?" Edel sat limply at the wardroom table.

"Not much of a plan." Becker took a deep breath. "We'll run as far as we can on the surface. We will alter course every ten kilometers or so. Stay down during the day and run surfaced at night.

"To France?"

"No, I think Germany."

Edel smiled. "Home."

"A long way to get there," Becker sighed.

Edel looked his Captain in the eye. "You think we'll make it?"

"We have to. We've come this far."

"We can leave when you say, Herr Kaleu." Edel tucked his head next to the thin cushion that lined the back of the seat.

"We'll give your black gang a few hours sleep, should be darker then." Becker then realized Edel had drifted off.

Becker studied the chart and thought,. *Germany seems so close.*

USS MIAMI SSN 755

"Okay, this is the last trip up till we make contact with the *Akula*," McKinnon said as he briefed his control room watch standers. "Guys, this is the real deal. You know your jobs. You know what's riding on this. Any questions, go ahead, ask. Something breaks, fix it. This is it. You all understand?" McKinnon studied the faces that stared back at him. "All right, let's do it." McKinnon clapped his hands like a football coach. "Officer of the deck, proceed to Periscope depth."

VEPR

Submerged to seventy meters, *VEPR* silently slipped past the north tip of Norway. Beneath her the ocean floor fell away at a steady sixty degrees till it leveled somewhat fifteen hundred meters below.

In the control room, Captain First Rank Danyankov studied the chart. "What is the best speed to the meeting area?"

"Fifteen knots," the on watch Navigator answered instantly.

"Diving command. Make turns for twenty knots. Get me down to three hundred meters. And you better do it smartly."

The throttle operator added steam to the GT3A turbines and the *Akula* leaped forward like a spurred horse.

"Maintain this course depth and speed," Danyankov ordered. "Watch Officer, find Shurgatov and bring the American to my cabin."

"Yes, Captain."

The VM-5 reactor purred silently while *VEPR* slid through the sea. All of her systems ran at peak performance. All of the seven million parts that made up this lethal warship operated as designed.

At the touch of the salt water, the dissimilar metals in the port stern plane connecting pin, the pintle, began disintegration. The heat of welding forced contaminates into the material, and as a result, microscopic pores opened soon after the new pintle submerged. Water slowly but steadily entered these pores and caused an electro-chemical reaction. As the port plane cycled, the reaction found more surface area to attack. The pores opened further, allowing more conductive seawater to surround the pintle.

By the time *VEPR* reached her cruising depth, fingernail size flakes of metal peeled away. Like tiny snowflakes, they swirled into the slipstream where they dissolved into the salt of the ocean.

USS MIAMI

"Downlink complete," the Radioman of the watch called over the 27MC.

"Very well," the Officer of the deck responded. "All stations going deep."

Miami dove into the cover of the deep sea. At her present speed of six knots, she seemed no more than a hole in the water.

"Dive, get us a good one-third trim. I want watch to watch compensations," McKinnon ordered. "I don't know when we'll get the chance again."

"Aye sir," the Chief in the dive seat answered.

"Sonar," he called over the open mike. "Do you hold any contacts?"

"Conn, sonar holds one sonar contact. Distant merchant - one, five-bladed screw. Designate Sierra two-two. Based on bottom bounce, estimated contact is greater the twenty-thousand yards."

"Sonar, conn aye," McKinnon replied. "Conn, radio, any new traffic?"

"Radio, Conn, nothing new on the latest broadcast."

"We're on our own." the XO whispered.

"Conn, Sonar," a voice came over the combat circuit, "Sonar holds ice noises bearing two-six-eight all the way to course north."

"Very well, sonar," McKinnon replied. "Looks like we've arrived."

"You figure out what we're listening for?" Gellor asked in a hushed voice.

"Not a clue," McKinnon sighed. "I've got a pissed

off German and a cocky Russian out there somewhere." McKinnon shrugged. "Simple mission really, if you break it down. Find a German U-boat that thinks World War II is still being fought. Find and *not* shoot at or get killed by an *Akula* whose captain hates Americans. Oh, and don't touch off Armageddon."

"We're gonna earn the paycheck this month," Gellor smiled.

VEPR

"He has ordered me to leave the cabin," Shurgatov said almost apologetically.

"I'll be fine." Blevins hoped his half smile hid his nervousness.

Shurgatov slowly shut the door like he closed the lid on a coffin.

With the door shut, Valerik Danyankov's eyes remained fixed on the retired Chief Petty Officer.

"You do speak some English," Blevins said.

"Mr..."

"It's Chief," Blevins interrupted.

Danyankov's eyes narrowed.

Blevins narrowed his.

Strong-willed, VEPR's Captain thought. *I hate to admit, but there's something about this man I like. Strange how my outlook and feelings have changed lately.* "Very well, Chief Blevins, we are near the meeting area. You will tell me what you know about this U-boat."

"You've read the report I sent," Blevins said in his best hard-ass voice, and one he perfected and often used when getting things done with his A-gang or Supply Officer or even a Squadron Commander or two.

"Yes, I have been briefed on this. What I want to know is where do you think your American submarine will enter the search area? Will they use active sonar? What depth do you think they'll use?"

"Well, Captain," Blevins folded his arms over his chest. "First of all, I was a Machinist Mate. The only time I went to Control was to stand my watch and grease the periscope. Second, I wouldn't tell you that if Jesus Christ himself ordered me too."

Valerik Danyankov leaned back in his seat. "Good."

"What?" Blevins asked.

"You are a loyal man. I can trust you."

"Trust me with what?"

Danyankov now leaned forward. "The truth."

"What truth?" Blevins asked honestly.

"You know of me?"

Blevins frowned. "Yes, I do. Most of the American Navy knows about you."

"Is it true what they call me?" Danyankov asked. "Am I *The Prince of Darkness*?"

"Well, there are a few other names they call you, but yes."

Danyankov laughed. "Good, good."

"Listen, Captain is there any point to this?"

"What do you think of my boat?"

Blevins shook his head. "What are you talking about?"

"My boat. Tell me, what do you think of her?"

"She's beautiful."

"My crew, what do you think of them?"

"They seem top shelf. Well trained, seem to know their stuff."

"You saw the condition of the base - no?" Danyankov asked.

"Yeah," Blevins forgot all formality. "It's pretty much a shit hole."

Danyankov grinned. "This is true."

"However, my ship is the best submarine in the Russian Navy."

"That's great, Captain, but with all due respect, you really are starting to babble."

Danyankov leaned closer. "Listen carefully, Chief Blevins, I am hard because I have to be. My men need to fear me. They do not desert as so many have. They perform their duties to the utmost. They do not steal from the ship or from each other. They keep this submarine from becoming one of those rusting hulks you saw along the waterfront. They make do with what they have."

"If that works for you, fine, but why are you telling me this?" Blevins asked.

"I need you to understand and I need your help."

"What do you need from me?" Blevins asked.

"This mission, this search, could mean the difference. My country and yours are once again ready to wipe one another from the face of the planet," Danyankov's voice lowered. "A month ago, I would have welcomed a war with America. Danyankov sat back, "But now that it is here, I have no more desire to see it. What I ask of you is simple - give me the truth."

"Yes sir," replied a stunned Blevins.

"I am not sure I believe a submarine from so long ago can come back, but I know that the American submarine out there is very real. Should this whole thing be true, I need you to not be fearful of giving me the truth."

Blevin's eyes seemed to twitch. "You can count on me, Captain," Blevins stood and took hold of the brightly polished doorknob.

"Wait," Danyankov called. "There is more I need of you."

Blevins returned and sat down. "Yes, Captain?"

"This is a personal matter," Danyankov said almost sheepishly.

"What can I do for you?"

"I am getting married soon and I ... "

Blevins smiled. "You need a best man? I'll check my schedule."

Danyankov's face broke into a wide grin. "No, you ass. I need some information on a place called Las Vegas."

"Is that before or after the wedding?"

"After, of course."

"Just checking," Blevins grinned. "If we get out of this alive, I'll be sure you get a great room on the strip."

Danyankov nodded. "Good. Now this conversation must be kept between you and me - yes?"

"Of course," Blevins smiled.

"Then, forgive me for what I must do now. Please stand up."

"What?"

"Please trust me," Danyankov whispered.

Blevins stood and as he did, Danyankov screamed in Russian.

The door flew open and Shurgatov stood with a look of horror on his young red face.

Still screaming, Danyankov gave Blevins a forceful shove that sent the American skidding into the wide-eyed Lieutenant.

Shurgatov's quick reflexes managed to catch Blevins before they both tumbled into the narrow passageway. Danyankov slammed the door so hard the steel frame seemed to vibrate.

"I see you made a friend," Shurgatov said sarcastically.

"What's that guy's problem?" Blevins panted. "What the hell was he saying to you in Russian?"

"It seems Captain Danyankov has questions about your parents being married when you were born," Shurgatov answered quietly.

"That son of a bitch," Blevins hissed. "I'll give him that answer." Blevins stepped toward the door.

The young Lieutenant grabbed Blevins's shirtsleeve just in time. "No. Please remember what he said he would do after he unscrewed my head?"

Blevins successfully stifled his laughter to keep from blowing his cover, and thought. *These Russians are some funny people.*"

U-761

The U-boat rose and fell in the slight swell. Small waves washed up and slapped against her port side. Thankfully, the wind eased and the fog settled over the foreboding blue water. The scene seemed one of peace and the joy of nature, but for the sound of the grind, snap and hiss of the ice.

The watch stood silently on the wooden planked deck of U-761's bridge. Becker stood at the front just to the side of the surface's aiming device mount (UZO). He scanned the waves and sky. Although the wind ebbed, the chill of the Arctic remained. Becker shivered as he tightened the fleece jacket around his neck.

Edel stuck his head from the bridge hatch. "She's ready, Herr Kaleu."

Becker smiled back. "Good work, Chief."

"Number-One," he smiled at Volker. "Start both main engines and head us for home."

Volker's cold reddened face broke into a wide grin. "With pleasure, Captain."

Becker leaned over the cone-shaped voice pipe that led to the Zentrale below. "Pass the word to all hands, we are making for Germany. I want to man actions stations each time we are surfaced. There are many miles between us and home. Every man must be alert."

VEPR

The sleek blue gray hull flowed like a part of the sea. The seven blades of the scimitar-like screw turned lazily when she slowed to the best listening speed.

In her rounded, almost bulbous bow, the powerful MGK-540 sonar system probed the audible and ultrasonic frequencies for anything manmade.

Danyankov followed his orders. *VEPR* entered the

meeting area at a depth of sixty-meters. A thermal layer stretching from ninety-meters to two-hundred and forty meters made finding the *Miami* difficult. He slowed to allow his array to droop below the layer.

The Commander prepared his weapon systems and order the battery of ten 553mm torpedo tubes loaded and ready. The weapons operators double-checked the status of both the weapon and launching tubes. The sonar systems linked by optic cables to data converters on the starboard side of *VEPR'S* torpedo room. At the push of a button, information about target speed range and course uploaded to the guidance computers for each tube-loaded torpedo.

System redundancy is key to a combat submarine. The ability to launch a torpedo needed two locations, first the control room, where the commanding officer could employ the weapons, second torpedo room or on the torpedo tube. If the weapon control console in the Command Center was damaged, a weapon could be launched from the torpedo room.

VEPR started her hunt and the weapon's operators ran one last series of checks. Every torpedo gave the electronic equivalent of a thumbs up. The test was run again, but, the slower but capable Emergency Firing Computer was used. The ten waiting torpedoes signified by a steady green light, happy and ready to serve the Motherland. Tube #4 refused to switch back to the normal command center computer.

The Warrant Officer in charge noted the fault and logged it. "Another relay gone out," he sighed to one of the Torpedoman.

"Yes sir, that happened last month also. Would

you like to take the tube from service till we repair it?" the senior Torpedoman asked.

"No, leave it as is for now. You know what will happen if I tell the Captain? Go draw the relay from supply."

"Yes sir," he replied. "I think that if we ever had to use all ten tubes, our asses would be hanging by a string."

The Warrant laughed. "And the same would hold true if the Captain found out about this."

On the pintle, holding the port stern plane to the stabilizer, a hairline crack started. The protective coating applied in the shipyard was gone, washed into the sea. *VEPR's* slower pace decreased stress on the pintle. Suddenly, a half-moon-shaped chunk of failed material fell out, which left one-third of the diameter of the original pintle.

USS MIAMI

"Conn sonar," came a voice over the 27MC. "Sonar holds new contact, designate Sierra two-three. Contact has two-three blades at eight-zero RPM. Contact just started."

McKinnon felt both fear and excitement. "Very well sonar. Designate contact as Master-One. Attention in the attack center," he called out so all could hear. "Designate Master-one as contact of interest. Tracking party, track Master-One."

"Conn, sonar aye. Sending bearings to fire control. Conn, be advised Master-One is intermittent due to ice noise. Hard to hold the tracker."

"Hold that contact," McKinnon watched the waterfall display mounted just above the periscope stand. "Okay sonar, I see it. Stay on as best you can. I'm maneuvering to put the array on it."

VEPR

"Sonar holds new contact. Initial contact is a merchant based on noise. Hold the contact on the bow sonar."

Danyankov moved slowly to the plot. His fingers traced over the chart. "Bearing to contact?" he asked.

"Contacts bear three-four-zero degrees," came the reply.

"Track that target," he ordered.

With a push of the button, the highly automated sonar system of the *Akula* analyzed the noise bouncing off its transducers. The information flashed by optic cable to the computers, converted to a display that the slow human mind could observe, geometric solutions then fed into the waiting torpedoes.

"Captain, hold new contact. Possible submerged contact. Bearing to new contact is one-nine-four. We are unable to track the new target. It appears to be blade tip cavitation."

"Diving control. Come left to new course two-zero-zero," Danyankov directed. "I found you first," he whispered to himself. "Sonar, prepare to go active - full power."

USS MIAMI

"Contact is in and out," Sonar reported. "Captain, we're getting more noises from the ice. I think the contact is maneuvering around some bergs."

"Very well, sonar. Keep me outta' trouble," McKinnon called back.

"Captain, Master One is making eight knots, course zero-eight-four," reported the plot coordinator.

"All right, we're almost steady on course again."

A excited voice shouted a warning, "Conn, Sonar gained a seventy-two hertz tonal on the array. Submerged contact, bearing one-nine-zero."

The interior of the *Miami* suddenly filled with the resonance of energy from a Russian active pulse. The early warning system chirped while the sound wave enveloped the hull.

McKinnon knew at once he'd been sloppy. The distraction was total and complete. The *Akula* found his ship and slipped into a perfect firing position. If this had this been a shooting war, the next sound *Miami's* BSY-2 sonar would have detected would have been a salvo of incoming Russian torpedoes.

"Conn, sonar, receiving active from *Shark-Gill* sonar. *Shark Gill* is carried on late model Russian Type 2-3 submarines," the voice said calmly with a hint of aggravation. "One-hundred percent probability of detection."

McKinnon held his cool. It was his fault, not sonar's. "Sonar conn, aye. Line up to go active. Go active when ready."

Gellor looked at McKinnon, but didn't say a word.

Grant McKinnon caught the look and offered a thin smile. "It won't happen again."

Gellor returned the smile. "This guy is the best."

"Sonar, I need underwater conn set up to the conn."

VEPR

"Captain we just received an active transmission from the contact."

"Scared the hell of him, I think," Danyankov smiled. "Well done to all."

"In receipt of underwater communication, Captain," the Sonar Officer reported.

"Bring the At Sea telephone on line," Danyankov ordered. He picked up the yellow handled handset. He reached in his pocket for his small notebook and flipped the pages until he found the page with his submarine's code name for this operation.

"Captain, you are ready to transmit," the Sonar Officer reported.

Danyankov held the handset to his ear and pressed the talk button. "Yankee-1, Yankee-1, this is Gray Ghost, do you copy?"

"Gray Ghost, Gray Ghost, this is Yankee-1. I read."

Chapter Thirty-Five

Voices

"The sword itself often incites a man to fight."
-Homer, Odyssey, XVI,c. 1000 B.C.

The Arctic Ocean
November 22

"Yes, we hold the same contact," Danyankov said into the mouthpiece.

"Recommend you proceed to periscope depth to investigate," McKinnon responded over the underwater intercom.

"I concur," Danyankov replied. "Yankee-1, this is Gray Ghost, have you received instructions for stopping this U-boat?"

A pause… "Gray Ghost, Gray Ghost, this is Yankee-1. We have recordings to play for contact. How, copy?"

"Yankee-1, Yankee-1, this is Gray Ghost. I do not think contact can hear while surfaced. I have a U-boat expert on board who says the contact needs to be submerged—over."

"Gray Ghost, Gray Ghost, this is Yankee-1, understand contact must be submerged—break. Any ideas?"

"Affirmative Yankee 1—break. We will proceed to periscope depth—break. Be ready with your recordings. Gray Ghost out."

VEPR

"Diving command," Danyankov bellowed. "Proceed to antenna depth. Plot, bring the ship to one-thousand meters ahead of contact."

The nose of the *Akula* started to rise when another communication came over the underwater sound system. "Gray Ghost, this is Yankee-1. Warning, contact has deck guns—repeat, contact has deck guns."

Danyankov's eyebrows rose. "Continue," he ordered.

VEPR angled toward the dull surface. She leveled off at the exact distance. Danyankov worked the men hard on reaching and maintaining proper depth.

"Report contact," he ordered. The large barrel of the attack scope slid up silently from deep within the submarine.

"Contact by plot bears one-nine-three. Range one-two-hundred meters," came the report.

"Stand by for periscope observation." Danyankov lowered the handles of the scope. He doubled-checked to make sure the scope power switch was on and pressed his eye to the rubber padded optic window.

The silence of the Command Center shattered as the Captain gasped, "My God. It is true." His words came out a bit shaky. "Stand by for observation on surfaced ... *surfaced* U-boat, bearing, mark. Get Blevins to the Command Center—now."

Blevins arrived in seconds, shepherded by Shurgatov.

"You need something?" Blevins asked gruffly.

"Take a look," Danyankov said, moving to the side.

Blevins placed his eye to the scope. His mouth dropped open. Only a gasp escaped his lips.

"Is that a U-boat?" Danyankov asked.

Blevins remained silent.

"Is that the U-boat?" Danyankov demanded.

A smile formed on his lips, though his eyes remained hidden by the periscope. "Sure as hell is. And she is a beauty."

"How do we get that thing to surrender without getting our asses blown off?" Danyankov asked quietly. "Can we contact her by radio?"

"That might work if she's monitoring her radio. My guess is she hasn't been able to contact anyone, so they may have it shut down, or it could be damaged. Worth a try though." Blevins again pressed his eye to the scope.

"Raise the radio mast," Danyankov ordered.

"Hang on there, cowboy." Blevins moved his eye from the scope. "These guys have very good optics and very good lookouts. I would be careful sticking too much out of the water. You spook this guy and he'll head right back for the ice."

"Stop the mast at the periscope window," Danyankov ordered.

"I'll give your radio room the frequencies." Blevins stepped away from the scope.

"The hell you will," Danyankov roared. "I will not allow an American into my radio room."

"Calm down. I'll write them down. Who here speaks German?"

"I had not thought of that," Danyankov admitted. "Still, I will not allow you in the radio room."

"This is your boat, Captain," Blevins shrugged.

"Could we use a flare to get him under water?" Danyankov asked.

Blevins shrugged. "It will get their attention."

"Launch signal flare," he ordered.

"You might consider sticking your sail out of the water," Blevins added.

"But what about spooking him?"

"This whole damn thing is a crap shoot."

U-761

The U-boat swayed gently while her bow sliced through the long rolling swells. Her diesels hummed, sending a slight vibration through the steel of her hull. At her stern, the mist of her exhaust formed a cloud that evaporated before reached the sky.

In the dim light of the Arctic noon, U-761 sailed into an empty horizon.

Volker had taken the watch when the U-boat departed from her bunker-like iceberg. His eyes, like the rest of his body, ached from fatigue and the constant threat of unknown death. He set his binoculars between the voice pipes and rubbed his eyes.

Suddenly the sea ahead of the U-boat seemed to erupt in a greenish orange flame. An object trailing a tail of sizzling red fire climbed high above the U-boat. The light from the comet-like tail of the object illuminated the U-boat in an eerie orange glow.

Fifty-meters high, the projectile exploded in a puff of angry black smoke followed by an intense glowing ball of burning gas. Volker and the other on the bridge craned their necks. The burning ball swayed in the wind.

"Star shell," one of the lookouts called.

Volker scanned the sea and sky in a quick, but practiced turn of his neck. "From where, Volker?" he shouted. The burning ball hissed.

As the object fell closer, the sea ahead of the U-boat boiled. Volker heard it before he saw it. His neck turned just as a massive hump emerged slowly in U-761's path.

The men gasped when the shape reared up. "Alarm," Volker screamed. The object turned directly for him. "Left hard rudder," he managed. His throat tightened with fear.

Rushing air from U-761's ballast tanks supplanted the sound of the falling shell and the swish from the object. Volker felt the bow dip sharply underwater. One last look to ensure the lookouts went below. Volker dropped down the hatch.

VEPR

"She's diving," Danyankov yelled. "Diving command right full rudder, new depth seven-zero meters."

Almost pitch black in the Command Center of the *Akula,* Danyankov snapped the handles of the scope up until they latched with a loud metallic click. "Lower the attack scope."

Defying her usual grace, the 12,770 ton *Akula* slipped awkwardly under the waves.

She nosed over and the streamlined hull regained its laminar flow. The screw beat a steady rhythm at this shallow depth. At twenty meters, water pressure overcame the bubbles while the screw bit cleanly into the sea. The beating stopped and she silenced.

"Contact?" Danyankov demanded.

"Lost in surface and ice noise," the Sonar Officer reported.

"Find that thing," Danyankov bellowed. "Turn the damn lights on in this coffin."

The fluorescents flickered and flashed until they returned to a dull pale, almost sickly glow. The *VEPR'S* Commander stepped from the chart to the remote sonar display.

"Regain contact," the Sonar Officer reported. His voice sounded somewhat relieved.

"Give me the bearing," Danyankov yelled.

"Bearing three-five-zero. I am isolating the sound and signal now, Captain."

"Ahead slow. Center the rudder," Danyankov ordered. He pivoted to the left, his hand reached for the underwater communication handset. "Yankee-1, Yankee-1, this is Gray Ghost, contact is submerged. Contact bears three-five-zero."

"Confirm regain of contact. Two three-blades, making five-zero RPM," Sonar reported.

Waves of sound struck the *VEPR'S* receiving transducer, then a blast of static that lasted only a few seconds, and McKinnon's voice came through the speaker. "Gray Ghost, this is Yankee-1...understand all—break. Beginning audio playback now—now—now."

Suddenly the sea went silent. The somewhat outdated, but effective noise and signal filters of the *Akula's* sonar system strained the incoming sound signals canceling out acoustic garbage.

As if the sea were haunted, a voice floated up from the dark. A voice strange to those listening aboard the two nuclear submarines and even stranger to those for whom the message was intended.

U-761

"Hold us here," Becker snapped. "Tell me again."

Volker peeled off the heavy oilskin coat. "I don't know what it was, Captain, but something I have never seen. Like a whale, or something. It has to be a submarine."

"Why didn't it shoot at us?" Becker asked. A cold fear struck him.

"Holding depth at twenty-meters," Edel announced.

Becker's mind raced. His brain's catalog of instinct, experience, and common sense came up with no answers.

"We're heading for the ice, sir," Hamlin gently reminded.

Becker nodded. "Both motors ahead, dead slow." Becker's head twisted toward the sound room. "*Unterwasserhorche*?"

Veldmon, the sound operator nodded that he had heard. He slowly moved the steering wheel sized hydrophone control. "Nothing sir," he whispered. Just the..." Veldmon's mouth dropped open. His lips moved, but nothing came out.

"What is it?" Becker hissed. "Veldmon,"

Struck by the force of his Captain's voice the hydrophone operator shook his head to clear his mind. His eyes shot toward Becker's. "Voices."

"What?" Becker stepped to the tiny sound room.

The hydrophone operator turned his head. "They know your name," he managed. Without looking, Veldmon reached above his head and toggled a switch. A small, but powerful speaker crackled. The sound came into the control room, faint at first, barely audible. Veldmon reached up and adjusted the gain. He moved the hydrophone wheel to the left. The voice came in clear, not perfect, but understandable.

Becker's mouth dropped open. A voice from the ocean flowed into his ears, perfect German with a slight hint of being from the Alsberg region.

"Kapitanleutnaunt Becker and the crew of the German submarine U-761. The war ended. Repeat. The war is over. This is United States submarine, USS MIAMI. We are operating below your vessel. Miami is in coordination with Russian submarine VIPER. You are to cease all hostile action and surface your ship. Repeat, cease all hostile action and surface your ship. No harm will come to you or your crew. If you refuse to surface or are perceived to make an attack, we have orders to destroy your vessel."

There was a pause before the message began again.

Becker looked around the control room at the expressions on his men's faces. He saw a few with a gleam of hope in their eyes, though most of the eyes peering at him contained only fear.

"A trick?" Hamlin asked.

Becker felt grateful someone asked what he thought. "I don't know," he answered.

"It's not a trick. They knew where to find us. They could have easily torpedoed us on the surface. Maybe the war *is* over, Herr Kaleu."

"Maybe they couldn't get a good bearing on us." Edel nervously stroked the stubble at his chin.

"Or maybe they want us alive," Hamlin countered.

Becker thought back to the radio broadcast. *If the war had ended, he and his crew were now war criminals.*

"We're nearing the ice, Captain," Hamlin warned.

Becker weighed information and options. Again the message started.

"Captain?" Volker asked.

Becker turned. "Left full rudder," he ordered. He picked up the microphone for the ship's address system. "Chief Baldric, reload tube two with the Leche."

Edel's head snapped around. "You're attacking?"

Becker remained silent.

Edel had been in the German Navy long enough to understand the meaning of that silence.

USS MIAMI

"Contact has changed bearing rate," Senior Chief Masters reported. "Master One is turning on a reciprocal bearing. Wait... uh-oh."

"What's the problem, sonar?" McKinnon asked.

"Looks like there might be a layer there, sir. I'm betting it's fresh water from the bergs."

"Conn, aye," the officer of the deck, Ken Wilson replied.

"Sonar, conn, I'm going to maneuver to the east," McKinnon announced.

"Conn sonar, I can hold Master on the array, that is no problem."

"Then, what is the problem?"

"Captain, we're receiving transits from Master One. Sounds like Master one is doing something with her tubes."

"Launch transits?" McKinnon asked nervously.

"Negative, Captain. Maybe tube loading or unloading."

"Damn," McKinnon swore. "You think *Viper* can hear?"

"I don't know, sir. We hold an intermittent seventy-two hertz tonal on her last good bearing. Appears *Viper* is on the right, drawing right."

Gellor moved beside the Captain. "You think they're loading that acoustic weapon?"

"I would," McKinnon replied quietly.

"That U-boat CO is running scared shitless right now."

"I know. If this guy thinks he's cornered, he'll take a shot."

"Yeah, but it'll have to be a lucky one. I mean, how good can that weapon be?"

"He's been real lucky so far," McKinnon, sighed.

"What if he does take a shot?"

"I'm not worried about us. What will that Russian do?"

VEPR

The *Akula* maneuvered to keep contact with the turning U-boat. Her stern plane pintle cracked wider and acted like a tuning fork. Water rushing by it caused a small vibration. As both sides reverberated a harmonic began. The ultrasonic sound started in the low Db range, but grew quickly when *VEPR* increased speed.

In the torpedo room, the Warrant Officer, along with the Torpedoman, were ready to repair the ailing Number 4 torpedo tube.

"We'll have to make this fast," the Warrant Officer warned.

"I've done this three times before," the Torpedoman replied with a cocky shrug of his shoulders.

"Just be sure the master circuit is bypassed when you replace the relay. There is a live weapon in there," the Warrant Officer warned.

"Don't be such an old woman," the Torpedoman smiled. He removed a flat head screwdriver from his pocket and removed the four screws that held the cover on the Emergency Firing Control.

In the Command Center, Captain First Rank Valerik Danyankov paced. He looked toward Blevins. "What do you think he'll do?"

"If I have done my homework correctly, and I have, this guy is no fanatic. Hell, he wants this thing to be over just as much as we do. So, if no one does anything stupid…"

"Exactly what does that mean?" Danyankov asked.

"I think he'll give it up and go home."

Danyankov continued to pace.

U-761

"Steady new course," the helmsman reported.

"Veldmon, anything?" Becker asked.

The hydrophone operator shook his head. "No, Herr Kaleu, just the ice."

"It could be below us," Hamlin offered.

Becker turned again toward the sound room. "Veldmon, you hear anything?"

"Nothing, Captain."

Baldric's voice crackled over the intercom. "Captain, Leche torpedo is loaded into tube-one."

"Chief, bring us up to periscope depth," Becker ordered.

The tension in the U-boat hung heavier than the stale air.

Edel looked over at Becker with their unspoken language that asked, "Are you sure about this?"

Becker understood and nodded.

The lights went out and for a moment, utter and total blackness filled the control room. Soon the lights came back, only this time they glowed a sickly dull red.

"Bow planes up ten, stern up fifteen," Edel ordered.

Chapter Thirty-Six

Deliverance

"They that go down to the sea in ships, and occupy their business
in great waters: these men see the works of the Lord
and his wonders in the deep."

-Psalm CVII

USS MIAMI

"Bearing shift on Master-One," Senior Chief Masters called from his perch in the blue lit sonar room. "Hang on. Yeah, I thought so. Master One is going to the roof. I hold hull pops from Master-One."

"Think he's giving up? Gellor asked.

Commander Grant McKinnon shrugged. "I hope so. Sonar, do we still hold master-two?" McKinnon asked of the *Akula*.

"Wait one, sir," Masters replied. "Okay, sonar also holds the *Akula* on passive narrow band. Weak seventy-two and a fifty-eight hertz tonal on …" Masters went silent.

"Conn, sonar?" McKinnon asked.

"Loud metallic transient from Master-two."

McKinnon felt a hot stab of fear land in the pit of his stomach. "Launch transients?"

The pause seemed hours. Then Master's voice came through the speaker, "Negative sir, negative. That *Akula* just broke something in a big way."

"A collision?" McKinnon asked.

"I don't think so, Captain. It sounds like a major part of her hull. Master-two is in trouble. Transits are getting louder now. Oh my God …."

VEPR

Danyankov had also heard the U-boat rising toward the surface. The plot showed *VEPR* nine-hundred meters from the U-boat. On his present course, the *Akula* would pass the German at a range of only two-hundred meters. That is, if the U-boat did not maneuver. Too close for comfort even for Valerik Danyankov. He ordered a twenty-five degree rudder shift.

When the rudder went over, the Russian submarine's blunt bow dropped eight degrees. The planes operator countered the rise by applying a ten-degree rise angle on his planes.

At her port stern, the harmonic rose in decibels. The frequency of the remaining metal reached the same as the generated frequency of the harmonic. The crack in the pintle spread like a spider web until chunks of steel and contaminated fill-material exploded. With the rudder turned, pressure of water flowing over the loose control surface doubled by the square root of the thousands of tons of hydrodynamic force. Gravity then pulled the stern plane downward. The slipstream of water caught the wobbly plane, and wrenched at the remaining inboard support shaft. The shaft held, but stretched. As it elongated, the moving water forced the jammed stern plane aft, toward the spinning nickel bronze screw. The hydraulic system sensed this problem and attempted to realign the control surfaces. The shaft and yoke which connected the two stern planes were now under the force of the rushing ocean and the ship's own five thousand pound per square inch hydraulic system. The yoke snapped at its midpoint. The undamaged starboard stern plane locked in the dive position. The nose of the *Akula* dropped as if she had fallen off a cliff.

In the Command Center, the plane's operator felt the control jerk in his hand. An electrical signal generated an alarm next to the plane operator.

The alarm sounded and the 12,500 ton submarine nosed over. The Torpedoman had only to swivel the contact pins of the new relay in place and push the unit down until plastic latches captured the inexpensive part. Out of instinct, he tried to withdraw his hand. The relay lodged the pins into the incorrect alignment. His sweaty fingers retracted, a ninety volt arc leaped from the command power transfer bus into the control switching relays for tube-four.

Outdated and far too complicated, the Emergency Firing Computer made events automatic and unstoppable. The ninety volts energized the tube control system, which sent signals to control valves. Torpedo tube four flooded and equalized with sea pressure.

A small part of the ninety volts isolated another set of relay switches from the Command Center. No further information would be accepted from the targeting computers. The voltage continued and a memory drive that sent last known targeting information to a flash memory. The memory detected the information and sent its own signal to another relay. A quarter second after it shut, power flowed into the waiting torpedo.

Instantly the torpedoes acoustic nose activated. Gyros spun as the torpedo became aware of where it was. The torpedoes on board, computer did a second long self-check. It noted the downward angle of the submarine, but the preset parameters were within tolerance. Satisfied, the torpedo signal demanded target information.

Back in the Emergency Firing Computer, the flash memory heard the signal. A burst of information flooded the torpedo. It took a quarter second for the computer to understand the inrush of information. The torpedo was happy enough to signal the submarine herself.

VEPR took control. Tube four's outer and inner door swung open. As the tube opened, a switch on the doors outer edge closed. A millisecond later, the tube, satisfied it obeyed its human masters, ordered valves atop three high-pressure air flasks to open. This air acted on the firing plunger. The plunger moved aft driving a column of water into the tube behind the weapon. The torpedo blocked the flow of the water. Pressure built rapidly until a pressure sensor was satisfied. A lug set into the top of the torpedo held it in place until it rolled out of the way.

Water pressure behind the torpedo pushed the weapon at almost four-Gs. The homing torpedo entered the sea.

The engine started at once, when the torpedo left the tube. As programmed, the torpedo turned to the set gyro angle. It banked slightly to starboard, slowed some as its computer recalled the search speed of twenty-eight knot. The computer measured shaft revolutions driving the counter rotating propellers, and calculated how many turns it took before it turned on the active sonar.

USS MIAMI

"We got big trouble," Senior Chief Masters called over the 27MC.

McKinnon looked at the waterfall display above his head. "What's going on?" he asked as calmly as he could.

"The *Akula* has suffered some type of casualty—wait—wait." Raw nerves tensed. Then Master's voice echoed through the speaker. "Conn, sonar torpedo in the water."

"What?" McKinnon yelled.

"Torpedo bears zero-four-zero," Masters called announced in a business-like voice.

"Who took a shot?" McKinnon yelled into the microphone.

"Definite Russian by nature of sound." Master's voice betrayed none of the fear that gripped those in the control room.

McKinnon opened his mouth to order a flank bell when Masters broke in, "Conn, sonar, Master-Two has launched against Master-One."

"Shit," McKinnon said as he watched the waterfall

display. The electronic image of the torpedo, a bright green line traveled across the screen.

"Not a damn thing we can do," Gellor sighed.

U-761

Veldmon heard the sudden grinding, wrenching noise. To his ear, it sounded like someone slowly crushed a tin can. He turned his head to report the sound to Becker when another sound emerged from the grinding noise. He pressed the headset to his ear. A whirring sound, familiar, but strange. He listened for only a second before his mind comprehended. His mouth opened, but unable to speak. He inhaled and forced the words out. "Torpedo."

Becker did not let surprise delay him. His mind flashed with numbers, questions and solutions. "A homing torpedo?" he gasped.

Veldmon answered his question a half second later. "The - the weapon is pinging," the hydrophone operator yelled more in amazement than fear.

"Launch BOLD. Ahead flank," Becker screamed.

Volker reached over the plot table and punched a button. From a small hole just aft of the conning tower, a small canister just over a meter long and half as wide dropped into the ocean. At once, the canister's chemical contents reacted with the seawater. Hydrogen bubbles erupted and the canister fell in lazy circles toward the sea floor.

"How far to the ice?" Becker asked quickly.

Hamlin did a quick guess, "Berg is three hundred meters bearing three-four zero."

"Chief, fifty meters, now. Twenty degree dive."

"Torpedo is closing," Veldmon hissed through clenched teeth.

The propellers bit deep into the water. The crew reached out for anything that might support them when the bow of the German submarine dropped.

"I can't hear anything, " Veldmon cried out.

Becker stood between the two periscopes, holding on to each as the angle increased. He felt it again. The anger he had fought so long, emerged from deep in his chest like a red snake. He shook his head to shake it loose, but it coiled around him, squeezed, and choked. "Not now," he growled.

VEPR

The jammed plane bent backwards while water continued to flow over the damaged surface. The control arm could no longer bear the strain and the seven-ton slab of steel broke away. The entire submarine shook like a toy. Hydrodynamic forces acted on the free plane, lifted it three meters before the ever-jealous force of gravity pulled down the fluttering steel. Only the screw blocked its path to the bottom of the sea.

The computer machined nickel-bronze and Type 3311 high tensile steel met with the explosive force of a torpedo warhead. Four of the *Akula's* propeller's blades sheared off under the weight and force of the falling stern plane. The remaining three blades bent at odd angles and the stern plane twisted around along its axis.

In the Command Center of the crippled submarine,

the crew remained calm, but groaned when the nose dipped to thirty degrees. Carl Blevins wedged himself between two consoles, until he thought his shoulders would break.

The ship fell on her side and a deep rumble swept through the straining steel of *VEPR's* hull. The angle grew larger and the entire stern bounced in a corkscrew motion. Those not braced were thrown into the air only to crash onto the unyielding deck.

A blur of stumbling and falling men, machines screamed in protest, lights flickered on and off with sparks and shrieks. In the blur, Blevins saw men tumbling almost lazily around him. The *Akula* bucked and the deck quaked as if it made of rubber.

Blevins closed his eyes and hoped the final act would be quick.

USS MIAMI

"Master-two, Master-two, damn," came the voice over the 27MC.

"What is it, sonar?" McKinnon demanded.

"Sounds like she's breaking up."

"Officer of the deck, periscope depth now," McKinnon ordered.

"Where's that torpedo?"

"Lost in the noise," came the reply.

"Okay, I can hear Master-One running. No, wait. Yes, that's her. Now I have active from the Russian weapon. Damn, now I have ... Wait. Sounds like a counter measure."

"Sonar, we're going to PD. Stay on top of it,"

McKinnon bellowed. He heard a rapid breathing sound and looked around. *Now is not the time to panic,* he thought, *whoever is having trouble controlling themselves is a threat to the ship.* Then he realized with a shock, it was his own lungs pumping.

The Torpedo

Confusion lasted only a second. The sea alive with noises, provided a number of possible targets. The sophisticated computer sorted and filtered information sent by the unsophisticated sonar. On either side of its seeker's head, the torpedo heard the rumble, but was instructed to ignore the sound due to the fact the Mother Ship was back there. It pinged and analyzed the returning waves of sound. The reflection from the U-boat's hull matched the target profile. The torpedoes' computer adjusted the control surfaces, and the weapon turned East and pitched down to three degrees. It listened.

Sound energy transmitted by the screws of the fleeing U-boat struck the weapon's passive transducers, but a sudden cloud of noise blanked them. Instantly, the active sonar adjusted its pulse and beam direction, and let go a full power surge of acoustic energy.

The thick noise cloud let the concentrated sounds pass through intact and decided to ignore the cloud and continue onward. A possible target loomed into the weapon's acoustic eye. A blend of signals swept in for analysis. The received signals were in both high and low frequencies. Unsure, the torpedo pinged again. The hull of the U-boat gave a fuzzy return, but this new object almost blanked the system. It listened again. The frequencies shifted on almost all scales while its electronic mind still wondered. The computer ordered the influence section of the warhead to energize. An invisible field of magnetic energy surrounded the nose of the torpedo. Sensors at the top and bottom of the seeker measured the field looking for any disturbance. In the warhead, a tiny pellet of Dystol-7 explosive aligned with the top of a tiny electro-explosive squib. The torpedo was ready to fulfill its mission.

U-761

"Boat is level at fifty-meters." Edel wiped a bead of moisture from his forehead.

"Where is the torpedo?" Becker asked.

"Still astern, closing fast, Captain," Veldmon announced.

"We're under the berg," Hamlin called out from the plot table.

"Periscope depth," Becker ordered.

Edel looked at Becker, his mouth as wide as his eyes.

"Now, Chief," Becker screamed.

"Full rise on both planes," Edel ordered.

U-761 leveled for a moment, then the bow rose. Suddenly they could hear the ice just meters outside the thin skin of their submarine. It cracked and hissed, as if angry at the sudden intrusion.

Edel glanced again at Becker, but the Captain's eyes remained fixed on the depth gauge.

The Torpedo

Logic circuits processed the hundreds of acoustic signals as fast as the noise filters could send them. The object in the seeker's acoustic window flooded the receiver with sounds on every frequency, but none seemed interesting. The torpedo pinged again. Then the faint return that matched the target's last good bearing struck the receiver module. With only a minor command to the control surfaces, the torpedo aligned its active sonar and again pinged, this time the return was solid. The computer measured the distance and the rate of closure. As programmed, the weapon validated the target and switched to high speed. Another ping issued from the seeker just to be sure.

One more ping and the weapon would know the final range to the U-boat. The passive filters eliminated all noises except for the whirring propellers of the U-boat. The torpedo did a quick second check of its influence firing circuit. The successful self-test readied the torpedo for the final act.

The received signal matched the profile the weapon created for this target. A shift in the target's position noted in the weapon's computer. Within a nanosecond, the computer did a minor geometric calculation to finalize the attack vector.

The Russian torpedo tipped its nose up five degrees to follow. The weapon hit the bottom of the iceberg at a twenty-five degree angle. The explosion of nearly a ton of advanced explosives shattered the surrounding ocean in a flash of orange and white. Tons of torn and broken ice fell away and rushed to the surface. The shockwave from the expanding ball of superheated steam, plasma, and melted ice reflected off the still intact iceberg like the echo of an avalanche.

USS MIAMI

Five hundred feet below and two-thousand yards south, the shockwave from the explosion took only a quarter second to reach the American submarine. The wave of pressure hit *Miami's* sail square, forced the submarine almost on her side like a punching bag. The submarine attempted to right herself.

Senior Chief Masters tried to call out a warning, but the shock wave traveled much faster than he could move. "Hang on," he yelled.

Commander McKinnon felt the ship lurch to starboard and out of instinct, grabbed the slippery barrel of number two periscope. His feet slipped from under him when *Miami* rolled like a bathtub toy.

Gellor fell on his side, down the loping deck until his leg caught on the fire hose cabinet in front of sonar's door. His body spun around and twisted his trapped leg. A look of horror and pain flashed across his face as the tibia and fibula snapped.

In the rear of the Control Room, the Quartermasters reached for the inboard and outboard induction valve hand wheels. One of the junior members of the tracking team, Petty Officer Kensey Starks, tumbled over the plot tables and crashed into the BEEPS-15 radar set. His limp body collapsed in a tangle of limbs and blood.

Belted to their seats as regulations required, the

ship control party managed to stay where they belonged. The helmsman, a wiry kid, from a small town in Nebraska, ducked his head when a large battle lantern flew through the air. It missed his head by mere inches before smashing one of the fire control screens.

Throughout the ship, men and equipment tumbled and fell. Major equipment and consoles tilted and swayed on steel and rubber mounts. Sonar went offline, but self-protection circuits operated to keep the system's million fragile parts from being shaken to bits.

The wave passed and the submarine rolled back along her axis to an even keel.

A strange, unnatural silence filled the Control Room. The ventilation fans hummed as did the various cooling fans from fire control. Within a few seconds the first moans drifted up from the decks.

McKinnon let go of the periscope and picked up the microphone for the 1MC. "All stations, this is the Captain," he said calmly. "Report damage to control." A quick look around the Control Room determined the systems okay. "Sonar?" he asked over the open mike.

"Conn, sonar," replied Senior Chief Masters, his voice seemed distant and groggy. "I ... I need to cold start the system."

"Is everyone okay in there?" McKinnon inquired.

"Just shook up a bit, Captain. I'll have us back on line in about three minutes."

McKinnon looked down and saw Gellor trying to pull himself to a sitting position. The Captain stepped off the conn and bent down to help.

Gellor cried out as the leg flopped on its side away from his body.

"Get the Corpsman up here," McKinnon ordered. "Take it easy, XO."

"There goes my ski trip in February." The XO cringed in pain.

"Captain," a voice said from behind his back.

McKinnon turned to see First Class Electronics Technician, Burl Betts holding the limp body of Petty Officer Kensey Starks. The boy's hair matted with blood, his eyes shut and his mouth hung half-open. "Request permission to take him below," Betts asked.

"Is he... ?" McKinnon asked.

"Dead? No sir, not yet, but I think he has a fractured skull."

"Get him below." McKinnon felt tears well and swallowed hard. *There will be time for that later,* he told himself.

"Getting damage reports now," the Chief of the Watch called out. "Number two compressor motor shorted. Auxiliary fresh water tank, sight glass cracked. Controlled leak from shaft seals."

"Is that all?" McKinnon asked.

"No, sir. The cooks say we eat off paper plates for a while."

Grant McKinnon smiled. "Good. What about injuries?"

"Mess Decks say they have lots of cuts and bruises, maybe a few broken bones. The damage control team is on the way to Control to get the XO."

"Tell the Corpsman, Betts is on his way down with Starks."

VEPR

The damaged *Akula* was only a few degrees from standing on her nose. The reactor shut itself down like a turtle hiding in its shell. Emergency lights powered by the ship's still stable battery came on illuminating the horror on the crippled submarine.

The battered and broken propeller finally stopped. For a few moments, the *Akula* hung in the sea like a fish strung up at the market. Forces of nature acted on the hull. The extreme down angle caused the submarine to slide toward the bottom. She slipped deeper and the pressure on her hull increased, compressing the hull and offering less resistance to the surrounding water.

Danyankov inched his way, hand-over-hand, toward the ballast control panel. His hands slipped but his foot found a small toehold on a chart locker and he steadied himself. He felt the ship shudder and looked at the digital depth gauge. The numbers moved faster, ninety-meters, ninety-five, one-hundred meters.

He spotted a figure wedged between the radar control housing and the inertial navigation receiver. "Blevins," Danyankov shouted over the rumbling of the sinking submarine.

Carl poked his head from between the two consoles.

Danyankov wrapped his arm around one of the electronic cooling water pipes. "Three buttons on top," he shouted.

"These?" Blevins pointed.

Danyankov bobbed his head. "Yes, push the buttons." The numbers on the depth meter indicated one-hundred-thirty, one-hundred forty.

Carl Blevins grabbed a valve handle, and pulled his body from its tiny enclosure. Blevins let out a groan when he swung his weakened legs and managed to grab another valve and pulled himself forward. Although he felt his strength drain, he pumped his legs once more and swung toward the panel. He managed to slide his fingers under the protective plastic cover. His muscles strained but his fingers pressed the three large red buttons.

Inside *VEPR'S* ballast, tanks, the rocket motors fired. Searing exhaust gases flashed the surrounding water to steam. Pressure from the newly formed steam forced water out of the louvered flood grates on the bottom of the hull. Within seconds, thousands of tons of water emptied into the sea.

The *Akula's* downward movement slowed, then stopped while buoyancy overcame gravity and the nose of the damaged submarine started upward.

The strained hull creaked around them, and those still able, rose slowly.

The ship approached level, when the stern dropped.

"Vent the forward tanks," Danyankov bellowed.

A set of firm hands pushed Blevins out of the way. He tumbled back, almost losing his footing on the still slightly sloped deck. His feet back-peddled till his hand caught on another pipe and he steadied himself.

The stern dropped further. If the upward angle increased more than forty degrees, air in the ballast tanks would spill out and, *VEPR* would plummet to the sea floor.

Crewmen at the ballast control station, smoothly operated the maze of knobs and switches.

The lights for the ballast tank vents appeared like green circles. The six forward lights blinked off, then turned red. The forward end of the submarine vibrated when the gases and steam vented. *VEPR'S* bow gently fell to level again.

Danyankov ordered the vents shut. Dazed and bloodied sailors pulled themselves up. Some had to be helped to their feet, others remained motionless. Blevins walked forward to the first man on the deck. He knelt down and gently rolled the body over. Blevins was surprised by the young face. He had dark wavy hair, his jaw proud and defined, Blevins checked his neck for a pulse. The young sailor's face twitched, then the eyes slowly opened. He spoke something in Russian.

The eye blinked twice and the young sailor sat up. Blevins extended his hand and helped the young man to his feet. The young Russian sailor shook his head, then nodded to Blevins.

"I had kids like you in my division," Blevins said, but the sailor limped toward his post.

Chapter Thirty-Seven

Hope

"How are the weapons of war perished."
-II Saumuel, I, 27

VEPR K-157

Crippled and almost powerless, the Russian submarine bobbed clumsily to the surface. She wallowed in the slight swells of the ice-filled ocean.

"The reactor is shut down, Captain," the Engineering officer reported.

"Start the diesel," Danyankov ordered. "What else is broken?"

The Engineer wiped the stream of blood flowing from his nose. "The shaft is cracked, thrust bearings destroyed, reduction gears hopeless. We have partial hydraulics, but the control surfaces are jammed."

"We have no main propulsion?" Danyankov asked.

"The creeping motors will give us a few knots," replied the Engineer.

Then a report came over the Emergency announcing system, "Command Center, this is compartment one. We have indications of a launch from tube-four."

"What?" Danyankov yelled into the open microphone.

"Tube four is empty," the voice said, almost apologetically.

Captain First Rank Danyankov spun on his heels. "Sonar Officer, what is your status?"

The reply was sluggish, "Captain, we are operating under emergency power. We have limited broadband capabilities."

"Can we communicate with the American?"

"Yes sir, I can divert power to the transducer."

"Do it now," Danyankov ordered as he stepped toward the microphone for the underwater communications set.

"You have power," the Sonar Officer reported.

Danyankov snatched the microphone from its holder. "Yankee-1, Yankee-1, this is Gray Ghost."

The Navigator came next to the Captain. "Do you think our torpedo…"

"If we sank a United States nuclear submarine…" Danyankov hissed.

The Navigator's head had struck the plot table during the jam dive and his right eye was nearly swollen shut. "We've started World War III."

"Get the scopes up and see if there is any debris," Danyankov ordered.

"You put a weapon in the water?" Blevins asked from the other side of the command center.

"Keep quiet."

"The hell I will," Blevins shouted back. "You better hope to God or whatever you worship that you missed."

Danyankov remained silent. *God is about my only hope right now.* He keyed the mike again. "Yankee-1, Yankee-1, this is Gray Ghost, …Static and watery silence.

"Captain, the sea is clear," the Navigator reported.

Then a voice came over the underwater transducer. It was faint, spirit-like as it drifted from below. "Gray Ghost, Gray Ghost, this is Yankee-1—break. What the hell is going on?"

With his submarine crippled and wallowing in the Arctic Ocean, Valerik Danyankov had to smiled. "Yankee-1, Yankee-1, this is Gray Ghost—break. Have lost control of surfaces and propulsion—break. Accidental torpedo launch during casualty—break. We are on the surface—over."

"Gray Ghost, Gray Ghost, do you require assistance?"

"Negative Yankee-1, not at this time—break. What about the U-boat?" Danyankov asked.

"Gray Ghost, this is Yankee-1, status of U-boat unknown. Torpedo detonation near last good bearing of German submarine—over."

"It was an accident," Danyankov said almost apologetically.

"Understand, Gray Ghost—break. Yankee-1 will conduct search for U-boat—over."

"Understand, Yankee-1 will search for German submarine."

U-761

Blocked from the explosion by the iceberg, the

U-boat rose toward the dim light of the Arctic noon.

"Twenty meters," Edel called softly.

"Ease the angle," Becker growled.

Veldmon looked back toward his Captain. "Herr Kaleu."

"What is it?" Becker snapped, nerves on edge.

"Sounds like a submarine blowing its tanks."

"They came up to look for our dead bodies," Becker shouted and threw the cap from his head to the wet, greasy deck. "What is the bearing?"

Veldmon looked at his bearing indicator. "Contact bears one-six-eight."

"Captain, boat is at periscope depth," Edel announced.

Becker didn't seem to notice. He panted, his eyes wide with rage.

"Captain?" Volker asked gently.

"I heard you," Becker snapped. "Raise the scope. Helm right, full rudder."

The dull silver tube of the attack scope lifted from its well and slid toward the ice-filled surface of the Arctic.

Becker snapped the handles of the periscope down and shoved his eye to the optic window. "Give me a bearing, Veldmon," Becker demanded.

"Target now bears three-four-eight," Veldmon reported.

Becker swung the scope around. The small optic window which framed much of a submarine captain's world moved in a slow circle of the two bergs, a bit of floating ice, then an object filled the scope's window. His brows arched and his eyes widened. "My God, I have it." His fingers locked around the handles. The sight of the deadly efficient outline of the *Akula* nearly took his breath. "I've never seen anything like this." Becker decreased the scope's magnification. Still, the strange submarine filled the view. "Slow ahead," he ordered. Then, on the conning tower of the submarine, a hatch popped open and men stood in the dim light.

"Looking for us?" Becker hissed. "I'll show you exactly where I am." He snapped the handles on the periscope up. "Action stations. Flood tube-two."

Volker stepped up to his Captain. "Herr Kaleu, it might be better for us to turn East."

Becker's eyes blazed. "Run?"

"Captain, if we miss,…"

"Miss?" Becker yelled. "If we miss, we die. If we run, we die. This is where it ends."

"But, Herr Kaleu there is another submarine out there," Volker protested.

Becker trembled. "Yes, and another Destroyer and tomorrow, another plane."

Volker looked at the deck. "Then, maybe we should consider … "

"Consider what?" Becker hissed. "Surrender? Those bastards lured us up with promises and then shot at us. Do you want to die like a dog?"

"We can escape, Captain. We've done it before."

"There is no escape."

Volker silenced.

"Get back to your station." Becker picked up his dull and dirty commander's cap.

Volker lowered his head like a condemned man. "Aye sir," he said softly and took the few small steps to the Torpedo Data Computer.

The eyes of his men expressed doubt in his orders. Shocked by them Becker had second thoughts. *It doesn't matter whether I'm right or wrong, there will be no surrender. But…how much longer can we continue? The food is going fast and the boat itself won't last much longer.*

"I hear engine sounds," Veldmon called. "Sounds like a diesel."

MIAMI

"What's the bad news?" McKinnon asked.

"Not too bad, Captain," the Corpsman smiled. "XO was the worst. He got a bad break and we'll need to get him in as soon as we can, but he's stable."

"Starks?"

"Cut his head pretty good, a mild concussion. Petty Officer Jerod has a broken collar bone. The rest have cuts and bruises."

"Thanks, Doc," McKinnon smiled.

"I've got the XO pretty much doped up right now, so he won't be much good to you sir," the Corpsman added.

"Some people will do anything to get out of standing watch," Chief of the Boat, Danny Norse laughed.

They all chuckled.

Senior Chief Master's voice came through the speaker, "Conn, sonar, sonar is back on line. Conn, sonar holds a regain of Master-one - U-boat."

McKinnon's head snapped around toward the speaker. "Where is she, sonar?"

"Master-one now bears one-seven-zero. Sounds like she just rounded that berg."

"Conn, sonar aye," McKinnon responded. "Attention in the attack center. Regain of Master-one the German U-boat. She managed to avoid the torpedo. I inten…"

Master's voice cut him off, "Conn sonar, Master-two the *Akula*, just started her diesel. Captain Master-one is closing on Master-two."

"Dear God." McKinnon watched the waterfall display. "Officer of the Deck, come to new course North. Get the ship to periscope depth fast."

Once again *Miami's* blunt bow pointed toward the surface. "Conn, sonar be advised there's a lot of ice floating around up there."

McKinnon grabbed the microphone for the underwater telephone. "German submarine, German submarine, this is the United States submarine. The attack was an accident. Repeat, the attack was an accident. Russian submarine is damaged and on the surface. Do not attack. The war is over," McKinnon tried to keep his voice calm. "Sonar, can we warn the *Akula?"*

"Negative sir. Her diesel masks all signals."

"Shit," McKinnon swore. "Set up a firing solution on the U-boat. Flood tubes one and three."

Miami's Weapons Officer, Oliver Dennison stood from his console and stepped toward McKinnon. "Captain, the contacts are pretty close. If we shoot and lose the wire …"

"I know," McKinnon sighed.

U-761

"Range, nine-hundred meters. Gyro angle, starboard thirty. Set. Final bearing, three-four-eight, set," Becker called out as the Russian submarine grew larger in the window of the attack scope.

"Herr Kaleu," Veldmon called. "Another message." Veldmon did not wait for the order, he switched on the speaker. Distant and watery but still understandable, a voice spoke in English.

"Do not attack. Torpedo launch an accident. War is over."

"Shut that off," Becker shouted. "That was no accident."

"Firing solution set," Volker reported half-heartedly. "Open bow cap for tube-two."

The words played in Becker's mind. His brain warned him, but his heart wanted blood.

"Ship is ready," Volker reported.

"Standby tube—two." Becker paused as his mind fought with itself. "Tube two—los."

The torpedo left the tube with a slight thump.

"Weapon away—motor running," Veldmon reported.

The Leche Torpedo

The sea was filled with noise, but the low rhythmic drum of the diesel proved to be the target. The noise grew stronger when the torpedo closed on the helpless Russian submarine. It turned to its preset gyro angle and listened. The gyro fought to keep on course, due to the high latitude and magnetic flux. The torpedo adjusted three degrees off its preset axis. The noise of the diesel filled the oil lined ceramic transducers.

MIAMI

"Launch transits," Masters yelled. "It's an electric torpedo."

McKinnon grabbed the rail around the periscope stand. "Range from the torpedo to Master-two?"

"Two-K," Master responded.

"Weapons Officer. Solution to the iceberg—Now. Switch tube –one to acoustic off mode."

Seconds later, the Petty Officer reported, "Solution tube-one, set."

"Open outer doors—match bearings and shoot."

At the Mk-81 weapon control console, the Fire-Control Petty Officer waited till the door open indicator went from red to green. "Standby," he said as he moved the firing lever to the right. Power flowed into the ADCAP torpedo. Another indicator on the panel lit WEAPON READY. The lever was moved to the left.

A rush of air, and the ADCAP left Miami's torpedo tube.

"Motor start," Masters called from Sonar.

"Good wire," the Weapons Officer reported.

"Weps, kick it to high speed."

Dennison punched the button. A signal traveled through the computer and along the thousands of feet of thin command wire. The ADCAP torpedo received the signal and instantly, its engine revved to maximum speed.

"Give me the count," McKinnon yelled.

Dennison half turned his head. "Seven seconds."

"Helm right full rudder. Cut the wire, shut the outer door. Hang on everyone."

The Leche Torpedo

The low thump of the *Akula's* diesel grew strong as the German torpedo surged on. The gyro settled and the fins made small adjustments for current.

Making twenty-eight knots, The Leche was now only one-hundred meters from its target, when a high frequency noise rushed by, and, forced the torpedo off course by three degrees. The German weapon lost the diesel engine sound for three seconds, but as the wake of the unknown object passed, the transducers reacquired the low thump of the diesel.

The ADCAP Torpedo

Although it was the most advanced torpedo in the world, this ADCAP was dumber than the steel it was made from. At a speed that would get drivers on the interstate a ticket, the ADCAP slammed into the second iceberg. The contact detonator survived the collision long enough to perform its one and only function.

MIAMI

"Warhead detonation," Masters called over the speaker.

Again a wave of pressure struck the ship. This

time the shock wave found little when it reached the American submarine. McKinnon turned his submarine so only the narrow stern offered resistance to the forceful wave. The bow dipped some as the wave washed over.

"Let's pray to God almighty this works," McKinnon said softly. "Helm left full rudder. Steady course North."

The Leche Torpedo

Thirty meters from the end of its mission, the German torpedo's depth and yaw gyros were suddenly thrown to the near limit of their gimbals. The sound information went from steady to a jumble of high and low frequency signals. The low rhythmic thumping of the engine vanished as its transducers flooded with sound. As programmed, it turned toward the lowest frequency noise. Once again, the gyros steadied themselves and ordered the control surfaces to even out from the bucking and twisting.

Two seconds later it slammed into the ice.

MIAMI

"Second detonation," Masters called out again. "Same bearing as our weapon."

"What about Master-two?" McKinnon asked almost in a whisper.

"Too many reverbs from the explosions, Captain."

"Now what?" Dennison asked. "The U-boat might take another shot."

"I don't know," McKinnon suddenly felt drained of all strength. *This has to end,* he told himself. "Make tube-three ready in all respects."

"Conn, sonar regain of Master-two. Regain based on diesel lines. Hold Master-two on narrow and broad band."

"Good Senior. Anything from Master One?"

"Just picked him up on tracker three. Broad band, submerged two three-bladed screws. Looks like he's opening range on Master-two. Captain, he might come around for another shot."

"Conn, sonar aye." An idea entered his head. If it worked, everyone would go home; if not everyone would die.

U-761

"What happened?" Volker picked himself off the deck.

The pressure wave from the first explosion had thrown the U-boat around like a cork. Becker held on to the scope and managed to stay on his feet. He shook his head to clear the ring in his ears. He placed his eye against the optic window. "Missed," he said. "I'm going to open range and attack again. I…"

Veldmon cut him off, "Captain, listen. Another message." Without orders, Veldmon turned on the speaker. Again, the voice drifted out of the depths.

"Captain Becker, this is Commander Grant McKinnon USS Miami. I have detonated your torpedo. Do not attack again or I will destroy your ship. Germany and the United States are now allies. I have no desire to sink you, but I will defend my ship and the

Russian submarine. The attack on your ship was a mistake and I am prepared to prove that, but you must not attack. If I hear a tube flood or a door open, I will sink you. I ask you as Captain to Captain to give me the chance to prove to you the war is over. You and I can see our families again."

"They won't fool me again," Becker hissed. "Helm, continue to new course zero-seven-zero."

MIAMI

"I don't think he's buying it," Masters advised. "Master-one is maneuvering into firing position."

"Close on the *Akula*," McKinnon ordered. "Bring us within two hundred yards."

Miami's rudder went over to port and the great ship turned.

"What are your intentions?" Dennison asked.

"You don't want to know."

Dennison's thick brows furrowed. "Sir?"

McKinnon seemed not to notice. His eyes remained locked on the sonar waterfall display. He could see the lines of sound closing on one another. The noise of the dieseling *Akula* appeared as a fuzzy orange blot, while the slowly creeping U-boat a faint blue-green line.

"Five-hundred yards," the plot operator called out.

Grant McKinnon squared his shoulders. "Officer of the deck, parallel our course with the *Akula*. Come to all stop," McKinnon ordered quietly.

"Maneuvering answers all stop," the Helm reported.

"Three-hundred yards," the plot announced.

The Mk-81 operator spoke next, "Angle on the bow to Master-two is port zero-nine –zero."

"Officer of the Deck, conduct a three-second emergency blow."

Every head in the control room turned to look at the Captain. The looks ranged from fear to bewilderment.

"Get this boat on the surface," McKinnon repeated, hoping the urgency in his voice would convince the crew he hadn't gone insane.

"Surface the ship, aye," the Officer of the Deck responded.

Seconds later, blasts of high pressure air displaced seawater from *Miami's* ballast tanks.

VEPR

Air rushed past their heads with the noise of a jet engine, as the intake for the diesel sucked in the frigid air.

"Engineer," Danyankov called over the sound of the screaming air. "How long until the creeper motors are operational?" He leaned over placing his ear close to the bridge communication box.

"Captain, the port creeper motor has a damaged bearing," the Engineer called back.

"I don't give a damn. Get me moving."

Then the lookout raised a nervous hand to the South. "Periscope."

Danyankov twisted his head. "Where?"

The young lookout stuttered, "Th-the-there."

VEPR'S Captain raised his binoculars. At first all he could see was mist which hung over the surface of sea like a thin sheet. Then his eyes caught a glimpse of movement. A tiny feather of water moving against the current. Danyankov followed the feather to its source.

Jutting from the water, its head slightly thicker than its body, the periscope moved deliberately, brushing the chunks of floating ice aside.

"Command, do I have weapons control?" Danyankov yelled into the frosted microphone.

"No, sir," a static filled voice replied. "Data and weapons control circuits are off line. A bad power converter shorted the entire system."

"It's turning toward us," the lookout yelled.

Danyankov stood and looked around, ice to port and the U-boat to starboard. *VEPR* could not move nor shoot. For the first time in his life, Valerik Danyankov knew what it was like to be trapped.

"Captain," a voice called from the bridge communications box. "Sonar has detected tanks blowing."

Before he could reply, a huge dome of water reared from the sea. The perfectly formed dome rose almost a meter before it exploded, sending jets of freezing water over the men in *VEPR's* bridge. Another bubble rose, this one smaller, then another. The Russian submarine bobbed while the ocean frothed and boiled.

Danyankov wiped the stinging saltwater from his face. His mouth dropped open as a black shape rose from the center of the swirling hissing water. "My God."

The black square shape of *Miami's* sail rose like a building. Water cascaded down the shiny surface like a hundred waterfalls. Then the deck came out of the sea. The submarine's rounded hull shook itself free of the freezing ocean.

U-761

Becker flinched back from the periscope. The shape of the American submarine nearly blocked his vision. He squeezed his eyes shut, then opened them again, as if his brain didn't believe his eyes.

She's beautiful, Becker thought for a second. *Nothing to cause underwater drag, the blunt bow.* Becker felt the rage ease. His mariner's eye took in the streamlined shape of the two submarines in his periscope. Then the voice came through the hydrophone again.

"Captain Becker, this is Commander McKinnon, Commanding Officer of USS Miami. We have surfaced next to the Russian submarine. We are defenseless. Our weapons are unable to reach you. I ask you as Captain to Captain to surface.

"You can, if you decide, destroy us both. But, if you do shoot, the world will plunge into a third world war. Captain Becker, the war you fought has long been over. Your next action will decide if there is another. I know that the U-boat fleet fought a good fight. I tell you that the fate of all is now in your hands. Miami—out."

Becker stood back from the periscope. His mind jammed with a thousand thoughts. He looked at the faces staring back at him. Faces that had been with him through it all. Faces that trusted him and faces of men who would die for him.

Becker imagined the faces of the young men on the other two submarines. How their hopes and dreams now lay in his hands. *Is the American Captain telling the truth? If this is a trick, it's very poorly planned. My torpedoes can wipe both of the monstrous submarines from the sea. Why would the American surface directly in front of my tubes? The American is either insane or telling the truth.*

Becker looked at his hands. They looked tired, dirty and rough. He looked again at his men around him, all silent and waiting his orders. *They deserve life. They deserve families and so do I.*

Edel wiped his hands on his leather trousers and stepped to his Captain. "Sir?"

Becker looked into Edel's eyes and smiled. The secret language worked again and Edel grinned back. Becker reached out and placed his hand on his friend's shoulder. "Chief, surface the boat."

Chapter Thirty-Eight

Dinner and a Movie

"The sword within the scabbard keep,
And let mankind agree."
John Dryden: The secular Masque, 1700

USS MIAMI

"Conn, sonar air transients from master-one," Senior Chief Masters called nervously.

"Launch transients?" McKinnon asked softly, and prayed for no inbound torpedo.

"Negative, Captain. Submarine blowing tanks off the starboard side."

McKinnon stood and walked to the already raised periscope. "There she is," he smiled.

The sight of U-761's knife-like bow rose from a foaming patch of ocean. Without looking, *Miami's* Captain reached up and snatched the microphone of the 1MC from it's holder. "All hands, this is the Captain. The German U-boat has surfaced. Well done to all hands. Break rig for dive, man the bridge. Chief of the Boat, open the forward escape trunk."

"Conn, radio, receiving clear voice comms from the Russian submarine."

"Send it to the conn," McKinnon ordered.

Suddenly a blast of static screeched through the air, followed by a voice. "Commander McKinnon, this is Captain First Rank Danyankov of the Russian submarine K-157. Well done, Commander."

The thick huffy Russian accent made some of the words a bit hard to understand, but McKinnon understood. "Radio, am I lined up to go out, clear voice?"

"Conn, radio, yes sir."

McKinnon keyed the mike, "Captain Danyankov, this is Commander McKinnon, thank you sir. Do you require assistance?"

"*Miami* this is *VEPR,* negative. I have my secondary propulsion on line and can steam at five knots. We are unable to submerge due to control surface failure." He paused. "*Miami,* this is the Russian submarine *VEPR.* What now?"

McKinnon let the microphone dangle around his neck. *The answer seems easy enough, but nothing has been easy on this mission,* he thought. "*VEPR,* this is *Miami.* Request you join me to meet with U-boat commander."

"*Miami*, this is *VEPR.* It would be an honor, sir. I will launch a small boat to my starboard."

"*VEPR,* this is *Miami.* I understand and will meet you on this vessel. *Miami* out."

"Weps," McKinnon called. "You have the boat. Hold us here. Draft a *sitrep*, and transmit in the clear."

"Aye sir. Ready in five minutes," Dennison replied with a smile.

U-761

"All stop," Becker ordered. He took his own microphone and put it to his mouth. "Men, we have surfaced to surrender. I don't know what the future holds for us, but we could fight no longer. This is a chance at life, a life I want you all to have. I want to prepare each of you for some hard facts. We have been asleep in the ice for sixty years ... maybe more. I want you all to be proud of your service and your boat. Do not resist and comply with our captor's wishes. You are the finest crew in the German Navy and I am proud of each of you. I wish you all luck and I will do my best to ensure you are treated fairly."

Becker replaced the microphone slowly and again looked at Edel. "Well, my friend, it's over."

"Captain, would you like me to be the first on the bridge?"

Becker smiled. "You know I can't allow that."

"Are you sure about this?" Edel asked.

"It's too late now," Becker slowly stepped into the conning tower. "Volker, you have the watch. Have the off watch man the after casing."

"Yes, sir," Volker smiled.

Becker reached the upper bridge hatch and spun the dogging wheel. With a hiss, the foul air of the U-boat's interior rushed out. The hatch flopped open and Becker climbed into the dimming light.

MIAMI

Grant McKinnon stood on the rounded hull of his submarine, trying rather unsuccessfully not to shiver. The German U-boat floated close, less than a hundred yards away. The current eased and the drifting ships managed to keep their distance.

A slight vapor made the ocean seem as though it simmered. Commander McKinnon looked at the U-boat's fine and deadly lines.

A swish, washing sound caused McKinnon to turn. In the growing mist, a rather large rubber raft approached his port side. McKinnon counted the men, trying to spot Danyankov.

Chief of the Boat, Danny Norse stepped beside *Miami's* Captain. "What will you say?"

Although the chill of the Arctic air stung his face, McKinnon felt his himself flush. "I don't know, COB."

"You'll figure something out, Skipper," Norse smiled through the black scarf around his face. "Here comes your ride."

The rubber boat bumped along *Miami's* hull. The Jacobs ladder unrolled neatly down the rounded side of the American submarine. Norse threw a heaving line toward the Russian boat. To the COB's surprise, the third man from the front reached out for the line. "Got it, COB." The man said as he reeled the line around his arm.

"You speak pretty good English," Norse chuckled.

"Well, when you live in Connecticut most of your life, you pick up a few things," the man answered.

Norse lowered the scarf from his face and peered into the bobbing raft. "Connecticut?"

"How you been, Danny?" the man asked.

Norse leaned toward the boat in total shock. "How the hell do you know my name?"

The man laughed. "I know all about you. You like your beer cold, your favorite team is the Dolphins. Oh and three years ago, you tried to jump a golf cart over the canal in Puerto Rico."

"Hey, there's only one son-of-a-bitch who knows about that." Norse pulled the hood from his head. "Carl?"

"Yep."

"What in the name of God are you doing here?"

The boat bumped alongside, bobbing in the small swells. One of the men on *Miami's* deck held out the boat hook. Blevins took the cold brass end in his hand, forming a handrail for the Captain to steady himself as he descended into the Russian raft.

Carl Blevins smiled up at Norse. "Hell, Danny, I got sick of sitting on my ass, so I joined the Russian Navy."

His mouth fell open. "What the hell?"

Blevins burst into a deep heartfelt laugh. "Long story, Danny. I'll fill you in later."

"You're damn straight you will," Norse waved his finger at the boat.

McKinnon tried not to laugh. *After all, this was a serious moment, right?*

Danyankov moved to make room for the American Captain. He knew he should stand, but that might dump them all in the freezing ocean. Instead, he held out his hand and McKinnon crouched into the space next to him. "Captain," he nodded with the proper air of formality.

McKinnon took the Russian's hand. "A pleasure, sir." He thought. *God, the things I would like to ask you,*

The Russian sailors pushed off the rubber tiles of the American submarine's side. They paddled backwards and turned the bobbing raft toward *Miami's* stern.

"What do you think of this whole thing?" McKinnon asked.

Danyankov thought carefully before he spoke. "It is historical."

Carl Blevins placed his hand on Danyankov's shoulder, "Oh come on, Valerik, you think this is cool as hell."

Danyankov rolled his eyes. "Would you like this one back?" he asked McKinnon. "And don't call me that."

Grant McKinnon burst into laughter. "I thought you could use more of Chief Blevins's charm."

A rare but genuine smile crossed Danyankov's face. "No thank you, I've had my fill. How did you win the Cold War with men such as this?"

"Hey, I just saved your ass," Blevins called back. "I thought of transferring over till you said that."

The raft rounded Miami's rudder. U-761 sat motionless less than fifty yards away.

"She is impressive," Danyankov said admiringly.

U-761

The oarsmen panted by the time the rubber raft bumped with a rubbery squish into the side of the U-boat.

On the Bridge, Becker straightened his cap and ordered attention on deck. The German sailors stood rigid in perfect military style.

Becker watched the first man out of the boat pulled himself to the deck using the life line. *Tall for a submariner,* he thought. The man gained his footing on the U-boat's after casing. The next man on the deck was shorter, but his shoulders wider and his face seemed frozen in a permanent scowl. "That must be the Russian," Becker whispered.

Oberbootsmann Hamlin saluted each man that stepped on the U-boat's deck. Both men returned the salute. Hamlin directed them to the small ladder leading to the after flak deck. They stepped up, each seeming in awe of the flak guns. They paused only briefly and Hamlin guided them to the bridge.

Becker felt his throat tighten when he saw McKinnon's and Danyankov's faces. *Old to be submariners,* he thought and took one step forward and saluted. "I am Kapitanleutnaunt Manfred Becker, Commanding Officer of the German submarine U-761." Becker felt the tightness in his throat double into a knot. He paused as a hundred things passed through his mind. The next words came difficult. "I ...I formally surrender my ship and crew. I ask that you treat my men in accordance with the Geneva Convention."

McKinnon and Danyankov returned the salute. An awkward silence ensued, then McKinnon spoke, "Captain Becker, I do not accept your offer to surrender."

The silence carried a life of its own.

"What?" whispered Danyankov.

McKinnon dropped his salute. "The surrender occurred many years ago, even before I was born. Our nations have been allies for decades." McKinnon extended his hand and smiled. "Welcome to a new century, Captain."

Becker stared in shock and took McKinnon's hand. "Allies?"

"Captain, there are things you're going to learn that you will not even believe."

Danyankov stepped up, "In the name of the Russian people, I also welcome you, Captain."

Becker cocked his head, "You didn't say Soviet people."

"Like the American said, you have much to learn."

McKinnon shivered from the cold. "Captain, is there anything your crew needs? We will be happy to provide food and medical care."

"You have a doctor?" Becker asked.

"We have one," Danyankov announced.

"My First Watch Officer is injured."

Danyankov turned and spoke to those in the boat. The boat pulled away and toward *VEPR*. "The doctor will be here soon."

Becker bowed, "Thank you sir." He then turned to McKinnon. "My men are in need of food."

"I think tonight is Lobster night, Captain Becker."

"Lobsters?" Becker asked. "In German lobster means one's anus."

McKinnon laughed, "Or maybe it's steak night."

A shout came from the rear deck of the U-boat's after deck. "My God, she's beautiful."

Those on the bridge turned. Then, the man in a Russian Lieutenant's uniform stepped rather clumsily onto the bridge. "Look, there is the UZO, and there the radio direction finder."

McKinnon smiled. "Captain Becker, I would like to introduce retired Chief Petty Officer, Carl Blevins."

Becker extended his hand.

"My God. It is good to meet you Captain. Your

boat is a beauty."

"Ah, thank you," Becker answered. "You seem to know about U-boats."

"Yes sir, I do. Ever since I was a kid, I studied U-boats. Then, when I went to see U-505, I decided to join the Navy."

"U-505? Where did you see U-505?" Becker asked.

"In Chicago," Blevins smiled.

Becker's mouth dropped open. "Chicago? But—how?"

McKinnon laughed, "I told you Captain, you have a lot to learn."

The Pentagon
Washington DC.

The morning had been filled with an ever growing list of phone calls and meetings. Admiral Malroy already had a headache slipping from his neck to his forehead. He glanced at the clock made in the shape of a ship's wheel. It had been a gift from James. *Two hours and I go brief the President,* he thought. SECDEF usually did the briefing, but he was in Korea showing the world that no matter how bad the situation was on one side of the world, the United States could have its eyes everywhere.

Malroy sighed as he opened the folder with the latest report on forward deployed fighter squadron readiness. He was about to yawn when the Communication Watch Officer burst through the door.

"Admiral, a message from the *Miami.*"

Malroy snatched the message out of the officer's hand. His eyes scanned the paper as his lips moved silently.

"Hot damn," Malroy said leaning back in the large chair. "Captain, get me a line to the Kremlin and the President."

"Which President?"

"Our President, smart ass.

"I thought so," the Captain smiled.

U-761

The German sailors devoured the lobsters. The coleslaw and yeast rolls didn't last long either. The crew of U-761 had an introduction to soft serve chocolate ice cream.

Becker ate with the officers in *Miami's* wardroom. He marveled at the space and the size of this wonderful vessel . He felt a little embarrassed at the condition of his uniform and his unshaven face.

McKinnon whispered he could use his shower after the meal. U-761's Captain tried to remember his table manners, but gave up after the aroma of the food entered his nose. Becker looked at the faces of the young American and Russian Officers, so very much like his own men.

The conversation in the crew's mess mirrored the talk in the wardroom. All burned with curiosity, but they understood, now was a time to celebrate being alive.

As all sailors had done since there were Navies, the crews of the three submarines traded items, lighters for a U-boat badge, a U-boat hat for a set of American Dolphins, a Russian patrol pin for a U-boat Blanket. Each side positive they made the better trade.

A few at a time, the crew of U-761 were taken on a tour of the *Miami.* With a common language unnecessary among submariners, the Germans were indeed awed by the systems and especially the torpedoes. Although not allowed to show the engine room, *Miami's* Engineer explained to their counterparts what made the American and Russian submarines work.

Edel shook his head in disbelief. "Nu-cl-er," he pronounced. He laughed at himself, the word sounded so strange.

After the tours and *MIAMI's* mess decks cleared from the meal, they asked the German guests to choose tonight's movie.

After Milo Stephens suggested *Das Boot,* followed by *The Hunt for Red October*. One of the Russian sailors laughed at the last mentioned movie.

"We have seen that picture," he said in heavily accented English. "It is not good. All Officers in film wear decorations on wrong side of coat."

"Wanna really blow their minds?" Milo smiled. "Show'em *Star Wars*."

"What about the *Exorcist?"* asked Petty Officer Rowe.

"Hell Rowe, if we wanted to scare 'em, we would show videos of your family reunion," Stephens yelled across the crowded mess deck.

After the laughter died, they picked *Star Wars* for their entertainment.

McKinnon invited Becker and Danyankov to his

stateroom. A plate of hot chocolate chip cookies waited on the small desk for the three officers.

Miami's Captain motioned for the two commanders to be seated.

"You have been most kind," Becker said softly.

"Think nothing of it, Captain," McKinnon smiled back.

Becker's face turned serious. "What happens now?" he asked.

McKinnon glanced over at Danyankov. "Our three countries are figuring that out now."

A soft rap at McKinnon's door broke the tense silence.

"Excuse me," McKinnon said. "Enter."

The door opened and the Radioman of the watch held out a covered clipboard. "Flash traffic," the Radioman announced.

McKinnon took the message board. "Thank you," he nodded to the young sailor.

The Radioman paused, "Excuse me again, Captain. I also have a message for Captain Danyankov."

"For me?" The *VEPR's* surprised Captain asked.

"With your permission?" The Radioman looked at McKinnon.

"Of course."

The radioman reached behind his back, pulling another covered clipboard from his belt. He handed the board to the wide-eyed Russian.

"How did you?"

"I can't say," replied McKinnon with a smile.

Danyankov grunted and took the board.

Both Captains crossed their legs, letting the

message board rest on the bent knee. They flipped the covers open and read.

Becker felt a twinge of fear creep into his mind while the two Captains read. Their serious looking faces added to his worry.

McKinnon closed the black plastic cover of the message board. Danyankov followed a few seconds later. The Russian and American Captains looked at each other, the seriousness in both faces seemed to route lines in their brows.

"Well, Captain Becker, we have received orders," McKinnon said softly.

The Russian's face seemed as cold and unemotional as a statue.

Fear turned to ice in his stomach. *What have I done?* Becker asked himself. *Should I have fought it out. Is this all a trap—complete with a last meal?*

McKinnon's serious look faded and a smile cracked his lips, "You're going home."

"Home?" Becker asked. "The word sounds so good."

"Yes, Captain, home," McKinnon said as he re-opened the folder and read the message. "*VEPR* and *MIAMI* are to escort U-761 to port of Wilhelmshaven to arrive on the twenty-fifth of this month."

Becker's bearded face opened with a wide grin. His tired blue eyes brightened.

Danyankov nodded, "I have received the same orders." He then offered a thin smile. "I have never been to another country."

"Captain Danyankov, can you sail?" McKinnon asked.

"My boat can travel on the surface. Our screw is damaged and we will be required to use our secondary electric motors."

McKinnon looked at Becker. "And you, sir?"

"U-761 is fully operational."

"Good, then if we all agree, we can remain surfaced here through the night. Captain Becker, you and your crew can get some rest. Captain Danyankov can conduct repairs. We will begin our transit at first light. All agreed?"

Becker and Danyankov nodded.

"Then Gentlemen, it is agreed."

Chapter Thirty-Nine

A New Flag

"How are the weapons of war perished."

-II Samuel, I, 27

The North Sea

November 25th

A ribbon of pale orange appeared just above the horizon when Becker climbed the ladder to the bridge, the stiffness in his legs gone like some of the gray hair.

Although the frozen Arctic was behind them, the chill followed them. Becker fastened the top button of his coat and his eyes adjusted to the pre-dawn darkness. Around him, silhouetted in the struggling sun, the bridge watch scanned the still star studded night.

Becker turned and looked aft. To the port side, the American submarine kept station, two-hundred meters off the U-boat's after quarter. Becker admired the powerful ship. A wave formed over her bow, as if she herself were part of the sea. On her sail - Becker liked that Americans called their conning towers sails - an amber light flashed, warning all ships that this was not an ordinary vessel.

On the after starboard side, Becker made out the ominous and somewhat sinister shape of the Russian that seemed to sweep the sea from its path.

"Morning, skipper," said the voice of the retired American Chief.

Becker smiled. He liked Blevins. The American almost begged to be allowed on U-761 for its homeward journey. This American knew almost as much about his ship as he did. *"Guten Morgen,Oberbootsmann Blevins,"* Becker replied.

Blevins moved over to make room for the U-boat Captain. "Are you ready for today?" Blevins asked quietly.

"I don't know. So much ... maybe too much time." Becker stared at the passing sea. The black water changed in the growing light to a shade of blue-green. "Tell me, what will we find?"

Blevins folded his elbows over the forward windscreen. "I don't really know, Captain. Like you said, it may be too much. You are about to enter a new time and a new world. I wish I could say a better world. The dumb asses that started the last world war are still around. Only the names and countries changed. Same ole bullshit, just a different time."

"No one learned from the war?"

"Oh, we learned. We learned to make weapons that kill millions. We learned to use germs and chemicals. Now we can destroy any city in the world in less than an hour. But did we learn to stop war? Hell no. Never will." Blevins paused. "But you'll find out for yourself. Besides, today is a great day. Any day you come home from sea is a great day."

"True," Becker nodded.

"Sailors are a strange bunch," Blevins shrugged. "We can't wait to get to sea, then when we're there we think about nothing but getting back to shore."

Becker looked worried. "This gas—this Forever Project, it is far more dangerous than beneficial. Look at what almost happened." Becker turned toward the American. "There is a difference between life and living."

"I never thought of it like that, but I guess you're right." Blevins squinted into the new dawn.

"Does the world know about this gas?"

Blevins reached in his coat and brought out the CD. He smiled at Becker, then flipped the disc over the side. "Now only one person knows, but he'll never talk."

The forward port lookout lifted his right arm and pointed across the water. "Land."

Becker turned his eyes to the thin strip of shore, stretched out along the sea. The light grew some brighter while the last of night retreated. He lifted his chin and let warm rays play across his face.

"I guess this is as good a time as any," Blevins smiled.

"Time for what?" Becker asked.

"Captain, will you stop your boat?"

"What?" Becker asked surprised.

"Formalities need to be taken care of before we hit port. Please Captain, stop the boat."

Becker eyed the smiling American cautiously but he ordered the U-boat to a halt.

Carl Blevins reached in his jacket and pulled a small two way radio, "*Miami,* this is *Gray Wolf.* How copy?—over."

"Good morning, Chief," the voice of Commander McKinnon came over the radio.

"*Miami,* this is *Gray Wolf,* we are in position—over."

"Roger, *Gray Wolf,*—break. Look off your starboard bow."

Blevins turned to Becker. "Take a look out there." He pointed into the water.

A shape rose from the water, bubbles frothed and the small conning tower of another submarine rose quickly, a sleek craft, more streamlined than the Russian. Smaller than the two modern submarines, sleek an deadly.

Becker stared in disbelief. The submarine approached his U-boat, with U-212 neatly painted in white on the side of the submarine's conning tower.

"That, Captain Becker, is the newest German U-boat."

Becker's mouth dropped open, as did the lookouts. "She's German?"

"Sure is," Blevins nodded. "Her Captain needs a word with you."

Men appeared on the U-212's tiny bridge. They smiled and waved. Becker returned the wave, as did the lookouts.

Soon a rubber raft slid over the calm sea toward U-761. "Lookouts to the forward casing," Becker ordered when the raft came alongside.

Becker watched from his bridge and a single figure climbed the limber holes, onto the forward Deck. Becker noted the white cap of a U-boat commander. "Attention on Deck," he ordered.

The Officer saluted and made his way around the conning tower and up the ladder to the bridge. His hands ran over the flak guns. Purpose seemed to remind him of his mission and the officer came to attention.

He saluted Becker. "I am Kapitanleutnaunt Hans Brinkermon, Commanding Officer of the U-212. It is an honor to welcome you home. U-212 will escort you into port." Brinkermon dropped his salute and extended his hand. "Captain Becker, this is a great day and I still have trouble believing it," U-212's Commander smiled.

Becker took the hand.. "You look old for a U-boat Commander."

"Times have changed, Captain. We need to proceed carefully." U-212's Commander pointed over U-761's bow.

Every type boat, yacht, and small ship covered the once empty ocean.

Becker and his crew ducked low and a loud whirr and whooshing sound vibrated the deck. Above their heads three German F-4 Phantom Fighters screamed over the submarines.

"The Luftwaffe also welcomes you," Brinkermon shouted over the roar of the jets.

"Our planes?" Becker's mind swam.

"Yes Captain, our planes. American-built, but piloted by Germans."

"My God." The jets now dots over the sea.

"Captain Becker, I would like to present U-761 with the Ensign of our country," Brinkermon said and reached inside his heavy overcoat and handed Becker the neatly folded German flag.

Becker took the flag, letting his hands gently run over the smooth nylon. "This is our flag?" Becker asked as he looked down at the black, red, and yellow stripes.

Then his head snapped up. He walked to the voice tube at the front of the bridge. "Send up the flag," he ordered.

Volker appeared out of the hatch. His hand carried the flag under which U-761 fought so many battles and killed so many ships and men. Becker held out his hand. Volker passed him the aging and now dulled Nazi flag.

Becker held the old cloth flag in his hand. The cotton material felt rough and heavy. The new flag was smooth and light. Becker stepped to the side of the tower. With a sudden extension of his arm, the Nazi flag flew into the waiting sea. Becker didn't notice the cheers from the other submarines when he walked to the flag staff at the after end of the flak deck. Carefully, almost reverently, Becker attached the flag to the lanyard and hauled up the new flag. The slight breeze caught the folds of the flag and it unfurled.

"Beautiful," Becker whispered.

"Yes, Captain, it is." Brinkermon smiled. "Now with your permission, Captain U-212 will escort you home."

Becker came to attention and saluted, "Thank you, Captain."

Wilhelmshaven, Germany

Hundreds, if not thousands of boats, lined the outer harbor. Flags of Germany, the United States, even Russia flew from a number of vessels. Helicopters buzzed like flies around the four submarines as they passed into the mouth of the channel.

Becker lined the crew on deck in the tradition of a returning U-boat. When U-761 rounded the turn just off the sea wall, he heard a band playing. The roaring cheers of thousands of people who lined the quays and shores, drowned out the sound of the band. Cameras flashed at the sight of the returning U-boat. The people waved and shouted, older ones threw flowers toward the barely moving U-boat.

One group of elderly men caught Becker's attention. They stood, some with canes, others proud and tall. Some of the men were bald and others bore the silver crown of age and wisdom. These men did not cheer. They stood in line and saluted. Their faces wrinkled, some of their bodies portly and frail, still they seemed familiar. "Those men?" Becker asked.

"U-Boat veterans," Blevins explained.

"My God," Becker whistled softly then he came to attention and rendered a salute. Becker could not help the tears that rolled down his face, nor could the old men he saluted.

U-761 slowed as the channel narrowed. Becker's felt an almost electric surge as his eyes took in a submarine so large it filled the entire end of the long quay. The submarine three times the size of *MIAMI,* featured a high flat after casing and a sail that towered over the entire base. Toward the stern, the flag of the United States waved lazily in the wind.

"What is that?" His voice betrayed his amazement.

"That, Captain Becker, is the *USS West Virginia.* I am a friend of her Captain."

The throng of people thinned some as U-761 was guided to her berth. White tents had been erected near the quay head. Becker spotted a group of long black cars a short distance from the tents. On the front fenders, tiny flags of at least a dozen nations also waved in the breeze.

"You see that tall man in the black suit with the slightly gray hair—the one talking with the lady in the green dress?" Blevins asked.

"Yes, I see."

"That is the President of the United States."

"What?"

"Oh and the lady he is talking to—she is the Chancellor of Germany."

Becker shook his head as if trying to clear a hangover. "The world has indeed changed."

As was tradition, the IWO (First Watch Officer) Volker brought the ship into port. Becker and his crew knew this place and docking the ship seemed almost routine. U-761 slipped along the quay. Neatly uniformed American, German and Russian sailors, passed lines to the U-boat.

The band stopped and the crowds fell silent. An electric crane silently lifted a brow through a small arc and onto the U-boat's deck.

Blevins placed his hand on Becker's shoulder. "You're home, Captain."

"Thank you for getting us here."Becker smiled.

Becker climbed slowly down the flak deck ladder. He turned to his crew and saluted.

"You men have made history. I can't tell you how proud and grateful I am to each of you. Nor can I tell what awaits you. I ask God look down on each of you and let you live in peace. My final order is that you make the most of this chance you have. I hope to see you all again. Dismissed."

Becker walked to the gangway, Blevins close behind. At the end of the brow, Becker looked down at firm ground. *How long has it been since I actually walked on land?*

Becker looked up at the curious smiling faces staring at him. Slowly, he stepped down.

A uniformed man walked up and rendered a salute. His uniform was strange but the braid and stars were not. Becker snapped again to attention. "Admiral," Becker began. "I report the return to port of U-761. My casualties are one dead and five wounded. We have expended ten torpedoes."

The Admiral smiled. "Welcome home, Captain." He pumped Becker's hand. "Please, come with me."

As they neared, the group of men and women stood. Becker again saluted.

The lady was around fifty or so. Her face was round and her cheeks bounced a bit as she walked forward. Her once blonde hair seemed dulled, but her eyes were bright and her smile warm. "In the name of the German people and I think I speak for the entire world, I welcome you home," Becker winced as the voice was broadcast over loud speakers.

Applause erupted and ships' whistles and horns blared. Becker felt like in a dream. He felt a hand grab his arm and hand gripped by the other. The grip was strong.

"Captain Becker, I would like to introduce the President of the United States."

The President spoke. "You have given the world hope, Captain. I, along with the men and women of the United States Navy and our entire nation, welcome you."

On queue, the crowd quieted. Carl Blevins and Commander McKinnon walked up, and another man walked between them.

Blevins and McKinnon rounded the crowd through a line of ropes set up to keep the path clear.

The three stopped in front of Becker. The tall, thin man in the middle wore the uniform of a Naval Officer, an American Naval Officer.

A look of worry crossed McKinnon's face. He cleared his throat. "Captain Becker, this is the Commanding Officer of the United States Ballistic Missile Submarine *USS WEST VIRGINIA*."

The Officer held out his hand.

Becker noticed how the hand trembled. He looked at the man's face. *Those eyes, I know those eyes*. He scanned down the uniform over the right pocket and noticed a name tag. White letters on a black background read BECKER.

Manfred Becker felt his own hand tremble. *Those eyes, they looked like Ada's eyes...his dear Ada....I wonder if she is here. Is she alive?....but....*

On the verge of tears, in a broken voice, the man spoke, "I am Commander Peter Becker, Commanding Officer *USS WEST VIRGINIA*. Welcome home, Grandpa."

ABOUT THE AUTHOR

Don Meadows

Don Meadows served nearly twenty years on nuclear submarines. He served on the nuclear Fast Attack submarines USS RAY, USS DALLAS, and USS SPRINGFIELD. His writing includes numerous articles dealing with submarine history. This is his first novel. He lives in Charleston, South Carolina.